THE ATTACK

THE ATTACK IN the story room two nights later took her by surprise.

Even in the moments afterwards Bitterblue was unaware of it having happened, and wondered why Saf had pushed in front of her protectively, clutching at the arm of a hooded man, and why Teddy was leaning on Saf looking vague and ill. The entire struggle was so silent and the movements so furiously controlled that when the hooded man finally broke away and Saf whispered to Bitterblue, "Give Teddy your shoulder. Act normal. He's only drunk," Bitterblue thought Teddy actually was drunk. She didn't understand until they'd passed out of the story room, Teddy's weight heavy between them, that his problem was not drink. His problem was the knife in his gut.

FIREBIRD
WHERE FANTASY TAKES FLIGHT™

KRISTIN CASHORE

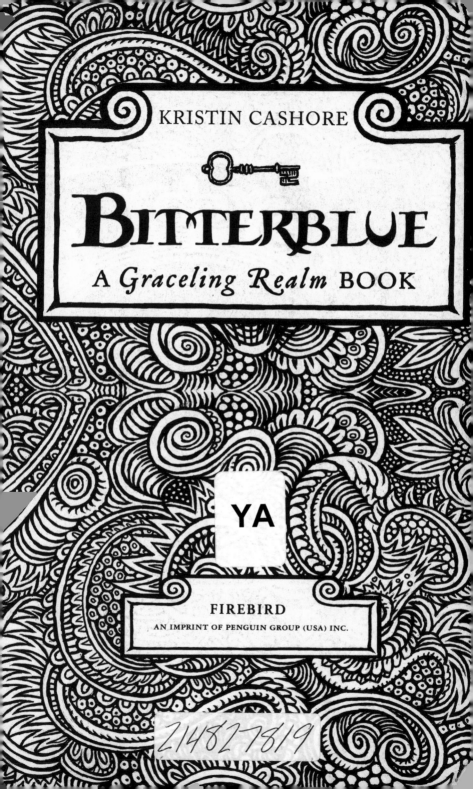

BITTERBLUE

A *Graceling Realm* BOOK

FIREBIRD

AN IMPRINT OF PENGUIN GROUP (USA) INC.

FIREBIRD
Published by the Penguin Group
Penguin Group (USA) Inc.
375 Hudson Street
New York, New York 10014, U.S.A.

USA / Canada / UK / Ireland / Australia / New Zealand / India / South Africa / China
Penguin Books Ltd, Registered Offices: 80 Strand, London WC2R 0RL, England

For more information about the Penguin Group visit www.penguin.com

First published in the United States of America by Dial Books,
an imprint of Penguin Group (USA) Inc., 2012
Published by Firebird, an imprint of Penguin Group (USA) Inc., 2013

Text copyright © Kristin Cashore, 2012
Maps and illustrations copyright © Ian Schoenherr, 2012
Text and photographs of "Pictures of a Book Being Made" copyright © Kristin Cashore, 2012

THE LIBRARY OF CONGRESS HAS CATALOGED THE DIAL BOOKS EDITION AS FOLLOWS:
Cashore, Kristin.
Bitterblue/ by Kristin Cashore.
p. cm.
Companion book to Graceling and Fire.
Summary: Eighteen-year-old Bitterblue, queen of Monsea, realizes her heavy responsibility and the
futility of relying on advisers who surround her with lies as she tries to help her people to heal from
the thirty-five-year spell cast by her father, a violent psychopath with mind-altering abilities.
ISBN 978-8037-3473-9 (hardcover)
[1. Fantasy.] I. Title.
PZ7.C26823Bit 2012 [Fic]—dc23 2011035026

Firebird ISBN 978-0-14-242601-2

Printed in the United States of America

3 5 7 9 10 8 6 4

The publisher does not have any control over and does not assume
any responsibility for author or third-party websites or their content.

This one was always for Dorothy

Bitterblue·City
with·a·detail·of·the·east·city

To·tunnel·to·ESTILL

River·Dell   Winged   Monster   Winter
              Bridge   Bridge   Bridge

Castle   Silver   Lumber   Fish   Merchant
              Docks   Docks   Docks   Docks

Printing·Shop

To·Silverhart

To·forest·and·mountain·pass

LIENID

Ror City

THE SEVEN KINGDOMS

CONTENTS

BITTERBLUE

PROLOGUE

WHEN HE GRABS Mama's wrist and yanks her toward the wall-hanging like that, it must hurt. Mama doesn't cry out. She tries to hide her pain from him, but she looks back at me, and in her face, she shows me everything she feels. If Father knows she's in pain and is showing me, Father will take Mama's pain away and replace it with something else.

He will say to Mama, "Darling, nothing's wrong. It doesn't hurt, you're not frightened," and in Mama's face I'll see her doubt, the beginnings of her confusion. He'll say, "Look at our beautiful child. Look at this beautiful room. How happy we are. Nothing is wrong. Come with me, darling." Mama will stare back at him, puzzled, and then she'll look at me, her beautiful child in this beautiful room, and her eyes will go smooth and empty, and she'll smile at how happy we are. I'll smile too, because my mind is no stronger than Mama's. I'll say, "Have fun! Come back soon!" Then Father will produce the keys that open the door behind the hanging and Mama will glide through. Thiel, tall, troubled, bewildered in the middle of the room, will bolt in after her, and Father will follow.

When the lock slides home behind them, I'll stand there trying to remember what I was doing before all of this happened. Before Thiel, father's foremost adviser, came into Mama's rooms looking for Father. Before Thiel, holding his hands so tight at his sides that they shook, tried to tell Father something that made Father angry, so that Father stood up from the table, his papers scattering, his pen dropping, and said, "Thiel, you're a fool who cannot make sensical decisions. Come with us now. I'll show you what happens when you think for yourself." And then crossed to the sofa and grabbed Mama's wrist so fast that Mama gasped and dropped her embroidery, but did not cry out.

"Come back soon!" I say cheerily as the hidden door closes behind them.

I REMAIN, STARING into the sad eyes of the blue horse in the hanging. Snow gusts at the windows. I'm trying to remember what I was doing before everyone went away.

What just happened? Why can't I remember what just happened? Why do I feel so—

Numbers.

Mama says that when I'm confused or can't remember, I must do arithmetic, because numbers are an anchor. She's written out problems for me so that I have them at these moments. They're here next to the papers Father has been writing in his funny, loopy script.

46 into 1058.

I could work it out on paper in two seconds, but Mama always tells me to work it out in my head. "Clear your mind of everything but the numbers," she says. "Pretend you're alone with the numbers in an empty room." She's taught me shortcuts. For example, 46 is almost 50, and 1058 is only a little more than 1000. 50 goes into 1000 exactly 20 times. I start there and work with what's left. A minute later, I've figured out that 46 into 1058 is 23.

I do another one. 75 into 2850 is 38. Another. 32 into 1600 is 50. Oh! These are good numbers Mama has chosen. They touch my memory and build a story, for fifty is Father's age and thirty-two is Mama's. They've been married for fourteen years and I am nine and a half. Mama was a Lienid princess. Father visited the island kingdom of Lienid and chose her when she was only eighteen. He brought her here and she's never been back. She misses home, her father, her brothers and sisters, her brother Ror the king. She talks sometimes of sending me there, where I will be safe, and I cover her mouth and wrap a hand in her scarves and pull myself against her because I will not leave her.

Am I not safe here?

The numbers and the story are clearing my head, and it feels like I'm falling. Breathe.

Father is the King of Monsea. No one knows he has the two different colored eyes of a Graceling; no one wonders, for his is a terrible Grace hidden beneath his eye patch: When he speaks, his words fog people's minds so that they'll believe everything he says. Usually, he lies. This is why, as I sit here now, the numbers are clear but other things in my mind are muddled. Father has just been lying.

Now I understand why I'm in this room alone. Father has taken Mama and Thiel down to his own chambers and is doing something awful to Thiel so that Thiel will learn to be obedient and will not come to Father again with announcements that make Father angry. What the awful thing is, I don't know. Father never shows me the things he does, and Mama never remembers enough to tell me. She's forbidden me to try to follow Father down there, ever. She says that when I am thinking of following Father downstairs, I must forget about it and do more numbers. She says that if I disobey, she'll send me away to Lienid.

I try. I really do. But I can't make myself alone with the numbers in an empty room, and suddenly I'm screaming.

The next thing I know, I'm throwing Father's papers into the fire. Running back to the table, gathering them in armfuls, tripping across the rug, throwing them on the flames, screaming as I watch Father's strange, beautiful writing disappear. Screaming it out of existence. I trip over Mama's embroidery, her sheets with their cheerful little rows of embroidered stars, moons, castles; cheerful, colorful flowers and keys and candles. I hate the embroidery. It's a lie of happiness that Father convinces her is true. I drag it to the fire.

When Father comes bursting through the hidden door I'm still standing there screaming my head off and the air is putrid, full of the stinky smoke of silk. A bit of carpet is burning. He stamps it out. He grabs my shoulders, then shakes me so hard that I bite my own tongue. "Bitterblue," he says, actually frightened. "Have you gone mad? You could suffocate in a room like this!"

"I hate you!" I yell, and spit blood into his face. He does the strangest thing: His single eye lights up and he starts to laugh.

"You don't hate me," he says. "You love me and I love you."

"I hate you," I say, but I'm doubting it now, I'm confused. His arms enfold me in a hug.

"You love me," he says. "You're my wonderful, strong darling, and you'll be queen someday. Wouldn't you like to be queen?"

I'm hugging Father, who is kneeling on the floor before me in a smoky room, so big, so comforting. Father is warm and nice to hug, though his shirt smells funny, like something sweet and rotten. "Queen of all Monsea?" I say in wonderment. The words are thick in my mouth. My tongue hurts. I don't remember why.

"You'll be queen someday," Father says. "I'll teach you all the important things, for we must prepare you. You'll have to work hard, my Bitterblue. You don't have all my advantages. But I'll mold you, yes?"

"Yes, Father."

"And you must never, ever disobey me. The next time you destroy my papers, Bitterblue, I'll cut off one of your mother's fingers."

This confuses me. "What? Father! You mustn't!"

"The time after that," Father says, "I'll hand you the knife and *you'll* cut off one of her fingers."

Falling again. I'm alone in the sky with the words Father just said; I plummet into comprehension. "No," I say, certain. "You couldn't make me do that."

"I think you know that I could," he says, trapping me close to him with hands clasped above my elbows. "You're my strong-minded girl and I think you know exactly what I can do. Shall we make a promise, darling? Shall we promise to be honest with each other from now on? I shall make you into the most luminous queen."

"You can't make me hurt Mama," I say.

Father raises a hand and cracks me across the face. I'm blind and gasping and would fall if he weren't holding me up. "I can make anyone do anything," he says with perfect calm.

"You can't make me hurt Mama," I yell through my face that is stinging and running with tears and snot. "One day I'm going to be big enough to kill you."

Father is laughing again. "Sweetheart," he says, forcing me back into his embrace. "Oh, see how perfect you are. You will be my masterpiece."

When Mama and Thiel come through the hidden door, Father is murmuring to me and I'm resting my cheek on his nice shoulder, safe in his arms, wondering why the room smells like smoke and why my nose hurts so much. "Bitterblue?" Mama says, sounding scared. I raise my face to her. Her eyes go wide and she comes to me and pulls me away from Father. "What did you do?" she hisses at Father. "You struck her. You animal. I'll kill you."

"Darling, don't be silly," Father says, standing, looming over us. Mama and I are so small, so small wound together, and I'm confused because Mama is angry at Father. Father says to Mama, "I didn't strike her. You did."

"I know that I did not," Mama says.

"I tried to stop you," Father says, "but I couldn't, and you struck her."

"You will never convince me of that," Mama says, her words clear, her voice beautiful inside her chest, where I'm pressing my ear.

"Interesting," Father says. He studies us for a moment, head tilted, then says to Mama, "She is a lovely age. It's time she and I became better acquainted. Bitterblue and I will start having private lessons."

Mama turns her body so that she's between me and Father. Her arms around me are like iron bars. "You will not," she says to Father. "Get out. Get out of these rooms."

"This really could not be more fascinating," Father says. "What if I were to tell you that Thiel struck her?"

"You struck her," Mama says, "and now you'll leave."

"Brilliant!" Father says. He walks up to Mama. His fist comes out of nowhere, he punches her in the face and Mama plummets to the floor, and I'm falling again, but for real this time, falling down with Mama. "Take some time to clean up, if you like," Father suggests as he stands over us, nudging us with his toe. "I have some thinking to do. We'll continue this discussion later."

Father is gone. Thiel is kneeling, leaning over us, dripping bloody tears onto us from the fresh cuts he seems to have acquired on either cheek. "Ashen," he says. "Ashen, I'm sorry. Princess Bitterblue, forgive me."

"You didn't strike her, Thiel," my mother says thickly, pushing herself up, pulling me into her lap and rocking me, whispering words of love to me. I cling to her, crying. There is blood everywhere. "Help her, Thiel, won't you?" Mama says.

Thiel's firm, gentle hands are touching my nose, my cheeks, my jaw; his watery eyes are inspecting my face. "Nothing is broken," he says. "Let me look at you now, Ashen. Oh, how I beg you to forgive me."

We are all three huddled on the floor together, joined, crying. The words Mama murmurs to me are everything. When Mama speaks to Thiel again, her voice is so tired. "You've done nothing you could help, Thiel, and you did not strike her. All of this is Leck's doing. Bitterblue," Mama says to me. "Is your mind clear?"

"Yes, Mama," I whisper. "Father hit me, and then he hit you. He wants to mold me into the perfect queen."

"I need you to be strong, Bitterblue," Mama says. "Stronger than ever, for things are going to get worse."

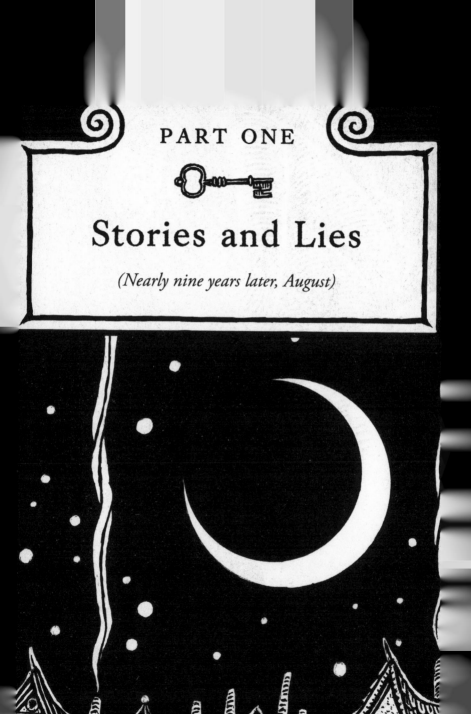

PART ONE

Stories and Lies

(Nearly nine years later, August)

1

QUEEN BITTERBLUE NEVER meant to tell so many people so many lies.

IT ALL BEGAN with the High Court case about the madman and the watermelons. The man in question, named Ivan, lived along the River Dell in an eastern section of the city near the merchant docks. To one side of his house resided a cutter and engraver of gravestones, and to the other side was a neighbor's watermelon patch. Ivan had contrived somehow in the dark of night to replace every watermelon in the watermelon patch with a gravestone, and every gravestone in the engraver's lot with a watermelon. He'd then shoved cryptic instructions under each neighbor's door with the intention of setting each on a scavenger hunt to find his missing items, a move useless in one case and unnecessary in the other, as the watermelon-grower could not read and the gravestone-carver could see her gravestones from her doorstep quite plainly, planted in the watermelon patch two lots down. Both had guessed the culprit immediately, for Ivan's antics were not uncommon. Only a month ago, Ivan had stolen a neighbor's cow and perched her atop yet another neighbor's candle shop, where she mooed mournfully until someone climbed the roof to milk her, and where she was compelled to live for several days, the kingdom's most elevated and probably most mystified cow, while the few literate neighbors on the street worked through Ivan's cryptic clues for how to build the rope and pulley device to bring her down. Ivan was an engineer by trade.

Ivan was, in fact, the engineer who'd designed, during Leck's reign, the three city bridges.

Sitting at the high table of the High Court, Bitterblue was a trifle annoyed with her advisers, whose job it was to decide what court cases were worth the queen's time. It seemed to her that they were always doing this, sending her to preside over the kingdom's silliest business, then whisking her back to her office the moment something juicy cropped up. "This seems like a straightforward nuisance complaint, doesn't it?" she said to the four men to her left and the four to her right, the eight judges who supported her when she was present at this table and handled the proceedings themselves when she was not. "If so, I'll leave it to you."

"Bones," said Judge Quall at her right elbow.

"What?"

Judge Quall glared at Bitterblue, then glared at the parties on the floor awaiting trial. "Anyone who mentions bones in the course of this trial will be fined," he said sternly. "I don't even want to hear mention of the word. Understood?"

"Lord Quall," said Bitterblue, scrutinizing him through narrowed eyes. "What on earth are you talking about?"

"In a recent divorce trial, Lady Queen," said Quall, "the defendant kept mumbling about bones for no reason, like a man off his head, and I will not sit through that again! It was distressing!"

"But you often judge murder trials. Surely you're accustomed to talk of bones."

"This is a trial about watermelons! Watermelons are invertebrate creatures!" cried Quall.

"Yes, all right," said Bitterblue, rubbing her face, trying to rub away her incredulous expression. "No talk of—"

Quall flinched.

Bones, finished Bitterblue in her own mind. *Everyone is mad.* "In addition to the findings of my associates," she said, standing to go, "the people on Ivan's street near the merchant docks who cannot read shall be taught to do so at the court's expense. Is that understood?"

Her words were met with a silence so profound that it startled her; her judges peered at her in alarm. She ran through her words again: The people shall be taught to read. Surely there was nothing so strange in that?

"It is in your power to make such a declaration," said Quall, "Lady Queen." He spoke with an implication in every syllable that she'd done something ridiculous. And why should he be so condescending? She knew perfectly well that it was within her power, just as she knew it was within her power to remove any judge she felt like removing from the service of this Court. The watermelon-grower was also staring at her with an expression of sheerest confusion. Beyond him, a scattering of amused faces brought the heat crawling up Bitterblue's neck.

How typical of this Court for everyone else to act mad and then, when I've behaved in a perfectly reasonable manner, compel me to feel as if I were the mad one.

"See to it," she said to Quall, then turned to make her escape. As she passed through the exit at the back of the dais, she forced her small shoulders straight and proud, even though it was not what she felt.

IN HER ROUND tower office, the windows were open, the light was beginning to change to evening, and her advisers weren't happy.

"We don't have limitless resources, Lady Queen," said Thiel, steel-haired, steel-eyed, standing before her desk like a glacier. "A declaration like that, once you've made it public, is difficult to reverse."

"But, Thiel, why should we reverse it? Shouldn't it distress us to hear of a street in the east city where people can't read?"

"There will always be the occasional person in the city who can't read, Lady Queen. It's hardly a matter that requires the direct intervention of the crown. You've now created a precedent which intimates that the queen's court is available to educate any citizen who comes forward claiming to be illiterate!"

"My citizens *should* be able to come forward. My father saw that they were deprived of education for thirty-five years. Their illiteracy is the responsibility of the crown!"

"But we don't have the time or the means to address it on an individual basis, Lady Queen. You're not a schoolteacher; you're the Queen of Monsea. What the people need right now is for you to behave like it, so that they can feel that they're in good hands."

"Anyway," broke in her adviser Runnemood, who was sitting in one of the windows, "nearly everyone can read. And has it occurred to you, Lady Queen, that those who can't might not want to? The people on Ivan's street have businesses and families to feed. When do they have time for lessons?"

"How would I know?" Bitterblue exclaimed. "What do I know about the people and their businesses?"

Sometimes she felt lost behind this desk in the middle of the room, this desk that was so big for her smallness. She could hear every word they were being tactful enough not to say: that she'd made a fool of herself; that she'd proven the queen to be young, silly, and naïve about her station. It had seemed a powerful thing to say at the time. Were her instincts so terrible?

"It's all right, Bitterblue," said Thiel, more gently now. "We can move on from this."

There was kindness in the use of her name rather than her title. The glacier showing its willingness to recede. Bitterblue looked into the eyes of her top adviser and saw that he was worried, anxious that he'd harangued her too much. "I'll make no more declarations without consulting you first," she said quietly.

"There now," said Thiel, relieved. "See? That's a wise decision. Wisdom is queenly, Lady Queen."

FOR AN HOUR or so, Thiel kept her captive behind towers of paper. Runnemood, in contrast, circled along the windows, exclaiming at the pink light, bouncing on the balls of his feet, and distracting her with tales of consummately happy illiterate people. Finally, mercifully, he went away to some evening meeting with city lords. Runnemood was a pleasant man to look at and an adviser she needed, the one most adept at warding away ministers and lords who wished to talk Bitterblue's ear off with requests, complaints, and obeisances. But that was because he himself knew how to be pushy with words. His younger brother, Rood, was also one of Bitterblue's advisers. The two brothers, Thiel, and her secretary and fourth adviser, Darby, were all about sixty or so, though Runnemood didn't look it. The others did. All four had been advisers to Leck. "Were we short-staffed today?" Bitterblue asked Thiel. "I don't remember seeing Rood."

"Rood is resting today," said Thiel. "And Darby is unwell."

"Ah." Bitterblue understood the code: Rood was having one of his nervous episodes and Darby was drunk. She rested her forehead on the desk for a moment, afraid that otherwise she'd laugh. What would her uncle, who was the King of Lienid, think of the state of her advisers? King Ror had chosen these men as her team, judging them, on the basis of their previous experience, to be the men most knowledgeable about the kingdom's needs for recovery. Would their behavior today surprise him? Or were Ror's own advisers equally colorful? Perhaps this was the way in all seven kingdoms.

And perhaps it didn't matter. She had nothing to complain of when it came to her advisers' productivity, except perhaps that they were *too* productive. The paper that piled itself on her desk every day, every hour, was the evidence: taxes levied, court judgments rendered, prisons proposed, laws enacted, towns chartered; paper, paper, until her fingers smelled like paper and her eyes teared at the sight of paper and sometimes her head pounded.

"Watermelons," Bitterblue said into the surface of her desk.

"Lady Queen?" said Thiel.

Bitterblue rubbed at the heavy braids wound around her head, then sat up. "I never knew there were watermelon patches in the city, Thiel. On my next yearly tour, may I see one?"

"We intend your next tour to coincide with your uncle's visit this winter, Lady Queen. I'm no expert on watermelons, but I don't believe they're particularly impressive in January."

"Could I go out on a tour now?"

"Lady Queen, it is the very middle of August. When do you imagine we could make time for such a thing in August?"

The sky all around this tower was the color of watermelon flesh. The tall clock against the wall ticked the evening away, and above her, through the glass ceiling, the light darkened to purple. One star shone. "Oh, Thiel," Bitterblue said, sighing. "Go away, won't you?"

"I will, Lady Queen," said Thiel, "but first, I wish to discuss the matter of your marriage."

"No."

"You're eighteen, Lady Queen, with no heir. A number of the six kings have sons yet unmarried, including two of your own cousins—"

"Thiel, if you start listing princes again, I'll throw ink at you. If you so much as whisper the names of my cousins—"

"Lady Queen," Thiel said, talking over her, completely unperturbed, "as little as I wish to upset you, this is a reality that must be faced. You've developed a fine rapport with your cousin Skye in the course of his ambassadorial visits. When King Ror comes this winter, he'll probably bring Prince Skye with him. Between now and then, we'll have to have this discussion."

"We won't," Bitterblue said, clutching her pen hard. "There's nothing to discuss."

"We will," said Thiel firmly.

If she looked closely enough, Bitterblue could make out the lines of healed scars on Thiel's cheekbones. "There's something I'd like to discuss," she said. "Do you remember the time you came into my mother's rooms to say something to my father that made him angry and he brought you downstairs through the hidden door? What did he do to you down there?"

It was as if she'd blown out a candle. He stood before her, tall, gaunt, and confused. Then even the confusion faded and the light went out of his eyes. He smoothed his impeccable shirtfront, staring down at it, tugging, as if tidiness mattered greatly in this moment. Then he bowed once, quietly; turned; and walked out of the room.

LEFT ALONE, BITTERBLUE shuffled papers, signed things, sneezed at the dust—tried, and failed, to talk herself out of a small shame. She'd done it on purpose. She'd known full well that he wouldn't be able to bear her question. In fact, almost all of the men who worked in her offices, from her advisers to her ministers and clerks to her personal guard—those who had been Leck's men—flinched away from direct reminders of the time of Leck's reign—flinched away, or fell apart. It was the weapon she always used when one of them pushed her too far, for it was the only weapon she had that worked. She suspected that there'd be no more marriage talk for a while.

Her advisers had a single-mindedness that left her behind sometimes. That was why the marriage talk frightened her: Things that started as mere talk among them seemed to become real institutions, suddenly, forcefully, before she'd ever managed to comprehend them or form an opinion. It had happened with the law that gave blanket pardons for all crimes committed during Leck's reign. It had happened with the charter provision that allowed towns to break free of their governing lords and rule themselves. It had happened with the suggestion—just a suggestion!—to block off Leck's old living chambers, take down his animal cages in the back garden, and burn his belongings.

And it wasn't that she was necessarily opposed to any of these measures, or regretted her approval once things settled down enough for her to comprehend that she'd approved. It was only that she didn't *know* what she thought, she needed more time than they did, she couldn't always be rushing ahead the way they were, and it frustrated her to look back and realize that she'd let herself be pushed into something. "It's deliberate, Lady Queen," they'd told her, "a deliberate philosophy of forward-thinkingness. You're right to encourage it."

"But—"

"Lady Queen," Thiel had said gently, "we're trying to lift people out of Leck's spell and help them move on, you understand? Otherwise, people will wallow in their own upsetting stories. Have you spoken to your uncle about it?"

Yes, she had. Bitterblue's uncle, after Leck's death, had come half-way across the world for his niece. King Ror had created Monsea's new statutes, formed its ministries and courts, chosen its admin-istrators, then passed the kingdom into Bitterblue's ten-year-old hands. He'd seen to the burning of Leck's body and mourned the murder of his own sister, Bitterblue's mother, who was gone. Ror had brought order out of chaos in Monsea. "Leck is still lodged in too many people's minds," he had said to her. "His Grace is a sick-ness that lingers, a nightmare you must help people to forget."

But how was forgetting possible? Could she forget her own father? Could she forget that her father had murdered her mother? How could she forget the rape of her own mind?

Bitterblue laid her pen down and went, cautiously, to an east-facing window. She put a hand to the frame to steady herself and rested her temple against the glass, closing her eyes until the falling sensation receded. At the base of her tower, the River Dell formed the city's northern boundary. Opening her eyes, she followed the river's south bank east, past the three bridges, past where she guessed the silver docks and lumber docks, fish and merchant docks to be. "Watermelon patch," she said, sighing. Of course, it was too far and too dark to see any such thing.

The River Dell here, as it lapped at the castle's north walls, was slow-moving and wide as a bay. The boggy ground on the opposite shore was undeveloped, untraveled except by those who lived in Monsea's far north, but still, for some unaccountable reason, her father had built the three bridges, each higher and more magnifi-cent than any bridge needed to be. Winged Bridge, the closest, had a floor of white and blue marble, like clouds. Monster Bridge, the highest, had a walkway that rose as high as its highest arch. Winter Bridge, made of mirrors, was eerily hard to distinguish from the sky during the day, and sparkled with the light of the stars, the water, the city at night. They were purple and crimson shapes now in the sunset, the bridges, unreal and almost animal. Huge, slender creatures that stretched north across flashing water to useless land.

The falling sensation crept up on her again. Her father had told her a story of another sparkling city, also with bridges and a river—a rushing river whose water leapt off a cliff, plummeted through the air, and plunged into the sea far below. Bitterblue had laughed in delight to hear of that flying river. She had been five or six. She'd been sitting in his lap.

Leck, who tortured animals. Leck, who made little girls and hundreds of other people disappear. Leck, who became obsessed with me and chased me across the world.

Why do I push myself to these windows when I know I'll be too dizzy to get a good look at anything? What is it that I'm trying to see?

She entered the foyer of her rooms that night, turned right to her sitting room, and found Helda knitting on the sofa. The servant girl Fox was washing the windows.

Helda, who was Bitterblue's housekeeper, ladyservant, and spymaster, reached a hand into a pocket and passed Bitterblue two letters. "Here you are, dear. I'll ring for dinner," she said, heaving herself up, patting her white hair, and leaving the room.

"Oh!" Bitterblue flushed with pleasure. "*Two* letters." She broke open the plain seals and peeked inside. Both were ciphered and both written in hands she knew instantly, the messy scrawl belonging to Lady Katsa of the Middluns, the careful, strong markings belonging to Prince Po of Lienid, who was Skye's younger brother, and, with Skye, one of the two unmarried sons of Ror who would make Bitterblue dreadful husbands. Truly, comically dreadful.

She found a corner of the sofa to curl up in and read Po's first. Po had lost his sight eight years ago. He could not read words on paper, for while the part of his Grace that allowed him to sense the physical world around him compensated for many aspects of his blindness, he had trouble demystifying differences on flat surfaces, and he could not sense color. He wrote in large letters with a sharp piece of graphite, because graphite was easier to control than ink, and he wrote with a ruler as a guide, since he could not see what he was writing. He also used a small set of movable wooden letters as a reference to help him keep his own ciphers straight in his mind.

Just now, his letter said, he was in the northern kingdom of Nander, stirring up trouble. Switching letters, Bitterblue read that Katsa, who was an unparalleled fighter and Graced with survival skills, had been dividing her time among the kingdoms of Estill, Sunder, and Wester, where she was also stirring up trouble. That was what they did with themselves, those two Gracelings, along with a small band of friends: They stirred up trouble on a serious scale—bribery, coercion, sabotage, organized rebellion—all directed at stopping the worst behavior of the world's most seriously corrupt kings. "King Drowden of Nander has been imprisoning his nobles randomly and executing them, because he knows some are disloyal, but isn't sure which," wrote Po. "We're going to spring them from prison. Giddon and I have been teaching townspeople to fight. There's going to be a revolution, Cousin."

Both letters ended the same way. Po and Katsa hadn't seen each other in months, and neither of them had seen Bitterblue in over a year. Both intended to come to Bitterblue as soon as their work could spare them, and stay as long as they could.

Bitterblue was so happy that she curled herself up in a ball on the sofa and hugged a pillow for a full minute.

At the far end of the room, Fox had managed to climb to the very top of the tall windows, bracing her hands and feet against the window frames. There, she rubbed at her own reflection vigorously, polishing the surface to a high shine. Wearing a divided skirt of blue, Fox matched her surroundings, for Bitterblue's sitting room was blue, from the carpet to the blue-and-gold walls to the ceiling, which was midnight blue and stenciled with gold and scarlet stars. The royal crown sat on a blue velvet cushion in this room, always, except when Bitterblue wore it. A hanging of a fantastical sky-blue horse with green eyes marked the hidden door that had once given passage down to Leck's rooms below, before people had come in and done something to block off the stairway.

Fox was a Graceling, with one eye pale gray and the other dark gray, and she was startlingly pretty, almost glamorous, red-haired and strong-featured. Her Grace was a strange one: fearlessness. But it was not fearlessness combined with recklessness; it was only a lack of the unpleasant sensation of fear; and, in fact, Fox had what Bitterblue interpreted to be an almost mathematical ability to calculate physical consequences. Fox knew better than anyone what was likely to happen if she slipped and fell out of the window. It was that knowledge that kept her careful, rather than the feeling of fear.

Bitterblue thought such a Grace was wasted in a castle servant, but in post-Leck Monsea, Gracelings were not the property of the kings; they were free to work where they liked. And Fox seemed to like doing odd jobs in the upper north floors of the castle—though Helda did talk about trying her as a spy sometime.

"Do you live in the castle, Fox?" asked Bitterblue.

"No, Lady Queen," answered Fox from her perch. "I live in the east city."

"You work strange hours, don't you?"

"It suits me, Lady Queen," Fox responded. "Sometimes, I work the night through."

"How do you get in and out of the castle at such odd hours? Does the Door Guard ever give you a hard time?"

"Well, it's never any trouble getting out; they'll let anyone out, Lady Queen. But to come in at the gatehouse at night, I show a bracelet that Helda's given me, and to get past the Lienid at your own doors, I show the bracelet again and give the password."

"The password?"

"It changes every day, Lady Queen."

"And how do you get the password yourself?"

"Helda hides it for us somewhere, in a different place every day of the week, Lady Queen."

"Oh? What is it today?"

"'Chocolate pancake,' Lady Queen," said Fox.

Bitterblue lay on her back on the sofa for a while, giving this its due consideration. Every morning at breakfast, Helda asked Bitterblue to name a word or words that could serve as the key for any ciphered notes they were likely to pass to each other during the day. Yesterday morning, Bitterblue had chosen "chocolate pancake." "What was yesterday's password, Fox?"

"'Salted caramel,'" said Fox.

Which had been the key Bitterblue had chosen two days ago. "What delicious passwords," Bitterblue said idly, an idea forming in her mind.

"Yes, Helda's passwords always make me hungry," Fox said.

A hood lay draped on the edge of Bitterblue's sofa, deep blue, like the sofa. Fox's hood, certainly; Bitterblue had seen her wear simple coverings like that before. It was much plainer than any of Bitterblue's coats.

"How often do you suppose the Lienid Door Guard changes guard?" Bitterblue asked Fox.

"Every hour on the hour, Lady Queen," Fox responded.

"Every hour! That's quite often."

"Yes, Lady Queen," replied Fox blandly. "I don't suppose there's much continuity in what any of them sees."

Fox stood on the solid floor again, bent over a bucket of suds, her back to the queen.

Bitterblue took the hood, tucked it under her arm, and slipped out of the room.

BITTERBLUE HAD WATCHED spies enter her rooms at night before, hooded, hunched, unrecognizable until they'd removed their covering garments. Her Lienid Door Guard, a gift from King Ror, guarded the castle's main entrance and the entrance to Bitterblue's living quarters, and did so with discretion. They were under no obligation to answer the questions of anyone but Bitterblue and Helda, not even the Monsean Guard, which was the kingdom's official army and police. This gave Bitterblue's personal spies the freedom to come and go without their presence being noted by her administration. It was a strange little provision of Ror's, to protect Bitterblue's privacy. Ror had a similar arrangement in Lienid.

The bracelet was no problem, for the bracelet Helda gave her spies was a plain leather cord on which hung a replica of a ring Ashen had worn. It was a proper Lienid ring in design: gold, inset with tiny, sparkly, deep gray stones. Every ring worn by a Lienid represented a particular family member, and this was the ring Ashen had worn for Bitterblue. Bitterblue had the original. She kept it in her mother's wooden chest in the bedroom, along with all of Ashen's rings.

It was strangely affecting to tie this ring to her wrist. Her mother had shown it to her many times, explained that she'd chosen the stones to match Bitterblue's eyes. Bitterblue hugged her wrist to her body, trying to decide what her mother would think of what she was about to do.

Well. And Mama and I snuck out of the castle once too. Though not this way; by the windows. And with good reason. She was trying to save me from him.

She did save me. She sent me on ahead and stayed behind to die.

Mama, I'm not sure why I'm doing what I'm about to do. Something is missing, do you see? Piles of paper at my desk in my tower, day in, day out. That can't be all there is. You understand, don't you?

SNEAKING WAS A kind of deceit. So was disguise. Just past midnight, wearing dark trousers and Fox's hood, the queen snuck out of her own rooms and stepped into a world of stories and lies.

SHE'D NEVER SEEN the bridges close up. Despite her yearly tours, Bitterblue had never been on the streets of the east city; she only knew the bridges from the heights of her tower, looking out at them from across the sky, not even certain they were real. Now, as Bitterblue stood at the base of Winged Bridge, she ran her fingers along a seam where pieces of cold marble joined to form the gargantuan foundations.

And attracted some attention. "Move along there," said a gruff man who'd come to the doorway of one of the dirty white stone buildings squeezed between the bridge's pillars. He emptied a bucket into the gutter. "We've no need of crackpots."

This seemed harsh for a person whose only crime was the touching of a bridge, but Bitterblue moved along obediently to avoid interaction. An awful lot of people were walking the streets at this hour. Every one of them gave her a fright. She skirted them when she could, pulling her hood low over her face, happy to be small.

Tall, narrow buildings leaned together, propping each other up, occasionally offering glimpses of the river in between. At every intersection, roads branched off in several directions, multiplying possibilities. She decided to stay within sight of the river for now, because she suspected that otherwise, she'd become lost and over-whelmed. But it was hard not to turn down some of those streets that wound away or stretched into darkness, promising secrets.

The river brought her to the next behemoth on her list, Monster Bridge. Bitterblue was absorbing more details now, even daring to glance into people's faces. Some were furtive and hurried, or exhausted, full of pain, and others were empty and expressionless. The buildings, many white stone, some clapboard, all washed with yellow light and rising into shadow, also impressed her, with how gaunt and run-down they seemed.

It was a misstep that landed her in the strange story place under Monster Bridge, though Leck also played a part. Hopping sideways into an alleyway to avoid a pair of large, lumbering men, she found herself trapped when the men turned into the alleyway too. She could have just pushed her way back out again, of course, but not without drawing attention to herself, so she scuttled on ahead, pretending she knew where she was going. Unfortunately, the alleyway ended abruptly, at a door in a stone wall, guarded by a man and a woman.

"Well?" the man said to her as she stood there in confusion. "What do you want, then? In or out?"

"I'm just going," said Bitterblue in a whisper.

"All right," said the man. "Off you go."

As she turned to obey, the men who'd followed her came upon them and moved past. The door opened to admit them, then closed, then opened again to release a small, cheerful group of young people. A voice escaped from inside: a deep, raspy rumble, indecipherable but melodic, a sort of voice she imagined a wizened old tree would speak with. It had the tone of someone telling a story.

And then it spoke a word she understood: Leck.

"In," she said to the man, deciding in a mad split second. He shrugged, not seeming to care, as long as she went someplace.

And so Bitterblue followed Leck's name into her first story room.

* * * * *

IT WAS A pub of some sort, with heavy wooden tables and chairs and a bar, lit by a hundred lamps and packed with men and women, standing, sitting, moving about, dressed plainly, drinking from cups. Bitterblue's relief that she had walked into nothing but a pub was so palpable that it gave her chills.

The room's attention was fixed on a man who stood on the bar telling a story. He had a crooked face and pitted skin that turned beautiful, somehow, as he spoke. The story he told was one Bitterblue recognized but didn't immediately trust, not because anything in the story itself seemed off, but because the man had one dark eye and one that shone pale blue. What was his Grace? A lovely speaking voice? Or was there something more sinister about it, something that kept this room in thrall?

Bitterblue multiplied 457 by 228 randomly, just to see how she felt afterwards. It took her a minute. *104,196.* And no feeling of blankness or fog around the numbers; no sense that her mental grip on the numbers was in any way superior to her mental grip on anything else. It was no more than a lovely voice.

Some traffic around the entrance had shuffled Bitterblue straight to the bar. A woman stood before her suddenly, asking her what she wanted. "Cider," Bitterblue said, grasping for something a person might want, for she didn't suppose it was normal to ask for nothing. Oh—but here was a dilemma, for the woman would expect payment for the cider, wouldn't she? The last time Bitterblue had carried money was—she couldn't remember. A queen had no need for money.

A man beside her at the bar belched, fumbling with some coins spread before him that his fingers were too clumsy to collect. Without thinking, Bitterblue rested her arm on the bar, letting her wide sleeve cover two of the coins closest to her. Then she slipped the fingers of her other hand under her sleeve and fished the coins into her fist. A moment later, the coins were in her pocket and her empty hand rested innocently on the bar. When she glanced around, trying to look nonchalant, she caught the eyes of a young man who was staring at her with the smallest grin on his face. He leaned on a part of the bar that was at a right angle to hers, where he had a perfect view of her, her neighbors, and, she could only assume, her transgressions.

She looked away, ignoring his smile. When the bar lady brought the cider, Bitterblue plunked her coins on the counter, deciding to trust to fate that they were the right amount. The woman picked up the coins and put a smaller coin down. Grabbing it and the cup, Bitterblue slipped away from the bar and moved to a corner in the back, where there were more shadows, a wider view, and fewer people to notice her.

Now she could lower her guard and listen to the story. It was one that she'd heard many times; it was one she'd told. It was the story—true—of how her own father had come to the Monsean court as a boy. He'd come begging, wearing an eye patch, saying nothing of who he was or where he was from. He'd charmed the king and queen with tall tales he'd invented, tales about a land where the animals were violently colored, and the buildings were wide and tall as mountains, and glorious armies rose out of rock. No one had known who his parents were, or why he wore an eye patch, or why he'd told such stories, but he'd been loved. The king and queen, childless, had adopted him as their own son. When Leck had turned sixteen, the king, having no living family, had named Leck his heir.

Days later, the king and queen were dead from a mysterious illness that no one at court felt the need to question. The old king's advisers threw themselves into the river, for Leck could make people do things like that—or could push them into the river himself, then tell the witnesses that they'd seen something other than what they'd seen. Suicide, rather than murder. Leck's thirty-five-year reign of mental devastation had begun.

Bitterblue had heard this story before as an explanation. She had never once heard it presented as a *story,* the old king and queen coming alive with loneliness and gentleness, love for a boy. The advisers, wise and worried, devoted to their king and queen. The storyteller described Leck partly the way he'd been and partly the way Bitterblue knew he hadn't. He hadn't been a person who cackled and leered and rubbed his hands together villainously like the storyteller said. He'd been simpler than that. He'd spoken simply, reacted simply, and performed acts of violence with a simple, expressionless precision. He'd calmly done whatever he'd needed to do to make things the way he wanted them.

My father, thought Bitterblue. Then she reached for the coin in her pocket suddenly, ashamed of herself for stealing. Remembering that her hood was stolen too. *I also take what I want. Did I get that from him?*

The young man who knew she was a thief was a distracting sort of person. He seemed to have no wish to keep still, always moving, slipping past people who shuffled aside to let him by. Easy to keep track of, for he happened to be one of the most conspicuous people in the room, both Lienid and not-Lienid at the same time.

The Lienid, almost without exception, were a dark-haired, gray-eyed people with a certain handsome set to their mouths and a certain sweep to their hair, like Skye, like Po, and gold in their ears and on their fingers, men and women, nobles and citizens alike.

Bitterblue had inherited Ashen's dark hair and gray eyes and, though its effects were rather plainer on her than on others, something of the Lienid aspect. At any rate, she looked more Lienid than this fellow did.

His hair was brown like wet sand, sun-bleached almost white at the ends, his skin deeply freckled. His facial features, though nice enough, were not particularly Lienid, but the gold studs that flashed in his ears and the rings on his fingers—those were unquestionably Lienid. His eyes were impossibly, abnormally purple, so that one knew at once he wasn't just a plain person. And then, as one adjusted to his overall incongruity, one saw that of course the purple was of two different shades. He was a Graceling. And a Lienid, but he had not been born Lienid.

Bitterblue wondered what his Grace was.

Then, as he slipped past a man who was swigging from a cup, Bitterblue saw him dip into the man's pocket, remove something, and tuck it under his arm, almost faster than Bitterblue could believe. Raising his eyes, accidentally catching hers, he saw that she saw. This time, there was no amusement in the expression he directed at her. Only coldness, some insolence, and the hint of a high-eyebrowed threat.

He turned his back to her and made his way to the door, where he placed a hand on the shoulder of a young man with floppy dark hair who was apparently his friend, for the two of them left together. Getting it into her head to see where they were going, she abandoned her cider and followed, but when she stepped out into the alley, they were gone.

Not knowing the time, she returned to the castle, but paused at the foot of the drawbridge. She had stood in this very spot once, almost eight years ago. Her feet remembered and wanted to take her into the west city, the way she'd gone with her mother that night; her feet wanted to follow the river west until the city was far behind, cross the valleys to the plain before the forest. Bitterblue wanted to stand in the spot where Father had shot Mama in the back, shot her from his horse, in the snow, while Mama tried to run away. Bitterblue hadn't seen it. She'd been hiding in the forest, as Ashen had told her to do. But Po and Katsa had seen it. Sometimes Po described it for her, quietly, holding her hands. She'd imagined it so many times that it felt like a memory, but it wasn't. She hadn't been there, she hadn't screamed the way she imagined it. She hadn't jumped in front of the arrow, or knocked Mama out of the way, or thrown a knife and killed him in time.

A clock, striking two, brought Bitterblue back. There was nothing for her to the west except for a long and difficult walk, and memories that were sharp even from this distance. She pushed herself across the drawbridge.

In bed, exhausted, yawning, she couldn't understand, at first, why she wasn't falling asleep. Then she felt it, the streets thick with people, the shadows of buildings and bridges, the sound of the stories and the taste of cider; the fright that had pervaded all she'd done. Her body was thrumming with the life of the midnight city.

3

REGULAR WORK IS ruined for me now.

This was Bitterblue's thought the next morning, bleary-eyed at her desk in her tower. Her adviser Darby, returned from his drunken bender that everyone knew about but no one mentioned, kept running up from the lower offices, bringing paper up the spiral staircase for her to do boring things with. With every arrival, he exploded through the door, catapulted across the room, and stopped on a pin before her desk. Every departure was the same. Darby, when he was sober, was always wide awake and full of vim—always, for he had one yellow eye and one green and was Graced with not needing sleep.

Runnemood, in the meantime, lazed around the room being handsome, while Thiel, too stiff and grim to be handsome, glided around Runnemood and loomed over the desk, deciding in which order Bitterblue should be tortured by the paper. Rood was still absent.

Bitterblue had too many questions, and there were too many people here whom she couldn't ask. Did her advisers know that there was a room under Monster Bridge where people told stories about Leck? Why weren't the neighborhoods under the bridges relevant to her yearly tours? Was it because the buildings were falling apart? That had been a surprise to her. And how could she get her hands on some coins without arousing suspicion?

"I want a map," she said out loud.

"A map?" said Thiel, startled, then, rustling a sheaf of papers at her: "Of the location of this charter town?"

"No. A street map of Bitterblue City. I want to study a map. Send someone to get one, will you, Thiel?"

"Does this have anything to do with watermelons, Lady Queen?"

"Thiel, I just want a map! Get me a map!"

"Gracious," said Thiel. "Darby," he said, turning to that bright-eyed personage as he burst once more into the room. "Send someone to the library for a street map of the city—a *recent* map—for the queen's perusal, would you?"

"A recent street map. Indeed," Darby said, spinning around and taking off again.

"We're procuring a map, Lady Queen," reported Thiel, turning back to Bitterblue.

"Yes," said Bitterblue sarcastically, rubbing her head. "I was here when it happened, Thiel."

"Is everything all right, Lady Queen? You seem a bit—ruffled."

"She's tired," Runnemood announced, perched in a window with his arms crossed. "Her Majesty is tired of charters and judgments and reports. If she wishes a map, she shall have one."

It annoyed Bitterblue that Runnemood understood. "I want to have more say in where I go on my tours from now on," she snapped.

"And so you shall," said Runnemood grandly. Honestly, she did not know how Thiel could stand him. Thiel was so plain and Runnemood so affected, yet the two of them worked together so comfortably, always capable of becoming a united front the moment Bitterblue stepped over the line of which only they knew the position. She decided to keep her mouth shut until the map arrived, to prevent herself from betraying the stratospheric heights of her irritability.

When it did arrive, it brought with it the royal librarian and a member of the Queen's Guard, Holt, for the librarian delivered so much more than she'd asked for that he couldn't carry it up the stairs without Holt's help. "Lady Queen," the librarian said. "As Your Majesty's request was disobligingly unspecific, I thought it best to deliver a range of maps, to increase the odds that one pleases you. It's my fervent wish to return to my work uninterrupted by your little people."

Bitterblue's librarian was Graced with the ability to read inhumanly fast and remember every word forever—or so he said, and certainly he seemed to have this skill. But Bitterblue wondered sometimes if he mightn't also be Graced with unpleasantness. His name was Death. It was pronounced to rhyme with "teeth," but Bitterblue liked to mispronounce it by accident on occasion.

"If that will be all, Lady Queen," said Death, dumping an armload of scrolls onto the edge of her desk, "I'll be going."

Half of the scrolls rolled away and hit the floor with hollow thuds. "Really," said Thiel crossly, bending to collect them, "I was quite clear to Darby that we wished a single, recent map. Take these away, Death. They're unnecessary."

"All paper maps are recent," said Death with a sniff, "when one considers the vastness of geological time."

"Her Majesty merely wishes to see the city as it is today," said Thiel.

"A city is a living organism, always changing—"

"Her Majesty wishes—"

"I wish you would all go away," said Bitterblue desolately, more to herself than to anyone else. Both men continued arguing. Runnemood joined in. And then Holt, the Queen's Guard, placed his maps on the desk, neatly so they would not fall, tipped Thiel over one shoulder, tipped Death over the other, and stood under his load. In the astonished silence that followed, Holt lumbered toward Runnemood, who, understanding, let out a snort and stalked from the room of his own accord. Then Holt carried his outraged burdens away on either shoulder, just as they got their voices back. Bitterblue could hear them screaming their indignation all the way down the stairs.

Holt was a guard in his forties with lovely eyes of gray and silver. A large, broad man with a friendly, open face, he was Graced with strength.

"That was odd," Bitterblue mused aloud. But it was nice to be alone. Opening a scroll randomly, she saw that it was an astronomical map of the constellations above the city. Cursing Death, she pushed it aside. The next one was a map of the castle before Leck's renovations, when the courtyards had numbered four instead of seven, and the roofs of her tower, the courtyards, and the upper corridors had contained no glass. The next was, amazingly, a street map of the city, but a strange map with words obliterated here and there and no bridges at all. The fourth, finally, was a modern-day map, for the bridges were shown. Yes, it was quite clearly present-day, for it was titled "Bitterblue City," not "Leck City" or the name of any previous king.

Bitterblue shifted the stacks of paper on her desk so that they held down the corners of her map, spitefully pleased to find a use for them that didn't involve her having to read them. Then she settled in to study the map, determined, at least, to have a better sense of geography the next time she snuck out.

EVERYONE REALLY IS *odd,* she thought to herself later, after another encounter with Judge Quall. She'd come upon him in the foyer outside the lower offices, balancing on one foot, then the other, scowling into the middle distance. "Femurs," he'd muttered, not noticing her. "Clavicles. Vertebrae."

"For someone who doesn't like to talk about bones, Quall," Bitterblue had said without prologue, "you bring them up an awful lot."

His eyes had passed over her, empty; then sharpening and momentarily confused. "Indeed, I do, Lady Queen," he'd said, seeming to pull himself together. "Forgive me. Sometimes I get lost in thought and lose track of the moment."

Later, at dinner in her sitting room, Bitterblue asked Helda, "Do you notice any peculiar behavior at this court?"

"Peculiar behavior, Lady Queen?"

"Like, for example, today Holt picked up Thiel and Death and carried them out of my office on his shoulders because they were annoying me," said Bitterblue. "Isn't that a bit odd?"

"Very odd," declared Helda. "I'd like to see him try that with me. We've a couple of new gowns for you, Lady Queen. Would you like to try them this evening?"

Bitterblue was indifferent to her gowns, but she always agreed to a fitting, for she found it soothing to be fussed over by Helda—Helda's soft, quick touches and her mutterings through a mouthful of pins. Her careful eyes and hands that considered Bitterblue's body and made the right decisions. Fox helped tonight too, holding fabric aside or smoothing it as Helda asked her to. It was centering to be touched. "I admire Fox's skirts that are divided into trousers," said Bitterblue to Helda. "Might I try some?"

Later, after Fox had gone and Helda had retired to bed, Bitterblue unearthed her trousers and Fox's hood from the floor of the dressing room. Bitterblue wore a knife in her boot during the day and slept with knives in sheaths on each arm at night. It was what Katsa had taught her to do. That night, Bitterblue strapped on all three knives, as security against the unpredictable.

Just before leaving, she rummaged through Ashen's chest, where she kept not only Ashen's jewelry but some of her own. She had so many useless things—pretty, she supposed, but it wasn't in her nature to wear jewelry. Finding a plain gold choker that her uncle had sent from Lienid, she tucked it into the shirt inside her hood. There were such things as pawnshops under the bridges. She'd noticed them last night, and one or two had been open.

"I only work with people I know," said the man at the first pawnshop.

At the second pawnshop, the woman behind the counter said exactly the same thing. Still standing in the doorway, Bitterblue pulled the choker out and held it up for her to see. "Hm," the woman said. "Let me take a look at that."

Half a minute later, Bitterblue had traded the choker for an enormous pile of coins and a terse "Just don't tell me where you got it, boy." It was so many more coins than Bitterblue had reckoned for that her pockets sagged and jingled in the streets, until she thought to jam some of them into her boots. Not comfortable, but far less conspicuous.

She saw a street fight she didn't understand, nasty, abrupt, and bloody, for barely had two groups of men started pushing and shoving each other than knives came out flashing and thrusting. She ran on, ashamed but not wanting to see how it ended. Katsa and Po could have broken them up. Bitterblue should have, as the queen, but she wasn't the queen right now, and she would've been mad to try.

The story under Monster Bridge that night was told by a tiny woman with a huge voice who stood stock-still on the bar, grasping her skirts in her hands. She wasn't Graced, but Bitterblue was mesmerized anyway, and nettled with the sense that she'd heard this story before. It was about a man who'd fallen into a boiling hot spring in the eastern mountains, then been rescued by an enormous golden fish. It was a dramatic story involving a bizarrely colored animal, just like the tales Leck had told. Was that how she knew it? Had Leck told her it? Or had she read it in a book when she was little? If she'd read it in a book, was it a true story? If Leck had told it, was it false? How could anyone know, eight years later, what was which?

A man near the bar smashed his cup over the head of another man. In the time it took Bitterblue to register her surprise, a brawl had erupted. She watched in amazement as the entire room seemed to enter into the spirit of the thing. The tiny woman on the bar used her advantage of height to deliver a few admirable kicks.

At the edge of the brawl, where a civilized minority was trying to keep out of the way, someone knocked against someone brown-haired, who pitched his cider onto Bitterblue's front.

"Oh, ratbuggers. Look, lad, I'm awfully sorry," Brown Hair said, grabbing a dubious bit of towel from a table and using it to dab at Bitterblue, much to her alarm. She recognized him. He was the companion of the purple-eyed Graceling thief from the previous night, whom she now recognized as well, beyond Brown Hair, launching himself cheerily into the melee.

"Your friend," Bitterblue said, pushing Brown Hair's hands away. "You should help your friend."

He came back at her determinedly with the towel. "I expect he's having a marvelous—time," he said, ending on a note of bewilderment as he uncovered a corner of braid under Bitterblue's hood. His eyes dropped to her chest, where, apparently, he found enough evidence to elucidate the situation.

"Great rivers," he said, snatching his hand back. He focused for the first time on her face, with no great success, for Bitterblue pulled her hood even lower. "Forgive me, miss. Are you all right?"

"I'm perfectly fine. Let me pass."

The Graceling and the man trying to kill the Graceling bashed into Brown Hair from behind, wedging Brown Hair more firmly against Bitterblue. He was a pleasant-looking fellow, with a lopsided face and nice hazel eyes. "Allow my friend and me to escort you safely from this place, miss," he said.

"I don't need escort. I just need you to let me by."

"It's past midnight and you're small."

"Too small for anyone to bother with."

"If only that were the way of things in Bitterblue City. Just give me a moment to collect my rather overly enthusiastic friend," he said as he was buffeted again from behind, "and we'll see you get home. My name is Teddy. His is Saf, and he isn't really the block-head he seems just now."

Teddy turned and waded heroically into the fray, and Bitterblue scuttled along the room's perimeter, making her escape. Outside, knives gripped in both hands, she ran, cutting through a graveyard, slipping into an alleyway so narrow that her shoulders touched the sides.

Her mind tried to tick off streets and landmarks from the map she'd memorized, but it was difficult on true ground, rather than paper. Her vague direction was south. Slowing to a walk, she entered a street of buildings that seemed broken all to pieces and decided never again to put herself in a situation in which she had to run with so much change in her boots.

Some of these buildings looked as if they'd been cannibalized for their wood. A shape in a gutter that formulated itself into a corpse startled her, then scared her even more when it snored. A man who smelled dead but apparently wasn't. A hen snoozed against his chest, his arm curled around it protectively.

When she came upon a whole new storytelling place, she knew somehow what it was. It had the same setup as the other place, a door in an alley, people passing in and out, and two tough-looking characters standing at the door with arms crossed.

Bitterblue's body decided for her. The watchdogs loomed but didn't stop her. Inside the door, steps led down into the earth, to another door that, when opened, dropped her into a room glowing with light, smelling of cellars and cider, and warm with the hypnotic voice of another storyteller.

Bitterblue bought a drink.

The story was, of all things, about Katsa. It was one of the horrible true stories from Katsa's childhood, when Katsa's uncle Randa, king of the seven kingdoms' most central kingdom, the Middluns, had used her for her fighting skill, forcing her to kill and maim his enemies on his behalf.

Bitterblue knew these stories; she'd heard them from Katsa herself. Parts of this storyteller's version were correct. Katsa had hated having to kill for Randa. But other parts were exaggerated or untrue. The fights in this story were more sensational, more bloody than Katsa had ever allowed them to become, and Katsa was more melodramatic than Bitterblue could imagine her ever being. Bitterblue wanted to yell at this storyteller for getting Katsa wrong, yell in Katsa's defense, and it confused her that the crowd seemed to love this wrong version of Katsa. To them, that Katsa was real.

As Bitterblue approached the castle's eastern wall that night, she noticed a few things at once. First, two of the lanterns atop the wall had gone out, leaving a section in such pitch darkness that Bitterblue glanced around the street, suspicious, and found that her suspicions were justified. The streetlamps along that stretch had also gone out. Next, she saw movement, nearly imperceptible, midway up the dark, flat wall. A moving shape—surely a person?—that stilled its movement as a member of the Monsean Guard marched past above. The movement started up again once the guard had gone.

Bitterblue realized that she was watching a person climb the east castle wall. She stepped into the seclusion of a shop doorway and tried to work out whether she should start shouting now, or wait until the perpetrator had made it to the top of the high wall, where he would be stuck, and the guards would be more likely to be able to catch him.

Except that the person didn't climb onto the wall. He stopped climbing just below the top—just below a small stone shadow that Bitterblue assumed, from its placement, was one of the many gargoyles that balanced on ledges or hung over the edge to stare at the ground below. A sort of scraping noise commenced that she couldn't identify, then stopped, momentarily, as the guard passed again above. Then started up again. This went on for quite some time. Bitterblue's mystification was turning to boredom when suddenly the person said, "Oof," a cracking noise followed, and the person slid, in a somewhat-controlled fall, down the wall again, with the gargoyle. A second person, whom Bitterblue hadn't noticed until this point, moved in the shadows at the base of the wall and caught the first person, more or less, though a grunt and a series of whispered curses suggested that one of them had gotten the worst of it. The second figure produced some sort of sack into which the first figure lowered the gargoyle, and then, sack over the shoulder of the first figure's back, they snuck away together.

They passed directly in front of Bitterblue, shrinking back against her doorway. She recognized them easily. They were the pleasant brown-haired fellow, Teddy, and his Graceling friend, Saf.

4

"LADY QUEEN," SAID Thiel sternly the next morning. "Are you even paying attention?"

She wasn't paying attention. She was trying to come up with a casual way to broach an unapproachable topic. *How is everyone feeling today? Did you all sleep well? Anyone missing any gargoyles?* "Of course I'm paying attention," she snapped.

"I daresay that if I asked you to describe the last five things you've signed, Lady Queen, you'd be at a loss."

What Thiel didn't understand was that this kind of work required no attention. "Three charters for three coastal towns," Bitterblue said, "a work order for a new door to be fitted to the vault of the royal treasury, and a letter to my uncle, the King of Lienid, requesting him to bring Prince Skye when he comes."

Thiel cleared his throat a bit sheepishly. "I stand corrected, Lady Queen. It was your unhesitant signing of that last that led me to wonder."

"Why should I hesitate? I like Skye."

"Do you?" said Thiel, then hesitated himself. "Really?" he added, beginning to look so thoroughly pleased about things that Bitterblue began to regret goading him, for that was what she was doing.

"Thiel," she said. "Are your spies good for nothing? Skye favors men, not women, and certainly not me. Understand? The worst is that he's practical, so he might even marry me if we asked him. Maybe that would be fine with you, but it wouldn't with me."

"Oh," Thiel said with obvious disappointment. "That is a relevant piece of information, Lady Queen, if it's true. Are you certain?"

"Thiel," she said impatiently, "he's not secretive about it. Ror himself has recently come to know. Haven't you wondered why Ror has never suggested the match?"

"Well," Thiel said, then resisted saying anything further. The threat of Bitterblue's cruelty if he persisted on the topic still lingered in this room. "Shall we review some census results today, Lady Queen?"

"Yes, please." Bitterblue liked reviewing the kingdom's census results with Thiel. The gathering of the information fell under Runnemood's jurisdiction, but Darby prepared the reports, which were organized neatly by district, with maps, showing statistics for literacy, employment, population numbers, lots of things. Thiel was good at answering her many questions; Thiel knew everything. And the entire endeavor was the closest Bitterblue ever came to feeling that she had a grasp on her kingdom.

THAT NIGHT AND the two nights following, she went out again, visiting the two pubs she knew, listening to stories. Often, the stories were about Leck. Leck torturing the little cut-up pets he'd kept in the back garden. Leck's castle servants walking around with cuts in their skin. Leck's death at the end of Katsa's dagger. These late-night story audiences had gory tastes. But it was more than that; in the spaces between the blood, Bitterblue noticed another kind of recurring, bloodless story. This kind always began in the usual way of stories—perhaps two people falling in love, or a clever child trying to solve a mystery. But just as you thought you knew where the story was going, it would end abruptly, when the lovers or the child vanished with no explanation, never to be seen again.

Aborted stories. Why did people come out to hear them? Why would they choose to listen to the same thing over and over, crashing up against the same unanswerable question every time?

What had happened to all the people Leck had made disappear? How had their stories ended? There had been hundreds of them, children and adults, women and men, taken by Leck, presumably killed. But she didn't know, and her advisers had never been able to tell her, where, why, or how, and it seemed as if the people in the city had no idea either. Suddenly, it wasn't enough for Bitterblue to know they were gone. She wanted to know the rest about them, because the people in these story places were her people, and it was clear that they wanted to know. She wanted to know so that she could tell them.

There were other questions pushing themselves forward too. Now that it occurred to her to look, Bitterblue noticed places where three more gargoyles, in addition to the one she'd seen carried away, were missing from the east wall. Why hadn't any of her advisers brought these thefts of property to her attention?

"Lady Queen," Thiel said severely in her office one morning, "don't sign that."

Bitterblue blinked. "What?"

"That charter, Lady Queen," said Thiel. "I've just spent fifteen minutes explaining why you shouldn't sign it, and there you are with a pen in your hand. Where is your mind?"

"Oh," Bitterblue said, dropping her pen, sighing. "No, I heard you. The lord Danhole—"

"Danzhol," corrected Thiel.

"Lord Danzhol, the lord of a town in central Monsea, objects to the town being taken from his governance. You think I should grant him an audience before deciding."

"I regret that it is his right to be heard, Lady Queen. I regret as well—"

"Yes," said Bitterblue in distraction. "You've told me he also wishes to marry me. Very well."

"Lady Queen!" said Thiel, then tucked his chin to his chest, studying her. "Lady Queen," he said gently, "I ask a second time. Where is your mind today?"

"It's with the gargoyles, Thiel," said Bitterblue, rubbing her temples.

"Gargoyles? What can you mean, Lady Queen?"

"The ones on the east wall, Thiel. I overheard some chatter among the clerks in the lower offices," she lied, "about there being four gargoyles missing from the east wall. Why has no one informed me?"

"Missing!" said Thiel. "Where have they gone, Lady Queen?"

"Well, how should I know? Where do gargoyles go?"

"I highly doubt this is true, Lady Queen," said Thiel. "I feel certain you misheard something."

"Go ask them," said Bitterblue. "Or have someone go check. I know what I heard."

Thiel went away. He came back sometime later with Darby, who carried a short stack of papers through which he was madly shuffling. "There *are* four gargoyles missing from the east wall, Lady Queen," Darby said briskly, reading, "according to our records of castle decoration. But they are missing merely in the sense that they were never there in the first place."

"Never there!" said Bitterblue, knowing perfectly well that at least one had been there mere nights ago. "None of the four were ever there?"

"King Leck never got around to commissioning those four, Lady Queen. He left the spaces blank."

What Bitterblue had seen, when she'd counted, had been rough, broken places on the wall where it very much looked as if something stone had been present and then been hacked away—namely, gargoyles. "You're certain of those records?" she said. "When were they made?"

"At the start of your reign, Lady Queen," said Darby. "Records were made of the state of every part of the castle; I supervised them myself, at the request of your uncle, King Ror."

It seemed a strange little thing to lie about, and not important enough for it to matter if Darby had gotten the records wrong. And yet, it unsettled her. Darby's eyes as he blinked at her, yellow and green, efficient and certain as he gave her incorrect information, unsettled her. She found herself tracing her mind back through all the recent things Darby had told her, wondering if he was the type to lie.

Then she caught herself, knowing that she was suspicious only because she was generally unsettled, and that she was unsettled because everything these days seemed designed to disorient her. It was like the maze she'd discovered last night, looking for a new, more isolated route from her high rooms at the castle's farthest north edge to the gatehouse in the castle's south wall. The glass ceilings of the castle's top level corridors made her nervous about being seen by guards patrolling above. So she'd dropped straight down a narrow staircase near her rooms to the level below, then found herself trapped in a series of passageways that always seemed promisingly straight and well lit but then veered or branched, or even came to dark dead ends, until she was hopelessly confused.

"Are you lost?" an unfamiliar voice had asked behind her, male and sudden. Bitterblue had frozen, turned, and tried not to look too hard at the man who was gray-haired and dressed in the black of the Monsean Guard. "You're lost, aren't you?"

Not breathing, Bitterblue had nodded.

"So is everyone I find here," the man said, "mostly. You're in King Leck's maze. It's all corridors leading nowhere, with his rooms in the middle."

The guard had led her out. Following on tiptoe, she'd wondered why Leck had built a maze around his rooms, and why she'd never known about it before. And began to wonder too about the other strange landscapes within her castle walls. To get to the grand foyer and the gatehouse exit beyond, Bitterblue had to cross the great courtyard that sat flush against the foyer at the castle's far south. Leck had arranged for the shrubberies in the great courtyard to be cut into fantastical shapes: proud, posing people with flowers for eyes and hair; fierce, monstrous flowering animals. Bears and mountain lions, enormous birds. A fountain in one corner poured noisy water into a deep pool. Balconies stretched up the courtyard walls, all five stories. Gargoyles, more gargoyles, perched on high ledges, scaled walls, leering, poking heads out shyly. The glass ceiling reflected the courtyard lanterns back at Bitterblue, like large muddy stars.

Why had Leck cared so much about his shrubberies? Why had he fitted glass ceilings to the courtyards and to so many of the castle's roofs? And what was it about the dark that made her question things she'd never questioned before, in the day?

In the great courtyard late one night, a man strode in from the grand foyer, pushing back his hood, crossing the floor with the sharp sound of boots on marble. Her adviser Runnemood's self-possessed walk; Runnemood's jeweled rings glittering and Runnemood's handsome features moving in and out of shadow.

In a panic, Bitterblue had dived behind a shrubbery of a rearing horse. Then her Graced guard Holt had followed Runnemood in, supporting Judge Quall, who was shivering. All of them had passed into the castle, heading north. Bitterblue had run along, too frightened at almost having been seen to wonder, then, what they'd been doing out in the city at such an hour. It had occurred to her to wonder later.

"Where do you go at night, Runnemood?" she'd asked him the next morning.

"Go, Lady Queen?" he'd said with narrowed eyes.

"Yes," Bitterblue said, "do you ever go out late? I hear you do. Forgive me; I'm curious."

"I do have late meetings in the city now and then, Lady Queen," he said. "Late dinners with lords who want things—like appointments to one of your ministries, or your hand in marriage, for example. It is my job to humor such people and put them off."

Until midnight, with Judge Quall and Holt? "Do you take a guard?"

"Sometimes," Runnemood said, pushing himself up from his seat in the window and coming to stand before her. His fine, dark eyes flashed with curiosity. "Lady Queen, why are you asking these questions?"

She was asking because she couldn't ask the questions she wanted to ask. *Are you telling me the truth? Why do I feel that you're not? Do you ever go to the east city? Do you ever hear the stories? Can you explain to me all the things I see at night that I don't understand?*

"Because I wish you would take a guard," Bitterblue lied, "if you must be out so late. I worry for your safety."

Runnemood's smile flashed, broad and white. "What a dear, kind queen you are," he said, in a patronizing manner that made it difficult for her to keep the dear, kind expression on her face. "I will take a guard if it eases your mind."

She went out on her own again for a few more nights, unremarked by her own Lienid Door Guard, who barely looked at her, caring only for her ring and her password. And then, on the seventh night since she'd seen them stealing the gargoyle, she crossed paths again with Teddy and his Graceling Lienid friend.

She'd just discovered a third story place, near the silver docks, in the cellar of an old, leaning warehouse. Tucked into a back corner with her drink, she was alarmed to find Saf bearing down upon her. He eyed her blandly, as if he'd never seen her before. Then he stood beside her, turning his attention to the man on the bar.

The man was telling a story that Bitterblue had never heard and was too anxious to attend to now, so distressing was it to have been singled out by Saf. The hero of the story was a sailor from the island kingdom of Lienid. Saf seemed quite riveted. Watching him while trying to appear not to, noticing how his eyes lit up with appreciation, Bitterblue made a connection that had eluded her before. She'd been on an ocean vessel once; she and Katsa had fled to Lienid to escape Leck. And she'd seen Saf climb the east wall; she'd noted his sun-darkened skin and bleached hair. Suddenly now, the way he carried himself became acutely familiar. He had a certain ease of movement and a gleam in his eyes that she'd seen before in men who'd been sailors, but not just sailors. Bitterblue wondered if Saf might be that particular brand of sailor who volunteered to climb to the top of the mast during a gale.

She wondered what he was doing so far north of Monport, and, again, what his Grace was. From the bruising around his eyebrow tonight and the raw skin on one cheekbone, it looked neither to be fighting nor quick mending.

Teddy wove through the tables bearing a mug in each fist, one of which he handed to Saf. He set himself up at Bitterblue's other side, which, as her stool was in the corner, meant that they had trapped her.

"The polite thing," Teddy murmured to her sidelong, "would be for you to tell us your name, as I've given ours."

Bitterblue did not mind Saf's proximity so much when Teddy was near, near enough that she could see the smudged ink on his fingers. Teddy had the feeling of a bookkeeper, or a clerk, or at any rate, a person who would not transform suddenly into a renegade. She said quietly, "Is it polite for two men to trap a woman in a corner?"

"Teddy would have you believe we're doing it for your own safety," Saf said, his accent plainly Lienid. "He'd be lying. It's pure suspicion. We don't trust people who come to the story rooms in disguise."

"Oh, come now!" Teddy said, loudly enough that a man or two nearby grunted at him to shush. "Speak for yourself," he whispered. "I, for one, am concerned. Fights break out. There are lunatics in the streets, and thieves."

Saf snorted. "Thieves, eh? If you'd stop prattling, we could hear the tale of this fabler. Rather close to my heart, this one."

"*Prattle,*" Teddy repeated, his eyes lit up like stars. "*Prattle.* I must add it to my list. I believe I've overlooked it."

"Ironic," Saf said.

"Oh, I haven't overlooked *ironic.*"

"I meant it's ironic that you should've overlooked *prattle.*"

"Yes," Teddy said huffily, "I suppose it would be something like you overlooking an opportunity to break your head pretending you're Prince Po reborn. I'm a writer," he added, turning back to Bitterblue.

"Shut your mouth, Teddy," said Saf.

"And printer," Teddy continued, "reader, speller. Whatever folks need, as long as it has to do with words."

"Speller?" said Bitterblue. "Do people really pay you to spell things?"

"They bring letters they've written and ask me to turn them into something legible," Teddy said. "The illiterate ask me to teach them how to sign their names to documents."

"Should they be signing their names to documents if they're illiterate?"

"No," Teddy said, "probably not, but they do, because they're required to, by landlords or employers, or lien holders they trust because they can't read well enough to know not to. That's why I serve as reader too."

"Are there so many illiterate people in the city?"

Teddy shrugged. "What would you say, Saf?"

"I'd guess thirty people in a hundred can read," Saf said, his eyes glued to the fabler, "and you talk too much."

"Thirty percent!" Bitterblue exclaimed, for these were not the statistics she'd seen. "Surely it's more than that!"

"Either you're new to Monsea," Teddy said, "or you're still stuck in King Leck's spell. Or you live in a hole in the ground and only come out at nights."

"I work in the queen's castle," Bitterblue said, improvising smoothly, "and I suppose I'm used to the castle ways. Everyone who lives under her roof reads and writes."

"Hm," Teddy said, squinting doubtfully at this. "Well, most people in the city read and write well enough to function in their own trades. A metalsmith can read an order for knives and a farmer knows how to label his crates *beans* or *corn*. But the percentage who could understand this story if it were handed to them on paper," Teddy said, tilting his floppy hair at the storyteller—fabler, Saf had called him—"is probably close enough to what Saf said. One of Leck's legacies. And one of the driving forces behind my book of words."

"Book of words?"

"Oh, yes. I'm writing a book of words."

Saf touched Teddy's arm. Instantly, almost before Teddy had finished his sentence, they left her, too quickly for Bitterblue to ask whether any book had ever been written that was not a book of words.

Near the door, Teddy looked an invitation back at her. She declined with a shake of her head, trying not to reveal her exasperation, for she was certain she'd just seen Saf slip something out from under a random man's arm and slide it up his own sleeve. What was it this time? It had looked like a roll of papers.

It didn't matter. Whatever those two were up to, they were up to no good, and she was going to have to decide what to do about them.

The fabler began a new story. Bitterblue was startled to find that it was, again, the story of Leck's origins and rise to power. Tonight's fabler told it just a bit differently than the last had. She listened hard, hoping that this man would say something new, a missing image or word, a key that would turn in a lock and open a door behind which all her memories and all she'd been told would make sense.

THEIR SOCIABILITY—OR, Teddy's—bolstered her courage. This, in turn, terrified her, though not enough to stop her seeking them out over the next few nights. *Thieves,* she reminded herself whenever she crossed paths with them in the story rooms, exchanged greetings, said a few words. *Wretched, ingrate thieves, and what I'm doing, trying to put myself in their way, is dangerous.*

August was coming to an end. "Teddy," she said one night as the two of them wandered toward her, then huddled with her at the back of the dark, crowded, cellar story room near the silver docks, "I don't understand your book. Isn't every book a book of words?"

"I must say," Teddy responded, "that if we're to run into each other so often, and if you're to call us by name, then we must have a name for you."

"Call me whatever you like."

"Hear that, Saf?" Teddy said, leaning across Bitterblue, his face brightening. "A word challenge. But how shall we proceed, when we know neither what she does for her bread nor what she looks like under that hood?"

"She's part Lienid," Saf said, not taking his eyes off the fabler.

"Is she? You've seen?" Teddy asked, impressed, stooping, and trying, unsuccessfully, to get a better look at Bitterblue's face. "Well then, we should give her a color name. What about Redgreenyellow?"

"That's the stupidest thing I've ever heard. It makes her sound like a pepper."

"Well, what about Grayhood?"

"First of all, her hood is blue, and secondly, she's not a grandmother. I doubt she's more than sixteen."

Bitterblue was tired of Teddy and Saf crushing her between them, having a whispered conversation about her, practically in her face. "I'm as old as both of you," she said, even though she suspected she wasn't, "and I'm smarter, and I can probably fight as well as you can."

"Her personality is not gray," Saf said.

"Indeed," Teddy said. "She's all sparks."

"How about Sparks, then?"

"Perfect. So, you're curious about my book of words, Sparks?"

The absurdity of the name tickled, flummoxed, and annoyed her all at once; she wished she hadn't given them free rein to choose, but she had, so there was no use complaining. "I am."

"Well, I suppose it'd be more accurate to say it's a book *about* words. It's called a dictionary. Very few have ever been attempted. The idea is to set down a list of words and then write a definition for each word. *Spark,*" he said grandly. "A small bit of fire, as in, 'A stray spark burst from the oven and ignited the curtains.' You see, Sparks? A person reading my dictionary will be able to learn the meanings of all the words there are."

"Yes," Bitterblue said, "I've heard of such books. Except that if it uses words to define words, then don't you already need to know the definitions of words in order to understand it?"

Saf seemed to be expanding with glee. "With one stroke," he said, "Sparks fells Teddren's blasted book of words."

"Yes, all right," Teddy said, in the forbearing tone of one who's had to hold up his side of this argument before. "In the abstract, that's true. But in practice, I'm certain it'll be quite useful, and I mean it to be the most thorough dictionary ever written. I'm also writing a book of truths."

"Teddy," said Saf, "go get the next round."

"Sapphire told me you saw him steal," continued Teddy to Bitterblue, unconcerned. "You mustn't misunderstand. He only steals back that which has already been—"

Now Saf's fist grabbed Teddy's collar and Teddy choked over his words. Saf said nothing, only stood there, holding Teddy at his throat, looking daggers into Teddy's eyes.

"—stolen," spluttered Teddy. "Perhaps I'll go get the next round."

"I could kill him," Saf said, watching Teddy go. "I think I will later."

"What did he mean, you only steal that which has already been stolen?"

"Let's talk about your thievery instead, Sparks," said Saf. "Do you steal from the queen, or only poor sods trying to have a drink?"

"What about you? Do you steal both on land and on sea?"

This made Saf laugh, quietly, which was a thing Bitterblue had never seen him do before. She was rather proud of herself. He nursed his drink, ran his eyes over the room, and took his time answering.

"I was raised on a Lienid ship by Lienid sailors," he admitted finally. "I'm about as likely to steal from a sailor as I am to put a nail in my head. My true family is Monsean, and a few months ago I came here to spend some time with my sister. I met Teddy, who offered me a job in his printing shop, which is good work, until I get the urge for leaving again. There. You've had my story."

"Great chunks of it are missing," said Bitterblue. "Why were you raised on a Lienid ship if you're Monsean?"

"All of yours is missing," said Saf, "and I don't trade my secrets for nothing. If you recognize me for a sailor, then you've spent some time working on a ship."

"Maybe," said Bitterblue testily.

"Maybe?" said Saf, amused. "What do you do in Bitterblue's castle?"

"I bake bread in the kitchens," she said, hoping he wouldn't ask any specifics about those kitchens, because she couldn't remember ever seeing them.

"And is it your mother who's Lienid, or your father?"

"My mother."

"And does she work with you?"

"She does fine needlework for the queen. Embroidery."

"Do you see much of her?"

"Not when we're working, but we live in the same rooms. We see each other every night and morning."

Bitterblue stopped, suddenly needing to catch her breath. It seemed to her a beautiful daydream, one that could easily be true. Perhaps there was a baker girl in the castle with a mother who was alive, touching her, every day, with thoughts, seeing her every night. "My father was a traveling Monsean fabler," she continued. "One summer he went to Lienid to tell stories and fell in love with my mother. He brought her here to live. He was killed in an accident with a dagger."

"I'm sorry to hear that," Saf said.

"It was years ago," Bitterblue said breathlessly.

"And why does a baker girl sneak out at night to steal drink money? A bit dangerous, isn't it?"

She suspected that the question contained a reference to her size. "Have you ever seen Lady Katsa of the Middluns?" she asked archly.

"No, but everyone knows her story, of course."

"She's dangerous without being big as a man."

"Fair enough, but she's a Graced fighter."

"She's taught many of the girls in this city to fight. She taught me."

"You've met her, then," Saf said, clapping his cup down onto the ledge and turning to her, all bright-eyed attention. "Have you met Prince Po too?"

"He's in the castle sometimes," Bitterblue said with a vague flap of her hand. "My point is, I'm able to defend myself."

"I'd pay to watch either of them fight," he said. "I'd give gold to watch them fight each other."

"Your own gold? Or someone else's? I think you're a Graced thief."

Saf seemed to enjoy this accusation immensely. "I'm not a Graced thief," he said, grinning. "Nor am I a Graced mind reader, but I know why you sneak out at nights. You can't get enough of the stories."

Yes. She couldn't get enough of the stories. Or of these exchanges with Teddy and Saf, for they were the same as the stories, the same as the midnight streets and alleys and graveyards, the smell of smoke and cider, the crumbling buildings. The monstrous bridges, reaching up into the sky, that Leck had built for no reason.

The more I see and hear, the more I realize how much I don't know. I want to know everything.

THE ATTACK IN the story room two nights later took her completely by surprise.

Even in the moments afterwards Bitterblue was unaware of it having happened, and wondered why Saf had pushed in front of her protectively, clutching at the arm of a hooded man, and why Teddy was leaning on Saf looking vague and ill. The entire struggle was so silent and the movements so furiously controlled that when the hooded man finally broke away and Saf whispered to Bitterblue, "Give Teddy your shoulder. Act normal. He's only drunk," Bitterblue thought Teddy actually was drunk. She didn't understand until they'd passed out of the story room, Teddy's weight heavy between them, that his problem was not drink. His problem was the knife in his gut.

If Bitterblue had had any doubt that Saf was a sailor, his language now as he carried his gasping, glass-eyed friend up the steps laid those doubts to rest. Saf lowered Teddy to the ground, whipped his own shirt over his head and ripped it in half. In one motion that caused Teddy—and Bitterblue—to cry out, he yanked the blade from Teddy's abdomen. Then he pressed a wadded piece of shirt to the wound and snarled up at Bitterblue.

"Do you know the intersection of White Horse Alley and Bow Street?"

It was a location close to the castle, by the east wall. "Yes."

"A healer named Roke lives on the second story of the building on the southeast corner. Run and wake him and bring him to Teddy's shop."

"Where is Teddy's shop?"

"On Tinker Street near the fountain. Roke knows it."

"But that's very near here. Surely there's a healer closer—"

Teddy stirred and began to whimper. "Roke," he cried. "Tilda— tell Tilda and Bren—"

Saf barked at Bitterblue, "Roke is the only healer we can trust. Stop wasting time. Go!"

Bitterblue turned and tore through the streets, hoping that Saf's Grace, whatever it was, was a kind to help him keep Teddy alive for the next thirty minutes, because that was how long this relay was going to take her. Her mind spun. Why would a hooded man in a story room attack a writer and a thief of gargoyles and things already stolen? What had Teddy done for someone to want to hurt him this badly?

And then, after a few minutes of running, the question dropped away, her head cooled, and she began to realize the true desperation of the situation. Bitterblue knew about knife wounds. Katsa had taught her how to inflict them, and Katsa's cousin Prince Raffin, the heir to the Middluns throne and a medicine maker, had explained to her the limits of what healers could do. The knife in Teddy's gut had been low. Perhaps his lungs and his liver and maybe even his stomach were safe, but still, it had probably at least cut into his intestine. This could mean death even with a healer skilled enough to patch the holes, for the contents of Teddy's intestine even now could be spilling into his abdomen, and this would lead to an infection—fever, swelling, pain—that people rarely survived. If it came to that. He could also bleed to death.

Bitterblue had never heard of the healer Roke, and was in no position to judge his abilities. But she did know of one healer who had kept alive people with knives in their bellies: her own healer,

Madlen, who was Graced, and who had a reputation for marvelous medicines and impossible surgical successes.

When Bitterblue reached the intersection of White Horse Alley and Bow Street, she kept running.

THE CASTLE INFIRMARY was on the ground floor, east of the great courtyard. Not knowing her way around, Bitterblue scurried like the shadow of a rat down a hallway and took a chance, thrusting Ashen's ring into the face of a member of the Monsean Guard who was drowsing under a wall lantern.

"Madlen!" she whispered. "Where?"

Startled, the man cleared his throat and gestured. "Down that corridor. Second door on the left."

A moment later she was in a dark bedroom shaking her healer out of sleep. Madlen woke, grunting strange, incomprehensible words that Bitterblue cut through sharply. "Madlen, it's the queen. Wake up, and dress for running, and bring whatever you need for a man with a blade in his gut."

There was the noise of fumbling, then a spark as Madlen lit a candle. She exploded out of bed, glared at Bitterblue with her single amber eye, and blundered across the room to her wardrobe, where she yanked on a pair of trousers. The ends of her nightgown hanging to her knees, her face glowing as palely as the gown, she began to toss a great number of vials and packages and horrible-looking sharp metal implements into a bag. "What part of his gut?"

"Lowish, and rightish, I think. The blade long and wide."

"How old the man, how big, and how far are we going?"

"I don't know, nineteen, twenty, and he's no unusual size— neither tall nor short, neither fat nor thin. Near the silver docks. Is it bad, Madlen?"

"Yes," she said, "it's bad. Lead the way, Lady Queen. I'm ready."

She was, perhaps, not ready in the traditional court sense of the word. She hadn't bothered with the eye patch she usually wore over her empty eye socket, and her white hair stood out in wild knots and snarls. But she'd shoved the bunchy ends of her nightgown into the waist of her trousers. "You mustn't call me Queen tonight," Bitterblue whispered as they raced along hallways and through the shrubberies of the great courtyard. "I'm a baker in the castle kitchens and my name is Sparks."

Madlen made a disbelieving noise.

"Above all else," Bitterblue whispered, "you must never tell a single soul even the smallest part of what happens tonight. I speak as your queen, Madlen. Do you understand?"

"I understand perfectly," Madlen said, "Sparks."

Bitterblue wanted to thank the seas for sending this ferocious, astonishing Graceling to her court. But it seemed too early in the night yet for thanks.

They ran to the silver docks.

ON TINKER STREET near the fountain Bitterblue stopped, breathing hard, turning in circles, looking for a place that was lit up, squinting at the pictures on the shop signs. She had just made out the words *Teddren's* and *Print* above a dark doorway when the door opened and the gold in Saf's ears flashed at her.

His hands and forearms were covered in blood, his bare chest rising and falling, and as Bitterblue yanked Madlen forward, the panic on his face turned to fury. "That is not Roke," he said, finger extended toward Madlen's white mane, apparently the portion of her anatomy identifying her most readily as someone other than Roke.

"This is the Graced healer Madlen," Bitterblue said. "No doubt you've heard of her. She's the very best, Saf, the queen's most favored healer."

He seemed to be hyperventilating. "You brought one of the queen's own healers *here*?"

"I swear to you that she won't speak of anything she sees. You have my word."

"Your word? Your word, when I don't even know your true name?"

Madlen, younger than her hair suggested and strong as any healer must be, shoved at Saf's chest with both hands, pushing him bodily back into the shop. "*My* true name is Madlen," she said, "and I may be the only healer in all seven kingdoms who can save whoever you've got dying in there. And when this girl asks me to keep something quiet," she said, pointing a steady finger back at Bitterblue, "I do. Now get out of my way, you daft, muscle-brained nitwit!"

She elbowed past him toward the light leaking from a partly open door in the back. Barging through it, she slammed the door shut behind her.

Saf reached beyond Bitterblue to pull the shop door closed, plunging them into darkness. "I'd love to know what the seas is going on in that castle of yours, Sparks," he said with bitterness, derision, accusation, and every other nasty feeling his voice could throw into it. "The queen's own healer jumping to the will of a baker girl? What kind of healer is she anyway? I don't like her accent."

Saf smelled like blood and sweat: a sour, metallic combination that was instantly familiar to her. Saf smelled like fear. "How is he?" she whispered.

He didn't answer, only made a sound something like a disgusted sob. Then he grabbed her arm and yanked her across the room to the door with edges seeping light.

* * * * *

When one has no occupation to pass the time while a healer determines whether she can patch up a friend's dying body, that time moves slowly. And indeed, Bitterblue had little occupation, for though Madlen required a stoked fire and boiling water and good light and extra hands as she dug her implements into Teddy's side, she did not require as many helpers as were available to her. Bitterblue had a long time to observe Saf and his two companions as the night wore on. She decided that the blond woman must be Saf's sister. She wore no Lienid gold and, of course, her eyes were not purple, but still, she had Saf's look, his lightish hair, and anger sat on her face the same way it sat on Saf's. The other one might be Teddy's sister. She had exactly Teddy's mop of brown hair and clear hazel eyes.

Bitterblue had seen both women before, in the story rooms. They'd chatted, sipped drinks, laughed, and had never given the slightest indication, whenever their brothers walked by, that they were acquainted.

They and Saf hovered at Madlen's elbows at the table, following her directions exactly: scrubbing their hands and arms; boiling implements and handing them to her without touching them directly; standing where she indicated. They didn't seem concerned by Madlen's odd surgical attire that nearly concealed her, her hair clamped down under a scarf and another scarf tied over her mouth. Nor did they seem tired.

Bitterblue stood nearby, waiting, struggling at times to keep her eyes open. The tension in the room was exhausting.

The place was small, undecorated, roughly furnished with a few wooden chairs and the wooden table Teddy lay on. A small stove, a couple of closed doors, and a narrow staircase leading upstairs. Teddy breathed shallowly, unconscious on the table, his skin damp and off-color, and the one time Bitterblue tried to focus closely on Madlen's work, she found her healer, head tilted to compensate for her missing eye, placidly taking needle and thread to a mucusy mass of pink stuff protruding from Teddy's abdomen. After that, Bitterblue stayed close, ready to jump if anyone needed anything, but content enough not to watch.

Her hood fell back once while she was struggling with a cauldron of water. They all saw her face. Her breathlessness at that moment had to do with a good deal more than the heavy load she was carrying, but it became clear enough, after a second or two, that Madlen was the only person in the room who'd ever laid eyes on the queen.

IN THE EARLY morning, Madlen set down the bottle of ointment with which she'd been working and stretched her neck to left and right.

"There's nothing more we can do. I'll sew the wound closed, and then we must wait and see. I'll stay with him through the morning, just for caution's sake," she said, with a quick, bold glance at Bitterblue that the queen understood to be a request for permission. Bitterblue nodded.

"How long must we wait?" asked Teddy's sister.

"If he's to die, we may know quite soon," Madlen said. "If he's to live, we won't know it for certain until several days have gone by. I'll give you medicines to fight infection and restore his strength. He must take them regularly. If he doesn't, I can promise you he will die."

Teddy's sister, so composed during the surgery, now spoke with a violence that startled Bitterblue. "He's careless. He talks too much; he befriends people he shouldn't. He always has and I've warned him, I've begged him. If he dies, it'll be his own fault and I'll never forgive him." Tears streamed down her face and Saf's startled sister embraced her. The distraught woman sobbed against her friend's breast.

Suddenly feeling as if her presence was an intrusion, Bitterblue crossed the room and went into the shop, pulling the door shut behind her. There, she flattened herself against the wall, breathing carefully, confused to find that the other woman's tears had brought her own tears close.

The door beside her opened. Saf stood in the half-light, fully clothed now, the blood cleaned from his skin and a dripping white cloth in his hands.

"Checking to see if I'm snooping around?" said Bitterblue, her voice coming harshly from her throat.

Saf wiped the doorknob clean of its bloody smears. He went to the front of the shop and cleaned that door handle too. As he walked back toward the light, she saw his expression clearly but didn't know what to make of it, for he seemed angry and happy and bewildered all at once. He stopped beside her and shut the door to the back room, cutting off the light.

Bitterblue didn't care to be alone with him in the dark, whatever his expression. Her hands moved to the knives in her sleeves and she took a step away from him, bumping into something pointy that made her yelp.

He spoke then, not seeming to notice her distress. "She had an ointment that slowed his bleeding," he said wonderingly. "She cut him open, pulled part of him out, fixed it, and stuck it back in again. She's given us so many medicines that I can't keep track of what they're all for, and when Tilda tried to pay her, she would only take a few coppers."

Yes, Bitterblue could share Saf's wonder. And she was pleased with Madlen for taking the coppers, for Madlen was the queen's healer, after all. If she'd refused payment, it might have seemed as if she'd performed this healing on behalf of the queen.

"Sparks," Saf said, surprising her with the intensity of his voice. "Roke could not have done what Madlen did. Even when I sent you to Roke, I knew Roke couldn't save him. I thought no healer could."

"We don't know yet if he's saved," she reminded him gently.

"Tilda is right," he said. "Teddy is careless and too trusting. You're the classic example. I couldn't believe the way he took to you, knowing nothing of you—and when we learned you came from the castle, there was such a fight. Did no good, of course; he sought you out the same as always. And the truth is, if he hadn't, he'd be dead now. It's your castle Graceling who's saved his life."

At the end of a long night of forced wakefulness and worry, the notion that these friends were the queen's enemy was deeply depressing. How she wished she could set her spies on them without arousing Helda's suspicions as to how she knew them.

She said, "I suppose I don't need to tell you that Madlen's presence here tonight must be kept quiet. Take care no one notices her when she leaves."

"You're quite the riddle, Sparks."

"You're one to talk. Why would anybody need to kill a gargoyle thief?"

Saf's mouth went hard. "How did you—"

"I watched you do it."

"You're a sneak."

"And you're partial to a fight. I've seen it. You're not going to try anything stupid in revenge, are you? If you start knifing people—"

"I don't knife people, Sparks," Saf said, "except to stop them knifing me."

"Good," she said weakly, relieved. "Me neither."

At this, Saf began to laugh, a soft chuckle that grew until Bitterblue was also smiling. A gray light seeped through the edges of the shutters. Shapes were beginning to take form in this room: tables piled high with paper; vertical stands with strange cylindrical attachments; an enormous structure in the center of the room, like a night ship rising from water, gleaming dimly in places as if parts of it were made of metal. "What is that thing?" she asked, pointing. "Is that Teddy's printing press?"

"A baker starts work before the rising sun," Saf said, ignoring her. "You'll be late to work this morning, Sparks, and the queen will have no fluffy morning bread."

"A bit dull for you, is it, honest office work, after a life on the sea?"

"You must be tired," he said blandly. "I'll walk you home."

Bitterblue took a perverse comfort in his lack of trust. "All right," she said. "Let's just look in on Teddy first."

Pushing away from the wall, following Saf back through the doorway, legs heavy, Bitterblue suppressed a yawn. This was going to be one long day.

TRUDGING THE STREETS toward the castle, Bitterblue was relieved that Saf seemed not to expect conversation. In the growing light, his face was alert, his arms swinging from strong, straight shoulders. *He probably gets more sleep in one night than I do in a week,* Bitterblue thought crossly. *He probably goes home after his late nights and sleeps until the next day's sunset. Criminals don't have to wake at six so they can start signing charters at seven.*

He rubbed his head vigorously then, until his hair stood out like the feathers of an addled river bird, then muttered something under his breath that sounded both desolate and angry. Her irritation vanished. Teddy had looked only slightly better than dead when they'd gone in to check on him, his face mask-like, his lips blue. The line of Madlen's mouth had been grim.

"Saf," Bitterblue said, reaching for his arm to stop him. "Get what rest you can today, won't you? You must take care of yourself if you're to be any use to Teddy."

A corner of his mouth turned up. "I've limited experience with mothers, Sparks, but that strikes me as a rather motherly thing to say."

In the light of day, one of his eyes was a soft reddish purple. The other, just as soft and deep, was purplish blue.

Her uncle had given her a necklace with a stone of that purplish blue hue. In daylight or firelight the gem was alive with a brilliance that shifted and changed. It was a Lienid sapphire.

"You were given your name after your eyes settled," she said, "and by the Lienid."

"Yes," he said, simply. "I've a Monsean name too, of course, given to me by my true family when I was born. But Sapphire is the name I've always known."

His eyes were rather too pretty, she thought, his entire freckled, innocent aspect was too pretty, for a person she wouldn't trust to safekeep anything she ever hoped to see again. He was not like his eyes. "Saf, what is your Grace?"

He grinned. "It's taken you a good week to come out and ask, Sparks."

"I'm a patient person."

"Not to mention that you only believe what you've worked out for yourself."

She snorted. "Which is as it should be, where you're concerned."

"I don't know what my Grace is."

This earned him a skeptical look. "What's that supposed to mean?"

"Just what I said. I don't know."

"Balls. Don't Graces become plain during childhood?"

He shrugged. "Whatever it is, it must be a thing I've never had any use for. Like, oh, I don't know, eating a cake the size of a barrel without getting indigested, except that's not it, because I've tried that one. Trust me," he said, with a roll of his eyes and an apathetic, long-suffering wave. "I've tried everything."

"Right," said Bitterblue. "At least I know it's not telling lies people believe, because I don't believe you."

"I don't lie to you, Sparks," said Saf, not sounding particularly offended.

Subsiding into silence, Bitterblue began walking again. She'd never seen the east city lit by the sun. A dirty stone flower shop leaned perilously to one side, buttressed with wooden beams and slapped over in some places with bright white paint. Elsewhere, sloppy wooden planks covered a hole in a tin roof, the planks painted silver to match. A bit farther on, broken wooden shutters had been mended with strips of canvas, the wood and canvas alike painted blue like the sky.

Why would anyone go to the trouble of painting shutters—or a house, or anything—without repairing them properly first?

WHEN BITTERBLUE SHOWED her ring to the Lienid Guard at the gatehouse and entered the castle, it was full light. When, hood pulled low, she showed the ring again and whispered yesterday's cipher key, "maple tart," to the guards outside her rooms, they cracked the big doors open for her, their own heads bowed.

Inside her entrance foyer, she took stock. Far down the hallway to the left, the door to Helda's apartments was closed. To the right, Bitterblue heard no one moving about in the sitting room. Turning left and entering her bedroom, she pulled her cloak over her head. When her eyes emerged from the garment, she jumped, almost screamed, for Po sat on the chest against the wall, gold gleaming in his ears and on his fingers, arms crossed, appraising her evenly.

"Cousin," Bitterblue said, taking hold of herself. "Would it kill you to be announced, like a normal guest?"

Po raised an eyebrow. "I've known since I arrived last night that you weren't where everyone supposed you to be. As the night wore on, that state of affairs did not change. At what point would you have liked me to rustle up a clerk and demand to be announced?"

"All right, but you've no right to sneak into my bedroom."

"I didn't sneak in. Helda sent me in. I told her you wanted me to wake you with breakfast."

"If you lied your way in, then you snuck your way in." Then she saw, out of the corner of her eye, a breakfast tray piled high with dirty dishes and used cutlery. "You've eaten everything!" she said indignantly.

"It's hungry work," he said blandly, "sitting up in my rooms all night, waiting and worrying."

A long moment of silence stretched out between them. Her conversation to this point had mostly been an attempt to distract him while she gathered her feelings: gathered them and ejected them, so that she could face him with a mind that was blank and smooth, with no thoughts for him to read. She was fairly good at this. Even bleary-headed and shaky with fatigue, she was good at emptying her mind.

Head tilted now, he seemed to be watching her. Only six people in the world knew that Po had no eyesight and that his Grace was not hand-fighting, as he claimed; that it was a kind of mind reading instead, that allowed him to sense people and the physicality of things. In the eight years since the fall that had lost him his sight, he'd perfected the technique of pretending he could see, and tended to make it his habit even with the six who knew he couldn't. The deceit was a necessity. People didn't like mind readers, and kings exploited them; Po had been pretending not to be one all his life. It was a bit too late to stop pretending now.

She thought she knew what Po was doing, sitting there, his silver-gold eyes glimmering at her softly. He very much wanted to know where she'd been all night and why she was disguised—but Po didn't like to steal the thoughts of his friends. His mind reading had limits: He could only ever read thoughts that bore some relation to himself; but, after all, most of a person's thoughts during an interrogation bore some relation to the interrogator. And so right now, he was trying to come up with a nonaggressive way to ask her for an explanation: vague and non-leading words that would allow her to answer as she wished, and not force an emotional reaction that he would be able to read.

She went to inspect the breakfast tray and, scavenging, found half a piece of toast he'd spared. Famished, she bit into it. "I must order *you* a breakfast now," she said, "and eat it as heartlessly as you ate mine."

"Bitterblue," he began. "That Graceling you parted ways with outside the castle. That splendid fellow with the muscles and the Lienid gold—"

She spun back to face him, understanding quite well what he was implying, appalled at the range of his Grace, and furious, because this was not a nonaggressive question. "Po," she snapped, "I advise you to abandon that tack and try a different approach altogether. Why don't you tell me the news from Nander?"

He set his mouth, not pleased. "King Drowden is deposed," he said.

"What?" squawked Bitterblue. *"Deposed?"*

"There was a siege," Po said. "He lives in the dungeons now, with the rats. There's going to be a trial."

"But why have I received no messenger?"

"Because I'm your messenger. Giddon and I came straight to you the moment things stabilized. We rode eighteen hours every day and changed horses more often than we ate. Just imagine my gratification when we rode in, on the verge of collapse, and then I got to stay up all night, wondering where the seas you'd gotten to and whether I should be raising the alarm and how I was going to explain your disappearance to Katsa."

"What's happening in Nander? Who's ruling?"

"A committee of Council members."

The Council was the name for the undercover association of Katsa and Po, Giddon and Prince Raffin, and all their secret friends devoted to organized mayhem. Katsa had started it years ago, to stop the world's worst kings from bullying their own people. "The *Council* is ruling Nander?"

"Everyone on the committee is a Nanderan lord or lady who played some role in Drowden's overthrow. When we left, the committee was electing its leaders. Oll is keeping a close watch on things, but it seems to me—and Giddon agrees—that for the moment, this committee is the least disastrous option while all of Nander sorts out how to proceed. There was some talk of plopping Drowden's closest relative straight onto the throne—Drowden has no heir, but his younger half brother is a sensible man and a long-standing Council ally—but there's a lot of outrage among the lords who want Drowden back—emotions are high, as I'm sure you can imagine. On the morning of our departure, Giddon and I broke up a fistfight, ate breakfast, broke up a swordfight, and got on our horses." He rubbed his eyes. "No one is safe as King of Nander right now."

"Seas, Po. You must be tired."

"Yes," Po said. "I came here for a vacation. It's been lovely."

Bitterblue smiled. "When is Katsa coming?"

"She doesn't know. No doubt she'll come flying in just when we've given her up. She's managed Estill, Sunder, and Wester practically on her own, you know, while the rest of us were in Nander. I long for a few days of quiet with her before we overthrow the next monarch."

"You're not doing it again!"

"Well," he said, closing his eyes, leaning back against the wall. "It was a joke, I think."

"You think?"

"Nothing is certain," said Po with maddening vagueness, then opened his eyes and squinted at her. "Have you been having any problems?"

Bitterblue snorted. "Could you be any less specific?"

"I mean, things like challenges to your sovereignty."

"Po! Your next revolution isn't going to be here!"

"Of course not! How can you even ask that?"

"Do you realize how opaque you're being?"

"Well, what about unexplained attacks?" he said. "Have there been any of those?"

"Po," she said firmly, fighting against the memory of Teddy so that Po would not see it; crossing her arms, as if that would help her defend her thoughts. "Either tell me what on earth you're talking about, or get out of the range of my thinking."

"I'm sorry," he said, raising a hand in apology. "I'm tired and I'm mucking things up. We've got two separate worries on your account, see. One is that news of the recent events in Nander has been stirring up a lot of discontent everywhere, but especially in kingdoms with a history of tyrannous kings. And so we worry that you're perhaps at greater risk than you were before of one of your own people, maybe someone injured by Leck, trying to hurt you. The other is that the kings of Wester, Sunder, and Estill hate the Council. For all our secrecy, they know who its ringleaders are, Cousin. They'd love to strike us a blow—which they could do in any number of ways, including hurting our friends."

"I see," Bitterblue said, suddenly uncomfortable, and trying to remember the details of the attack on Teddy without linking them to Po in her mind. Was there any chance that the knife that had stabbed Teddy had been meant for her? She couldn't remember the particulars clearly enough to know. It would mean, of course, that someone in the city knew who she was. It seemed unlikely.

"No one has hurt me," she said.

"I'm relieved," he said, a bit doubtfully, then paused. "Is something wrong?"

Bitterblue let out a breath. "A number of things have seemed wrong in the past two weeks," she admitted. "Mostly small things, like a bit of confusion over some of the castle records. No doubt it's nothing."

"Let me know if I can help you," he said, "in any way."

"Thank you, Po. It's lovely to see you, you know."

He stood, gold flashing. Such a beautiful man, with those eyes that glowed with his Grace, and with the feeling in his face that he was never good at hiding. Coming to her, he took her hand, bowed his dark head over it, and kissed it. "I've missed you, Beetle."

"My advisers think we should marry," said Bitterblue wickedly.

Po shouted a laugh. "I shall enjoy explaining that one to Katsa."

"Po," she said. "Please don't tell Helda I was gone."

"Bitterblue," he said, still holding her hand, tugging on it. "Should I be worried?"

"You've got the wrong idea about that Graceling. Forget it, Po. Get some sleep."

Po gazed, or seemed to gaze, into her hand for a moment, sighing. Then he kissed it again and said, "I won't tell her about it *today*."

"Po—"

"Don't ask me to lie to you, Bitterblue. Just now, this is all I can promise."

"ARE YOU HAPPY that your cousin has arrived, Lady Queen?" asked Helda that morning, peering at Bitterblue, who'd just entered the sitting room bathed and dressed for the day.

"Yes," Bitterblue said, blinking through bloodshot eyes. "Of course."

"So am I," said Helda smartly, in a way that made Bitterblue obscurely uneasy about her late-night secrets. It also took away her courage to ask for any breakfast, seeing as she was supposed to have already eaten.

"The queen will have no fluffy morning bread," she muttered, sighing.

When she entered the lower offices, through which she had to pass to get to her tower, dozens of men milled around or scribbled at desks, poring over long, tiresome-looking documents, their faces blank and bored. Four of her Graceling guards, sitting against the wall, lifted unmatching eyes to her. The Queen's Guard, who numbered eight, had been Leck's guard too. All were Graced with hand-fighting or swordplay, strength, or some other skill befitting the protector of a queen, and it was their job to guard the offices and tower. Holt, one of the four on duty just now, studied her expectantly. Bitterblue made a mental note not to seem annoyed with anyone.

Her adviser Rood was also present, happily recovered, at last, from his nervous episode. "Good morning, Lady Queen," he said timidly. "Can I do anything for you, Lady Queen?"

Rood looked not like his elder brother Runnemood but like Runnemood's shadow, faded and old, as if, were he poked with something sharp, he would pop, and vanish. "Yes, Rood," she said. "I'd love some bacon. Could someone arrange for some bacon and eggs and sausages? How are you?"

"A shipment of silver being transported from the silver docks to the royal treasury at seven o'clock this morning was pilfered, Lady Queen," said Rood. "The loss was only a pittance, but it seems to have disappeared while the cart was in transit, and of course, we are both mystified and concerned."

"Inexplicable," Bitterblue said dryly. She had parted ways with Sapphire well before seven that morning, but she hadn't expected that he'd be out thieving with Teddy's condition so serious. "Had that particular silver ever been stolen before?"

"Forgive me, Lady Queen, but I don't follow. What are you asking?"

"To be honest, I couldn't say."

"Lady Queen!" said Darby, appearing before her out of nowhere. "Lord Danzhol is waiting above. Thiel will attend the meeting with you."

Danzhol. The one with the marriage proposal and the objections to the town charter in central Monsea. "Bacon," Bitterblue muttered. "Bacon!" she repeated, then carefully made her way up the spiral stairs.

GRANTING CHARTERS OF independence to towns like Danzhol's had been the idea of Bitterblue's advisers, and King Ror had agreed. During Leck's time, more than a few lords and ladies of Monsea had behaved badly. It was hard to know which had acted under Leck's influence, and which had acted out of pure clear-headedness, seeing how much they stood to gain from calculated exploitation while the rest of the kingdom was distracted. But it was apparent, when King Ror visited a few nearby estates, that there were lords and ladies who had set themselves up as kings, taxing and legislating their people unwisely, often cruelly.

How forward-thinking, then, to reward every victimized town with freedom and self-governance? Of course, an application for independence required motivation and organization on the part of a town's residents—not to mention literacy—and lords and ladies were allowed to object. They hardly ever did, though. Not many people seemed keen on the court poking too hard at past behavior.

Lord Danzhol was a man in his forties with a wide-mouthed face and clothing that sat strangely on his form, too big in the shoulders, so that his neck seemed to be emerging from a cave; too tight around the middle. He had one silver eye and the other pale green.

"Your citizens claim that you starved them with your taxes during Leck's reign," Bitterblue said, pointing to the relevant passages in the charter, "absconding with their property if they couldn't pay. Their books, the products of their trade, ink, paper, even farm animals. It's hinted here that you had, and still have, a gambling problem."

"I don't see how my personal habits come into it," Danzhol said pleasantly, arms hanging awkwardly from the broad shoulders of his coat, as if they were new arms and he hadn't gotten used to them yet. "Believe me, Lady Queen, I know the people who've drawn up this charter and the ones who've been elected to serve on the town council. They won't be able to keep order."

"Perhaps not," Bitterblue said, "but they're allowed a trial period to prove otherwise. I see here that since my reign began, you've eased back on taxes, only to default on a number of loans to businesses in your town. Don't you have farms and artisans? Isn't your estate prosperous enough to keep you moneyed, Lord Danzhol?"

"Have you noticed that I'm Graced, Lady Queen?" asked Danzhol. "I can open my mouth as wide as my head. Would you like to see?"

Danzhol's lips parted and began to stretch open, his teeth drawing back. His eyes and nose slid to the back of his head and his tongue flopped out—then his epiglottis, taut and red, and none of it stopping, only becoming more stretched, more red, more open and flopping. Finally, his face was all glistening viscera. It was as if he'd turned his head inside out.

Bitterblue pushed against the back of her chair, trying to get away, her own mouth ajar with mingled fascination and horror. Beside her, Thiel scowled in the most supreme annoyance. And then in one smooth motion, Danzhol's teeth swung over again, closing, pulling the rest of his face back into position.

He smiled and gave her a cheeky twitch of the eyebrows, which was almost too much for Bitterblue. "Lady Queen," he said cheerfully, "I would revoke my each and every objection to the charter if you would consent to marry me."

"I'm told you have wealthy relations," said Bitterblue, pretending not to be rattled. "Your family won't lend you any more money, am I right? Perhaps there's talk of debtor's prison? Your only true objection to this charter is that you're bankrupt and you need a town to overtax, or, preferably, a rich wife."

Something nasty flickered across Danzhol's face. He did not seem entirely balanced, this man, and Bitterblue found herself wanting to get him out of her office.

"Lady Queen," he said, "I don't believe you're giving my objections—or my proposal—the proper consideration."

"You're lucky I'm not giving this *entire matter* closer consideration," said Bitterblue. "I might ask for the details of how you spent these people's money while they were starving, or what you did with the books and farm animals you took from them."

"Ah," he said, smiling again, "but I know that you won't. A town charter is a guarantee of the queen's considerate inattention. Ask Thiel."

At her side, Thiel turned the charter to its signature page and thrust a pen into Bitterblue's hand. "Just sign, Lady Queen," he said, "and we'll get this boor out of here. This meeting was a bad idea."

"Yes," Bitterblue said, grasping the pen, barely noticing it. "A town charter is most certainly no such guarantee," she added, to Danzhol. "I can order an investigation of any lord I wish."

"And how many have you ordered, Lady Queen?"

Bitterblue hadn't ordered any investigations. The appropriate circumstances had never arisen before and it wasn't a forward-thinking thing to do; her advisers had never suggested it. "I don't think we need an investigation, Lady Queen," said Thiel, "to determine that Lord Danzhol is unfit to govern this town. It's my advice that you sign."

Danzhol smiled, bright and toothy. "Are you quite dead set against marrying me, then, Lady Queen?"

Bitterblue plunked her pen down onto her desk, not signing. "Thiel," she said, "take this unhinged man out of my office."

"Lady Queen," Thiel began—then stopped as Danzhol swung out with a dagger he'd pulled from nowhere, slamming Thiel on the head with its hilt. Thiel's eyes rolled up. He toppled to the floor.

Bitterblue sprang to her feet, too amazed at first to think or speak or do anything but gape in astonishment. Before she could collect herself, Danzhol had reached across the desk, grabbed the back of her neck, yanked her forward, opened his mouth, and begun to kiss her. It was awkward positioning, but she fought him, truly frightened now, pushing at his eyes and his face, wrestling his iron-strong arms, finally crawling onto the desk and kneeing him. His stomach was hard and didn't give at all. *Po!* she cried, for it was possible to get his attention if he was in range. *Po, are you awake?* She reached for the knife in her boot but Danzhol dragged her off the desk and pulled her against him, twisting her back to his front, holding his dagger to her throat.

"Scream and I'll kill you," he said.

She couldn't have screamed, not with her head jerked back as it was. The pins in her hair pulled and cut at her scalp. "Do you imagine," she choked out, "that this is the way to get what you want?"

"Oh, I'll never have what I want. And the marital approach

seemed not to be working," he said, one of his hands raking her arms and chest, hips and thighs for weapons, which set her ablaze with indignation and made her hate him, truly hate him. His chest and stomach were strange and bulky against her back.

"And you think that killing the queen *will* work?" she said. "You won't even make it out of this tower." *Po. Po!*

"I'm not going to kill you, unless I have to," he said, dragging her easily across the room to the northernmost window, pressing his knife so hard against her throat that she daren't even squirm, then struggling one-handed with his coat in some awkward manner that she couldn't see but that resulted in a bunched-up pile of rope, attached to a grappling hook, clattering to the floor around his feet. "My plan is to kidnap you," he said, pulling her closer, his body soft and human-feeling now. "There are people who would pay a fortune for you."

"Who are you working for?" she cried. "Who are you doing this for?"

"Not for myself," he said. "Not for you. Not for anyone alive!"

"You're mad," she gasped.

"Am I?" he said, almost conversationally. "Yes, I probably am. But I did it to save myself. The others don't know that it made me mad. If they knew, they wouldn't let me near you. I saw them!" he cried out. "I saw!"

"You saw what?" she said, tears running down her face. "What did you see? What are you talking about? Let me go!" The rope was knotted at regular intervals. Bitterblue began to understand what he was doing, and with her comprehension came the sheerest, blankest refusal. *Po!* "There are guards on the grounds," she said. "You will not get me past them."

"I have a boat on the river, and some friends. One of them is

Graced with disguise—we slipped right by the river guards. I think she'll impress you, Lady Queen, even if I haven't."

Po! "You won't—"

"Shut your mouth," he said with a press of the dagger that effectively made his point. "You talk too much. And stop moving around." He was having some trouble with the grappling hook. It was too small for the sill and kept clunking to the stone floor. He sweated and yammered to himself, shaking a bit, his breath rasping and uneven. Bitterblue knew, with a fundamental, unshakable sort of knowledge, that she was not capable of stepping with this man out of the kingdom's highest window onto a badly attached rope. If Danzhol wanted her to leave by this window, he was going to have to throw her out of it.

She tried Po one last, hopeless time. Then, when Danzhol dropped the hook again, she took advantage of his need to bend down to attempt something desperate. Lifting one foot up, reaching one hand down—crying out, as she had to push her throat right into the dagger in order to reach—she groped for the tiny knife in her boot. Finding it, she jabbed backward, stabbing Danzhol in the shin as hard as she could.

He yelled out in pain and fury and loosened his hold on her, just enough for Bitterblue to spin around. She plunged the knife into his chest as Katsa had taught her, under the breastbone and up with all her strength. It was horrible going in, unimaginably horrible; he was too solid and giving, too real, and suddenly too heavy. Blood ran down her hands. She pushed hard at his weight. He crashed to the floor.

A moment passed.

Then footsteps thundered on the stair and Po exploded into the room, others behind him. Bitterblue was in his arms but didn't feel it; he asked questions she couldn't comprehend, but she must have opened the answers to him, because barely a moment had passed before he'd let her go, attached Danzhol's hook to the sill, flung the rope out the window, and flung himself out after it.

She couldn't stop looking at Danzhol's body. She found herself against the opposite wall, vomiting. Someone kind was holding her hair out of the way. She heard the rumble of the person's voice above her. It was Lord Giddon, the Middluns lord, Po's traveling companion. She began to cry.

"There," Giddon said quietly. "That's all right." She tried to wipe her tears but saw that her hands were covered with blood; she turned to the wall and was sick again. "Bring me some of that water," she heard Giddon say, then felt him cleaning her hands with a dripping wet cloth.

There were so many people in this room. Every one of her advisers was here, and ministers and clerks, and her Graced guards kept jumping out the window, which made her dizzy. Thiel sat up, moaning. Rood knelt beside him, holding something to Thiel's head. Her guard Holt stood nearby, watching her, worry flickering in his silver-gray eyes. Then, suddenly, Helda was there, enfolding Bitterblue into her arms, soft and warm. And then, the most amazing thing yet, Thiel came to her and fell on his knees before her, taking her hands, holding them to his face. In his eyes, she saw something naked and broken that she didn't understand.

"Lady Queen," he said, his voice shaking. "If that man has hurt you, I will never forgive myself."

"Thiel," she said. "He didn't hurt me. He hurt you much more. You should lie down." She began to shiver. It was terribly cold in here.

Thiel stood and, still holding her hands, said calmly to Helda, Giddon, and Holt, "The queen has had a shock. She must go to bed and rest as long as she needs to. A healer must come and tend her cuts and brew an infusion of lorassim tea, which will calm her shivers and replace some of the water she's lost. Do you follow?"

Everyone followed. It was done as Thiel said.

7

Bɪᴛᴛᴇʀʙʟᴜᴇ ʟᴀʏ ᴜɴᴅᴇʀ blankets, shivering and too tired to sleep. Her mind would not be still. She pulled at the embroidered edge of her bedsheet. Ashen had always been embroidering, endlessly embroidering the edges of sheets and pillowcasings with these cheerful little pictures, boats and castles and mountains, compasses and anchors and falling stars. Her fingers flying. It was not a happy memory.

She threw her sheets off and went to Ashen's chest. Kneeling before it, she placed her palms on its dark wooden lid, its top carved with rows and rows of precious decorations very like those Ashen had liked to embroider. Stars and suns, castles and flowers, keys, snowflakes, boats, fish. She had a memory of having liked this when she was little: the way Ashen's embroidery matched parts of Ashen's chest.

Like puzzle pieces fitting together, she thought. *Like things that make sense. What's wrong with me?*

She found a roomy red robe that matched her carpet and her bedroom walls, then challenged herself, for no reason she could have explained, to go to the window and look down at the river. She'd climbed out a window before with Ashen. It might even have been this window. And there hadn't been a rope that time, just sheets knotted together. On the grounds, Ashen had killed a guard with a knife. She'd had to. The guard would never have let them pass. Ashen had snuck up on him and stabbed him from behind.

I had to kill him, Bitterblue thought.

Looking out, she saw Po in the castle's back garden far below, leaning on the wall with his head in his hands.

Bitterblue went to her bed and laid herself down, touching her face to Ashen's sheets. After a moment, she rose, dressed in a plain green gown, and strapped her knives to her forearms. Then she went out to find Helda.

HELDA SAT IN a plush blue chair in Bitterblue's sitting room, pushing needle through fabric that was the color of the moon. "You're meant to be sleeping, Lady Queen," she said, peering at Bitterblue worriedly. "Was that not working for you?"

Bitterblue wandered from place to place in the room, touching her fingertips to the vacant bookshelves, not certain what she was looking for, but at any rate, finding no dust. "I can't sleep. I'll go mad if I keep trying."

"Are you hungry?" asked Helda. "We've had a delivery of some breakfast things. Rood came, pushing the cart himself, and insisted you would want it. I couldn't turn him away. He seemed so desperate to do something to comfort you."

BACON IMPROVED THINGS dramatically. But she was still too scattered for sleep.

A never-used spiral staircase near her rooms wound down to a small door guarded by a member of the Monsean Guard. The door opened to the castle's back garden.

When had she last visited this garden? Had she been here even once since Leck's cages had been removed? Stepping into the garden now, she came face-to-face with a sculpture of a creature that seemed to be a woman, with a woman's hands, face, body, but that had the claws, teeth, ears, the posture almost, of a mountain lion rearing on its hind legs. Bitterblue stared into the woman's eyes, which were vital and frightened—not blank, the way she might have expected a sculpture's eyes to be. The woman screamed. There was a tension in her stance, an out-throwing of arms and a curvature of spine and neck, that somehow created the impression of tremendous physical pain. A living vine with golden flowers wrapped around one hind leg tightly, seeming to tether her to her pedestal. *She's a woman turning into a mountain lion,* Bitterblue thought, *and it hurts, horribly.*

High shrubbery walls on either side enclosed the garden, which was unruly with trees and vines, flowers. The ground sloped down to the low stone wall that fronted the river. Po still stood there, elbows propped, eyes staring—or seeming to stare—at the long-legged birds that preened themselves on the pilings.

As she walked toward him, he dropped his head into his hands again. She understood. Po was never particularly hard to read.

The very day that Bitterblue had lost her mother, this man, this cousin, had found Bitterblue. In the hollow of a fallen tree trunk, he'd found her. He'd carried her to safety, running full-tilt through the forest with her tipped over his shoulder. He'd tried to kill her father for her, failed, nearly died, and that was how he'd lost his sight. Trying to protect her.

"Po," she said softly, coming to stand beside him. "It's not your fault, you know."

Po took a breath, let it go. "Are you always armed?" he asked, his voice quiet.

"Yes. I wear a knife in my boot."

"And when you sleep?"

"I sleep with knives strapped to my forearms."

"And do you ever come home and sleep in your own bed?"

"Always," she said a bit sourly, "except last night. Not that it's any of your business."

"Would you consider wearing the arm holsters during the day always, as you're doing now?"

"Yes," she said, "and anyway, why must it all be hidden? If men are to attack me in my own office, why shouldn't I wear a sword?"

"You're right. You should wear a sword. Are you out of practice?"

She hadn't had a moment to pick up a sword in the last—she calculated—three or four years. "Very."

"I or Giddon or one of your guards will train with you. And all such visitors will be searched from now on. I crossed paths briefly with Thiel just now and found him consumed with his concern for you; he hates himself, Cousin, for not having had Danzhol searched. Your guards did manage to catch two of the accomplices, but neither accomplice could tell me whom Danzhol was planning to ransom you to. I'm afraid the other accomplice, a girl, got away. This girl, Bitterblue—she could do some extensive damage if she wanted to, and I don't even know how to advise you to watch out for her. She's Graced with—I guess you could call it hiding."

"Danzhol mentioned someone Graced with disguise."

"Well, from what I gather, you'd be impressed with the way she'd hidden the boat. It was all rigged up to look like a big, leafy, floating tree branch. Or so I understand. It involved mirrors, and I wish I could've seen the effect myself. When we got closer and your guards recognized it for a boat, they were quite bowled over, and thought I was some kind of genius, of course, for marching straight up to it with no confusion whatsoever. I left them to chase after the two Ungraced fellows and I went after her, and I tell you, Bitterblue, what she could do was not normal. I was chasing her up the river-bank, I felt her directly in front of me, and I sensed her planning to hide from me, and then all at once, we reached a pier and she jumped up onto it, lay down, and expected me to mistake her for a pile of canvas."

"What?" Bitterblue said, scrunching her nose at him. "What does that even mean?"

"She believed herself to be hiding from me," Po repeated, "in the guise of a pile of canvas. I stopped, knowing I was supposed to seem fooled, but confused, because I wasn't fooled. There was no canvas at all! So I went to a couple of men on the pier and asked them if they could see any canvas nearby, and if so, please not to stare at it or point at it in a demonstrative manner."

"You said that to strangers?"

"Yes," said Po. "They thought I was completely barmy."

"Well, of course they did!"

"Then they told me that yes, there was a pile of canvas right where I knew her to be, gray and red, which I'm told were the colors she'd been wearing. I had to leave her there, which killed me, but I'd already made enough of a scene, and anyway, I needed to get back and see how you were. Do you know, she even felt a bit like canvas to me? Isn't that wild? Isn't it marvelous?"

"No, it isn't marvelous! She could be in this garden this very minute. She could be this wall we're leaning on!"

"Oh, she isn't," Po said. "She isn't anywhere in the castle, I assure you. I wish she were—I want to meet her. She didn't feel malevolent to me, you know. She felt quite sorry about the whole thing."

"Po. She tried to kidnap me!"

"But she felt as if she were friends with your guard Holt," said Po. "I'll try to find her. Maybe she can tell us what Danzhol was up to."

"But Po, what about the scene you made? And what about my

guards who saw you unfazed by the boat? Are you sure no one was suspicious of you?"

The question seemed to subdue him. "I'm sure. They only thought I was peculiar."

"I don't suppose there's any point in asking you to be more careful."

He closed his eyes. "It's been so long since I've had a break from society. I'd love to go home for a bit." Rubbing his temples, he said, "The man you were with this morning, the Lienid who wasn't born a Lienid . . ."

Bitterblue bristled. "Po—"

"I know," he said. "Sweetheart, I know, and I've only got an innocent question. What's his Grace?"

Bitterblue snorted. "He says he doesn't know."

"A likely story."

"Could you tell anything about it from the feel of him?"

Po paused, considering, then shook his head. "There's a certain feeling to a mind reader, and he didn't have it. But I did feel something unusual about him. Something about his mind, you understand, that I don't feel with cooks or dancers, or your guard, or Katsa. He may have some mental power."

"Could he be prescient?"

"I don't know. I met a woman in Nander who calls birds with her mind, and calms them. Your friend—he's called Saf, is he?—Saf felt a bit like that woman, but not exactly."

"Could he have a malevolent power like Leck's?"

Po let out an explosive breath of air. "I've never encountered anyone with a mind like Leck's. We must hope I never do." He shifted position and changed his tone. "Introduce me to Saf, why don't you, and I'll ask him what his Grace is."

"Oh, certainly, why not? They wouldn't think it at all strange if I showed up with a Lienid prince in tow."

"So, he doesn't know who you are? I wondered."

"I suppose you're going to lecture me now about telling lies."

He began to laugh, which confused her at first, until she remembered to whom she was speaking. "Yes," she said, "all right. How *did* you explain your mad rush to my office today, by the way? The spy excuse?"

"Naturally. Spies are always telling me things in the strictest confidence at exactly the last moment."

She giggled. "Oh, but it's awful, isn't it, Po, so much lying? Especially to people who trust you."

He didn't answer this and turned back to the wall, the humor still in his face, but something else there too, that silenced her, and made her wish she hadn't been so flip. Po's particular web of lies was not, in fact, very funny. And the longer it went on—the more Council work Po did—the more people who gained his trust—the less funny it became. The lie he told when pressed to explain his inability to read—that an illness had damaged his close vision—stretched credibility and occasionally raised eyebrows. Bitterblue didn't like to imagine what would happen if the truth were to come out. Bad enough that he was a mind reader, but a mind reader who'd been lying about it for more than twenty years and who was admired and praised all seven kingdoms over? In Lienid, flatly revered? And what of his closest friends who didn't know? Katsa did, and Raffin, and Raffin's companion, Bann; Po's mother, and Po's grandfather. That was all. Giddon didn't know, nor did Helda. Nor did Po's father and brothers. Skye didn't know, and Skye adored his younger brother.

Bitterblue didn't like to think how Katsa would react if people began to be vicious to Po. She thought that Katsa's ferocity in his defense might be frightening.

"I'm sorry I couldn't spare you having to do what you did today, Beetle," Po said.

"There's nothing to forgive. I managed, didn't I?"

"More than that. You were marvelous."

He was so like her mother in profile. Ashen had had that straight nose, that promise around the mouth of a quick smile. His accent was like Ashen's, and so was the fierce, loyal feeling of him. Perhaps it had made sense that Po and Katsa had dropped into her life just when her mother was torn out of it. Not justice, but sense. "I did as Katsa taught me," she said quietly.

He reached his arm out and pulled her in, hugging her tight, centering her around herself again with his embrace.

BITTERBLUE WENT NEXT to the infirmary to find out about Teddy.

Madlen was snoring fit to drown out an invasion of geese, but when Bitterblue pushed the door open, she sat bolt upright in bed. "Lady Queen," she said hoarsely, blinking. "Teddy's holding on."

Bitterblue fell into a chair, then pulled her knees up, and hugged her legs hard. "Do you think he'll live?"

"I think it's highly possible, Lady Queen."

"Did you give them all the medicines they need?"

"All I had, Lady Queen, and I can give you more for them."

"And did you . . ." Bitterblue wasn't sure how to ask this. "Did you see anything . . . *odd* while you were there, Madlen?"

Madlen didn't seem surprised by the question, though she peered at Bitterblue keenly, from Bitterblue's sloppy, knotted hair all the way to her boots, before answering. "Yes," she said. "There were some strange things said and done."

"Tell me," Bitterblue said, "everything. I want to know it all, strange or not."

"Well," Madlen said, "where to begin? I suppose the strangest thing was the excursion they made after Sapphire got back from walking you home. He came into the room rather obviously happy about something, Lady Queen, shooting significant looks at Bren and Tilda—"

"Bren?"

"Bren. Sapphire's sister, Lady Queen."

"And Tilda is Teddy's?"

"I'm sorry, Lady Queen—I assumed—"

"Assume I know nothing," said Bitterblue.

"Well," said Madlen, "yes. They are two brother-sister pairs. Teddy and Sapphire live in the rooms behind the shop, where we were, and Tilda and Bren in the apartments above. The women are older and have lived together for some time, Lady Queen. Tilda seems to be the owner proper of the printing shop, but she told me that she and Bren are teachers."

"Teachers! What kind?"

"I'm sure I couldn't say, Lady Queen," said Madlen. "The kind who would slip into the shop with Sapphire, shut the door, have a muttered conversation that I can't hear, then leave me alone with their half-dead friend without telling me."

"So, you were in their house, alone," said Bitterblue, sitting up straight.

"Teddy woke up, Lady Queen, so I went into the shop to let them know the good news. That's when I discovered they'd gone."

"What a shame Teddy woke before you knew you were alone," exclaimed Bitterblue. "You could have gone through all their things and found the answers to so many questions."

"Hm," said Madlen wryly. "That's not generally my first line of action when left alone in a stranger's home with a sleeping patient. Anyway, Lady Queen, you'll be glad Teddy woke, because he was quite forthcoming."

"Really!"

"Have you seen his arms, Lady Queen?"

Teddy's arms? She'd seen Saf's arms; Saf had had Lienid markings on his upper arms like the ones Po had. Less ornate than Po's, though no less effective at drawing the eye. And no less attractive. *More,* she thought sternly, just in case Po was awake and having his ego stroked. "What about Teddy's arms?" she asked, rubbing her eyes, sighing.

"He has scars on one arm, Lady Queen. They've the look of burns—as if he's been branded. I asked him how it happened, and he said it was the press. He'd been trying to wake his parents, he said, and failed, and fell asleep himself, lying against the printing press, until Tilda dragged him out. It didn't sound like anything sensical to me, Lady Queen, so I asked him if his parents had had a printing shop that had burned. He began to giggle—he was drugged, you understand, Lady Queen, and perhaps saying more than he would otherwise, and making less sense—and told me that his parents had had *four* printing shops that had burned."

"Four! Was he hallucinating?"

"I can't be certain, Lady Queen, but when I challenged him, he was adamant that they'd had four shops, and that one after another, they'd burned. I said it seemed a remarkable coincidence, and he said no, it was exactly what was bound to have happened. I asked if his parents were particularly incautious, and he giggled again, and said yes, in Leck City it had been particularly incautious to run a printing shop."

Oh. And now Bitterblue understood the story; she saw the level on which it made perfect sense. "His parents," she said. "Where are they?"

"They died in the fire that scarred him, Lady Queen."

She had known it would be the answer, and still, it was difficult to hear. "When?"

"Oh, ten years ago. He was ten."

My father killed Teddy's parents, thought Bitterblue. *I couldn't blame him if he hated me.*

"And then," Madlen said, "he said something I could make so little sense of that I wrote it down, Lady Queen, so I wouldn't mix it up when I told you. Where is it?" Madlen asked herself, poking crossly at the mountain of books and papers on her bedside table. She leaned out of bed and grabbed at the discarded clothing on the floor. "Here it is," she said, fishing a folded paper from a pocket and flattening it against the mattress. "He said, 'I suppose the little queen is safe without you today, for her first men can do what you would. Once you learn cutting and stitching, do you ever forget it, whatever comes between? Even if Leck comes between? I worry for her. It's my dream that the queen be a truthseeker, but not if it makes her someone's prey.'"

Madlen stopped reading and looked across at Bitterblue, who stared back at her blankly.

"That's what he said?"

"That's it, as best I could remember, Lady Queen."

"Who are my 'first men'?" Bitterblue asked. "My advisers?" *And—prey?*

"I've no idea, Lady Queen. Given the context, perhaps your best male healers?"

"It's probably drug-induced nonsense," Bitterblue said. "Let me see it."

Madlen's handwriting was big and careful, like a child's. Bitterblue sat with her legs curled in the chair, puzzling over the message for some time. Cutting and stitching? Did that mean healing work? Or sewing work? Or something terrible, like what her father had used to do to rabbits and mice with knives? *It's my dream that the queen be a truthseeker, but not if it makes her someone's prey.*

"He did speak a lot of gibberish, Lady Queen," said Madlen, plucking her eye patch from its hook on her bedpost and tying it behind her head. "And when the other three returned, they had the look of young people quite pleased with themselves."

"Oh, right." Bitterblue had forgotten about the antics of the other three. "Were they carrying anything?"

"Indeed. A small sack that Bren brought upstairs before I could get a close look at it."

"Did it make any noise? A clinking? A jingle?"

"No noise, Lady Queen. She held it close and carefully."

"Could it have been silver coins?"

"Just as surely as it could have been flour, Lady Queen, or coal, or the jewels from the crowns of all six kings."

"Five kings," Bitterblue informed her. "Drowden is deposed. I found out this morning."

Madlen sat up straight and dropped her feet to the floor. "Great floods," she said, staring at Bitterblue solemnly. "This is a day for astonishment. When you tell me King Thigpen is deposed, I'll fall off my bed."

Thigpen was the King of Estill. Estill was the kingdom Madlen said she'd escaped from, though Madlen was rather close-mouthed about her past, and spoke with an accent that Bitterblue couldn't match to any part of the seven kingdoms she knew. Madlen had come to Bitterblue's court seeking employment seven years ago, alluding to the fact, during her interview, that in all the seven kingdoms but Lienid and Monsea, and particularly in Estill, Gracelings were enslaved to their kings, a circumstance she did not find acceptable. Bitterblue had had the tact not to ask Madlen if she had taken out her own eye to hide her Graceling identity during her escape. If she had—well, Madlen's Grace was healing, so she'd probably known the best way to do it.

DINNER TOOK PLACE in her sitting room, early. A clock gently ticked and her crown caught the white light of a sun that wasn't even thinking about setting yet. *I must stay awake,* thought Bitterblue, *so that I can go see Teddy.*

Po joined her and Helda for dinner. Helda had once been Katsa's ladyservant in the Middluns, and had been a Council ally for some time now. She fussed over Po like he was a long-lost grandson.

I must not think about how I need to sneak out tonight without Po knowing. I can think about sneaking out. I must only avoid thinking about sneaking out without him knowing, for then he'll know immediately. Of course, the other side of Po's Grace was that he sensed the physicality of everyone and everything, so he would probably sense the departure of her body whether or not he knew her thoughts. Which he probably did by now, anyway, so determinedly had she been thinking about how she mustn't think about them.

And then, mercifully, Po got up to take his leave. Giddon appeared, ravenous, slapping Po on the shoulder, falling into Po's chair. Helda went off somewhere with a pair of spies who'd arrived. Bitterblue sat across from Giddon, nodding over her plate. *I must ask him about Nander,* she thought to herself. *I must make polite conversation and I must not tell him my plans for sneaking out. He's nice-looking, isn't he? A beard quite suits him.* "Puzzles," she said stupidly.

"What's that, Lady Queen?" he asked, putting his knife and fork down, looking into her face.

"Oh," she said, realizing she'd spoken aloud. "Nothing. I'm plagued by puzzles, is all. I'm sorry for the state I was in when we met earlier today, Giddon. It's not how I would have preferred to welcome you to Monsea."

"Lady Queen," he said with instant sympathy, "you mustn't apologize for that. I was in much the same state the first time I was involved in someone's death."

"Were you?" she said. "How old were you?"

"Fifteen."

"Forgive me, Giddon," she said, embarrassed to find herself fighting off a yawn. "I'm exhausted."

"You must rest."

"I must stay awake," she said—then apparently dozed off, for she woke sometime later in confusion, in her bed, to which Giddon had presumably helped her. He seemed to have taken her boots off, unbound her hair, and tucked her under the sheets. The memory came to her: her own voice saying, "I cannot sleep with all these pins in my hair." Lord Giddon's deep voice responding: He would go and get Helda. And Bitterblue, half asleep, saying forcefully, "No, it cannot wait," and yanking at her wound-up braids, and Giddon reaching to stop her, sitting beside her on her own bed and helping her, saying things to calm her. She leaning against him as he took down her hair, he murmuring with gentlemanly sympathy as she sighed against his chest, "I'm so tired. Oh, I haven't slept in ever so long."

Oh, she thought. *How mortifying.* And now her throat stung; her muscles ached, as if she'd been through one of Katsa's fighting lessons. *I killed a man today,* she thought, and with that thought, tears began to run down her face. She cried freely, hugging a pillow, pressing her face into Ashen's embroidery.

After a while, her feelings solidified themselves around an odd little comfort. *Mama had to kill a man once too. I've only done what she's done.*

Paper crinkled in the pocket of her gown. Dashing tears away, Bitterblue pulled out Teddy's strange words and held them tight in one fist. A small determination flared in her breast. She was a puzzle solver, and a truthseeker too. She didn't know what Teddy had meant by it, but she knew what she meant. Fumbling to light a lamp, finding pen and ink, she turned the paper to its back and wrote.

LIST OF PUZZLE PIECES

Teddy's words. Who are my "first men"? What did he mean by cutting and stitching? Am I in danger? Whose prey am I?

Danzhol's words. What did he SEE? Was he complicit with Leck in some way? What was he trying to say?

Teddy and Saf's actions. Why did they steal a gargoyle, and other things too? What does it mean to steal what's already been stolen?

Darby's records. Was he lying to me about the gargoyles never having been there?

General mysteries. Who attacked Teddy?

Things I've seen with my own eyes. Why is the east city falling apart but decorated anyway? Why was Leck so peculiar about decorating the castle?

What did Leck DO?

Here, she scribbled a few notes.

Tortured pets. Made people disappear. Cut. Burned printing shops. (Built bridges. Did castle renovations.) Honestly, how can I know how to rule my kingdom when I have no idea what happened in Leck's time? How can I understand what my people need? How can I find out more? In the story rooms? Should I ask my advisers again, even though they won't answer?

She added one more question, slowly and in small letters.

What is Saf's Grace?

Then, returning to her larger list, she wrote:

Why is everybody insane? Danzhol. Holt. Judge Quall. Ivan, the engineer who switched the gravestones and the watermelons. Darby. Rood. Although, she wondered, was it insane to drink too much from time to time, or to be susceptible to nerves? Bitterblue crossed out the word *insane* and replaced it with *strange.* Except that that opened the list to everybody. Everybody was strange. In a fit of frustration, she scratched out *strange* and wrote the word *CRACKPOTS* in big letters. Then she added Thiel and Runnemood, Saf, Teddy, Bren, Tilda, Death, and Po, just to be thorough.

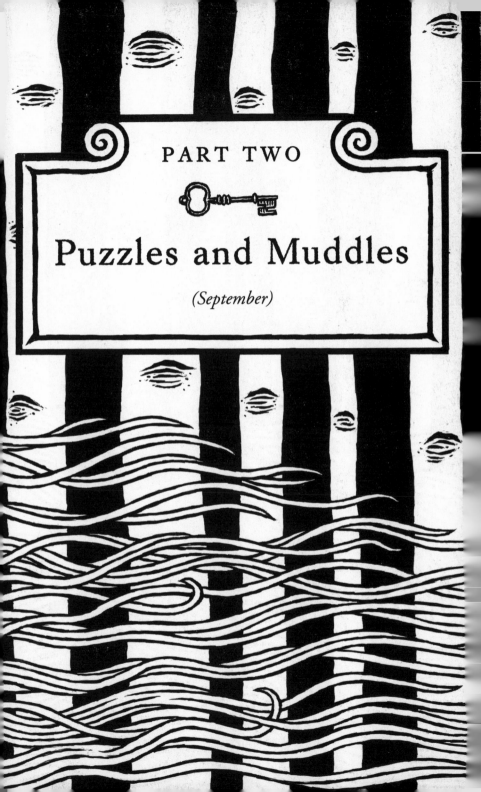

PART TWO

Puzzles and Muddles

(September)

8

Some wonderful person had gotten every trace of Danzhol's blood out of the stone of her office floor. Even looking for it, Bitterblue couldn't find it.

She read the charter once more, carefully, letting each word sink in, and then she signed it. There was no point not to now.

"What will we do with his body?" she asked Thiel.

"It has been burned, Lady Queen," said Thiel.

"What? Already! Why was I not informed? I would have liked to go to the ceremony."

The door to the tower room opened. Death the librarian came in.

"I'm afraid the body couldn't wait for burning, Lady Queen," said Thiel. "It's only just September."

"And it was no different from any other burning ceremony, Lady Queen," added Runnemood from the window.

"That is not the point!" said Bitterblue. "I killed the man, for rot's sake. I should have been at the burning."

"It's not actually Monsean tradition to burn the dead, you know, Lady Queen," Death put in. "It never has been."

"Nonsense," said Bitterblue, really quite upset. "We all perform fire ceremonies."

"I suppose it's not politic to contradict the queen," Death replied with such undisguised sarcasm that Bitterblue was surprised into looking at him hard. This man, nearing seventy, had the paper-thin skin of a man in his nineties. His mismatched eyes were always dry and blinking, one green like seaweed, the other purplish like his pinched lips. "Many people in Monsea do burn the dead, Lady Queen," he went on, "but it is not the Monsean way, as I'm sure your advisers know. It was King Leck's way. It's his tradition we honor when we burn our dead. Monseans before King Leck wrapped the body in a cloth infused with herbs and buried it in the ground at midnight. They've done so for as long as records have been kept. Those who know as much still do."

Bitterblue thought, suddenly, of the graveyard she ran through most nights, and of Ivan the engineer, who'd replaced watermelons with gravestones. What was the point of looking at things if she couldn't see them? "If this is true," she said, "then why have we not gone back to the Monsean ways?"

Her question was directed at Thiel, who stood before her looking patient and concerned. "I suppose we have not wanted to upset people unnecessarily, Lady Queen," he said.

"But why should it be upsetting?"

Runnemood answered. "There's no reason to disturb our mourners, Lady Queen. If people like the fire ceremonies, why should we stop them?"

"But, how is that forward-thinking?" said Bitterblue in confusion. "If we want to move away from Leck, why not teach people that it's the Monsean way to bury their dead?"

"It's a little thing, Lady Queen," said Runnemood. "It barely matters. Why remind people of their grief? Why give them reason to feel that perhaps they've been honoring their dead wrongly?"

It is not a little thing, thought Bitterblue. *It has to do with tradition and respect, and with recovering what it means to be Monsean.* "Was my mother's body burned or buried?"

The question seemed both to startle Thiel and bewilder him. He sat down hard in one of the chairs before her desk and did not answer.

"King Leck burned Queen Ashen's body," announced Death the librarian, "at the top of the high walkways on Monster Bridge at night, Lady Queen. It was how he preferred to perform such ceremonies. I believe he liked the grandness of the setting and the spectacle of the bridges lit up with fire."

"Was anyone there who actually cared?" she asked.

"Not that I know of, Lady Queen," said Death. "I, for one, was not."

It was time to change the subject, for Thiel was worrying her, sitting there with that empty look in his eyes. Like his soul had gone away. "Why are you here, Death?" Bitterblue snapped.

"Many people have forgotten the Monsean ways, Lady Queen," said Death obstinately. "Especially inhabitants of the castle, where Leck's influence was strongest, and especially the many in both city and castle who cannot read."

"Everyone in the castle can read," said Bitterblue.

"Can they?" Death dropped a small roll of leather onto her desk and, in the same motion, bowed, somehow making a mockery of the gesture. Then he turned and left the room.

"What has he given you?" asked Runnemood.

"Have you been lying to me about literacy statistics, Runnemood?" Bitterblue countered.

"Of course not, Lady Queen," said Runnemood in exasperation. "Your castle is literate. What would you like? Another survey on the matter?"

"Yes, another survey, of both the castle and the city."

"Very well. Another survey, to dispel the slander of an antisocial librarian. I hope you won't expect us to furnish evidence every time he makes an accusation."

"He was right about the burying," said Bitterblue.

Releasing a breath, Runnemood said patiently, "We've never denied the truth about the burying, Lady Queen. This is the first we've ever discussed it. Now, what has he given you?"

Bitterblue pulled at the tie that held the small roll closed. The leather flattened itself before her. "Just another useless map," she said, rolling it up again and shoving it aside.

Later, when Runnemood had gone to an appointment somewhere and Thiel stood stiffly at his stand, his back to her and his mind somewhere else, Bitterblue slipped the little map into the pocket of her gown. It wasn't a useless map. It was a lovely, soft miniature of all the major streets in the city, perfect for carrying on one's person.

IN THE EAST city that night, she sought out the graveyard. The paths were lit, but dimly, and there was no moon; she couldn't make out the inscriptions. Walking among the nameless dead, she tried to find a way to fit "burning versus burial" onto her list of puzzle pieces. It was starting to seem to her that being "forward-thinking" too often involved avoiding any kind of thought at all—especially about things that might benefit from a great deal of thinking. What had Danzhol said about the town charters being a promise of the queen's considerate inattention? Clearly, her inattention to Danzhol had led to disastrous results. Were there people at whom she should be looking more closely?

She stumbled across a grave with loose soil in the shape of a mound. Someone newly dead. *How sad,* she thought. *There's something horribly sad, but also right, about the body of someone who has died disappearing into the ground.* Burning a body was sad too. And yet Bitterblue felt deeply that burning was also right.

No one who loved Mama was there to mark her passing. She burned alone.

Bitterblue felt her feet planted in the ground of this graveyard, as if she were a tree, unable to move; as if her body were a gravestone, dense and heavy.

I left her behind, for Leck to pretend to mourn. I shouldn't still feel this way, she thought with an unexpected flash of fury. *It was years ago.*

"Sparks?" said a voice behind her. She turned to find herself staring into the face of Sapphire.

Her heart flew into her throat. "Why are you here?" she cried. "Not Teddy!"

"No!" Saf said. "Don't worry. Teddy's well enough, for a man who's been cut open."

"Then why?" she said. "Are you a grave robber?"

He snorted. "Don't be daft. It's a shortcut. Are you all right, Sparks? I'm sorry if I interrupted something."

"You didn't."

"You're crying."

"I'm not."

"Right," he said mildly. "I suppose you got rained on."

Somewhere, one of the city clocks began to strike midnight. "Where are you going?" Bitterblue asked.

"Home."

"Let's go, then," she said.

"Sparks," he said, "you're not invited."

"Do you burn your dead," she said, ignoring this, leading him out of the graveyard, "or bury them?"

"Well, it depends where I am, doesn't it? It's Lienid tradition to bury people at sea. In Monsea, it's tradition to bury them in the ground."

"How do you know the old Monsean traditions?"

"I could ask you the same question; I wouldn't have expected you to know. Except that I never expect the expected from you, Sparks," he added, a tired sort of dreariness coming over his voice. "How is your mother?"

"What?" she said, startled.

"I hope the tears are nothing to do with your mother. Is she well?"

"Oh," Bitterblue said, remembering that she was a castle baker girl. "Yes, she's well. I saw her tonight."

"Then that's not what's wrong?"

"Saf," she said. "Not everyone who lives in the castle can read."

"Huh?"

She didn't know why she was saying this now; she didn't know why she was saying it at all. She hadn't even realized until this moment that she believed it. It was just that she had the need to tell him something honest, something honest and unhappy, because cheerful lies tonight were too depressing and too sharp, turning in on her like pins. "I said before that everyone under the queen's roof reads," she said. "I've—developed doubts."

"All right," he said warily. "I knew that for a corker when you first said it. So did Teddy. Why are you admitting it now?"

"Saf," she said, stopping in her tracks in the middle of the street to face him, needing at this moment to know. "Why did you steal that gargoyle?"

"Hm," he said, amused in an unamused sort of way. "What's your game tonight, Sparks?"

"I don't have a game," Bitterblue said miserably. "I just want things to start making sense. Here," she said, pulling a small parcel from her pocket and shoving it into Saf's hand. "These are from Madlen."

"More medicines?"

"Yes."

Musing over the medicines, his feet square in the street, Saf seemed to be considering something. Then he glanced at her. "What about a game of trading truth for truth?" he said.

This struck her as a terrible idea. "How many rounds?"

"Three, and we must both swear to be honest. You must swear on your mother's life."

Well then, she thought. *If he presses me too hard, I can lie, for my mother is dead. He would lie, if pressed, too,* she added stubbornly, arguing with the part of her that rose up to insist that a game like this should be played in good faith. "All right," she said. "Why did you steal the gargoyle?"

"No, I go first, because the game was my idea. Are you a spy for the queen?"

"Great seas!" Bitterblue said. "No."

"That's all I get? A 'no'?"

She glared into his grinning face. "I'm not anyone's spy but my own," she said, realizing, too late, that her own spy would inevitably be the queen's spy. Annoyed to find herself lying already, she said, "My turn. The gargoyle. Why?"

"Hm. Let's walk," he said, motioning her up the street.

"You're not allowed to avoid my question."

"I'm not avoiding it. I'm just trying to come up with an answer that doesn't incriminate others. Leck stole," he said, startling her with the randomness of it. "Anything he wanted—knives, clothing, horses, paper—he took. He stole people's children. He destroyed people's property. He also hired people to build the bridges and never paid them. He hired artists to decorate his castle—never paid them either."

"I see," said Bitterblue, working through the implications of his statement. "Did you steal a gargoyle from the castle because Leck never paid the artist who made it?"

"Essentially," said Saf.

"But—what did you do with it?"

"We return things to their rightful owners."

"So, there's a gargoyle artist somewhere and you're bringing him back his gargoyles? What possible use could he have for them now?"

"Don't ask me," said Saf. "I've never understood the use of a gargoyle. They're creepy."

"They're lovely!" said Bitterblue in indignation.

"All right!" said Saf. "Whatever. They're creepily lovely. I don't know what he wants with them. He only asked us for a few of his favorites."

"A few? Four?"

"Four from the east wall. Two from the west and one from the south that we haven't managed to steal yet, and possibly won't, now. The guard presence on the walls has increased since we stole the last one. They must've finally noticed that gargoyles are going missing."

Noticed, because Bitterblue had pointed it out? Were her advisers the ones who'd arranged for more guards? Why would they do that, unless they believed the gargoyles actually were being stolen? And if they believed it, why had they lied?

"Where's your mind, Sparks?" asked Saf.

"So, people ask you for things," Bitterblue repeated. "They make requests for specific items Leck stole, and you steal the items back for them?"

Saf considered her. There was something new in his expression tonight. For some reason, it frightened her. His eyes, which used to be hard and suspicious, were softer, touching her face and hood and shoulders, wondering something about her.

She recognized what was happening. He was deciding whether or not to trust her. When he reached into the pocket of his coat and handed her a small bundle, she found that suddenly, whatever it was, she didn't want it.

"No," she said, pushing it back at him.

Stubbornly, he pressed it back into her hands. "What's wrong with you? Open it."

"It'll be too much truth, Saf," she insisted. "It'll make us unequal."

"Is this an act?" he said. "Because it's a stupid one. You saved Teddy's life: We'll never be equal. It's not any deep, dark secret, Sparks. It won't tell you anything I haven't already said."

Uncomfortable, but counting on this promise, she untied the bundle. It contained three papers, folded small. She moved closer to a streetlamp. Then she stood there, in rising distress, as the papers told her a thousand things Saf hadn't said, immediately.

It was a chart, three pages long, composed of three columns. Running down the left column was an alphabetical list of names, straightforward enough. The right-hand column listed dates, all falling in the years of Leck's reign. The items in the middle column, each one presumably corresponding to the name on the left, were more difficult to characterize. Across from the name "Alderin, farmer" was written, "3 farm dogs, 1 pig." Across from the second instance of the name "Alderin, farmer" was written, "Book: The Kissing Traditions of Monsea." Across from the name "Annis, teacher" was written "Grettel, 9." Across from "Barrie, ink-maker": "Ink, every kind, too much to quantify." Across from "Bessit, scribe": "Book: Monsean Ciphers and Codes; paper, too much to quantify."

It was an inventory. Except that the middle column of inventoried items seemed to be as crowded with people—"Mara, 11," "Cress, 10"—as it was with books, paper, farm animals, money. Almost all of the people named as inventory were children. Girls.

And that wasn't all this paper told her, not by a far shot, for Bitterblue recognized the handwriting. The paper, even, and the ink. One remembered such particulars when one had killed a lord with a knife; one remembered accusing the lord, before killing him, of stealing his people's books and farm animals. She drew the list to her nose, knowing how the paper would smell: just like the charter of the people from the town of Danzhol.

One lonely puzzle piece clicked into place. "This is an inventory of items *Leck* stole?" asked Bitterblue shakily.

"In this case, someone else stole them, but it's clear that it was on Leck's behalf. Those are the types of things Leck liked to collect, and the little girls clinch it, wouldn't you say?"

But—why hadn't Danzhol simply *told* her that he'd stolen from his townspeople on Leck's behalf? That his ruin had begun with Leck's greed? Why hide behind hints when he could have defended himself with that truth? She would have listened to that defense, no matter how mad or disgusting he was. And why had the people of Danzhol mentioned missing farm animals in their charter, but not their missing daughters? She had imagined that Leck had taken castle people, city people. Those were the people the fablers talked about in their stories. She hadn't known that his reach had extended to the distant country estates of his lords.

And that wasn't all. "Why would *you* be stealing these things back?" she asked, almost frantically. "Why would this list make its way to *you*, not to the queen?"

"What could the queen do?" asked Saf. "These items were stolen during Leck's reign. The queen has issued blanket pardons for all crimes committed during Leck's reign."

"But, surely, she hasn't pardoned *Leck's* crimes!"

"What did Leck ever do for himself? You don't think he marched around smashing windows and grabbing books? I told you, these things were stolen by someone else. That lord who just tried to kidnap the queen, actually, and ended up poked in the gizzard," he added, as if this piece of trivia should amuse her.

"It makes no sense, Saf," she said. "If these people sent this list to the queen, she would find some legal way to provide remuneration."

"The queen is looking ahead," Saf said glibly, "haven't you heard? She has no time for all the lists she would receive, and we manage it quite well, you know."

"How many lists are there?"

"I expect every town in the kingdom could provide one, if pressed," he said. "Don't you?"

The names of children crowded thick before her eyes. "It's wrong," she insisted. "There must be a legal recourse."

Saf took the papers from her hands. "If it's any comfort to your law-abiding heart, Sparks," he said, folding the papers up again, "we cannot steal what we cannot find. It's rare that we locate any of the items on these lists."

"But you just told me that you manage it quite well!"

"Better than the queen could," he said, sighing. "Have I answered your question?"

"What question!"

"We're playing a game, remember?" said Saf. "You asked me why I stole a gargoyle. I told you. Now I believe it's my turn. Were your people part of the resistance? Is that how your father was killed?"

"I don't know what you're talking about. What resistance?"

"You don't know about the resistance?"

"Perhaps I call it by a different name," she said, doubting this but not caring, for her mind was still wrapped up in the last matter.

"Well, it's no secret," he said, "so I'll explain it for free. There was a resistance movement in the kingdom while Leck was alive. A small group of people who knew what he was—or who knew it part of the time, at least, and kept it in writing—tried to spread the word, remind each other of the truth whenever his lies grew too strong. The most powerful among them were mind readers, who had the advantage of always knowing what Leck was trying to do. A lot of the members of the resistance were killed. Leck knew they existed and was always trying to stamp them out. Especially the mind readers."

Bitterblue was paying attention now.

"You really didn't know," Saf said, noting her surprise.

"I had no idea," she said. "That's why Leck kept burning Teddy's parents' print shop, isn't it? And that's how you knew about burying. Your family was part of this resistance and kept written records of the old traditions, or something. Right?"

"Is that your second question?" asked Saf.

"No. I'm not wasting a question on something I already know the answer to; I want to know why you grew up on a Lienid ship."

"Ah. That's an easy one," he said. "My eyes settled when I was six months old. Leck was king then, of course. Gracelings in Monsea were not free, but as you've already guessed, my mother and father were in the resistance. They knew what Leck was, most of the time. They also knew that Gracelings in Lienid were free. So they took me south to Monport, snuck me aboard a Lienid ship, and left me on the deck."

Bitterblue's mouth dropped open. "You mean they abandoned you. To strangers who could've decided to throw you overboard!"

He shrugged, smiling lightly. "They saved me from Leck's service, Sparks, in the best way they could manage. And after Leck died, my sister went to great lengths to find me—even though all she knew about me was my age, my eye colors, and the ship they'd left me on. Also, Lienid sailors do not throw babies overboard."

They turned onto Tinker Street and drew up outside the shop door. "They're dead now, aren't they," she said. "Your parents. Leck killed them."

"Yes," he said, then reached out to her when he saw her expression. "Sparks, hey—it's all right. I never really knew them."

"Let's go in," she said, pushing him off, too frustrated with her own helplessness to show him the sorrow she felt. There were crimes for which a queen could never provide enough remuneration.

"We've got one more round of questions, Sparks," he said.

"No. No more."

"I'll ask a nice one, Sparks, I promise."

"A nice one?" Bitterblue snorted. "What's your idea of a nice question, Saf?"

"I'll ask about your mother."

It was the very last thing she had the energy to lie about. "No."

"Oh, come on. What's it like?"

"What's what like?"

"To have a mother."

"Why should you want to ask me that?" she snapped at him, exasperated. "What's wrong with you?"

"Why are you biting my head off, Sparks? The closest thing I ever had to a mother was a sailor named Pinky who taught me to climb a rope with a dagger in my mouth and piss on people from the topmast."

"That's disgusting."

"Well? That's my point. Your mother probably never taught you anything disgusting."

If you had any idea what you were asking me, she thought. *If you had the slightest idea to whom you were speaking.* She could see nothing sentimental or vulnerable in his face. This wasn't his prologue to pouring out the heart-rending tale of a child sailor on a foreign ship who'd yearned for a mother. He was merely curious; he wanted to know about mothers, and Bitterblue was the only one made vulnerable by the question.

"What do you mean, you want to know about her?" she asked with slightly more patience. "Your question is too vague."

He shrugged. "I'm not picky. Is it she who taught you to read? When you were young, did you live together in the castle and eat your meals together? Or do castle children live in the nurseries? Does she talk of Lienid? Is she the person who taught you to bake bread?"

Bitterblue's mind flickered around all the things he said, images coming to her. Memories, some of them wanting precision. "I did not live in the nurseries," she said honestly. "I was with my mother most of the time. I don't think it was she who taught me to read, but she taught me other things. She taught me mathematics and all about Lienid." Then Bitterblue spoke another certainty that came to her like a thunderbolt. "I believe—I remember—my *father* taught me to read!"

Grasping her head, she turned away from him, remembering Leck helping her spell out words, in her mother's rooms, at the table. Remembering the feel of a small, colorful book in her hands; remembering his voice, his encouragement, his pride at her progress as she struggled to put letters together. "Darling!" he'd said. "You're fabulous. You're a genius." She'd been so small that she'd had to kneel in the chair to reach the table.

It was an utterly disorienting memory. For a moment, in the

middle of the street, Bitterblue was lost. "Give me a mathematics problem, would you?" she said to Saf unsteadily.

"Huh?" he said. "You mean like, what's twelve times twelve?"

She glared at him. "That's just insulting."

"Sparks," he said, "have you quite lost your mind?"

"Let me sleep here tonight," she said. "I need to sleep here. Can I sleep here?"

"What? Of course not!"

"I won't snoop around. I'm not a spy, remember?"

"I'm not certain you should come in at all, Sparks."

"At least let me see Teddy!"

"Don't you want to ask your last question?"

"You'll owe me one."

Sapphire considered her skeptically. Then, shaking his head, sighing, he produced a key. He opened the door a Sparks-sized crack and motioned her inside.

TEDDY LAY FLAT and limp on a cot in the corner, like a leaf in the road that's been snowed on all winter and rained on all spring; but he was awake. When he saw her, the sweetest of smiles spread across his face. "Give me your hand," he whispered.

Bitterblue gave him her hand, tiny and strong. His own hands were long, beautifully formed, with ink rimming the fingernails. And strengthless. She used her own strength to move her hand where he pulled it. He brought her fingers to his mouth. He kissed them.

"Thank you for what you did," he whispered. "I always knew you'd be lucky for us, Sparks. We should have called you Lucky."

"How are you feeling, Teddy?"

"Tell me a story, Lucky," he whispered. "Tell me one of the stories you've heard."

There was only one story in her mind: the tale of Princess Bitterblue's escape from the city eight years ago with Queen Ashen, who'd hugged the princess hard and kissed her, kneeling in a field of snow. And then given her a knife and sent her on ahead, telling her that though she was only a little girl, she had the heart and the mind of a queen, strong and fierce enough to survive what was coming.

Bitterblue pulled her hand away from Teddy's. She pressed her temples and rubbed them, breathing carefully to calm herself.

"I'll tell you the story of a city where the river jumps into the sky and takes flight," she said.

SOMETIME LATER, SAF shook her shoulder. She woke, startled, to find herself snoozing in the hard chair, neck twisted and rigid with pain. "What is it?" she cried. "What happened?"

"Shh!" said Saf. "You were crying out, Sparks. Disturbing Teddy's sleep. I figured it was a nightmare."

"Oh," she said, becoming conscious of a monumental headache. She reached up to bring down her braids, releasing her hair, rubbing at her aching scalp. Teddy slept nearby, his breath a gentle whistle. Tilda and Bren were climbing the stairs together to the apartments above. "I think I was dreaming that my father was teaching me to read," Bitterblue said vaguely. "It was making my head hurt."

"You're a strange one," Saf said. "Go sleep on the floor by the fire, Sparks. Dream something nice, like babies. I'll bring you a blanket, and wake you before dawn."

She lay down and fell asleep, dreaming of herself as a baby in her mother's arms.

BITTERBLUE RAN BACK to the castle in a thick, gray dawn. She raced the sun, hoping, fervently, that Po wasn't planning to ruin her breakfast again. *Find something useful to do with your morning,* she thought to him as she neared her chambers. *Do something heroic in front of an audience. Knock a child into the river while no one's looking and then rescue him.*

Entering her rooms, she found herself face-to-face with Fox, who stood in the foyer with a feather duster. "Oh," said Bitterblue, calculating fast, but not coming up with much in the way of a creative excuse. "Balls."

Fox regarded the queen calmly with unmatching gray eyes. She wore a new hood that was just like the old one, the one Bitterblue was wearing at this moment. The difference between the two women was marked: Bitterblue small, plain, guilty, and not particularly clean; Fox tall and striking, with nothing to be ashamed of.

"Lady Queen," she said, "I won't tell a soul."

"Oh, thank you," Bitterblue said, almost light-headed with relief. "Thank you."

Fox bowed her head, stepped aside, and that was that.

Minutes later, soaking in the bath, Bitterblue heard rain, thudding on the castle roofs.

She was grateful to the skies for waiting until she'd gotten home.

* * * * *

RAIN STREAMED DOWN the canted glass roofs of her tower office and raced into the gutters.

"Thiel?"

He was at his stand, pen scritching across paper. "Yes, Lady Queen?"

"Thiel, Lord Danzhol said some things after he knocked you out that worry me."

"Oh?" Thiel set his pen down and came to stand before her, all concern. "I'm sorry to hear that, Lady Queen. If you'll tell me what he said, I'm confident that we'll be able to resolve it."

"He was some sort of crony of Leck's, wasn't he?"

Thiel blinked. "Was he, Lady Queen? What did he tell you?"

"Do you know what it meant to be a crony of Leck's?" Bitterblue asked. "I know you don't like questions like that, Thiel, but I must know the basics of what happened, you see, if I'm to know how to help my people."

"Lady Queen," said Thiel, "my reason for disliking such a question is that I don't know the answer. I had my own run-ins with King Leck, as you know, as I expect we all did, and would all prefer not to talk about. But he would disappear for hours, Lady Queen, and I haven't the foggiest notion where he would go. I know nothing beyond the bare fact that he *would* go. None of your advisers do. I hope you'll trust me on that, and not trouble the others. We've only just got Rood back into the offices. You know he's not strong."

"Danzhol told me," Bitterblue lied, "that everything he stole from his people, he stole for Leck's sake, and that other lords stole from their people for Leck too. That means there are other lords and ladies out there like Danzhol, Thiel, and it also means that there are citizens from whom Leck stole who could benefit from remuneration. You do understand that the crown is liable to these people, Thiel? It will help us all move forward to settle such debts."

"Oh, dear," Thiel said, steadying a hand on her desk. "I see," he said. "Lord Danzhol, of course, was mad, Lady Queen."

"But I've asked my personal spies to make some inquiries, Thiel," Bitterblue improvised smoothly. "It seems that Danzhol was right."

"Your personal spies," Thiel repeated. His eyes were beginning to shift to confusion, then to a kind of blankness, so quickly that she reached out to stop him.

"No," she said, pleading with the fading feeling in his eyes. "Please, Thiel, don't. Why do you do that? I need your help!"

But Thiel was wrapped in himself, not speaking, not seeming to hear.

It's like being left alone in a room with a shell, thought Bitterblue. *And it happens so fast.* "I'll just have to go down and ask one of the others," she said.

A rough voice came out of the middle of him somewhere. "Don't leave me quite yet, Lady Queen," he said. "Please wait. I have the right answer. May I—may I sit, Lady Queen?"

"Of course!"

Heavily, he did so. After a moment, he said, "The trouble lies with the blanket pardons, Lady Queen. The blanket pardons, and the impossibility of ever proving, beyond doubt, that those who stole, stole for Leck and not for themselves."

"Wasn't the very reason for the blanket pardons the assumption that Leck was the true cause of all crime?"

"No, Lady Queen," said Thiel. "The reason for the blanket pardons was the acknowledgment of the impossibility of our ever knowing the truth about anything."

What a depressing notion. "Nonetheless, someone needs to provide reparation to those who were victimized."

"Don't you think, Lady Queen, that if citizens wished your reparation, they would tell you so?"

"Do they have means?"

"Anyone may write the court a letter, Lady Queen, and every letter is read by your clerks."

"But do they know how to write?"

The eyes Thiel trained on her face were awake now, and filled with a perfect comprehension of her meaning. "After yesterday's argument, Lady Queen," he said, "I challenged Runnemood on the matter of the literacy statistics. I'm sorry to say that he admitted that he has, in fact, been embellishing them. He has a habit of . . . erring on the side of optimism in his representations. It is," said Thiel, clearing his throat delicately, "one of the qualities that makes him a valuable agent of the court in the city. But of course, he must be transparent with *us*. He will be from now on. I've made that plain to him. And, yes, Lady Queen," Thiel added firmly. "Enough of your citizens know how to write; you've seen the charters. I maintain that if they wished reparation, they would write."

"Well then, I'm sorry, but it's not good enough, Thiel. I can't bear to walk around knowing how much this court owes people. I don't care whether they want it from me or not. It's not fair for me not to give it."

Thiel considered her silently, hands folded before him. She didn't understand the peculiar hopelessness in his eyes. "Thiel," she said, almost begging. "Please. What is it? What's wrong?"

After a moment, he said quietly, "I understand you, Lady Queen, and I'm pleased you came to me about this. I hope you always will come to me first with such matters. Here is what I recommend: Write to your uncle and ask his advice. When he visits, perhaps we can discuss the way to proceed."

It was true that Ror would know what to do and how best to do it. It wasn't terrible advice. But Ror's visit was scheduled for January, and it was only just September.

Perhaps, if she wrote to him, he could send suggestions ahead of his visit, in letters.

THE RAIN WAS soporific, throwing itself against her glass roof and the stone of her round walls. She wondered what it was like in the great courtyard today, where water pounded on the glass ceilings and overflow from the gutters poured into a fat rain pipe that snaked down the courtyard wall, ending with a gargoyle that vomited rainwater into the fountain pool. On days like this, the pool overflowed onto the courtyard floor. No water was wasted: It found drains in the floor that led to cisterns in the cellars and the prison.

It was impractical, the courtyard flood that accompanied rainy days. It was a strange design, easy enough to reverse. Except that it did no structural damage in a courtyard that had originally been built to be rained on; and except that Bitterblue loved it, on the rare occasions when she was able to escape her office to see it. The tiles on the floor surrounding the fountain were adorned with mosaics of fish that seemed to flop and swim under the sheen of water. Leck had intended the courtyard to be dramatic in the rain.

When Darby pushed into the room with a pile of papers so high that he needed both arms, Bitterblue announced that she was taking a walk to the royal smithy to order a sword.

But good heavens, they responded, did she realize that to reach the smithy, one must cross the grounds, in the rain? Had it not occurred to her that it would save time to summon a smith to her tower, rather than go herself? Had she not considered that it might be viewed as unusual—

"Oh, for mercy's sake," Bitterblue snapped at her advisers. "I'm proposing a walk to the smithy, not an expedition to the moon. I'll be back in a matter of minutes. In the meantime, you can all return to work and stop being annoying, if such a thing is possible."

"At least take an umbrella, Lady Queen," pleaded Rood.

"I won't," she said, then swept out of the room as dramatically as possible.

STANDING IN THE east vestibule, peeking through an arch at the pounding water of the fountain, the swirling water on the floor, the gurgling water in the drains, Bitterblue allowed the noise and the earthy smell of it all to soothe her irritation.

"Lady Queen," said a quiet voice to her side. "How are you?"

Bitterblue was mildly embarrassed to find herself in the company of Lord Giddon. "Oh," she said. "Giddon. Hello. I'm all right, I suppose. I'm sorry about the other night. The falling asleep, I mean," she bumbled, "and—the hair."

"Don't apologize, Lady Queen," he said. "An ordeal like the one with Danzhol is bound to be exhausting; it was the end of an extraordinary day."

"That it was," she said, sighing.

"How is your puzzle going?"

"Dreadfully," she said, grateful to him for remembering. "I have lords like Danzhol, who stole for Leck, connecting with thieves who are stealing the things back, connecting with a strange piece of misinformation about gargoyles my advisers gave me, connecting with other kinds of knowledge my advisers seem to prefer to discourage, connecting with knowledge the thieves would like to keep from me as well, such as why someone would stick knives in their guts. I don't understand the courtyard decoration either," she said grouchily, glaring at the shrubberies that a moment before had been delighting her.

"Hm," said Giddon. "I confess, it doesn't sound very illuminating."

"It's a disaster," Bitterblue said.

"Well," said Giddon with mild amusement. "Your great courtyard is lovely in the rain."

"Thank you. Did you know that my being here to look at it, alone, in the middle of the day, requires a lengthy debate? And I'm not even alone," she added, indicating, with a nod, the man tucked behind an arch in the south vestibule. "That's one of my Graced guards, Alinor, pretending not to watch us. I bet you my crown that they sent him along to spy on me."

"Or perhaps to keep an eye out for your safety, Lady Queen?" suggested Giddon. "You were recently attacked while in their care. They might be feeling a bit twitchy, not to mention guilty."

"It's just—I did something today that I should be happy about, Giddon. I proposed a policy of remuneration from the crown for those who were robbed during Leck's reign. But all I feel is impatience, fury for the opposition I anticipate and the lies I'm going to have to tell to make it happen, and frustration that I can't even take a walk without them sending someone to hover. Attack me," she said.

"I beg your pardon, Lady Queen?"

"You should attack me, and we'll see what he does. He's probably quite bored—it'll be a relief to him."

"Mightn't he run me through with his sword?"

"Oh." Bitterblue chuckled. "Yes, I suppose he might. That would be a shame."

"I'm gratified that you think so," said Giddon dryly.

Bitterblue squinted at a muddy person wading into the court-yard from the west vestibule, which was the route from the stables. Her heart leapt; she jumped forward. "Giddon!" she cried. "It's Katsa!"

Suddenly Po shot into the courtyard from the north vestibule, whooping. Katsa, seeing him, broke into a run and they tore at each other through the wash. Just before the moment of impact, Po shifted to one side, crouched, scooped Katsa up, and, with admirable precision, propelled them both sideways into the pool.

THEY WERE STILL thrashing around and laughing and screaming, and Bitterblue and Giddon were still watching, when a stiff little clerk spotted Bitterblue, trotted up to her, and said, "Good day, Lady Queen. Lady Katsa of the Middluns has arrived at court, Lady Queen."

Bitterblue raised an eyebrow. "You don't say?"

The clerk, who seemed not to have risen to his position on the merits of his powers of observation, confirmed his announcement humorlessly, then added, "Prince Raffin of the Middluns has accompanied her this time, Lady Queen."

"Oh! Where is he?"

"He is finding his rooms, Lady Queen."

"Is Bann with him?" asked Giddon.

"He is, My Lord," said the clerk.

"They'll be exhausted," said Giddon to Bitterblue as the clerk slipped away. "Katsa'll have ridden them hard through the rain."

Katsa and Po were trying to drown each other and, judging from their hoots of laughter, enjoying it immensely. People had begun to gather in archways and on balconies—servants, guards—pointing, staring.

"I expect this will make a good story for the rumor mills," Bitterblue ventured.

"Another chapter in *The Heroic Adventures Of*?" Giddon asked quietly. Then he shot her a grin that reached all the way to his very nice, but ordinary, matching brown eyes, and Bitterblue had the feeling suddenly of not being so alone. She'd forgotten, in her first joy, what this was always like. Preoccupied with Po, Katsa hadn't even noticed her.

"I was actually headed to the royal smithy," Bitterblue said to Giddon, in the way of also having preoccupations and places to go, "but the truth is that I'm not certain where it is. I wasn't going to admit that to my advisers, of course."

"I've been there, Lady Queen," Giddon said. "It's on the western grounds, north of the stables. Shall I point you in the right direction or would you like company?"

"Join me."

"It looks like the entertainment is breaking up, anyway," Lord Giddon said. And indeed, the splashing and the noise seemed to have calmed. Katsa and Po had their arms around each other. It was difficult to tell if they were still wrestling or if the kissing had begun.

Bitterblue turned away with a small flash of resentment.

"Wait!"

It was Katsa's voice; it slapped against Bitterblue's back and spun her around. Katsa had climbed out of the fountain and out of Po's arms. Katsa was running toward her, eyes shining blue and green, clothes and hair streaming. She slammed into Bitterblue and gathered her into a hug. She picked Bitterblue up, put her down, squeezed her harder, kissed the top of her head. Crushed painfully against Katsa, Bitterblue heard the wild, strong thump of Katsa's heart. She held Katsa tight. Tears pricked her eyes.

Then Katsa was gone, flying back to Po.

As Bitterblue and Giddon moved through the western castle to the exit nearest the smithy, Giddon told her that remuneration for a king's thefts was one of the Council's specialties. "It can be quite beautiful in execution, Lady Queen," he said. "Of course, when we do it, it involves trickery, and our thieving kings are still alive. But I think you'll feel the same satisfaction we do."

He was a big man beside her, as tall as Thiel and broader. "How old are you?" she asked bluntly, deciding that queens had the privilege of asking nosy questions.

"Twenty-seven last month, Lady Queen," he answered, not seeming to mind the question.

Then they were all of a similar age—Giddon, Po, Katsa, Bann, and Raffin. "How long have you been Katsa's friend?" she asked, remembering, with mild indignation, that Katsa hadn't greeted him in the courtyard.

"Oh," he said, calculating, "well, some ten or eleven years? I offered myself to her and Raffin as soon as the Council began. Of course, I knew of her before that; I'd seen her at court many times. I used to watch her practices."

"Did you grow up at King Randa's court, then?"

"My family's estate is near to Randa's court, Lady Queen. As a boy, I spent as much time at court as I did at home. My father, while he was alive, was a great friend of Randa's."

"Your priorities differed from your father's."

He glanced at her in surprise, then made an unamused noise. "Not really, Lady Queen."

"Well, you chose the Council over any allegiance to Randa, didn't you?"

"I joined the Council more out of fascination for its founder than anything else, Lady Queen. Katsa, and the promise of adventure. I don't think I much cared what it was for. At the time, I was one of Randa's most reliable bullies."

Bitterblue remembered then that Giddon was among those excluded from the truth of Po's Grace. Was this why? Was he a bully? But Giddon was one of Po's closest friends now, wasn't he? How did a man who was crony to a bad king undo that entanglement while the king was still alive?

"Giddon?" she said. "Do you care about the Council's purpose now?"

When he looked into her face, she saw his answer before he gave it. "With all my heart."

They stepped into a dimly lit foyer where tall, gray windows rattled with rain. A pair of Monsean Guards stood to either side of a postern doorway. When Bitterblue passed through, she found herself on a covered slate terrace, looking out over a field of soggy snapdragons. Beyond the flowers sat a squat stone building with smoke rising from several chimneys. The musical clangs of metal, in various pitches and rhythms, suggested that they'd succeeded in their search for the smithy.

"Giddon," she said. "Wasn't it a bit rude for Katsa not to greet you in the courtyard just now? It's been some time since you've seen each other, hasn't it?"

His smile was sudden and enormous; he began to chuckle. "Katsa and I don't like each other very much," he said.

"Why? What did you do?"

"Why must it be something *I* did?"

"Well? Wasn't it?"

"Katsa will hold a grudge," Giddon said, still grinning, "for years."

"You're the one who seems to be holding a grudge," Bitterblue said hotly. "Katsa's heart is true. She would not dislike you for no reason."

"Lady Queen," he said mildly, "I meant no offense to you, or to her. Any courage I have, I learned from her example. I would go so far as to say that her Council has saved my life. I can work with Katsa whether she greets me in the courtyard or not."

His tone, and his words, brought her back to herself. She unclenched her fists and wiped her hands on her skirts. "Giddon. Forgive my temper."

"Katsa is fortunate to have your loyalty," said Giddon.

"Yes," Bitterblue said, confused, then gesturing through the downpour to the smithy, more than ready to put an end to the conversation. "Shall we make a dash for it?"

Within seconds, she was soaked through. The snapdragon bed was a swamp and one of her boots sunk deep in the mud, nearly toppling her. When Giddon came to her and took her arms in an attempt to pull her free, his own boots stuck. With a vague expression of impending disaster, he plummeted backward into the flowers, his falling momentum popping her out of the mud but also sending her sprawling.

On her stomach amidst snapdragons, Bitterblue spat out dirt. And there really wasn't any use for decorum after that. Covered with mud and snapdragon carcasses, they dragged each other up and staggered, gasping with laughter, into the lean-to that comprised the front half of the smithy building. A man came stomping out whom Bitterblue recognized, small, with a sharp, sensitive face, dressed in the black of the Monsean Guard with distinctive silver chains on his sleeves. "Wait," Bitterblue said to him, trying to wipe mud from her skirts. "You're my Captain of the Monsean Guard, aren't you? You're Captain Smit."

The man's eyes flicked across her bedraggled appearance, then absorbed Giddon's as well. "I am, Lady Queen," he said with crisp correctness. "It's a pleasure to see you, Lady Queen."

"Indeed," said Bitterblue. "Is it you who decides the number of guards patrolling the castle walls?"

"Ultimately, yes, Lady Queen."

"May I ask why you've increased their number recently?"

"Of course, Lady Queen," he said. "It was in response to the news of unrest in Nander. In fact, now that we've heard that the Nanderan king is deposed, I may increase their number even more, Lady Queen. Such news has the potential to encourage unruly behavior. The castle's security—and yours, Lady Queen—are among my highest priorities."

When Captain Smit had gone, Bitterblue frowned after him. "That was a perfectly reasonable explanation," she said grumpily. "Perhaps my advisers don't lie to me."

"Isn't that what you'd want?" asked Giddon.

"Well, yes, but it doesn't elucidate my puzzle!"

"If I may say so, Lady Queen," said Giddon, "it's not always easy to follow your conversation."

"Oh, Giddon," she said, sighing. "If it's any comfort, I don't follow it either."

A second man came from inside the smithy then, and stood blinking at them. He was youngish and sooty, his sleeves rolled up to reveal muscular forearms, and he held in both hands the most massive sword Bitterblue had ever seen, dripping with water from the slack trough and gleaming like lightning.

"Oh, Ornik," Giddon said, going to the smith, trailing snapdragons and slime. "This is good work." He took the sword from the man carefully, balanced it, and held the hilt out to Bitterblue. "Lady Queen?"

The sword was nearly Bitterblue's height and so heavy that she needed to throw her shoulders and legs into the lifting of it. She muscled it gamely into the air and gazed at it in admiration, liking its fine, simple hilt and its even gleam; liking the solid, steady weight of it pushing her into the floor. "It's beautiful, Ornik," she said. And then, "We're muddying it up, which is shameful." And finally, "Help me, Giddon," because she didn't trust herself to lower it without crashing the tip into the stone floor. "Ornik," she said, "we've come about a sword for myself."

Ornik stood back, hands on hips, looking her small frame up and down in a way only Helda ever did, and then only when Bitterblue was trying a new gown.

She said defensively, "I like heft, and I am not weak."

"As I saw, Lady Queen," Ornik said. "Allow me to present you with a few possibilities, Lady Queen. If we have nothing to suit you, we'll design something that does. Excuse me."

Ornik bowed and went inside. Alone with Giddon again, Bitterblue considered him, rather liking the mud streaks on his face. He looked like a handsome sunken rowboat. "How is it that you know my smiths by name, Giddon? Have you been ordering swords?"

Giddon glanced at the door to the inner forge. He lowered his voice. "Has Po spoken to you yet about the situation in Estill, Lady Queen?"

Bitterblue narrowed her eyes. "Nander, yes. Estill, no. What's going on?"

"I think it's time we included you in a Council meeting. Perhaps tomorrow's, if your schedule allows it."

"When is it?"

"Midnight."

"Where do I go?"

"Katsa's rooms, I believe, now that she's here."

"Very well. What's the situation in Estill?"

Giddon glanced again at the doorway and pitched his voice even lower. "The Council anticipates a popular uprising against King Thigpen, Lady Queen."

She stared at him in astonishment. "As in Nander?"

"As in Nander," he said, "and the rebels are asking the Council for help."

T HAT NIGHT, PADDING through the great courtyard, Bitterblue
tried to come to terms with her own unease.

She trusted her friends in their work. But, for a group of people
who claimed to be concerned for her safety, they did seem to have
developed rather a habit of encouraging uprisings against monarchs.
Well, she would see what they meant by it tomorrow at midnight.

The rain had turned to mist by the time she knocked on the door
at Tinker Street, infinitesimal beads soaking her clothing and hair
so thickly that she dripped like a forest of trees. It was some time
before her knock was answered—by Saf, who hauled her across the
shop by one arm. "Hey! Hands off!" she said, trying to get a good
look at the room, which was lit so violently that it hurt her eyes. He
had rushed her through this room on her way out that morning as
well. Tonight she glimpsed paper, everywhere, rolls of it, sheets of it;
high tables cluttered with mysterious objects; a row of jars containing what must be ink; and that large, oddly shaped structure in the
middle of the room that creaked and thumped and stank of grease
and metal and was so enthralling that Bitterblue actually kicked
Saf—not hard—to make him stop pulling her away.

"Ow!" he yelled. "Everyone abuses me!"

"I want to see the press," she said.

"You're not allowed to see the press," he said. "Kick me again and
I'll kick you back."

Tilda and Bren stood together at the press, working companionably. Turning their faces in tandem to see what the fuss was about; rolling their eyes at each other.

A moment later, Saf had yanked her into the back room and shut the door; and finally, she took a good look at him. One of his eyes was swollen half shut, blackish purple. "Balls," she said. "What happened to you?"

"Street fight."

She squared her shoulders. "Tell the truth."

"Why? Is it your third question?"

"What?"

"If you must go out again, Saf," said Teddy's voice weakly from the bed, "avoid Callender Street. The girls told me a building came down and brought two others with it."

"Three buildings down!" Bitterblue exclaimed. "Why is the east city so fragile?"

"Is *that* your third question?" asked Saf.

"I'll answer both your questions, Lucky," said Teddy. In response to this, Saf stormed into another room and slammed the door in disgust.

Bitterblue went to Teddy's corner and sat with him in his little circle of light. Papers were strewn all over the bed where he lay. Some had found their way to the floor. "Thank you," he said as Bitterblue collected them. "Did you know that Madlen stopped in on me this morning, Lucky? She says I'm going to live."

"Oh, Teddy," said Bitterblue, hugging the papers to herself. "That's wonderful."

"Now, you wanted to know why the east city is falling apart?"

"Yes—and why there are some strange repairs. Broken things repainted."

"Ah, yes. Well, it's the same answer for both questions. It's the crown's ninety-eight percent employment rate."

"What!"

"You're aware that the queen's administration has been aggressive about finding people work? It's part of their philosophy for recovery."

Bitterblue was aware that Runnemood had told her that nearly everyone in the city had work. These days, she wasn't so quick to believe any of his statistics. "Are you saying that the ninety-eight percent employment rate is real?"

"For the most part, yes. And some of the new work has to do with repairing structures that were neglected during Leck's reign. Each part of the city has a different team of builders and engineers assigned to the job, and, Lucky, the engineer leading the team in the east city is an absolute nutpot. So is his immediate underling and a few of his workers. They're just hopeless."

"What's the leader's name?" asked Bitterblue, knowing the answer.

"Ivan," said Teddy. "He was a phenomenal engineer once. He built the bridges. Now it's lucky if he doesn't kill us all. We do what we can to repair things ourselves, but we're all working too, you know. No one has time."

"But, why is it allowed to go on?"

"The queen has no time," said Teddy simply. "The queen is at the helm of a kingdom that's waking up from the thirty-five-year spell of a madman. She may be older now than she was, but she still has more headaches and more complications and confusions to deal with than the other six kingdoms combined. I'm sure she'll get to it when she can."

She was touched by his faith, but baffled by it too. *Will I?* she thought numbly. *Do I? I'll grant that I'm dealing with confusions. The confusions push themselves in from everywhere, but I don't particularly feel like I'm dealing with anything; and how can I correct problems I don't even know about?*

"As far as Saf's injuries go," Teddy continued, "there's this group of four or five idiots we cross paths with now and then. Brains the size of buttons. They never liked Saf to begin with, because he's Lienid and has those eyes and, well, has some tendencies they don't like. And then one night they told him to demonstrate his Grace, and of course he couldn't demonstrate a thing. So they decided he's hiding something. That he's a mind reader, I mean," Teddy explained. "Whenever they see him now, they punish him as a matter of course."

"Oh," whispered Bitterblue. She couldn't stop her mind from playing it out for her, the punching and kicking that probably constituted their kind of punishment. Punching and kicking of *Saf,* of his face. She pushed it away. "So then—it wasn't the same people who attacked you?"

"It wasn't, Lucky."

"Teddy, who did attack you?"

Teddy answered this with a quiet smile, then said, "What did Saf mean about you asking your third question? Are you two playing a game?"

"Sort of."

"Sparks, if I were you, I wouldn't agree to play Saf's games."

"Why?" asked Bitterblue. "Do you think he lies to me?"

"No," said Teddy. "But I think there are ways in which he could be dangerous to you without ever telling a single lie."

"Teddy," said Bitterblue, sighing. "I don't want to talk riddles with you. Could we please not talk riddles?"

Teddy smiled. "All right. What should we talk about?"

"What are these papers?" she asked, passing them to him. "Is this your book of words or your book of truths?"

"These are my words," said Teddy, holding the papers to his chest, hugging them protectively. "My dear words. Today I was thinking about the *P*'s. Oh, Lucky, how will I ever think of every word and every definition? Sometimes, when I'm having a conversation, I become unable to pay attention, because all I can do is tear apart other people's sentences and obsess over whether I've remembered to include all their words. My dictionary is destined to have great gaps of meaning."

Great gaps of meaning, thought Bitterblue, taking a breath, breathing air through the phrase. *Yes.* "You're going to do a wonderful job, Teddy," she said. "Only a person with the true heart of a dictionary-writer would be lying in bed, three days after being stabbed in the gut, worrying about his *P*'s."

"You only used one word beginning with *P* in that sentence," said Teddy dreamily.

The door opened and Saf stuck his head in, glaring at Teddy. "Have you divulged our every secret yet?"

"There were no *P*-words in that sentence," said Teddy, half asleep.

Saf made an impatient noise. "I'm going out."

Teddy woke right up, tried to sit up, then winced. "Please don't go out if it's only to look for trouble, Saf."

"When do I ever have to look for it?"

"Well, at least bandage that arm," he insisted, proffering a bandage from the small table beside his bed.

"Arm?" said Bitterblue. "Did they hurt your arm?" She saw, then, the way he was holding his arm close to his chest. She got up and went to him. "Let me see," she said.

"Go away."

"I'll help you bandage it."

"I can do it."

"One-armed?"

After a moment, with an irritated snort, Saf stalked to the table, hooked his foot around a chair leg, yanked the chair out, and sat. Then he pushed his left sleeve to his elbow and scowled at Bitterblue, who tried to keep her face from showing what she felt at the sight of his arm. The entire forearm was bruised and swollen. A long, even cut, fully the length of her hand, ran along the top, neatly stitched together with thread, the dark reddish tinge of which came, she knew, from Saf's own blood.

So, pain was at the base of Saf's fury tonight. And perhaps humiliation? Had they held him down and cut him deliberately? The incision was long and neat.

"Is it deep?" Bitterblue asked as she bandaged it. "Did someone clean it properly and give you medicines?"

"Roke may not be a queen's healer, Sparks," Saf said sarcastically, "but he does know how to keep a person from dying of a flesh wound."

"Where are you going, Saf?" asked Teddy wearily.

"To the silver docks," said Saf. "I got a tip tonight."

"Sparks, I'd feel better if you went with him," Teddy said. "He's more likely to behave if he knows he needs to look after you."

Bitterblue was of a different opinion. Touching Saf's arm, she could almost feel the tension humming in his body. He had an instinct toward recklessness tonight, and it was rooted in his anger.

And that was why she went with him—not so that he would have someone to look after, but so that someone, no matter how small and reluctant, would be there to look after him.

IT WAS GOOD that she was a strong runner, or Saf might have left her behind.

"Word is that Lady Katsa arrived in the city today," Saf said. "Is that true? And is Prince Po still at court?"

"Why do you care? Planning to rob them or something?"

"Sparks, I'd sooner rob myself than rob my prince. How is your mother?"

His strange, persistent courtesy toward her mother seemed almost funny tonight, what with his rough appearance and his madcap way of barreling through the wet streets as if he were looking for something to smash. "She's well," Bitterblue said. "Thank you," she added, not certain, at first, what she was thankful for. Then realizing, with a small implosion of shame, that it was for his adamant belief in her mother.

At the silver docks, the river wind pushed the rain right through to their skin. The ships shivered and dripped, their sails tied up tight. They were not really as tall as they looked in the darkness. Bitterblue knew that; they were not ocean vessels but river ships, designed to carry heavy loads north against the current of the River Dell, from the mines and refineries in the south. But they seemed massive at night, looming over the piers, silhouettes of soldiers lining their decks, for this was the landing place of the kingdom's wealth.

And the treasury, where that wealth is kept, is mine, Bitterblue thought. *And the ships are mine, and they're manned by my soldiers, and they bear my fortune from the mines and refineries that are also mine. This is all mine, because I am queen. How strange it is to think it.*

"I wonder what it would take to storm one of the queen's treasure ships," Saf said.

Bitterblue smirked. "Pirates make attempts now and then—or, so I've heard—near the refineries. Catastrophic attempts. For the pirates, I mean."

"Yes," Saf said, an irritable edge to his voice. "Well, each of the queen's ships contains a small army, of course, and the pirates wouldn't be safe with their loot anyway, until they'd escaped into the sea. I bet the sweep of river from the refineries to the bay is well-patrolled by the queen's water police. It's no easy task to hide a pirate ship on a river."

"How do you know all that?" Bitterblue asked, suddenly uneasy. "Great seas. Don't tell me you're a pirate! Your parents snuck you aboard a pirate ship! They did! I can tell just by looking at you!"

"Of course they didn't," he said with a long-suffering sigh. "Don't be daft, Sparks. Pirates murder and rape, and sink ships. Is that what you think of me?"

"Oh, you make me crazy," Bitterblue said tartly. "The lot of you sneak around thieving and getting knifed, except for when you're writing abstract books or printing Lienid-knows-what in your printing shop. You tell me nothing and then you get all huffy when I try to understand it on my own."

Saf turned away from the docks into a dark street Bitterblue didn't know. Near the entrance to what was obviously a story room, he faced her, grinning in the darkness.

"I've done a bit of treasure hunting," he said.

"Treasure hunting?"

"But I've never been a pirate, and never would, as I like to think you'd know without me having to tell you, Sparks."

"What is treasure hunting?"

"Well, ships go down, you know. They're wrecked in storms, or they burn, or they founder. Treasure hunters come later and dive to the floor of the sea, looking for treasure to salvage from the wreck."

Bitterblue studied his battered face. His conversation was amiable enough; fond, even. He liked to talk to her. But he had not lost any of his earlier anger. Something hard and hurt sat in his eyes, and he held his injured arm close to his body.

This sailor, treasure hunter, thief—whatever he was—should be in a warm, dry bed tonight, recovering his health and his temper. Not thieving, or treasure hunting, or whatever he'd come out here to do.

"It sounds dangerous," she said with a sigh.

"It is," he said. "But it's not illegal. Now, come inside. You're going to like what I steal tonight." Swinging the door open, he gestured her into the yellow light and the steam, the smell of bodies and musty wool, and a low-throated rasp that pulled Bitterblue forward: the voice of a fabler.

ON THE COUNTERS and tables of this story room, pots and buckets pinged with a tinny rhythm of falling drops. Bitterblue shot a dubious glance at the ceiling and kept to the edges of the room.

The fabler was a squat woman with a deep, melodious voice. The story was one of Leck's old animal tales: a boy in a boat on a frozen river. A fuchsia bird of prey with silver claws like anchor hooks—a gorgeous, mesmerizing, vicious creature. Bitterblue hated the story. She remembered Leck telling it to her, or one very similar. She could almost see Leck right there on the bar, one eye covered, the other gray, keen, and careful.

An image flickered then and flashed bright: the terrible wreck of the eye behind Leck's eye patch.

"Come on, let's go," Saf was saying. "Sparks. I'm done here. Let's go."

Bitterblue didn't hear him. Leck had removed the patch for her, just once, laughing, saying something about a horse that had reared and kicked him. She had seen the globe of his eyeball swollen purple with blood and had thought that the vivid crimson of the pupil was a bloodstain, not a clue to the truth of everything. A clue that explained why she felt so plodding and stupid and forgetful so much of the time—especially every time she sat with him, wanting to show off how well she read, hoping to please him.

Saf took hold of her wrist and tried to tug her away. Suddenly she was awake, galvanized. She swung out at him but he grabbed that wrist too, held her in a double grip, and muttered low, "Sparks, don't fight me here. Wait till we're outside. Let's go."

When had the room gotten so crowded and hot? A man sidling too close to her said in a voice too smooth, "Is this golden fellow giving you a hard time, boy? Do you need a friend?"

Saf spun on the man with a growl. The man backed away, hands raised, eyebrows raised, conceding defeat, and now it was Bitterblue grabbing on to Saf as Saf pushed after the man, Bitterblue grasping Saf's injured arm intentionally to cause him pain, to turn his fury back onto her, whom she knew he would not hurt, and away from everyone else in the room, whom she was less certain about.

"None of that," she said. "Let's go."

Saf was gasping. Tears brightened his eyes. She'd hurt him more than she'd meant to, but perhaps not more than she'd needed to; and anyway, it didn't matter, because they were leaving now, pushing through the people and scrambling out into the rain.

Outside, Saf ran, turned into an alleyway, and crouched low under the shelter of an awning. Bitterblue followed him and stood above him as he cradled his arm to his chest, swearing bloody murder.

"I'm sorry," she said, when he finally seemed to be switching from words to deep breaths.

"Sparks." A few more deep breaths. "What happened in there? I lost you. You weren't hearing a word I said."

"Teddy was right," she said. "It helped you to have me to look after. And I was right too. You needed someone to look after you." Then she heard her own words and shook her head to clear it. "I really am sorry, Saf—I was somewhere else. That story transported me."

"Well," Saf said, standing carefully. "I'll show you something that'll bring you back."

"You had time to steal something?"

"Sparks, it only takes a moment."

He pulled a gold disc from his coat pocket and held it under a guttering streetlamp. When he flicked the disc open, she took the edge of his hand, adjusting the angle so that she could see what she thought she saw: a large pocket watch with a face that had not twelve, but fifteen hours, and not sixty, but fifty minutes.

"Feel like explaining this to me?"

"Oh," he said, "it was one of Leck's games. He had an artist who was brilliant with small mechanics and liked to tinker with timepieces. Leck got her to make pocket watches that divided the half day into fifteen hours, but ran through them more quickly to make up the difference. Apparently, he liked to have all the people around him talking gibberish about the time, and believing their own gibberish. 'It's half past fourteen, Lord King. Would you like your lunch?' That sort of thing."

How creepy that this should sound familiar as he said it. Not a memory, not anything specific, just a feeling that she'd always known pocket watches like these but hadn't thought them worth considering for the past eight years. "He had a perverted sense of humor," she said.

"They're popular now, in certain circles. Worth a small fortune," Saf said quietly, "but considered to be stolen property. Leck compelled the woman to build them without compensating her. Then, presumably, he murdered her, as he did most of his artists, and hoarded the watches for himself. They made their way to the black market once he died. I'm recovering them for the woman's family."

"Do they keep good time?"

"Yes, but you need to work through some tricky arithmetic to figure out the real time."

"Yes," Bitterblue said. "I suppose you could convert everything into minutes. Twelve times sixty is seven hundred twenty, and fifteen times fifty is seven hundred fifty. So our seven-hundred-twenty-minute half day equals its seven-hundred-fifty-minute half day. Let's see . . . Right now, the watch reads a time of *nearly* twenty-five past two. That's one hundred twenty-five total minutes, which, divided by seven hundred fifty, should equal our time in minutes divided by seven hundred twenty . . . so, seven hundred twenty times one hundred twenty-five is . . . give me a moment . . . ninety thousand . . . divided by seven hundred fifty . . . is one hundred twenty . . . which means . . . well! The numbers are quite neat, aren't they? It's just about two o'clock. I should go home."

Saf had begun to chuckle partway through this litany. When, right on cue, a distant clock tower chimed twice, he burst into laughter.

"I, for one, would find it simpler to memorize which time signifies what," Bitterblue added.

"Naturally," Saf said, still chuckling.

"What's so funny?"

"I should know by now not to be surprised by anything you say or do, shouldn't I, Sparks?"

His voice had gone gentle somehow. Teasing. They stood close, heads bent together over the watch, her fingers still holding his hand. She understood something suddenly, not with her mind, but in the air that touched her throat and made her shiver when she looked up into his bruised face.

"Ah," she said. "Good night, Saf," then she slipped away.

NOTHING HAD HAPPENED. Still, the next day, she couldn't
stop thinking about it. Astonishing, how much thought could
be generated about nothing. Heat came upon her at the most
inconvenient moments, so that she was certain everyone who
looked into her eyes knew exactly what she was thinking about. It
was a good thing, really, that the Council meeting was planned for
that night. She needed to cool down before she went out again.

Katsa burst into her rooms far too early. "Po tells me you need
sword practice," she said, then committed an outrage by pulling
Bitterblue's sheets away.

"I don't even have a sword yet," Bitterblue moaned, trying to
burrow back under. "They're making it."

"As if we'd be starting with anything but wooden swords. Come
on! Get up! Think how satisfying it'll be to attack me with a sword."

Katsa rushed out again. For a moment, Bitterblue lay there,
bemoaning all existence. Then she rolled up and out of bed, the plush
red softness of the carpet swallowing her toes. Bitterblue's bedroom
walls were upholstered with a fabric woven in exquisite patterns of
scarlet, russet, silver, and gold. The ceiling was high, deep, and dark
blue like in her sitting room, scattered with gold and scarlet stars. The
tile of the bathing room shone gold through a doorway across from
her. It was a room like a sunrise.

As she pulled off her shift, she caught her own reflection in the tall mirror. It stopped her. She stared at herself, suddenly thinking of two incongruous people: Danzhol, who had kissed her, and Saf.

I do not suit this dazzling room, she thought. *My eyes are big and dull. My hair is heavy and my chin pointy. I'm so small that my husband won't be able to find me in the bed. And when he does, he'll discover that my breasts are uneven and I'm shaped like an eggplant.*

She snorted, laughing at herself; then was suddenly close to tears, kneeling on the floor before the mirror, naked. *My mother was so pretty.*

Is an eggplant ever pretty?

Nothing came through the pith of her mind to answer that question.

She remembered every part of her body Danzhol had touched. How far removed his kiss had been from how she'd imagined kissing. She knew that wasn't how it was supposed to feel. She had seen Katsa and Po kissing, she'd stumbled upon them once in her own stables, one of them pushing the other against a tower of hay, and once at the end of a corridor late at night, where they'd been little more than dark shapes and glimmers of gold, making small noises, barely moving, oblivious. Plainly, they enjoyed it.

But Po and Katsa are so beautiful, Bitterblue thought. *Of course they know the right way to do it.*

She had an imagination, and she wasn't shy of her own body; she'd made discoveries. And she knew the mechanics of two people. Helda had explained it to her, and she was pretty sure her mother had too, a long time ago. But understanding want and understanding mechanics did not go far toward elucidating how you could invite someone else to see you, to touch you in that way.

She hoped that all the kisses of her life, and all the things beyond, would not be with lords who only wanted her money. How simple it would be if she really were a baker girl. Baker girls met kitchen boys, and no one was a lord after a queen's money, and maybe it didn't matter so much if you were plain.

She hugged herself.

Then she stood, ashamed of herself for dwelling on these things when there was so much else to worry about.

PRINCE RAFFIN, KING Randa's son and the heir to the Middluns throne, and his companion Bann were also at sword practice, not looking entirely awake.

"Lady Queen," Raffin said, bending down from great heights to place a kiss on Bitterblue's hand. "How are you?"

"I'm so glad you came," said Bitterblue. "Both of you."

"We are too," said Raffin. "Though I'm afraid we had no choice, Lady Queen. We were attacked by Nanderan enemies of the Council. Katsa convinced us we'd be safer joining her wherever she went." The yellow-haired prince then beamed down upon Bitterblue as if he hadn't a trouble in the world.

Bann, who took Bitterblue's other hand, was, like Raffin, a Council leader and medicine maker who radiated calm—a broad mountain of a man, with eyes like the gray sea. "Lady Queen," he said. "It's lovely to see you. I'm afraid they pulverized our workrooms."

"We'd spent almost a year on that nausea infusion," said Raffin grumpily. "Months of us heaving our guts up, all lost."

"I don't know, it sounds to me as if you were quite successful," said Katsa.

"It was meant to be an infusion for *reducing* nausea!" Raffin said. "Not inducing it. We were close, I'm sure of it."

"That last batch barely caused you to vomit at all," Bann said.

"Wait," Katsa said suspiciously. "Is this why you both vomited on me while I was rescuing you? You'd been guzzling down your own infusion? Why would anyone bother trying to kill you?" she said, throwing her hands in the air. "Why not just wait for you to kill yourselves? Here, take this," she said, shoving a wooden sword so hard against Raffin's chest that he coughed. "If I have anything to do about it, the next time someone comes across the world to kill you, you'll be ready."

Bitterblue had forgotten how good this could be: a project with straightforward, identifiable, and *physical* goals. An instructor whose confidence in one's ability was absolute—even when one caught one's sword in one's skirts, tripped, and fell on one's face.

"Skirts are an imbecilic invention," said Katsa, who always wore trousers and cut her hair short. Then she picked Bitterblue up and set her on her feet so quickly that Bitterblue was no longer certain she'd been lying on the floor in the first place. "I expect they were a man's idea. Don't you have any practice trousers?"

Bitterblue's single pair of practice trousers were also her midnight escape trousers and, as such, were currently muddy and soaking wet, drying as best they could on the floor of her dressing room, where she hoped Helda wouldn't find them. She supposed she could ask Helda for more trousers now, with these lessons as the excuse. "I thought I should practice in the clothing I was likely to be wearing when attacked," she improvised.

"That does make sense. Did you knock your head?" Katsa asked, smoothing Bitterblue's hair back.

"Yes," Bitterblue lied, to keep Katsa touching her.

"You're doing well," Katsa said. "You have quick instincts—you always have. Not like that nincompoop," she added, with a roll of her eyes at Raffin, who was sparring with Bann awkwardly at the other end of the practice room.

Raffin and Bann were far from evenly matched. Bann wasn't just bigger, he was faster and stronger. The cowering prince, who handled his own sword ponderously, as if it were an impediment, never seemed to see an attack coming, even if he'd been told exactly when to expect it.

"Raff," Katsa said, "your problem is that your heart's not in it. We need to find something to strengthen your defensive resolve. What if you pretended he's trying to smash your favorite medicinal plant?"

"The rare blue safflower," Bann suggested.

"Yes," Katsa said gamely, "pretend he's after your snaffler."

"Bann would never come after my rare blue *safflower*," Raffin said distinctly. "The very notion is absurd."

"Pretend he's not Bann. Pretend he's your father," Katsa said.

This did seem to have some effect, if not on Raffin's speed, then at least on his enthusiasm. Bitterblue focused on her own drills, soothed by the noises of productive work going on nearby, allowing herself to empty her mind. No memories, no questions, no Saf; only sword, sheath, speed, and air.

SHE WROTE A ciphered letter to Ror on the subject of remuneration and entrusted it to Thiel, who carried it gravely to his stand. It was hard to predict how long a letter would take to reach Ror City. It depended entirely on what ship carried it and on the weather. If conditions were ideal, she might look for a response in two months—the beginning of November.

In the meantime, something had to be done about Ivan in the east city. But Bitterblue couldn't claim to have learned of him through her spies as well, or her credibility would begin to wear thin. Perhaps if she were allowed to roam the castle every day, then she could reasonably pretend to have overheard conversations. She could claim a broader familiarity, with everything.

"Thiel," she said, "do you think I could have one task every day that took me out of this tower? If only for a few minutes?"

"Are you restless, Lady Queen?" asked Thiel gently.

Yes, and it was also that she was distracted and far away from here, in a rainy alleyway under a guttering lamp, with a boy. Embarrassed, she touched her flushing throat. "I am," she said. "And I don't want to fight every time. You must let me do more than shuffle paper, Thiel, or I'm going to go mad."

"It's a matter of finding the time, Lady Queen, as you know. But Rood says there's a murder trial in the High Court today," added Thiel benevolently, noting the disappointment on her face. "Why don't you go to that, and we'll look for something relevant for tomorrow?"

THE ACCUSED WAS a shaking man with a history of erratic behavior and an odor that Bitterblue pretended not to notice. He had stabbed a man to death, an utter stranger, in broad daylight, for no reason he was able to explain. He had just . . . felt like it. As he made no attempt to deny the charge, he was convicted unanimously.

"Are murderers always executed?" Bitterblue asked Quall to her right.

"Yes, Lady Queen."

Bitterblue watched the guards take the shaking man away, stunned at the brevity of the trial. So little time, so little explanation needed to condemn a man to death. "Wait," she said.

The guards to either side of the shaking man stopped, turning him around to face her again. She stared at the prisoner, whose eyes rolled in his head as he tried to look at her.

He was disgusting and he'd done a horrible thing. But did no one else feel in his gut that something was wrong here?

"Before this man is executed," she said, "I should like my healer Madlen to meet with him and determine whether he's in his right mind. I don't wish to execute a person incapable of rational thought. It's not fair. And at the very least, I insist on some greater attempt at finding his reason for doing something so senseless."

LATER THAT DAY, Runnemood and Thiel were carefully pleasant to her, but seemed to stiffen around each other, avoiding conversation between them. She wondered if they were having a row. Did her advisers have rows? She'd never witnessed one before.

"Lady Queen," said Rood near evening, when he and she were momentarily alone. Rood most certainly wasn't squabbling with anyone. He'd been walking around meekly, trying to avoid people altogether. "It pleases me that you're kind," he said.

Bitterblue was rendered speechless at this. She knew she wasn't kind. She was largely ignorant, she was trapped behind unknowable things, she was trapped behind things she knew but couldn't admit she knew, she was a *liar*—and what she wanted to be was useful, logical, helpful. If a situation presented itself in which the right and the wrong seemed clear to her, then she was going to grab on tight. The world presented too few anchors for her to let one pass.

She hoped that the Council meeting would be another anchor.

AT MIDNIGHT, BITTERBLUE slipped down stairways and through dim-lit corridors to Katsa's rooms. As Bitterblue approached Katsa's door, it opened and Po emerged. These were not Katsa's usual rooms. Normally Katsa took rooms abutting Po's, near to Bitterblue and all of her personal guests, but Po, for some reason, had arranged for

Katsa to occupy south castle rooms this time and sent Bitterblue directions.

"Cousin," Po said. "Do you know about the secret staircase behind Katsa's bathing room?"

Moments later, Bitterblue watched in astonishment as Po and Katsa climbed into Katsa's bath. The bath itself was rather astonishing, lined with bright tiles decorated with colorful insects that looked so real that Bitterblue didn't think it could possibly be relaxing to bathe. Po reached down to the floor behind the bath and pressed on something. There was a clicking noise. Then a section of the marble wall behind the bath swung inward, revealing a small, low doorway.

"How did you find it?" asked Bitterblue.

"It leads up to the art gallery and down to the library," said Po. "I was in the library when I noticed it. That's where we're going."

"Is it a staircase?"

"Yes. A spiral."

I hate spiral staircases.

Still standing in the bath, Po held out his hand. "I'll be before you," he said, "and Katsa will be behind."

SEVERAL COBWEBBY, DUSTY, sneezy minutes later, Bitterblue crawled through a small door in a wall, pushed a hanging aside, and stepped into the royal library. It was a back alcove somewhere. The bookcases, dark, thick wood, were tall as trees and had the musty, living, moldering smell of a forest. The copper, brown, and orange books were like leaves; the ceilings were high and blue.

Bitterblue turned in circles. It was the first time she'd been in the library for as long as she could recall, and it was exactly how she remembered it.

An odd little assortment of castle people were present for the meeting. Helda, of course, which didn't surprise her; but also Ornik the swordsmith, young and earnest-looking when not smeared with soot; an older woman with a weathered face, named Dyan, who was introduced to Bitterblue as her head gardener; and Anna, a tall woman with short, dark hair and strong, striking features, who was apparently the head baker in the kitchens. *In my imaginary world*, thought Bitterblue, *she is my employer.*

Finally, and most surprisingly, one of the judges on her High Court was here. "Lord Piper," Bitterblue said calmly. "I didn't know you had a yen for overturning monarchies."

"Lady Queen," he responded, mopping his bald pate with a handkerchief, swallowing uncomfortably, and looking for all the world as if the presence of a talking horse at the meeting would have been less alarming than the presence of the queen. Indeed, all four castle people seemed a bit taken aback at her presence.

"Some of you are surprised that Queen Bitterblue is joining us," Po said to the group. "You'll understand that the Council is composed of her family and friends. This is our first time holding a meeting in Monsea and inviting Monseans. We don't require the queen to involve herself in our dealings, but we are, of course, unlikely to operate at her court without her knowledge or permission."

These words seemed to mollify not a single person in the group.

Scratching his head, beginning to grin, Po put an arm around Bitterblue and cocked a significant eyebrow at Giddon. While Giddon led everyone through a row of bookshelves and into a dark corner, Po spoke quietly into Bitterblue's ear. "The Council is an organization of lawbreakers, Bitterblue, and you are the law to these Monseans. They've all snuck here tonight, then come face-to-face with their queen. It'll take them a little while to adjust to you."

"I understand completely," said Bitterblue blandly.

Po snorted. "Yes. Well, stop making Piper nervous on purpose just because you don't like him."

The carpet here was thick, shaggy, green. When Giddon sat directly on the floor and motioned for Bitterblue to do the same, the others, with a moment's hesitation, formed a loose circle and began to sit as well. Even Helda plunked herself down, pulled knitting needles and yarn from a pocket, and set to work.

"Let's start with the basics," Giddon began without preamble. "Whereas the overthrow of Drowden in Nander began with the dissatisfaction of the nobility, in Estill, what we're looking at is a popular revolution. The people are starving. They're the world's most overtaxed, by King Thigpen and by their lords. Lucky for the rebels, our success with army deserters in Nander has frightened Thigpen. He's tightened the screws on his own soldiers, severely, and an unhappy army is something rebels can work with. I believe, and Po agrees, that there are enough desperate people in Estill— and enough thoughtful, meticulous people—for something to come of this."

"What frightens me is that they don't know what they want," said Katsa. "In Nander, we essentially kidnapped the king for them, then a coalition of nobles that they'd chosen beforehand slipped into place—"

"It was a thousand times messier than that," said Giddon.

"I know that. My point is that powerful people had a plan," said Katsa. "In Estill, people with no power whatsoever know that they *don't* want King Thigpen, but what *do* they want? Thigpen's son? Or some kind of massive change? A republic? How? They've got nothing in place, no structure to take over once Thigpen is gone. If they're not careful, King Murgon will move in from Sunder and we'll be calling Estill East Sunder. And Murgon will become twice the bully he is now. Doesn't that terrify you?"

"Yes," Giddon said coldly. "Which is why I vote that we answer their call for our help. Do you agree?"

"Completely," Katsa said, glowering.

"Isn't it lovely to be all together again?" Raffin said, throwing one arm around Po and the other around Bann. "My vote is yes."

"As is mine," said Bann, smiling.

"And mine," said Po.

"Your face will freeze like that, you know, Kat," Raffin said helpfully to Katsa.

"Maybe I should rearrange your face, Raff," said Katsa.

"I should like smaller ears," Raffin offered.

"Prince Raffin has nice, handsome ears," Helda said, not looking up from her knitting. "As will his children. Your children will have no ears at all, My Lady," she said sternly to Katsa.

Katsa stared back at her, flabbergasted.

"I believe it's more that her ears won't have children," began Raffin, "which, you'll agree, sounds much less—"

"Very good," Giddon interrupted, loudly, though perhaps no more so than circumstances warranted. "In the absence of Oll, it's unanimous. The Council will involve itself in the Estillan people's overthrow of their king."

* * * * *

IT WAS, FOR Bitterblue, a statement that required some time to absorb. The others moved on to the whos, whens, and hows, but Bitterblue wasn't one of the people who was going to carry a sword into Estill, or tip King Thigpen merrily into a sack, or however they decided to do it. Thinking that perhaps Ornik the smith, Dyan the gardener, Anna the baker, and Piper the judge would be less shy with their input were she not part of the circle, she pushed herself to her feet. Waving away their hasty attempts to rise, she wandered into the bookshelves, toward the tapestry that hung over the opening she'd come through. She noticed, absentmindedly, that the woman in the hanging, dressed in white furs and surrounded by stark white forest, had eyes green as moss and hair bright and wild, like a sunset or like fire. She was too vivid, too strange to be human. Yet another odd decorative object of Leck's.

Bitterblue needed to think.

A monarch was responsible for the welfare of the people he ruled. If he hurt them deliberately, he should lose the privilege of sovereignty. But what of the monarch who hurt people, but not deliberately? Hurt them by not helping them. Not fixing their buildings. Not returning their losses. Not standing beside them as they grieved for their children. Not hesitating to send the mad or the troubled to be executed.

I know one thing, she thought, staring into the sad eyes of the woman in the hanging. *I would not like to be deposed. It would hurt like being skinned, or like being torn into pieces.*

And yet, what am I as a queen? My mother said I was strong and brave enough for this. But I'm not, I'm useless. Mama? What happened to us? How can this be, that you're dead and I'm queen of a kingdom I can't even touch?

There was a marble sculpture here, set on the floor with the hanging as its backdrop. A child, five or six, perhaps, whose skirts were metamorphosing into rows of brick, for the child was turning into a castle. Clearly, this was the work of the same sculptor whose woman-turned-mountain-lion was in the back garden. One of the child's arms, reaching up to the sky, shifted form at the elbow and became a tower. On the flat roof of the tower, where her fingers should have been, stood five tiny, finger-sized guards: four with arrows drawn and notched, one with a sword at the ready. All aiming upward, as if some threat came from above, from the sky. Perfect in form and absolutely fierce.

The voices of her friends came to her in snatches. Katsa said something about the length of time it took to travel north through the mountain pass to Estill from here. Days and days; weeks. An argument began about which kingdom would make the best base for an operation in Estill.

Half listening, half observing the castle child, Bitterblue was overtaken suddenly by a most peculiar sense of recognition. It crawled up the base of her spine. She *knew* the stubborn mouth and the small, pointy chin of the sculpture child; she knew those big, calm eyes. She was looking into her own face.

It was a statue of herself.

Bitterblue tottered backward. The end of a bookshelf stopped her and held her up as she stared at the girl who seemed to stare back at her; the girl who *was* her.

"A tunnel connects Monsea and Estill," a voice said. Piper, the judge. "It's a secret passage under the mountains. Narrow and unpleasant, but passable. The journey from here to Estill by that route is a matter of days, depending on how hard you like to push your horse."

"What!" Katsa exclaimed. "I can't believe it. Can you believe it? I can't believe it!"

"We've established that Katsa can't believe it," said Raffin.

"I can't believe it either," said Giddon. "How many times have I crossed those mountains at the pass?"

"I assure you, it exists, My Lady, My Lord," said Piper. "My estate is at Monsea's northwesternmost point. The tunnel begins on my land. We used it to smuggle Gracelings out of Monsea during King Leck's reign, and now we use it to smuggle Estillan Gracelings in."

"This is going to change our lives," said Katsa.

"If the Council based itself in Monsea during the initial planning," Piper said, "Estillans could come to you swiftly through the tunnel, and you to them. You could smuggle weapons north to them, and any other supplies they needed."

"Except that we're not going to base ourselves in Monsea," said Po. "We're not going to make Bitterblue into a target for every angry king's vengeance. She's enough of a target already; we still haven't determined whom Danzhol was planning to ransom her to. And what if one of the kings decides to be less subtle than that? What's to stop one of them from declaring war on Monsea?"

The sculpture-Bitterblue looked so defiant. The little soldiers on her palm were ready to defend her with their lives. Bitterblue was amazed that a sculptor had been able to imagine her that way once: so strong and certain, so steady on the earth. She knew she wasn't those things.

She also knew what would happen if her friends chose to base their operation someplace other than Monsea. Walking back to the group, waving them down again when they all moved to rise, she said quietly, "You must use my city as your base."

"Hm," Po said. "I don't think so."

"I'm only offering it as a temporary base as you get yourselves organized," Bitterblue said. "I will not provide you with soldiers, nor will I allow you to employ Monsea's craftworkers to make any arms you need." *Perhaps,* she thought to Po alone, calculating, *I'll write to your father. There are two ways for an army to invade Monsea: the mountain pass, which is easy to defend, and the sea. Lienid is the only kingdom with a proper navy. Do you think Ror would bring part of his fleet along this winter? I should like to see it. I think sometimes about building my own, and his will look very nice and threatening sitting in my harbor.*

Po rubbed his head vigorously at this. He even let out a small moan. "We understand, Bitterblue, and we're grateful," he said. "But some angry friends of Drowden crossed into the Middluns to kill Bann and Raffin in reparation for what we did in Nander, you do realize that? Estillans could just as easily cross into Monsea—"

"Yes," she said. "I know. I heard what you said about war, and about Danzhol."

"It isn't just Danzhol," Po snapped. "There may well be others. I won't risk involving you in this."

"I'm already involved," said Bitterblue. "My problems are already your problems. My family is your family."

Po was still clutching his head worriedly. "You're not invited to any more meetings."

"That's fine," she said. "It will look better if I'm not seen to be in on the planning."

The circle considered Bitterblue's words in silence. The four Monseans who worked in the castle seemed rather startled. Helda, stopping her knitting, peered upon Bitterblue with gratified approval.

"Well then," Katsa said. "Of course, we'll operate with the greatest possible secrecy, Bitterblue. And for what it's worth, we'll deny your involvement to our dying breaths, and I'll kill anyone who doesn't."

Bann began to laugh into Raffin's shoulder. Smiling, Raffin said sideways to him, "Can you imagine what it would be like to be able to say that and mean it?"

Bitterblue didn't smile. She may have impressed them with fine words and sentiments, but her true reason for offering her city as their base was that she didn't want them to leave. She wanted them near, even if they were subsumed by their own affairs, she needed them at sword practice in the morning, at dinner at night, moving and shifting around her, there and gone, back again, arguing, teasing, acting like people who knew who they were. They understood the world and how to mold it. If she could keep them near, maybe one day she'd wake up and discover that she'd become strong that way too.

ONE MORE UNSETTLING thing happened before Bitterblue left the library that night. It involved a book she found by accident, while returning to the secret passage. An awkward shape, square and flat, it protruded from a shelf, or perhaps a lantern caught the gleam of its cover; either way, when her eyes lit upon it, she knew, instantly, that she'd seen it before. That book, with the same scratch through the gold filigree on its spine, had used to sit on the bookshelves in her blue sitting room, back when that sitting room had been her mother's.

Bitterblue pulled the book down. The title on the cover, gold printing on leather, said *Book of True Things*. Opening it to the first page, she found herself looking at a simple but beautifully rendered drawing of a knife. Underneath the knife, someone had written the word *Medicine*. Turning the page, memory came to her like a dream, like sleepwalking, so that she knew what she would find: a drawing of a collection of sculptures on pedestals, and underneath, the word *Art*. On the next page, a drawing of Winged Bridge and the word *Architecture*. Next, a drawing of a strange, green, clawed, furry creature, a kind of bear, and the word *Monster*. Next, a person—a corpse? Its eyes were open, painted two different colors, but something was wrong with this person, its face was stiff and frozen—and the word underneath was *Graceling*. Finally, a drawing of a handsome man with an eye patch and the word *Father*.

She remembered an artist bringing this book of pictures to her father. She remembered her father sitting at the table in the sitting room and writing the words in himself, then bringing it to her and helping her read it.

Bitterblue shoved the book back onto the shelf, suddenly furious. This book, this memory did not help her. She didn't need more bizarre things to make sense of.

But she couldn't leave it here either, not really. It called itself *Book of True Things*. True things were what she wanted to know, and this book that she didn't understand had to be a clue to the truth about *something*.

Bitterblue reached for the book again. When she returned to her bedroom, she laid it on the table by her bed and stuck her list of puzzle pieces inside.

IN THE MORNING, Bitterblue pulled her list out of the book and read it again. There were some pieces she'd answered and others that remained unsolved.

Teddy's words. Who are my "first men"? What did he mean by cutting and stitching? Am I in danger? Whose prey am I?

Danzhol's words. What did he SEE? What was he trying to say?

Darby's records. Was he lying to me about the gargoyles never having been there?

General mysteries. Who attacked Teddy?

Things I've seen with my own eyes. Why is the east city falling apart but decorated anyway? Why was Leck so peculiar about decorating the castle?

What did Leck DO? Tortured pets. Made people disappear. Cut. Burned printing shops. (Built bridges. Did castle renovations.) Honestly, how can I know how to rule my kingdom when I have no idea what happened in Leck's time? How can I understand what my people need? How can I find out more? In the story rooms?

She stopped on this part. Last night, her friends' meeting had brought her to what was, essentially, the kingdom's biggest story room. What if there were more books like the *Book of True Things* she'd found, but that she could make sense of? Books that could touch her memory and fill in some of these great gaps of meaning? Could she learn more about what Leck had done? If she knew what he'd done and why, mightn't it be easier to understand some of the things people were doing now?

She added to her list two questions: *Why are there so many missing pieces everywhere? Will the library hold any answers?*

When Katsa dragged her out of bed for sword practice, Bitterblue found that she'd dragged not just Raffin and Bann, but Giddon and Po along as well. The lot of them waited in Bitterblue's sitting room, picking at her breakfast while she dressed. Giddon, muddy and rumpled in last night's clothing, showed every sign of having been out all night. Collapsing on her sofa, he actually fell asleep for a moment.

Raffin and Bann stood together, propped against the wall and against each other, half dozing. At one point, Raffin, not knowing he had one small, curious witness, gave Bann a sleepy kiss on the ear.

Bitterblue had wondered that about them. It was nice when something in the world became clear. Especially when it was a nice thing.

"THIEL," SHE SAID in her office later that morning. "Do you remember that mad engineer with the watermelons?"

"You mean Ivan, Lady Queen?" said Thiel.

"Yes, Ivan. When I was walking back from that murder trial yesterday, Thiel, I overheard a conversation that concerned me. Apparently, Ivan is in charge of the renovation of the east city and is doing a mad, useless job of it. Could we have someone look into that? It sounds as if there's actual danger of buildings collapsing and so on."

"Oh," said Thiel, then sat down randomly, rubbing his forehead in an absent manner.

"Are you all right, Thiel?"

"Forgive me, Lady Queen," he said. "I'm perfectly all right. This Ivan business is a dreadful oversight on our part. We'll see to it immediately."

"Thank you," she said, looking at him doubtfully. "And will I be going to another High Court case today? Or will it be some new adventure?"

"There's not much of interest in the High Court today, Lady Queen. Let me see what other extra-office task I can rustle up."

"That's all right, Thiel."

"Oh? Have you lost your wanderlust, Lady Queen?" he asked hopefully.

"No," she said, rising. "I'm going to the library."

WHEN APPROACHING THE library in the usual manner, one walked into the north vestibule of the great courtyard, then stepped straight through the library doors. The first room, Bitterblue discovered, had ladders that ran on tracks and led to balconied mezzanines connected by bridges. Everywhere, tall bookshelves cut into the window glare like dark tree trunks. Dust hung suspended in shafts of light from the high windows. As she had the night before, Bitterblue turned in circles, sensing the familiarity and trying to remember.

Why had it been so long since she'd come here? When had she stopped reading, aside from the charters and reports that crossed her desk? When she'd become queen, and her advisers had taken over her education?

She walked past Death's desk, covered with papers and one sleeping cat, the skinniest, most wretched creature Bitterblue had ever seen. It lifted its hoary head and hissed at her as she passed. "I expect you and Death get along quite well," she said to it.

Arbitrary steps, one or two here or there, seemed to be part of the library's design. The farther she advanced into the library, the more steps she descended or climbed. The farther into the shelves, the darker and mustier her landscape, until she needed to backtrack and remove a lantern from a wall to light her way. Entering a nook lit by dim lamps stretching from the walls on long arms, she reached up and traced a carving in the wooden end of a bookcase. Then she realized that the carving was a curiously shaped set of letters that spelled out large, floppy words: *Stories and Explorations, Monsea's East.*

"Lady Queen?" said a voice behind her.

She had been thinking of the story rooms, of tales of strange creatures in the mountains. The sneer of her librarian dragged her unceremoniously back into reality. "Death," she said.

"May I help you find anything, Lady Queen?" Death asked with an attitude of palpable unhelpfulness.

Bitterblue studied Death's face, his green and purple eyes that glinted with antagonism. "I found a book here," she said, "recently, that I remember reading as a child."

"That couldn't surprise me less, Lady Queen. Your father and mother both encouraged your presence in the libraries."

"Did they? Death, have you been the caretaker of this library all my life?"

"Lady Queen, I have been the caretaker of this library for fifty years."

"Are there books here that tell about the time of Leck's rule?"

"Not a one," he said. "Leck kept no records that I know of."

"All right, then," she said. "Let's focus on the last eighteen years. How old was I when I used to come here?"

Death sniffed. "As young as three, Lady Queen."

"And what kind of books did I read?"

"Your father directed your studies for the most part, Lady Queen. He presented you with books of every kind. Stories he himself wrote; stories by others; the journals of Monsean explorers; the written appreciation of Monsean art. Some, he wanted you to read most particularly. I would go to great lengths to find them, or him to write them."

His words flickered like lights just out of her grasp. "Death," she said, "do you recall *which* books I read?"

He had begun to dust the volumes on the shelf before him with a handkerchief. "Lady Queen," he said, "I can list them in the order in which you read them, and then I can recite their contents to you, one after the other, word for word."

"No," Bitterblue said, deciding. "I want to read them myself. Bring the ones he most particularly wanted me to read, Death, in the order he gave me them."

Perhaps she could find missing pieces by starting with herself.

IN THE NEXT few days, reading whenever she could, staying in at night and stealing time from her sleep, Bitterblue worked her way fast through a number of books in which pictures outnumbered words. Lots of them, as she reread them, climbed into her and spread to her edges in a way that felt obscurely familiar, as if they were comfortable inside her, as if they remembered being there before; and when this happened, she kept the book in her sitting room for the time being, rather than returning it to the library. Very few of them were as obscure as the *Book of True Things*. Most were educational. One described, in simple words, on thick, cream-colored pages, each of the seven kingdoms. It had a page with a colored illustration of a Lienid ship cresting a wave, from the up-high perspective of a sailor in the riggings—every sailor on the deck below with rings on each hand and studs in each ear, painted with the world's tiniest brush, the paint burnished with real gold. Bitterblue could remember having read it, over and over, and having loved it, as a child.

Unless it was her own journey on a Lienid ship, fleeing Leck, that touched something comfortable inside her? How frustrating to feel a familiarity yet not be able to trace the feeling back to why. Did this happen to everyone, or was it one of Leck's special bequests? Bitterblue squinted at the empty shelves lining the walls of this room, certain too that when these rooms had been her mother's, the shelves had not been empty. What books had her mother kept on these shelves, and where were they now?

The library became Bitterblue's default extra-office destination every day for a week, for Rood had no interesting High Court cases to offer and she didn't feel like inspecting the drains with Runnemood, or seeing the rooms where Darby filed paperwork, or whatever other task Thiel suggested.

She walked into the library on the fourth day to find the cat guarding the entrance. It bared its teeth at the sight of her, its hair standing in a ridge on its back, its ragged coat a mix of blotches and stripes that seemed to sit wrong, somehow, on its body. As if it were wearing a coat that was the wrong shape for it.

"It's my library, you know," Bitterblue said, stamping her foot. The cat shot away in alarm.

"Nice cat you have," she said to Death when she reached his desk.

Death extended a book toward her, dangled between two fingers as if it smelled.

"What is that?" asked Bitterblue.

"The next volume in your rereading project, Lady Queen," Death said. "Stories written by your father the king."

After the briefest hesitation, she took the book from him. Leaving the library, she found herself carrying it in the same manner, some distance from her body, then placing it at the farthest edge of her sitting room table.

She could only absorb it in small portions. It gave her nightmares, such that she stopped reading it in bed or keeping it at her bedside, as she was wont to do with the other books. His handwriting, with its large, slightly off-kilter letters, was so organically familiar that she had dreams that every word she'd ever read had been written in that handwriting. Dreams too of the veins of her own body standing blue under her skin, turning and looping into that handwriting. But then she had another dream: Leck big like a wall bent over his pages, writing all the time in letters that wound and dipped and, when she tried to read them, weren't actually letters at all. That dream was more than a dream: It was a memory. Bitterblue had thrown her father's strange scribbles into the fire once.

The stories in the book included the usual nonsense: colorful, flying monsters that tore each other apart. Colorful caged monsters that screamed for blood. But he'd written true stories too. He'd written down stories of Katsa! Of broken necks, broken arms, chopped-off fingers; of the cousin Katsa had killed by accident when she was a child. He'd written them with transparent awe for what Katsa could do. It made Bitterblue shudder to feel his reverence for things Katsa was so ashamed of.

One of his stories was about a woman with impossible red, gold, and pink hair who controlled people with her venomous mind, living her life forever alone because her power was so hateful.

Bitterblue knew this could only be the woman in the hanging in the library, the woman in white. But that woman had no venom in her eyes; that woman wasn't hateful. It calmed Bitterblue to stand before the hanging and gaze at her. Either Leck had described her wrong to the artist or the artist had changed her on purpose.

When she lay down at night to sleep, sometimes Bitterblue would comfort herself with that other dream she'd had, the night she'd slept in Teddy and Saf's apartment, about being a baby in her mother's arms.

A WEEK OF reading went by before she went out into the city again. Bitterblue had been trying to use the reading to get Saf out of her mind. It hadn't really worked. There was something Bitterblue was undecided about, something vaguely alarming, though she wasn't sure what it was.

When she finally returned to the shop, it wasn't because she'd decided anything; she just couldn't help herself any longer. Staying inside night after night was claustrophobic, she didn't like being out of touch with the night streets, and anyway, she missed Teddy.

Tilda was working at the press when she arrived. Saf was out, which was a tiny dart of disappointment. In the back room, Bren helped Teddy drink from a bowl of broth. He smiled beatifically at Bren when she caught the dribbles on his chin with a spoon, causing Bitterblue to wonder what feelings Teddy had for Saf's sister, and whether Bren returned them.

Bren was gentle, but firm, with Teddy's dinner. "You will eat it," she said flatly when Teddy began to shift and sigh and ignore the spoon. "You need to shave," she said next. "Your beard makes you look like a cadaver." Not particularly romantic words, but they brought a grin to Teddy's face. Bren smiled too, and, rising, kissed his forehead. Then she went to join Tilda in the shop, leaving them alone.

"Teddy," Bitterblue said to him, "you told me before that you were writing a book of words *and* a book of truths. I would like to read your book of truths."

Teddy grinned again. "Truths are dangerous," he said.

"Then why are you writing them in a book?"

"To catch them between the pages," said Teddy, "and trap them before they disappear."

"If they're dangerous, why not let them disappear?"

"Because when truths disappear, they leave behind blank spaces, and that is also dangerous."

"You're too poetic for me, Teddy," said Bitterblue, sighing.

"I'll give you a plainer answer," said Teddy. "I can't let you read my book of truths because I haven't written it yet. It's all in my head."

"Will you at least tell me what kind of truths it's going to be about? Is it truths of what Leck did? Do you know what he did with all the people he stole?"

"Sparks," said Teddy, "I think those people are the only ones who know, don't you? And they're gone."

Voices rose in the shop. The door opened, filling the room with light, and Saf stepped in. "Oh, wonderful," he said, glaring at the bedside tableau. "Has she been feeding you drugs, then asking you questions?"

"I did bring drugs, for *you*, actually," said Bitterblue, reaching into her pocket. "For your pain."

"Or as a bribe?" Saf said, disappearing into the small closet that served as a pantry. "I'm ravenous," came his voice, followed by a considerable clatter.

A moment later, he popped his head out and said with utter sincerity, "Sparks, thank Madlen, all right? And tell her she needs to start charging us. We can pay."

Bitterblue put her finger to her lips. Teddy was asleep.

LATER, BITTERBLUE SAT with Saf at the table while he spread cheese on bread. "Let me do that," she said, noticing his gritted teeth.

"I can manage," he said.

"So can I," Bitterblue said, "and it doesn't hurt me." In addition to which, it gave her something to do with her hands, something to occupy her attention. She liked Saf too much as he sat there bruised and chewing; she liked being in this room too much, both trusting and not trusting him, both prepared to tell him lies and prepared to tell him the truth. None of what she was feeling was wise.

She said, "I'd very much like to know what Tilda and Bren are printing in there every night that I'm not allowed to see."

He held a hand out to her.

"What?" she asked, suspicious.

"Give me your hand."

"Why should I?"

"Sparks," he said, "what do you think? I'm going to bite you?"

His hand was broad and calloused, like every sailor's hand she'd ever seen. He wore a ring on every finger—not fine, heavy rings like Po's, not a prince's rings, but true Lienid gold nonetheless, just like the studs in his ears. The Lienid didn't skimp on those things. He'd extended his injured arm, which had to be aching, waiting like that.

She gave him her hand. He took it in both of his and set to inspecting it with great deliberation, tracing each finger with the tips of his, examining her knuckles, her nails. He lowered his freckled face to her palm and she felt herself held between the heat of his breath and the heat of his skin. She no longer wanted him to give her hand back—but, now he straightened and let her go.

Somehow, she managed to inject sarcasm into her question. "What's wrong with you?"

He grinned. "You've got ink under your fingernails, baker girl," he said, "not flour. Your hand smells like ink. It's too bad," he said. "If your hand smelled like flour, I was going to tell you what we're printing."

Bitterblue snorted. "Your lies aren't usually so obvious."

"Sparks, I don't lie to you."

"Oh? You were never going to tell me what you're printing."

He grinned. "And your hand was never going to smell like flour."

"Of course not, when I made the bread some twenty hours ago!"

"What are the ingredients of bread, Sparks?"

"What is your Grace?" Bitterblue countered.

"Oh, now you're just hurting my feelings," said Saf, not looking remotely hurt about anything. "I've said it before and I'll say it again: I do not tell you lies."

"That doesn't mean you tell the truth."

Saf leaned back comfortably, smiling, cradling his injured forearm and chewing on more bread. "Why don't you tell me who you work for?"

"Why don't you tell me who attacked Teddy?"

"Tell me who you work for, Sparks."

"Saf," Bitterblue said, beginning to be sad and frustrated about all the lies and wanting very much, suddenly, to get past his willfulness that was keeping her questions from being answered. "I work for myself. I work alone, Saf, I deal in knowledge and truth and I have contacts and power. I don't trust you, but it doesn't matter;

176 — KRISTIN CASHORE

I don't believe that anything you're doing could make us enemies. I want your knowledge. Share what you know with me and I'll help you. We could be a team."

"If you think I'm going to jump at a vague offer like that, I'm insulted."

"I'll bring you proof," Bitterblue said, with no idea what she meant by it, but certain, desperately, that she would figure it out. "I'll prove to you that I can help you. I've helped you before, haven't I?"

"I don't believe you work alone," Saf said, "but I'm corked if I can place who you work for. Is your mother part of this? Does she know you come out at nights?"

Bitterblue thought about how to answer that. Finally, she said in a sort of a hopeless voice, "If she knew, I'm not sure what she would think."

Sapphire considered her for a moment, the purples of his eyes soft and clear. She considered him in return, then looked away, wishing she weren't so conscious of certain people sometimes, people who were more alive to her, somehow, more breathing, more invigorating, than other people. "Do you suppose that if you bring proof that we can trust you," Saf said, "you and I will start having conversations that move in straight lines?"

Bitterblue smiled.

Grabbing another handful of food, shooting to his feet, Saf cocked his head at the shop door. "I'll walk you home."

"There's no need."

"Think of it as my payment for the medicines, Sparks," he said, bouncing on his heels. "I'll deliver you safely to your mother."

His energy, and his words, too often, brought to mind things she wanted and couldn't have. She had nothing left to argue with.

*   *   *   *   *

IT WAS A great relief to leave Leck's stories behind and move on to the journals of Grella, the ancient Monsean explorer. The volume she was reading was called *Grella's Harrowing Journey to the Source of the XXXXXX,* and the name of the river, clearly the Dell by context, was obliterated every time it appeared. Odd.

She entered the library one day in mid-September to find Death scribbling at his desk, the cat glaring at his elbow. As Bitterblue stopped before them, Death pushed something toward her without looking up.

"The next book?" she asked.

"What else would it be, Lady Queen?"

The reason she'd asked was that the volume appeared to be not a book but a stack of papers, wrapped in a length of rough leather, tied shut. Now she read the card secured under its leather tie: *The Book of Ciphers.*

"Oh!" Bitterblue said, the hairs of her body suddenly standing on end. "I remember that book. Did my father really give it to me?"

"No, Lady Queen," said Death. "I thought you might like to read a volume your mother chose for you."

"Yes!" Bitterblue said, unfastening the ties. "I remember that I read this with my mother. 'It will keep our minds sharp,' she said. But—" Bitterblue flipped through the loose, handwritten pages, confused. "This is not the book we read. That book had a dark cover and was typeset. What is this? I don't know the handwriting."

"It is my handwriting, Lady Queen," said Death, not looking up from his work.

"Why? Are you the author?"

"No."

"Then why—"

"I have been rewriting, by hand, the books King Leck burned, Lady Queen."

Something tightened in Bitterblue's throat. "Leck burned books?"

"Yes, Lady Queen."

"From this library?"

"Yes, and other libraries, Lady Queen, and private collections. Once he'd decided to destroy a book, he sought out every copy."

"What books?"

"A variety. Books on history, the philosophy of monarchy, medicine—"

"He burned books about medicine?"

"A select few, Lady Queen. And books on Monsean tradition—"

"Such as burying the dead instead of burning."

Death managed to combine his nod with a frown, thus maintaining, in agreement, the appropriate level of disagreeableness. "Yes, Lady Queen."

"And books on ciphers that I read with my mother."

"It would seem so, Lady Queen."

"How many books?"

"How many books what, Lady Queen?"

"How many books did he destroy!"

"Four thousand thirty-one unique titles, Lady Queen," Death said crisply. "Tens of thousands of individual volumes."

"Skies," Bitterblue said, breathless. "And how many have you managed to rewrite?"

"Two hundred forty-five titles, Lady Queen," he said, "over the past eight years."

245, out of 4,031? She calculated: just over six percent; some thirty books a year. It meant that Death took an entire book down by hand, more than an entire book, every two weeks, which was a mammoth feat, but it was absurd; he needed help. He needed a row of printers at nine or ten presses. He needed to recite ten different books at once, feeding each typesetter one page at a time. Or, one sentence? How fast could a setter lay down type? How fast could someone like Bren or Tilda print multiple copies and move to the next page? And—oh, this was dreadful. What if Death took ill? What if he died? There were . . . 3,786 books that existed nowhere, no place but in the Graceling mind of this man. Was he getting enough sleep? Did he eat well? How old was he? At this rate, it was a project that would take him . . . over 120 years!

Death was speaking again. With effort, she pulled her thoughts back. "In addition to the books King Leck obliterated," he was saying, "he also forced me to alter one thousand four hundred forty-five titles, Lady Queen, removing or replacing words, sentences, passages he considered objectionable. The rectification of such errors waits until I've completed my current, more urgent project."

"Of course," Bitterblue said, barely hearing, progressing unstoppably to the conviction that no books in the kingdom were more important for her to read right now than the 245 that Death had rewritten, 245 books that had offended Leck so deeply that he'd destroyed them. It could only be because they'd contained the truth, about something. About anything; it didn't matter. She needed to read them.

"*Grella's Harrowing Journey to the Source of the River XXXXXX*," she added, suddenly realizing. "Leck forced you to cross out the word *Dell* throughout."

"No, Lady Queen. He forced me to cross out the word *Silver*."

"*Silver*? But the book is about the River Dell. I recognize the geography."

"The true name of the River Dell is the River Silver, Lady Queen," Death said.

Bitterblue stared at him, not comprehending. "But, everyone calls it the Dell!"

"Yes," he said. "Thanks to Leck, almost everyone does. They are wrong."

She leaned both hands against the desk, too overwhelmed, suddenly, to stand without support. "Death," she said with her eyes closed.

"Yes, Lady Queen?" he asked impatiently.

"Are you familiar with the library alcove that has a hanging of a red-haired woman and a sculpture of a child turning into a castle?"

"Of course, Lady Queen."

"I want a table moved into that alcove, and I want you to pile all the volumes you've rewritten on that table. I wish to read them and I wish that to be my workspace."

Bitterblue left the library, holding the cipher manuscript tight to her chest as if it might not actually be real. As if, if she stopped pressing it to herself, it might disappear.

THERE WAS LITTLE information in *The Book of Ciphers* that Bitterblue didn't already know. She wasn't sure if this was because she remembered it from reading it before or simply because ciphers, of various kinds, were part of her daily life. Her personal correspondence with Ror, Skye, with her Council friends, even with Helda was routinely ciphered. She had a mind for it.

The Book of Ciphers seemed to be a history of ciphers through time, beginning with the Sunderan king's secretary, centuries ago, who'd noticed one day that the unique designs in the molding along the wall of his office numbered twenty-eight, as did the letters in the alphabet at that time. This led to the world's first simple substitution cipher, one design assigned to each letter of the alphabet—and worked successfully for only as long as it took someone to notice the way the king's secretary stared at the walls while writing. Next came the notion of a scrambled alphabet that substituted for the real alphabet, and which required a key for decipherment. This was the method Bitterblue used with Helda. Take the key SALTED CARAMEL. First, one removed any repeating letters from the key, which left S A L T E D C R M. Then, one continued forward with the known twenty-six-letter alphabet from the place where the key left off, skipping any letters that had already been used, starting again at A once one had reached *Z*.

The resulting alphabet, S A L T E D C R M N O P Q U V W X Y Z B F G H I J K, became the alphabet for use in writing the ciphered message, like so—

S	A	L	T	E	D	C	R	M	N	O	P	Q
A	B	C	D	E	F	G	H	I	J	K	L	M

U	V	W	X	Y	Z	B	F	G	H	I	J	K
N	O	P	Q	R	S	T	U	V	W	X	Y	Z

—such that the secret missive "A letter has arrived from Lady Katsa," became "S P E B B E Y R S Z S Y Y M G E T D Y V Q P S T J O S B Z S."

Bitterblue's ciphers with Ror began with a similar premise but operated on a number of levels simultaneously, several different alphabets in use in the course of one message, the total number in use and the order in which they were used depending on a changing series of keys. Communicating these keys to Bitterblue in a subtle manner only she would understand was one of the jobs of Skye's own ciphered letters.

Bitterblue was astonished—utterly—at Death's Grace. She supposed she'd never quite considered before what Death could do. Now she held it in her hands: the regeneration of a book that introduced some ten or twelve different kinds of ciphers, presenting examples of each, some of which were dreadfully complicated in execution, most of which looked to the reader like nothing more than a senseless string of random letters. *Does he understand everything he reads? Or is it just the* look *of the thing he remembers—the symbols, and how they sit on the page in relation to each other?*

There seemed to be little in this rewritten book worth studying. And still, she read every line, letting each one linger, trying to resurrect the memory of sitting before the fire with Ashen, reading this book.

WHEN SHE COULD make the time, Bitterblue continued her nightly excursions. By mid-September Teddy was doing better, sitting up, even moving from room to room, with help. One night, when nothing was being printed, Teddy let Bitterblue come into the shop and taught her how to set type. The tiny letter molds were awkward to manage.

"You pick it up quickly," Teddy mused as she fought with an *i* that would not land base side down in the tray.

"Don't flatter me. My fingers are clumsy as sausages."

"True, but you have no trouble spelling words backwards with backward letters. Tilda, Bren, and Saf have good fingers, but they're always transposing letters and mixing up the ones that mirror each other. You haven't once."

Bitterblue shrugged, fingers moving faster now with letters that had a bit more heft, *m*'s and *o*'s and *w*'s. "It's like writing in cipher. Some part of my brain goes quiet and translates for me."

"Write in cipher much, do you, baker girl?" Saf asked, coming through the outside door, startling her, so that she dropped a *w* in the wrong place. "The castle kitchen's secret recipes?"

ON A MORNING a week later, Bitterblue climbed the stairs to her tower, entered, and found her guard Holt standing balanced inside the frame of an open window. His back to the room, he leaned out, nothing but a casual handhold on the molding keeping him from falling.

"Holt!" she cried, convinced, in that first irrational moment, that someone had fallen out the window and Holt was looking down at the body. "What happened?"

"Oh, nothing, Lady Queen," Holt said calmly.

"Nothing?" Bitterblue cried. "You're certain? Where is everyone?"

"Thiel is downstairs somewhere," he said, still leaning perilously out of the window, speaking loudly, but evenly, so that she could hear. "Darby is drunk. Runnemood is in the city having meetings and Rood is consulting with the judges of the High Court about their schedule."

"But—" Bitterblue's heart was trying to hammer its way out of her chest. She wanted to go to him and yank him back into the room, but she was afraid that if she got too close, she would touch him in the wrong way and send him plummeting. "Holt! Get down from there! What are you doing?"

"I was just wondering what would happen, Lady Queen," he said, still leaning out.

"You come back into this room this instant," she said.

Shrugging, Holt stepped down onto the floor, just as Thiel pushed into the room. "What is it?" Thiel asked sharply, looking from Bitterblue to Holt. "What's going on here?"

"What do you mean," said Bitterblue, ignoring Thiel, "you were wondering what would happen?"

"Don't you ever wonder what would happen if you jumped out a high window, Lady Queen?" asked Holt.

"No," cried Bitterblue, "I don't wonder what would happen! I know what would happen. My body would be crushed to death. Yours would too. Your Grace is strength, Holt, nothing else!"

"I wasn't planning to jump, Lady Queen," he said with a nonchalance that was beginning to make her furious. "I only wanted to see what would happen."

"Holt," said Bitterblue through gritted teeth. "I forbid you, absolutely forbid you, to climb into any more window frames and look down, wondering what would happen. Do you understand me?"

"Honestly," said Thiel, going to Holt and grabbing his collar, then pushing Holt to the door in a manner that was almost comical, as Holt was bigger than Thiel, almost twenty years younger, and enormously stronger. But Holt just shrugged again, making no protest. "Pull yourself together, man," said Thiel. "Stop giving the queen frights." Then he opened the door and shoved Holt through it.

"Are you all right, Lady Queen?" said Thiel, slamming the door shut, turning back to her.

"I don't understand anyone," Bitterblue said miserably, "or anything. Thiel, how am I to be queen in a kingdom of crackpots?"

"Indeed, Lady Queen," said Thiel. "That was an extraordinary display." Then he picked up a pile of charters from his stand, dropped them on the floor, picked them up again, and handed them to her with a grim face and shaking hands.

"Thiel?" Bitterblue said, seeing a bandage peeking out of one sleeve. "What did you do to yourself?"

"It's nothing, Lady Queen," he said. "Just a cut."

"Did someone competent look at it?"

"It doesn't warrant a healer, Lady Queen. I dealt with it myself."

"I'd like Madlen to examine it. It might need stitches."

"It needs nothing."

"That's a question for a healer to decide, Thiel."

Thiel made himself tall and straight. "A healer has already stitched it, Lady Queen," he said sternly.

"Well, then! Why did you tell me you'd dealt with it yourself?"

"I dealt with it by bringing it to a healer."

"I don't believe you. Show me the stitches."

"Lady Queen—"

"Rood," Bitterblue snapped at her white-haired adviser who'd just entered the room, puffing from the effort of the stairs. "Help Thiel unwrap his bandage so that I may see his stitches."

Not a little confused, Rood did as he was told. A moment later, the three of them gazed down upon a long, diagonal slice across Thiel's inner wrist and the base of his hand, neatly stitched.

"How did you do this?" Rood asked, clearly shaken.

"A broken mirror," Thiel said flatly.

"A wound like this left unattended would be quite serious," Rood said.

"This particular wound is rather over-attended," said Thiel. "Now, if you'll both allow me, there is much to do."

"Thiel," Bitterblue said quickly, wanting to keep him here beside her, but not knowing how. Would a question about the name of the river make things better or worse? "The name of the river," she ventured.

"Yes, Lady Queen?" he said.

She studied him for a moment, searching for an opening in the fortress of his face, the steel traps of his eyes, and finding nothing but a strange, personal misery. Rood put a hand on Thiel's shoulder and made *tut-tut* noises. Shaking him off, Thiel went to his stand. She noticed now that he was limping.

"Thiel?" said Bitterblue. She'd ask something else.

"Yes, Lady Queen?" whispered Thiel with his back to her.

"Would you happen to know the ingredients of bread?"

After a moment, Thiel turned to face her. "A yeast of some kind, Lady Queen," he said, "as a leavening agent. Flour, which is, I believe, the ingredient with the largest share. Water or milk," he said, gaining confidence. "Perhaps salt? Shall I find you a recipe, Lady Queen?"

"Yes, please, Thiel."

Thiel went off to find Bitterblue a recipe for bread, which was a ridiculous task for the queen's foremost adviser. Watching him as he limped through the door, she noticed that his hair was thinning on top. She'd never noticed that about him before, and it was somehow unbearable. She could remember Thiel dark-haired. She could remember him bossy and confident; she could also remember him broken and crying, confused, bleeding, on her mother's floor. She could remember Thiel a lot of ways, but she had never thought of him before as a man growing old.

SHE WENT TO the library next, stopping in her rooms to glare at her list of puzzle pieces. Snatching it out of the strange picture book and reading it again, she supposed that the list was a sort of cipher too, in the sense that each part of it meant something it wasn't saying yet. Fighting tears and fed up with worry, fed up with people who made no sense and lied, she wrote "BALLS" in big letters across the bottom, a general expression of dissatisfaction with the state of all things. *It could be a cipher, and "balls" could be the key. Wouldn't that be blessedly simple?*

Po, she thought as she stomped away to the library, the list clenched in her hand. *Are you around? I have questions for you.*

In the library, no one was at Death's desk except for the cat, curled tight in a ball, every vertebra sharp and visible. Bitterblue gave it a wide berth. Wandering room to room, she finally found Death standing between two rows of shelves, using a blank shelf before him as a desk for his furious scribbling. Pages and pages. He came to the end of one page, lifted the paper, shook it around to dry the ink, and pushed it aside, his writing hand already zipping across the next page before the last was disposed of. She almost couldn't

188 — KRISTIN CASHORE

believe how fast he was writing. He came to the end of that page and began another without pause. At the end of that page he began the next, then dropped his pen suddenly and stood with eyes closed, massaging his hand.

Bitterblue cleared her throat. Death jumped, flashing wide, uneven eyes at her. "Ah, Lady Queen," he said, not unlike the way someone checking a hole in an apple might say, "Ah, worms."

"Death," Bitterblue said, waving her list at him, "I have a list of questions. I want to know if you, as my librarian, know the answers or how to find them."

Death looked thoroughly put out by this, as if she weren't asking him to do his precise job. He continued rubbing his hand, which she hoped was in an agony of cramps. Finally, wordlessly, he reached out and snatched the paper from her.

"Hey!" Bitterblue said, startled. "Give that back!"

He glanced at it front and back, then returned it to her, not even looking at her, not seeming to look at anything, brow creased in thought. Bitterblue, remembering with alarm that once Death read something, he would recall it forever and never need to refer to it again, reread both sides of the paper herself, trying to assess the damage.

"A number of these questions, Lady Queen," Death said, still peering into empty air, "are a bit general, wouldn't you say? For example, the question 'Why is everybody crackpots?' and the question about why you're plagued by missing pieces everywhere—"

"That's not what I've come to you about," said Bitterblue testily. "I want to know if you know anything about what Leck did, and who, if anyone, is lying to me."

"Regarding the middle question, about man's reasons for stealing a gargoyle, Lady Queen," Death continued, "criminality is a natural form of human expression. We are all part light and part shadow—"

"Death," Bitterblue interrupted. "Stop wasting my time."

"Is 'BALLS' a question, Lady Queen?"

Bitterblue was now dangerously on the verge of doing something she would never forgive herself for: laughing. She bit her lip and changed her tone. "Why did you give me that map?"

"Map, Lady Queen?"

"The little, soft leather one," said Bitterblue. "Why, when your work is so important and can bear no interruption, did you make a special trip to my office to deliver that map?"

"Because Prince Po asked me to, Lady Queen," said Death.

"I see," Bitterblue said. "And?"

"And, Lady Queen?"

Bitterblue waited patiently, holding his eyes.

Finally, he relented. "I have no idea who might be lying to you, Lady Queen. I have no reason to think that anyone would, beyond that it is a thing people do. And if you're asking me what King Leck did in secret, Lady Queen, you would know better than I. You spent more time with him than I did."

"I don't know his secrets."

"Nor do I, Lady Queen, and I've already told you that I know of no records he kept. Nor do I know of records kept by anyone else."

She didn't like to give Death the satisfaction of knowing he'd caused her disappointment. She tried to turn away before he could see it in her face.

"I can answer your first question, Lady Queen," he said to her back.

Bitterblue stopped in her tracks. The first question was *Who are my "first men"?*

"The question refers, quite conspicuously, to the words written on the back of your list, doesn't it, Lady Queen?"

Teddy's words. "Yes," said Bitterblue, turning to face him again.

"'I suppose the little queen is safe without you today, for her first men can do what you would,'" Death recited. "'Once you learn cutting and stitching, do you ever forget it, whatever comes between? Even if Leck comes between? I worry for her. It's my dream that the queen be a truthseeker, but not if it makes her someone's prey.' Were these words addressed to one of your healers, Lady Queen?"

"They were," whispered Bitterblue.

"May I assume then, Lady Queen, that you are unaware that forty-some years ago, before Leck came to power, your advisers Thiel, Darby, Runnemood, and Rood were brilliant young healers?"

"Healers! Trained healers?"

"Then Leck murdered the old king and queen," Death went on, "crowned himself, and made the healers part of his advising team— perhaps 'coming between' the men and their medical profession, if you will, Lady Queen. These words seem to suggest that a healer some forty years ago is still a healer today, rendering you safe in the company of your 'first men,' your advisers, Lady Queen, even when your official healers are unavailable."

"How do you know this about my advisers?"

"It's not a secret, Lady Queen, to anyone who can remember. My memory is aided by medical pamphlets in this library, written long ago by Thiel, Darby, Runnemood, and Rood, when they were students of the healing arts. I gather that they were, all four of them, considered to be stellar prospects, very young."

Bitterblue's mind was full of the memory of Rood and Thiel, moments ago, both staring at Thiel's wound. Full of her argument with Thiel, who'd first claimed to have dealt with the injury himself and then claimed to have brought it to a healer for stitching.

Could both claims have been true? He wouldn't have stitched it *himself*, would he? And then hidden his skill from her, as he had done for as long as she could remember?

"My advisers were healers," she said aloud, suddenly deflated. "Why would Leck choose healers to be his political advisers?"

"I haven't the foggiest notion," Death said impatiently. "I only know that he did. Do you wish to read the medical pamphlets, Lady Queen?"

"Yes, all right," she said with no enthusiasm.

Po appeared through the bookshelves then, carrying the cat and, of all things, making smooching noises into its crooked fur. "Death," he said, "Lovejoy is smelling excellent today. Did you bathe him?"

"Lovejoy?" Bitterblue repeated, staring at Death incredulously. "The cat's name is Lovejoy? Could you have named him anything more ironic?"

Death made a small, scornful noise. Then he took Lovejoy gently from Po's arms, scooped his papers up, and marched away.

"You shouldn't insult a man's cat," said Po mildly.

Ignoring this, Bitterblue rubbed her braids. "Po," she said. "Thank you for coming. May I use you?"

"Possibly," said Po. "What do you have in mind?"

"Two questions," Bitterblue said, "for two people."

"Yes?" said Po. "Holt?"

Bitterblue let out a short sigh. "I want to know what's wrong with him. Will you ask him why he was perched in my tower window today, and see what you think of his answer?"

"I suppose," said Po. "Perched how, exactly?"

Bitterblue opened the memory to Po.

"Hm," he said. "That is very odd, indeed." Then his eyes flashed at her, gentle lights. "You're not certain what question you want me to ask Thiel."

"No," she admitted. "I'm at a bit of a loss with Thiel. I'm finding him unpredictable. He's rattled too easily, and today he had the most horrific cut on his arm that he wouldn't be straight with me about."

"I can tell you he cares for you deeply, Beetle. But if you're finding yourself with actual reason to doubt his trustworthiness, I'll ask him an entire book of questions, whether you want me to or not."

"It's not that I don't trust him," said Bitterblue, frowning. "It's that he worries me, but I'm not sure why."

Po removed a small sack from his pocket and held it open to her. She reached in and pulled out a chocolate peppermint.

"I've learned that Danzhol had family and connections in Estill, Beetle," said Po, rocking on his heels and also eating a peppermint. "What do you think of that?"

"I think he's dead," Bitterblue said dully. "I think it doesn't matter."

"It does matter," said Po. "If he was thinking of selling you to someone in Estill, it means you have enemies in Estill, and that matters."

"Yes," said Bitterblue, sighing again. "I know."

"You know, but you don't care."

"I care, Po. It's just, I've got other things to worry about as well. If you wouldn't mind . . ."

"Yes?"

"Ask Thiel why he's limping."

THE NEXT DAY, Bitterblue found evidence of her usefulness to give to Saf.

She was in the library—again—wondering how many more times she could abandon her office for this alcove before her advisers lost their patience completely. On the alcove table were 244 handwritten manuscripts, stacked in towering piles, each manuscript enclosed in a soft leather wrapping and tied with soft leather strings. Under the ties of each book, Death had tucked a card with scribbles that indicated the book's title, author, date of first printing, date of destruction, and date of restoration. Bitterblue moved the manuscripts around, pushing and re-piling and lugging, reading all the titles. Books about Monsean customs and traditions, Monsean holidays, recent Monsean history pre-Leck. Books by philosophers who argued the merits of monarchy versus republic. Books about medicine. An odd little biographical volume about a number of Gracelings who were famous for having concealed their true Graces from the world, until their truths were discovered.

It was hard to know where to start. *Hard because I don't know what I'm looking for,* she thought, in the very moment that she found something. Not a big, mysterious something, just a small thing, but important, and she gaped at it, hardly believing she'd found it at all. *The Kissing Traditions of Monsea.*

That title had been on the list Saf had shown her, the list of items he was trying to recover for the people of Danzhol. And here that book was, sitting before her, returned to life.

I may as well take a look, she thought, unwinding the leather ties. Clearing a space in a patch of sunlight, she sat down and began to read.

"Lady Queen."

Bitterblue jumped. She'd been absorbed in a description of Monsea's four celebrations of darkness and light: the equinoxes in spring and fall and the solstices in winter and summer. Bitterblue was used to a party around the time of the winter solstice to celebrate the return of the light, but apparently, before the time of Leck, all four occasions had been times of festival in Monsea. People had used to dress up in bright clothing, decorate their faces with paint, and, traditionally, kiss everybody. Bitterblue's imagination had snagged itself on the kissing everybody part. It was less than delightful to look up into Death's sour face.

"Yes?" she said.

"I regret that I am unable to lend you the medical pamphlets written by your advisers after all, Lady Queen," he said.

"Why not?"

"They are missing, Lady Queen," he said, enunciating each syllable.

"Missing! What do you mean?"

"I mean that they're not on the shelves where they belong, Lady Queen," he said, "and now I shall have to take time away from my more important work to locate them."

"Hm," Bitterblue said, suddenly not trusting him. Perhaps the pamphlets had never existed. Perhaps Death had read her list of puzzle pieces and made up the entire tale for his own amusement. She certainly hoped not, since he claimed to be restoring—accurately—truths Leck had erased.

* * * * *

THE NEXT TIME Death interrupted her, Bitterblue had dozed off, her cheek pillowed on *The Kissing Traditions*.

"Lady Queen?"

Gasping, Bitterblue shot upright too fast, so that a muscle in her neck pulled and tightened. *Ow. Where—*

She'd been dreaming. As she woke, the dream fled, as dreams do, and she grabbed at it: her mother, embroidering, reading. Doing both at once? No, Ashen had been embroidering, her fingers like lightning, while Bitterblue had read aloud from a book Ashen had chosen, a difficult book, but fascinating in the moments that Bitterblue understood it. Until Leck had found them sitting together and asked about the book, listened to Bitterblue's explanation, then laughed and kissed Bitterblue's cheek and neck and throat and taken the book away and thrown it into the fire.

Yes. Now she remembered the destruction of *The Book of Ciphers*.

Bitterblue wiped at her throat, which felt dirty. She massaged the sore knot of muscle in her neck, slightly drunk with departing sleep and with the sense that she wasn't entirely attached to the earth. "What is it now, Death?"

"Pardon me for interrupting your nap, Lady Queen," he said, looking down his nose.

"Oh, don't be a twit, Death."

Death cleared his throat noisily. "Lady Queen," he said. "Is the rereading of your childhood books a project you still wish to pursue? If so, I have here a collection of tall tales about fabulous medical recoveries."

"From my father?"

"Yes, Lady Queen."

Bitterblue sat up straight and shuffled through the manuscripts on the table, looking for the two books about medicine that Death had rewritten. The rewritten books were not tall tales, but factual. "And so, he obliterated some medical books from existence but encouraged me to read others?"

"If it exists in my mind, Lady Queen," Death said, offended, "then it is not obliterated."

"Of course," she said, sighing. "Very well. I'll find time for it. What time is it now? I'd better go back to my office, before they come looking for me."

But when Bitterblue stepped into the great courtyard, she saw Giddon sitting on the edge of the pool, hands propped on knees. He was talking easily to a woman who seemed to be shaping the rump of a rearing shrubbery horse with shears. Dyan, the head gardener. Not far from them, Fox dangled from the high limbs of a tree, pruning the flowering ivy, dropping a shower of dark, overripe petals. "Fox," said Bitterblue, walking over with a pile of books and papers in her arms, craning her neck. "You work everywhere, don't you?"

"Wherever I'm useful, Lady Queen," said Fox, blinking down at her with those uneven gray eyes, her hair bright against the leaves. She smiled.

The green horse Dyan was working on rose from the bases of two shrubberies planted close together. Flowering ivy swirled across its rearing chest and trailed down its legs. "No, don't get up," Bitterblue said to Dyan and Giddon as she reached them, but Giddon already had, holding out a hand to help her with her armload. "Very well— here," she said, passing him the two medical rewrites and the reread, then sitting so that she could bind the pages of *The Kissing Traditions* safely back into their leather cover. "Are the shrubberies your design, Dyan?" she asked, glancing at the horse, which really was rather impressive.

"They were the design of King Leck's gardener, Lady Queen," Dyan said shortly, "and of King Leck himself. I merely maintain them."

"You were not King Leck's gardener?"

"My father was King Leck's gardener, Lady Queen. My father is dead," Dyan said, then gave an *oof* as she rose and stumped across the courtyard to a man-shaped shrubbery with flowering blue hair.

"Well," Bitterblue said to Giddon, a bit deflated. "It's always nice to hear of someone new one's father has murdered."

"She was rude to you," said Giddon apologetically, sitting back down beside her.

"I hope I didn't interrupt anything."

"No, Lady Queen," said Giddon. "I was only telling her about my home."

"You come from the grasslands of the Middluns, don't you, Giddon?"

"Yes, Lady Queen, west of Randa City."

"Is it very nice, your home?"

"I think so, Lady Queen. It's my favorite patch of land in all seven kingdoms," he said, leaning back, beginning to smile.

His face was transformed and quite suddenly, the more pleasant traditions of Monsea's light festivals came to her mind. She wondered if Giddon shared a woman's bed here at court, or a man's. Flushing now, she asked hastily, "How is your planning going?"

"It's coming along," Giddon said, pitching his voice low, directing his eyebrows significantly to where Fox was still pruning. The noise of the fountain muffled his voice. "We're going to send someone through Piper's tunnel to make contact with the Estillan rebels who asked for our help. And there may be a second tunnel that leads to a place near one of Thigpen's army bases in the eastern Estillan

198 — Kristin Cashore

mountains. One of us is going to see if that tunnel is a reality. It's been poked at from both ends, but no one seems to have followed it all the way through from one end to the other."

"Katsa?" said Bitterblue. "Or Po?"

"Katsa will search for the second tunnel," said Giddon. "Po or I will head through the first tunnel to make contact. More likely, we'll both go together."

"Is Po going to be a bit conspicuous, appearing suddenly in Estill, meeting with commoners and asking pointed questions? He's a bit of a glowing Lienid peacock, isn't he?"

"Po is impossible to disguise," he said. "But he also has a knack for sneaking around. And he's oddly good at getting people talking," he added, with something significant in his voice that made Bitterblue watch her hands for a beat, rather than his eyes, afraid of what her own eyes might convey.

She sent a burst of unpleasantness to Po. *You realize he puts himself into danger alongside you, don't you? Shouldn't he know the skills his partner possesses? Do you think he won't find out one day? Or that when he does, he won't mind?* Then she dropped her head into her hands and gripped her hair.

"Lady Queen," Giddon said. "Are you all right?"

She was not all right; she was having a crisis that had nothing to do with Po's lies and only with her own. "Giddon," she said, "I'm going to try an experiment on you that I've never tried on anyone else."

"Very well," he said good-humoredly. "Should I wear a helmet?"

"Maybe," she said, grinning, "if Katsa ever announces that she's trying an experiment. I only meant that I'd like to have someone I never lie to. From now on, you're it. I won't even equivocate to you. I'll either tell you the truth or say nothing at all."

"Huh," said Giddon, scratching his head. "I'll have to think up a lot of nosy questions."

"Don't push your luck. I wouldn't even try this if you were in the habit of asking me nosy questions. It also helps that you're not my adviser, my cousin, or my servant; you're not even Monsean, so you've no imaginary moral obligation to interfere with my business. Nor do I think you'll run off and tell Po all I say."

"Or even think about telling Po all you say," Giddon said, his tone so perfectly nonchalant that it raised hairs on the back of her neck. *Po*, she thought, shivering, *for goodness sake. Tell him what he already knows.*

"For what it's worth, Lady Queen," Giddon continued quietly, "I understand that your trust is a gift, not something I've earned. I promise to guard faithfully, as secret, anything you choose to tell me."

Flustered, she said, "Thank you, Giddon," then sat there, playing with the ties of *The Kissing Traditions of Monsea*, knowing that she ought to get up, that Runnemood was stewing somewhere, that Thiel was probably working too hard to deal with the paperwork she had abandoned. "Giddon," she said.

"Yes, Lady Queen?"

Trust is stupid, she thought. *What's the true reason I've decided I trust him? Certainly his Council work recommends him, his choice of friends. But isn't it just as much the timbre of his voice? I like to hear him say words. I trust the deep way he says "Yes, Lady Queen."*

She made a noise that was part snort, part sigh. Then, before she could ask her question, Runnemood stalked in from the grand foyer, saw her, and crossed to her.

"Lady Queen," he said sharply, crowding her, so that she had to crane her neck to look up at him. "You have been spending an inordinate percentage of each workday away from your desk."

He was looking quite sure of himself today, thrusting his jewel-ringed fingers through dark hair. Runnemood's hair showed no signs of thinning. "Have I?" Bitterblue said warily.

"I'm afraid I am a less indulgent man than Thiel," said Runnemood, flashing a smile. "Both Darby and Rood are indisposed today, yet I return from the city to find you chatting with friends and dabbling with dusty old manuscripts in a patch of sun. Thiel and I are quite overwhelmed with the work you're neglecting, Lady Queen. Do you take my meaning?"

Passing *The Kissing Traditions* to Giddon, Bitterblue stood, so that Runnemood had to jump backward in order to avoid them colliding. She took not just his meaning, but his condescending tone, and it was the tone that offended her. Nor did she like the way his eyes played over the books Giddon was holding, not as if he truly believed them to be harmless, dusty old manuscripts; more as if he were trying to assess each one and disliking all that he saw.

She wanted to tell him that a trained dog could do the work she was neglecting. She wanted to tell him that she knew somehow, in some way she could neither justify nor explain, that this time she spent outside her office was just as important to the kingdom as the work she did in her tower with charters, orders, and laws. But some instinct told her to protect these thoughts from him. To protect these books Giddon was guarding against his chest.

"Runnemood," she said instead, "I hear you're supposed to be good at manipulating people. Try a little harder to make me like you, all right? I'm the queen. Your life will be nicer if I like you."

She had the satisfaction of Runnemood's surprise. He stood with his eyebrows high and his mouth forming a small O. It was pleasant to see him looking silly, pleasant to see him struggling to regain his dignified scorn. Finally, he simply stalked away into the castle.

Bitterblue sat down again beside Giddon, who seemed to be having some trouble subduing an amused expression.

"I was about to ask you something unpleasant," Bitterblue said, "when he came along."

"Lady Queen," he said, still fighting with his face, "I'm all yours."

"Can you think of a reason why Leck would have chosen four healers as his advisers?"

Giddon thought about this for a moment. "Well," he said. "Yes."

"Go on," she said miserably. "It's nothing I'm not already thinking."

"Well," said Giddon again, "Leck is well known for his behavior with his animals. Cutting them, letting them heal, then cutting them again. What if he liked to hurt *people,* then let them heal? If it was a part of the way he liked to conduct his politics—as sick as it sounds—then it would've made sense for him to have had healers at his side all the time."

"They've lied to me, you know," whispered Bitterblue. "They've told me they don't know the secret things he did, but if they were mending his victims, then they saw, plainly, what he did."

Giddon paused. "Some things are too painful to talk about, Lady Queen," he said quietly.

"I know," she said. "Giddon, I know. Asking would be unpardonably cruel. But how can I help anyone now if I don't understand what happened then? I need the truth, don't you see?"

It was Saf who came barreling straight at her in an alleyway that night, Saf, who, gasping, grabbed her and hoisted her through some sort of broken doorway into a rank-smelling room and smashed her against a wall; Saf, who, through the entire enterprise, whispered to her fiercely, "Sparks, it's me, it's me, I beg you, don't hurt me, it's me"—but still, she'd whipped her knives out and also kneed him in the groin before she'd entirely comprehended what was happening.

"Arrhhlglm," he said, more or less, doubling over, still crushing her.

"What the high skies are you doing?" Bitterblue hissed, trying to wriggle out of his grip.

"If they find us," he said, "they're going to kill us, so shut your mouth."

Bitterblue was shaking, not just from her own shock and confusion, but from fear of what she could have done to him in those first moments, had he provided her with room to drive a knife. Then footsteps slapped in the alley outside and she forgot all that.

The footsteps pattered past the broken doorway, continued on, slowed. Stopped. When they reversed direction, creeping back toward the building where they hid, Saf swore in her ear. "I know a place," he said, hauling her across the dark room. When a low, deep, living exhalation of breath nearby caused her to jump nearly out of her wits, he whispered, "Climb." Bewildered, she groped forward and discovered a ladder. The smell of the place made sense to her suddenly. This was a barn of some sort, the thing that had breathed was a cow, and Saf wanted her to climb.

"Climb," he repeated when she hesitated, pushing her forward. "Go!"

Bitterblue reached up, took an iron grip, and climbed. *Don't think,* she said to herself. *Don't feel. Just climb.* She couldn't see where she was headed or how many rungs were left to climb. Nor could she see how high she'd gone so far, and she imagined only empty space below her.

Saf, at her heels, finally scuttled up around her and spoke low in her ear. "You don't like ladders."

"In the dark," she said, humiliated. "In the—"

"All right," he said. "Quick," and then he hoisted her up, turning her so that he was carrying her like a child, front to front. She wrapped her arms and legs around him as if he were the earth's pillar, because there did not seem to be any other alternative. He sped up the ladder. It was only when he lowered her onto some sort of solid ground that she was able to contemplate her outrage. And then there was no more time for that, because he was pulling her across what she suddenly recognized as a roof. He was pushing her up onto the higher roof of a higher building, and tugging her, running, they were swarming up a tinny, slippery slant, over an apex, down its opposite side, then down onto another roof, then up onto another and another.

He dragged her up the slant of the sixth or seventh roof to an adjoining wall and crouched against the siding. She dropped beside him, pressing up against the beautiful, solid wall, shaking.

"I hate you," she said. "I hate you."

"I know," he said. "I'm sorry."

"I'm going to kill you," she said. "I'm going—"

She was going to vomit. She turned her back to him, lopsided on her knees across the roof, hands clinging to slippery tin, trying to push the sourness down. A minute passed in which she successfully managed not to throw up. Miserably, she said, "How do we get down from here?"

"This is the shop," he said. "We step right through that window there into Bren and Tilda's bedroom. No more ladders, I promise. All right?"

The shop. Taking a gulp of air, she found that the tin of the roof seemed less like it was trying to buck her off. Shifting carefully, so that her back was to the wall, she sat, adjusting the *Kissing Traditions* manuscript, which was hanging in a bag across her front. Then she glanced over at Sapphire. He lay on his back, dark in profile, knees bent, considering the sky. She caught the faintest gleam in one of his ears.

"I'm sorry," she said quietly. "I'm not rational about heights."

He tilted his head to her. "No worries, Sparks. Let me know if there's anything I can do to help. Mathematics?" he suggested brightly, perking up, then reaching into his coat pocket and pulling out a gold disc she recognized. "Here," he said, tossing the heavy watch into her lap. "Tell me what time it is."

"I thought you were supposed to return this to the family of the watchmaker," said Bitterblue.

"Ah," he said, looking sheepish. "I was, and no doubt I will. It's just, I'm rather fond of that one."

"Fond of it," said Bitterblue, snorting. She opened the watch, read a time of half past fourteen, sat in an empty room with the numbers for a moment, then announced to Saf that it would be midnight in twenty-four minutes.

"It seems that the whole city got started early tonight," said Saf to that, dryly.

"I assume they didn't hear us? We wouldn't be sitting here stargazing if they were still after us, would we?"

"I threw a few chickens around before I came up that ladder," he said. "You didn't hear them making a racket?"

"I was distracted by the conviction that I was going to die."

A smile. "Well, they covered our noise, and the dogs were awake too by the time we reached the roof, which is what I was counting on. No one will have gotten past the dogs."

"You know that barn."

"It belongs to a friend. It was where I was headed when you appeared."

"I very nearly stuck a knife into you."

"Yes, I recall. I should've left you there in the alley. You could've driven them off for me all by yourself."

"Who were they? It wasn't just bullies this time, was it, Saf? It was the people who tried to kill Teddy."

"Let's talk about what's in the bag you're carrying tonight instead," said Saf, propping one ankle on the other knee and yawning at the stars. "Did you bring me a present?"

"I did, actually," she said. "It's something to prove that if you'll help me, I can help you."

"Oh? Bring it here, then."

"If you think I'm leaving this spot, you're mad."

He rolled to his feet on the uneven tin so fast, so easily, that she closed her eyes against the dizziness. When she opened them again, he'd settled down beside her, leaning his back against the wall, as she was doing.

"Perhaps your Grace is fearlessness," she said.

"I'm afraid of plenty of things," he said. "I just do them anyway. Let me see what you've got."

She extracted *The Kissing Traditions of Monsea* from the bag and placed it into his hands. He blinked at it. "Papers bound in leather?"

"It's something for you to make lots of copies of," she said. "A manuscript of a book called *The Kissing Traditions of Monsea*."

Humphing in surprise, he brought it closer to his nose to inspect the label in the dark.

"It was handwritten by the queen's own librarian," Bitterblue continued, "who's Graced with fast reading and with remembering every book and sentence and word—every letter—he's ever read. Did you know of his Grace?"

"We have heard of Death," Saf said, pulling the leather ties loose, throwing the leather flaps aside and flipping through the pages, squinting hard. "Are you telling me truth? This is what you say it is—and Death is rewriting the books King Leck made disappear?"

She thought that perhaps Sparks the baker girl wouldn't know too much about the business of the queen's own librarian. "I don't know what Death is doing. I don't know him personally. This was lent me by the friend of a friend. Death relinquished it only because he was promised that the person who wanted it was a printer who would make copies. Those are the conditions, Saf. You may borrow it, if you'll make copies. Death will see that you're paid for your labor and expenses, of course," she added, cursing herself for thinking up that sudden complication, but not certain how she could avoid it. It couldn't be cheap to print a book, and she couldn't expect them to finance the restoration of the queen's library, could she? Would it be so outlandish for a baker girl who'd never met Death to be the courier of the queen's money? And did this mean she was going to have to pawn more of her own jewelry?

"Sparks," Saf said. "Tie me with twine and mail me to Ror City. If this really is what you say it is—let's bring it down to the shop, shall we? I'm going blind here."

"Yes, all right," she said, "but . . ."

He looked up from the pages into her face. His eyes were black and full of stars. "I never wished I was a mind reader before I knew you," he said. "You know that, Sparks? What is it?"

"I'm frightened to move," she said, ashamed of herself.

"Sparks," Saf said. Then he slapped the *Kissing Traditions* manuscript shut and took hold of both of her small, cold hands. "Sparks," he said again, looking into her eyes, "I'll help you. I swear to you, you will not fall. Do you believe me?"

She did believe him. There on a roof with his familiar silhouette, his voice, all the things about him she was used to, holding tight to his hands, she believed him completely. "I'm ready to ask my third question," she said.

He exhaled. "Oh, weaselbugger," he said grimly.

"Who's trying to kill you and Teddy?" she asked. "Saf, I'm on your side. Tonight, I became their target too. Just tell me. Who is it?"

Saf didn't answer, just sat there, playing with her hands. She thought he wasn't going to answer. Then, as the moments passed, she stopped caring so much, because his touch began to seem more important than her question.

"There are people in the kingdom who are truthseekers," he finally said. "Not many people, but a few. People like Teddy and Tilda and Bren—people whose families were in the resistance and who place the highest value on knowing the truth of things. Leck is dead now, but there's still so much truth to uncover. That's their business, you understand, Sparks? They're trying to help people figure out what happened, sometimes reassemble memories. Return what Leck stole, and, when they can, undo what Leck did, through thievery, through education—however they can."

"You too," Bitterblue interjected. "You keep saying 'they,' but it's you too."

Saf shrugged. "I came to Monsea to know my sister better, and this is who my sister turned out to be. I like my friends here and I like to steal. While I'm here, I'll help. But I'm Lienid, Sparks. It's not my cause."

"Prince Po would be disgusted with that attitude."

"If Prince Po told me to fall off the earth, Sparks, I would," said Saf. "I told you. I'm Lienid."

"You make no sense whatsoever!"

"Oh?" said Saf, pulling on her hands, grinning wickedly. "And you do?"

Flustered, Bitterblue said nothing, just waited.

"There's a force in the kingdom working against us, Sparks," said Saf quietly. "The truth is that I can't answer your question, because we don't know who it is. But someone knows what we're doing. There's someone out there who hates us and will go to any length to stop us and people like us. Remember the new grave I found you standing in front of that night in the graveyard? That was our colleague, stabbed to death in broad daylight by a hired killer who's in no state to tell us who hired him. Our people are murdered. Or sometimes they're framed for crimes they didn't commit and get thrown into prison, where we'll never see them again."

"Saf!" Bitterblue said, appalled. "Are you serious about this? Are you sure?"

"Teddy was stabbed and you're asking me if I'm sure?"

"But, why? Why would someone go to so much trouble?"

"For silence," Saf said. "Is it really so surprising? Everyone wants silence. Everyone is happy forgetting Leck ever hurt anyone and pretending Monsea was born, fully formed, eight years ago. If they can't get their own heads to be silent, they go to the story rooms, get drunk, and start a fight."

"That's not why people go to the story rooms," Bitterblue protested.

"Oh, Sparks," Saf said, sighing, tugging at her hands. "It's not why you, I, or the fablers go to the story rooms. You go to hear the stories. Other people go to drown out the stories with drink. Remember, you asked me before why lists of stolen items make their way to us instead of to the queen? Often it's because no one ever even thinks about cataloging their losses until someone like Teddy comes around and suggests it. People aren't thinking. They want silence. The *queen* wants silence. And someone out there *needs* silence, Sparks. Someone out there is killing for it."

"Why haven't you taken this to the queen?" asked Bitterblue, trying to swallow the distress in her voice so that he wouldn't sense its extent. "People murdering people to silence the truth are breaking the law. Why haven't you taken your case to the queen!"

"Sparks," said Saf flatly. "Why do you think?"

Bitterblue was quiet for a moment, understanding him. "You think the queen is behind it."

A city clock began its midnight chime. "I'm not ready to say that," said Saf, shrugging. "None of us are. But we've gotten in the habit of warning people not to draw attention to any knowledge they might have of what Leck did, Sparks. Towns applying to the queen for independence, for example. They state their case against their lords plainly and refer to Leck as little as possible. They make no mention of the daughters that their lords mysteriously stole, or the people who disappeared. Whoever our villain is, it's someone with a very long arm. If I were you, Sparks, I would tread carefully in that castle of yours."

17

*L*ECK IS DEAD.

But if Leck is dead, why isn't it over?

Treading carefully through her corridors that night, up her staircases, Bitterblue tried to wrap her head around these murder attempts that baffled her. She could understand an instinct to move on, move ahead, leave the pain of Leck's time behind. But react by becoming like Leck himself? Kill? It was insane.

Her guards let her into her rooms. Hearing voices inside, she froze, panicking. Her brain caught up with her instincts: The voices, which came from her bedroom, belonged to Helda and Katsa. "Weaselbugger," she whispered under her breath. Then a male voice cleared its throat in her sitting room and she had a small heart attack before realizing it was Po.

Marching in to him, she said in a low voice, "You told them."

He sat in an armchair, making folds in a piece of paper against his thigh. "I didn't."

"Then what are they doing in my bedroom?"

"I believe they're having an argument," said Po. "I'm waiting for them to finish so that I can resume the argument I'm having with Katsa."

There was something funny about Po's face, about the way he was steadfastly not turning it to her. "Look at me," she said.

"Can't," he said glibly. "I'm blind."

"Po," she said. "If you could even begin to imagine the night I've had—"

Po turned. The skin under his silver eye was spectacularly bruised and his nose was swollen.

"Po!" she cried. "What happened? Katsa didn't hit you in the face!"

Making a final fold in the paper he was working with, Po raised it over his shoulder and hurled it across the room. Long, slender, and winged, it glided on air, swerved dramatically leftward, and crashed into a bookcase. "Hm," Po said with maddening calmness. "Fascinating."

"Po," said Bitterblue through clenched teeth. "You are being provoking."

"I have some answers to your questions," he said, getting up to recover his glider.

"What? You've asked them already?"

"No, I haven't asked any of them," he said, "but I've gathered some data." He smoothed the crumpled nose of the glider and flung the thing again, this time straight at the wall from a short distance. It crashed and fell. "Just as I thought," he said musingly.

Bitterblue collapsed on the sofa. "Po," she said, "take pity on me."

He came to sit beside her. "Thiel has a cut on his leg," he said.

"Oh!" said Bitterblue. "Poor Thiel. A bad cut? Do you know how it happened?"

"He's got a big broken mirror in his room," said Po, "but beyond that, I really couldn't say. Did you know he plays the harp?"

"Why does he keep that broken mirror around?" exclaimed Bitterblue. "Is the wound stitched?"

"Yes, and it's healing cleanly."

"It's a bit creepy what you can do," she said, leaning back, closing her eyes. "You know that, Po?"

212 — KRISTIN CASHORE

"I had time tonight to poke around," he said blandly, "while I was lying in bed with ice on my face. Next, you won't believe what Holt did earlier tonight."

"Oh," said Bitterblue, moaning. "Did he dive under a team of galloping horses, just to see what would happen?"

"Have you ever been to your art gallery?"

The art gallery? Bitterblue wasn't even entirely certain where it was. "Is it on the top floor, overlooking the great courtyard from the north?"

"Yes. Several floors directly above the library. It's quite neglected, did you know? Dust everywhere, except where pieces of art have been recently removed—which is why I was able to count the exact number of sculptures that have been stolen from the sculpture room. Five, in case you were wondering."

Bitterblue's eyes popped open. "Someone's stealing my sculptures," she said as a statement, not a question. "And returning them to the artist? Who's the artist?"

"Ah," said Po, pleased. "You seem already to be familiar with the overriding concept here. Excellent. I had to go have a chat with someone—Giddon—to understand it myself. Here's the situation: Holt had a sister named Bellamew who was a sculptor."

Bellamew. Bitterblue had an image of a woman in the castle: tall, broad-shouldered, with kind eyes. That woman had been a sculptor?

"Bellamew sculpted transformations for Leck," Po continued. "A woman turning into a tree. A man turning into a mountain, and so on."

"Ah," said Bitterblue, understanding now that not only did she have some familiarity with Bellamew's work, but Bellamew had had familiarity with her once. "Did Giddon tell you all this? Why does Giddon always know more about my castle than I do?"

Po shrugged. "He knows Holt. Really, you should be asking Giddon what's wrong with Holt, not me. Though I didn't tell Giddon what I witnessed."

"Well? What did you witness?"

Po smiled. "Are you ready for this? I witnessed Holt entering the castle from the city with a sack on his shoulder. He carried it up to the art gallery, removed a sculpture from the sack, and placed the sculpture in the sculpture room, right on the non-dusty spot it was missing from. That girl who disguised Danzhol's boat and turned into canvas, you remember her?"

"Oh, balls!" said Bitterblue. "I'd forgotten all about her. We need to find her and arrest her."

"I feel more and more that we don't," said Po. "She was with Holt tonight, because, guess what? She's Bellamew's daughter and Holt's niece. Her name is Hava."

"Wait," Bitterblue said. "What? I'm confused. Someone stole my sculptures to give back to Bellamew, but Holt and Bellamew's daughter are bringing them back to me?"

"Bellamew is dead," said Po. "*Holt* stole your sculptures. Holt brought them to Hava, Bellamew's daughter, but Hava told Holt, no, the sculptures had to go back to the queen. So Holt brought them back, with Hava supervising."

"What! Why?"

"Holt puzzles me," said Po, musing. "He may or may not be mad. He's certainly confused."

"I don't understand!" said Bitterblue. "Holt stole from me, then changed his mind?"

"I think he's trying to do the right thing," said Po, "but is confused about what the right thing is. I understand that Leck used

Bellamew, then killed her. Holt feels that Hava is the rightful owner of the sculptures."

"Is Giddon the one who told you about Hava?" asked Bitterblue. "Shouldn't something be done about Hava if she's floating around the castle? She tried to kidnap me!"

"Giddon doesn't know about Hava."

"Then how did you figure all this out?" cried Bitterblue.

"I just—did," said Po, looking sheepish.

"What do you mean, you just did? How can I be sure it's all true on the basis of 'you just did'?"

"I'm quite certain it's all true, Beetle. I'll explain why another time."

Bitterblue studied his battered face as he smoothed the glider against his leg. It was clear to her that he was upset about something he wasn't saying. "What are Helda and Katsa arguing about?" she asked quietly.

"Babies," he responded, flashing her a tiny grin. "As usual."

"And what are you and Katsa arguing about?"

His grin faded. "Giddon."

"Why? Is it about Katsa not liking him? I would love someone to explain that to me."

"Bitterblue, don't pry into the man's business."

"Oh, such commendable advice, coming from a mind reader. You can pry into his business whenever you like."

Po raised his eyes to her face. "As he well knows," he said.

"You told Giddon," she said, understanding everything now; understanding when he hung his head. "Giddon hit you," she continued. "And Katsa is angry with you for telling Giddon."

"Katsa is frightened," said Po quietly. "Katsa is too aware of the strain I'm under. It frightens her, knowing how many people I'd like to tell."

"How many people would you like to tell?"

This time, when he raised his eyes to her face, Bitterblue was also frightened. "Po," she whispered. "Please start small. If you're going to do this, tell Skye. Tell Helda. Maybe tell your father. Then wait, and get advice, and think. Please?"

"All I'm doing is thinking," he said. "I can't stop thinking. I'm so tired, Beetle."

His problems were so peculiar. Bitterblue's heart reached out to this cousin who slumped on the sofa looking weary, disgruntled, and sore. "Po," she said, going to him. She smoothed his hair and kissed the top of his head. "What can I do?"

Sighing, he said, "You could go comfort Giddon."

A VOICE ANSWERED her knock. When she entered Giddon's rooms, Giddon was sitting against the wall on the floor, in rapt contemplation of his left hand.

"You're left-handed," Bitterblue said. "I suppose I should have noticed that before."

He flexed the hand and spoke grimly, not looking up. "I spar sometimes with my right, just for practice."

"Have you hurt yourself?"

"No."

"Is left-handedness an advantage in fights?"

He shot Bitterblue a sardonic glance. "Against Po?"

"Against normal people."

A disinterested shrug. "Sometimes. Most fighters are better trained to defend against a right-handed assault."

Even Giddon's grumpy voice was nice in timbre. "Shall I stay?" Bitterblue asked lightly. "Or shall I go?"

He dropped his hand then and looked up at her, looked straight at her. His face softened. "Stay, Lady Queen." Then, seeming to remember his manners, he made a move to stand up.

"Oh, please," Bitterblue said. "It's a stupid custom," and she lowered herself to the floor beside him, putting her back to the wall for symmetry's sake, commencing an inspection of her own hands.

"Less than two hours ago," she said, "I sat beside a friend, just like this, on the roof of a shop in the city."

"What? Really?"

"We'd been chased there by people who wanted to kill him."

"Lady Queen," Giddon said, almost choking, "are you serious?"

"Don't tell anyone," Bitterblue said, "and don't interfere."

"You mean that Katsa and Po—"

"Don't think of him and think of it at the same time," Bitterblue said calmly. "Don't ever bring him up in any conversation or contemplation you don't wish him to be a part of."

Giddon made a noise of disbelief; then went quiet, working that over for a while. "Let's discuss what you've just told me another time, Lady Queen," he said, "for my thoughts are rather single-mindedly on Po right now."

"The only point I wanted to make," Bitterblue said, "is that I have an irrational terror of heights."

"Heights," Giddon said, sounding lost.

"On occasion," she said, "it is profoundly humiliating."

Giddon went quiet again. When he next spoke, he was not lost. "I've shown you my worst behavior, Lady Queen, and you respond with kindness."

"If that's really the worst you've got," Bitterblue said, "then Po has an excellent friend, indeed."

Giddon stared into his hands again, which were broad and big as plates. Bitterblue resisted the urge to hold hers up to his and marvel at the difference in size.

"I've been trying to decide which is the most humiliating," he said. "That I was only able to hit him because he let me—he stood there like a punching bag, Lady Queen—"

"Mm? And you know, you won't get the credit for it," said Bitterblue. "Everyone will think Katsa made a mistake in one of their practice fights. No one will believe you managed it."

"Don't feel the need to spare my feelings, Lady Queen," he said dryly.

"Go on," Bitterblue said, grinning. "You were enumerating the points of your humiliation."

"Yes, you're very thoughtful. Second, it's not pleasant to be the last person to know."

"Ah," Bitterblue said. "I'll just point out that you're far from the last person to know."

"But you understand me, Lady Queen. I spend more time with Po than any of the rest of you. Even Katsa. Though really, there's no contest."

"What do you mean?"

"The truest humiliation," he said, then stopped, suddenly stiff-jawed and miserable, drawing his arms and shoulders close to his body, as if it were a thing he could protect himself from physically, like a blow, or like cold weather. Which, of course, it wasn't.

Bitterblue stretched her legs out straight and made a quiet show of smoothing her trousers, to spare him the embarrassment of being watched. She said simply, "I know."

He nodded, once. "I've opened so much of myself to him. Especially in the early years, when I had no suspicions and never thought to take care with my thoughts—and also happened to hate him. He knew every point of resentment I bore against him; every jealous thought, he knew. And now I'm remembering all of it, every single piece of malice, and the humiliation is double, because as I relive it, he does too."

Yes. This *was* the worst, the most unfair and humiliating thing about any mind reader, especially a secret mind reader. It was the reason Katsa was so frightened: a great wellspring of wrath and humiliation, all focused on Po, especially if Po began telling his truth indiscriminately.

"Katsa has told me that she was also humiliated when Po first told her," Bitterblue said, "and furious. She threatened to tell everyone. She never wanted to see him again."

"Yes," Giddon said. "And then she ran away with him."

He spoke those words mildly, which interested her. Bitterblue considered his tone for an instant, then decided to seize it as justification for asking an utterly inappropriate question about something she'd been wondering. "Are you in love with her?"

He shot her an incredulous brown glare. "Is that any of your business?"

"No," she said. "Are you in love with him?"

Giddon rubbed his eyebrows in wonderment. "Lady Queen, where is this coming from?"

"Well, it fits, doesn't it? It explains the tension with Katsa."

"I hope you haven't been stirring up this sort of talk with the others. If you have nosy questions about me, ask *me*."

"I am," Bitterblue said.

"Yes," Giddon said, chewing on the word with admirable good humor, "you are."

"I haven't," she said.

"Lady Queen?"

"Asked anyone this question but you," she said. "And no one has said anything definitive about it to me. And I can keep a secret."

"Ah," he said. "Well, it's not much of a secret, really, and I suppose I don't mind telling you."

"Thank you."

"Oh, my pleasure. It's your delicacy, you know. It makes a fellow want to bare his soul."

Bitterblue grinned.

"I was—rather obsessed—with Katsa once," he said, "for a long time. I said some wrong-headed things I'm ashamed of and Katsa won't forgive me. In the meantime, I've recovered from my obsession."

"Is that true?"

"Lady Queen," he said patiently, "among my less attractive qualities is a certain pride that serves me well when I discover that a woman I love never would, and never could, give me the things I want."

"The things you want?" Bitterblue repeated acidly. "Is that what it's about: the things you want? What are these things?"

"Someone who can bear the grievousness of my company, to start with. I'm afraid I insist upon it."

Bitterblue burst into laughter. He watched her, smiling, then sighed. "Some bad feelings linger," he said quietly, "even when the thing that brought them into being has died. I've wanted to hit Po practically since the first time I laid eyes on him. I'm glad it's finally done. Now I can see what an empty wish it was."

"Oh, Giddon," Bitterblue said, then went quiet, because the things she wanted to say were things she couldn't articulate. Bitterblue loved Katsa and Po with a love as big as the earth. But she knew what it was like to be lost on the edges of their love for each other.

"I need your help," she said, thinking that distraction might be a comfort to him.

He looked at her in surprise. "What is it, Lady Queen?"

"Someone is trying to kill people who wish to bring Leck's crimes to light," she said. "If, in your wanderings, you hear anything about it, will you let me know?"

"Of course," he said. "Goodness. Do you think it's someone like Danzhol? Other nobles who stole for Leck and don't want the truths of their past to come out?"

"I have no idea," she said. "But at least that would make some sort of logical sense; yes, I'll have to look into that. Though I hardly know where to start," she added tiredly. "I've got hundreds of nobles I've never even heard of. Giddon, what do you think of my guard Holt?"

"Holt is a Council ally, Lady Queen," Giddon said. "He stood guard during the meeting that took place in the library."

"Did he?" Bitterblue said. "He's also been stealing my sculptures."

Giddon stared at her in the sheerest amazement.

"Then bringing them back," said Bitterblue. "Will you pay him close attention in your dealings, Giddon? I'm worried about his health."

"You want me to pay close attention to Holt, who is stealing your sculptures, because you're concerned for his health," Giddon repeated incredulously.

"Yes. His mental health. Please don't tell him I mentioned the sculptures. You do trust him, though, Giddon?"

"Holt, who is stealing your sculptures and is of questionable mental health?"

"Yes."

"I trusted him five minutes ago. Now I'm at a bit of a loss."

"Your opinion five minutes ago is good enough for me," Bitterblue said. "You have good instincts."

"Have I?"

"I suppose I should go back to my rooms now," Bitterblue said, sighing. "Katsa is there. I expect she intends to yell at me."

"I very much doubt that, Lady Queen."

"The two of them together can be so pushy, you know," said Bitterblue impishly. "Part of me hopes you broke his nose."

The knuckles of Giddon's left hand were darkening with bruises from their impact with Po's face. He did not rise to her bait. Instead, still studying his own hand, he said quietly, "I will never tell his secret."

BACK IN HER rooms, she looked in on Po. Finding him asleep on the sofa, snoring with the clogged snore of someone whose nose is swollen, she covered him with a blanket. Then, having no more excuses, she went to her bedroom.

Katsa and Helda were making up the sheets to her bed. "Thank goodness," Katsa said at the sight of her. "Helda's been trying to impress me with the embroidery on the sheets. One more minute and I thought I might use them to hang myself."

"My mother did the embroidery," Bitterblue said.

Katsa clapped her mouth shut and glared at Helda. "Thank you, Helda, for mentioning that detail."

Helda expertly snapped a blanket open so that it billowed over the bed. "Can I be blamed for forgetting details when I'm worried to distraction at finding the queen missing from her bed?" she said. Then she marched to the pillows and beat them mercilessly until they lay puffed out like obedient clouds.

Bitterblue thought it might be to her advantage to take control of this conversation from the start. "Helda," she said, "I need the help of my spies. People in the city who're trying to uncover truths about Leck's time are being killed. I need to know who's behind this. Can we find out?"

"Of course we can find out," said Helda with a self-righteous sniff. "And in the meantime, while killers are running around on the loose, you'll be moving among them dressed like a boy with no guard to look out for you and not even your own name to protect you. The two of you think I'm a foolish old woman whose opinions don't matter."

"Helda!" Katsa exclaimed, practically vaulting over the bed to be near her. "That's certainly not what we think."

"It's all right," Helda said, giving the pillows one last thrashing, then straightening to face her two young ladies with unapproachable dignity. "It hardly matters. Even if you thought me Graced with supreme knowledge, you'd none of you listen to me and every one of you do whatever harebrained thing you liked. You all think you're invincible, don't you? You think the only thing that doesn't matter is your own safety. It's enough to drive a woman wild." She reached deep into a pocket and flung a small bundle onto Bitterblue's bed. "I've known from the beginning that you sneak out nights, Lady Queen. The two nights you never came home were sleepless nights for me. You might remember that, the next time you contemplate lying in some bed other than your own. I won't pretend that I don't know the pressures you're under—and that goes for you too, My Lady," she added, gesturing at Katsa. "I won't deny but that your responsibilities differ from any I've ever known, and when push comes to shove, you're to be held to a different standard than other people. But that does not mean that it feels nice to be lied to and taken for a fool. Tell your young man that," she finished, raising her chin a notch to stare into Katsa's eyes. Then she marched from the room.

A long silence followed.

"She's rather good at keeping secrets, isn't she," Bitterblue said, somewhere between shame and alarm.

"She's your spymaster," said Katsa, dropping onto the bed, splaying out on her back. "I feel like mud."

"Me too."

"I wonder what she meant about Po, exactly. He's said nothing about her knowing. Is that true, Bitterblue, about the killing in your city? If it is, I don't want to leave."

"It is," said Bitterblue quietly, "and I don't want you to leave either, but I think you belong to Estill right now, don't you?"

"Bitterblue, come here, won't you?"

Bitterblue let Katsa grab her arm and pull her to the bed. They sat facing each other, Katsa holding her hand. Katsa's hands were strong, alive, and hot like a furnace.

"Where do you go at night?" Katsa asked.

Like that, the spell was broken. Bitterblue pulled away. "That's not a fair question."

"Then don't answer it," Katsa said, surprised. "I'm not Po."

But I can't lie to you, she thought. *If you ask me for something, I'll give it.* "I go to the east city," she said, "to visit friends."

"What kind of friends?"

"A printer, and a sailor who works with him."

"Is it dangerous?"

"Yes," she said, "sometimes. It's not your business and it's nothing I can't handle, so stop asking questions."

Katsa sat for a moment, frowning into the middle distance. Then she said quietly, "This printer and this sailor, Bitterblue. Have you—" She paused. "Have you lost your heart to either of them?"

"No," Bitterblue said, stunned and breathless. "Stop asking me questions."

"Do you need me? Is there anything you'll let me do?"

No. Go away.

Yes. Stay with me, stay here until I fall asleep. Tell me I'm safe and my world will make sense. Tell me what to do about how I feel when Saf touches me. Tell me what it means to lose your heart to somebody.

Katsa turned to her, pushed her hair back, kissed her forehead; pressed something into her hand. "This may be a thing you neither want nor need," she said. "But I'd rather you have it, wishing you didn't, than not have it and wish you did."

And Katsa left, closing the door behind her. Off to who knew what adventure. Her bed, most likely, with Po, where they would lose themselves to each other.

Bitterblue examined the item in her hand. It was a medicinal envelope with a label written clear across the front: "Seabane, for the prevention of pregnancy."

Numbly, she read the instructions. Then, setting the seabane aside, she tried to sort out what she felt, but got nowhere. Remembering the bundle Helda had thrown onto the blanket, she reached for it. It was a cloth pouch, which opened to reveal another medicinal envelope, also clearly labeled.

She laughed, not certain what was so funny about a girl with a muddled heart having enough seabane to last the entirety of her childbearing years.

Then, exhausted almost to dizziness, she stretched onto her side and pressed her face, where Katsa had kissed it, into Helda's impeccable pillows.

BITTERBLUE WAS HAVING a dream of a man, a friend. He began as Po, then turned to Giddon, then Saf. When he became Saf, he began to kiss her.

"Will it hurt?" Bitterblue asked.

Then her mother was there between them, saying to her calmly, "It's all right, sweetheart. He doesn't mean to hurt you. Take his hand."

"I don't mind if it hurts," Bitterblue said. "I just want to know."

"I won't let him hurt you," Ashen said, suddenly wild and frantic, and Bitterblue saw that the man had changed again. Now he was Leck. Ashen was standing between Bitterblue and Leck, guarding Bitterblue from him. Bitterblue was a little girl.

"I would never hurt her," said Leck, smiling. He was holding a knife.

"I won't let you near her," said Ashen, shaking but certain. "Her life will not be like mine. I will protect her from that."

Leck sheathed his knife. Then he punched Ashen in the stomach, pushed her to the floor, kicked her, and walked away, while Bitterblue screamed.

In her bed, Bitterblue woke in tears. The last part of the dream was more than a dream; it was a memory. Ashen had never let Leck talk Bitterblue into going away with him to his rooms, his cages. Leck had always punished Ashen for interfering. And whenever Bitterblue had run to her mother crumpled on the floor, Ashen had always whispered, "You must never go with him. Promise me, Bitterblue. It would hurt me more than anything he could ever do to me."

I never did, Mama, she thought, tears soaking into her sheets. *I never went with him. I kept my promise. But you died anyway.*

AT MORNING PRACTICE, sparring with Bann, she couldn't focus.

"What's wrong, Lady Queen?" he asked.

"I had a bad dream," she told him, rubbing her face. "It was a dream of my father hurting my mother. Then I woke up and realized it was true."

Bann paused his sword to consider this. His calm eyes touched her, reminding her of the beginning of the dream, the part where Ashen had comforted her. "Dreams like that can be awful," he said. "I have one that recurs sometimes, about the circumstances of my own parents' deaths. It can torment me cruelly."

"Oh, Bann," she said. "I'm sorry. How did they die?"

"Illness," he said. "They had terrible hallucinations and said cruel things I know now they didn't mean. But when I was a child, I didn't understand that they were being cruel only because of the illness. When I'm dreaming, it's the same."

"I hate dreams," said Bitterblue, angry now in his defense.

"What if you attacked your dream while you're awake, Lady Queen?" said Bann. "Could you act out what it would be like to fight back against your father? You could pretend I'm him and get your revenge right now," he said, raising his sword in preparation for her attack.

It did improve her swordplay for the morning, pretending to attack the Leck of her dream. But Bann was a big, kind man in the real world, and she could hurt him if she came at him too hard. Her imagination wouldn't quite allow her to forget that. At lesson's end, she had a muscle cramp in her hand and she was still out of sorts.

IN HER TOWER office, Bitterblue watched Thiel and Runnemood shift carefully around each other with silent, stiff faces. Whatever argument they were having today, it was as big as a third person in the room. She wondered what to say to them about the truthseekers under attack. She couldn't claim to have accidentally overheard a detailed conversation about knifings and bloody street murders; that would border on the absurd. She would have to use the spy excuse again, but spreading false information about things her spies supposedly knew, could she put her spies in danger? Also, Teddy, Saf, and their friends broke the law. Was it fair to bring that to Thiel and Runnemood's attention?

"Why don't I know more about my nobles?" she said. "Why are there hundreds of lords and ladies I wouldn't recognize if they walked through that door?"

"Lady Queen," said Thiel gently, "it's our job to prevent you from having to deal with every small matter."

"Ah. But as you're so overwhelmed with my work," she said significantly, "I think it best I learn what I can. I should like to know their stories and reassure myself that they aren't all mad like Danzhol. Are we three alone again today?" she added, then clarified, needing to force the point, "Is Rood having nervous fits and Darby still drunk?"

Runnemood rose from his perch in the window. "What an inconsiderate thing to say, Lady Queen," he said, sounding actually hurt. "Rood cannot help his nerves."

"I never said he could," said Bitterblue. "I only said he has them. Why must we always pretend? Wouldn't it be more productive to talk about the things we know?" Deciding there was something she wanted, needed, she stood up.

"Where are you going, Lady Queen?" asked Runnemood.

"To Madlen," she said. "I need a healer."

"Are you ill, Lady Queen?" asked Thiel in distress, taking a step forward, reaching out a hand.

"That's a matter for me to discuss with a healer," she said, holding his eyes to let it sink in. "Are you a healer, Thiel?"

Then she left, so that she wouldn't have to see him crushed—by nothing, by words that shouldn't matter—and feel her shame.

WHEN BITTERBLUE STEPPED into Madlen's room, Madlen was scribbling in symbols at a desk covered with papers. "Lady Queen," Madlen said, gathering her papers together and pushing them under her blotter. "I hope you're here to rescue me from my medical writing. Are you all right?" she asked, taking in Bitterblue's expression.

"Madlen," said Bitterblue, sitting on the bed. "I had a dream last night that my mother refused to let my father take me away, so he hit her. Only it wasn't a dream, Madlen; it was a memory. It's a thing that happened over and over, and I was never able to protect her." Shivering, Bitterblue hugged herself. "Maybe I could have protected her if I'd gone with him when he asked. But I never did. She made me promise not to."

Madlen came to sit beside her on the bed. "Lady Queen," she said with her own particular brand of rough gentleness. "It is not the job of a child to protect her mother. It's the mother's job to protect the child. By allowing your mother to protect you, you gave her a gift. Do you understand me?"

Bitterblue had never thought of it this way before. She found that she was holding Madlen's hand, her eyes full of tears.

Finally, after a while, she said, "The dream didn't start out bad."

"Oh?" said Madlen. "Did you come here to talk about your dream, Lady Queen?"

Yes. "My hand hurts," said Bitterblue, opening her hand and showing it to Madlen.

"Is it serious?"

"I think I was holding my sword too hard at practice this morning."

"Well," said Madlen, seeming to understand. She took Bitterblue's hand and explored it with light fingers. "That sounds easily mended, Lady Queen."

It did mend something, those few minutes of Madlen's gentle touch.

ON HER WAY back to her tower, Bitterblue encountered Raffin in the middle of the hallway, peering worriedly at a knife in his hands.

"What is it?" asked Bitterblue, stopping before him. "Has something happened, Raffin?"

"Lady Queen," he said, politely moving the knife far away from her and, in the process, nearly poking a passing member of the Monsean Guard, who jumped away in alarm. "Oh, dear," Raffin said. "That's just it."

"What's just it, Raffin?"

"Bann and I are taking a trip into Sunder, and Katsa says I must wear this on my arm, but I truly feel the danger is greater if I do. What if it falls out and impales me? What if it flings itself from my sleeve and lodges in someone else? I'm perfectly content poisoning people," Raffin muttered, pulling up his sleeve and holstering the knife. "Poison is civilized and controlled. Why must everything involve knives and blood?"

"It will not fly out of your sleeve, Raffin," said Bitterblue soothingly. "I promise. Sunder?"

"Only briefly, Lady Queen. Po will stay here with you."

"I thought Po and Giddon were taking the tunnel into Estill."

Raffin cleared his throat. "Giddon isn't desirous of Po's company just now, Lady Queen," he said delicately. "Giddon is going alone."

"I see," said Bitterblue. "Where will you go after Sunder? Not back home?"

"As it happens, Lady Queen," said Raffin, "that is not an option. My father has made it known that members of the Council aren't welcome in the Middluns at the moment."

"What?" said Bitterblue. "Even his own son?"

"Oh, it's only political bluster, Lady Queen. I know my father, regrettably. He's trying to appease the kings of Estill, Sunder, and Wester because they dislike him even more than they used to, now that Nander has fallen at the hands of an organization that likely includes me and Katsa. I don't expect he could keep any of us out without making more of a scene than he wants to. But it's no inconvenience to us at the moment, so we won't protest. It'll chafe at Giddon most, if it continues. He never likes to be away from his estate for too long. Is it really supposed to feel like this?" Raffin demanded, shaking his forearm.

"Like you have a blade against your skin?" asked Bitterblue. "Yes. And if someone tries to hurt you, you must use it, Raffin. Assuming there's no time to respond with poison, of course," she added dryly.

"I've done it before," Raffin said darkly. "It's only a matter of information. As long as I know an attack is being planned, I can foil the whole thing as well as anyone else. And usually no one needs to die." Then he sighed. "How have things come to this, Lady Queen?"

"Have things ever been any other way?"

"Peaceful, you mean, and safe?" he said. "I suppose not. And I suppose we may as well be in the thick of the violence, trying to take some control over the way it plays out."

Bitterblue considered this prince, the son of a bully king, the cousin of a fireball like Katsa. "Will you like to be king, Raffin?"

His answer was in the resignation that came over his face. "Does it matter?" he responded quietly. Then he added, shrugging, "I shall have less time for mayhem. And, sadly, less time for my medicines. And I will have to marry, because a king must produce heirs." Glancing into her face, he said with a small smile, "You know, I would ask you to marry me, except that it's not a thing I would ask anyone without Bann present, nor would I actually make you such an inadequate offer in earnest. It would solve a great many of my problems and create problems for you, hm?"

She couldn't help smiling. "I confess it's not a future I would wish for," she said. "On the other hand, it's no less romantic than any other proposal I've ever gotten. Ask me again in five years. Perhaps then I'll be in need of something complicated and strange that looks good to the rest of the world."

Chuckling, Raffin practiced straightening his arm, bending it, straightening it again. "What if I stick Bann by accident?" he asked grumpily.

"Just open your eyes wide and look where you're stabbing," said Bitterblue cheerfully.

RUNNING THROUGH THE east city that night, she wasn't certain what she was running toward. With truthseekers and truth killers on her mind she was alert, trusting no one she passed, conscious of the blades on her own arms, of how quickly she could whip them out if she needed to. When a hooded woman passed under a streetlamp

232 — KRISTIN CASHORE

and gold paint on her lips caught the light, it stopped Bitterblue like a shock. Gold paint, and glitter around her eyes.

Bitterblue stood, breathing hard. Yes, it was late September; yes, it could very well be the equinox. Yes, it did seem likely that some people in the city would celebrate, discreetly, those traditional rituals. For example, the same people who buried their dead and stole back truths.

For the merest instant, Bitterblue was uncertain. In that instant, she could have turned back. It wasn't thought; it didn't go that deep. It was in the fingertips she brought to her lips, and on her skin.

She ran on.

TILDA ANSWERED HER knock and pulled her into a room she barely recognized, so full was it of people and noise. Tilda bent down and kissed Bitterblue on the lips, smiling, wearing an ornament in her hair, more like a hat, really, made of hanging, swaying drops of glass.

"Come kiss Teddy," Tilda said. Or, at least, it was what Bitterblue thought she said, for two young men to her right were singing raucously, arms linked. One of them, seeing Bitterblue, leaned in, pulling the other along, and gave her a peck on the lips. Half of his face was painted with silver glitter, to dazzling effect—he was attractive, they were both attractive—and Bitterblue began to understand that it was going to be an alarming night.

Tilda led her through the doorway into Teddy and Saf's apartment, where light blazed on people's jewelry and face glitter, on the golden drinks they held in tumblers. The room was too small for so many people. Bren appeared out of nowhere, took Bitterblue's chin, and kissed her. Flowers were painted all across Bren's cheekbones and down her neck.

When Bitterblue finally reached Teddy's cot in the corner, she dropped into a chair beside him, breathless, relieved to find him unpainted and dressed just like his usual self. "I suppose I have to kiss you," she said.

"Indeed," he said cheerily. Pulling on her hand, drawing her near, he gave her a soft and sweet kiss. "Isn't it marvelous?" he said, smacking one last little kiss onto her nose.

"Well, it's something," said Bitterblue, whose head was spinning.

"I just love parties," he said.

"Teddy," she said, noticing the glass in his hand, full of some amber liquid, "should you be drinking that in your condition?"

"Perhaps not. I'm drunk," he said gleefully, then threw back his glass and held it out to a fellow nearby for a refill. The fellow gave him both a refill and a kiss. Someone took Bitterblue's hand and pulled her up from the chair. Turning, she was kissing Saf.

It was not like the other kisses, not at all. "Sparks," he whispered into the place beneath her ear, nuzzling her, pulling her hood back, which made her crane her face up and kiss him more. He seemed amenable to more kissing. When it occurred to her that eventually he might stop kissing her, her hands reached to take hold of his shirt and anchor him there, and she bit him.

"Sparks," he said, grinning, then chuckling, but staying right where he was. His eyelids and the skin around his eyes were painted gold in the shape of a mask, which was startling, and exciting.

Rough hands yanked them apart.

"Hello," said a man Bitterblue had never seen before, pale-haired and mean-looking and clearly not sober. He shoved his finger in Saf's face. "I don't think you understand the nature of this holiday, Sapphire."

"I don't think you understand the nature of our relationship,

Ander," Saf said with sudden ferocity, then smashed his fist into the other man's face so fast that Bitterblue was left gasping. An instant later, people had grabbed on to both of them and pulled them apart, pulled them away, taken them out of the room, and Bitterblue stood there, dazed and bereft.

"Lucky," said a voice.

Teddy was holding his hand out to her from the cot, like a rope to pull her to shore. Going to him numbly, Bitterblue took his hand and sat. After a moment of trying to figure it out on her own, she said, "What just happened?"

"Oh, Sparks," said Teddy, patting her hand. "Welcome to Sapphire's world."

"No, seriously, Teddy," she said. "Please don't talk in riddles. What just happened? Was that one of the bullies who like to beat him up?"

"No," said Teddy, shaking his head ponderously. "That was a different kind of bully. Saf keeps a vast range of bullies on hand at all times. That one seemed to be of the jealous variety."

"Jealous? Of me?"

"Well, you're the one who was kissing him in rather a non-holiday manner, weren't you?"

"But, is that man his—"

"No," Teddy repeated. "Not now. Unfortunately, Ander is a psychopath. Saf has the most bizarre taste, Sparks, present company excluded, of course, and I really cannot warn you strongly enough against getting involved, but what good will it do?" Teddy flapped his free hand in a gesture of despair, sloshing his drink. "It's clear you're already involved. I'll talk to him. He likes you. Maybe I can get through to him about you."

"Who else is there?" she heard herself ask.

Teddy shook his head unhappily. "No one," he said. "But he's not good for you, Sparks, do you understand that? He's not going to marry you."

"I don't want him to marry me," said Bitterblue.

"Whatever you want him to do to you," Teddy said flatly, "I beg you to remember that he is reckless." Then, taking another big sip of his drink, he added, "I fear that you're the one who's drunk."

SHE LEFT THE party with the feeling, physical and painful, that something was unfinished. But there was nothing to be done about it. Saf had not returned.

Outside, she pulled her hood close, for the night air held a chill and the promise of rain. When she stepped into the graveyard, a shape moved in the shadows. She reached for her knives—then saw that it was Saf.

"Sparks," he said.

As he moved toward her, she understood something all at once, something that had to do with his gold, his recklessness, the mad sparkle of his face paint. His aliveness and roughness and realness that reminded her too much, suddenly, of Katsa, of Po, of everyone she loved and fought with and worried about.

"Sparks," he said breathlessly, stopping before her. "I've been waiting for you so I can apologize. I'm sorry for what I did in there."

She looked up at him, unable to answer.

"Sparks," he said. "Why are you crying?"

"I'm not."

"I made you cry," he said in distress, closing the space between them and gathering her into a hug. Then he began kissing her and she lost her hold on what had been making her cry.

It was different this time, because of the silence and because they were alone. Standing in the graveyard, they were the only two people on earth. He shifted and began to be more gentle, too gentle, on purpose. He was making her crazy, on purpose, with want, teasing her, she knew it from his smile. Vaguely she was conscious that their clothing was in the way of the kind of touching she wanted.

"Sparks."

He'd murmured something she hadn't heard. "Huh?"

"Teddy's going to kill me," he said.

"Teddy?"

"The thing is, I like you. I know I'm a mess, but I like you."

"Mhm?"

"I know you don't trust me."

Thoughts came slowly. "No," she whispered, understanding, grinning. "You're a thief."

Now he was smiling too much to kiss properly. "I'll be the thief," he said, "and you can be the liar."

"Saf—"

"You're my liar," he whispered. "Will you tell me a lie, Sparks? Tell me your name."

"My name," she whispered, began to speak, then caught herself. Froze and stopped kissing him. She'd very nearly said her name aloud. "Saf," she said, jangling with the pain of abruptly, jaggedly becoming conscious. "Wait," she said, gasping. "Wait. Let me think."

"Sparks?"

She struggled against his hold; he tried to stop her, then he too came awake and understood. "Sparks?" he said again, releasing her, blinking, confused. "What is it?"

She stared at him, sober now to what she was doing in this graveyard with a boy who liked her and had no idea who she was. No idea of the magnitude of the lie he was begging her to tell.

"I have to go," she said, because she needed to be where he couldn't see her comprehension.

"Now?" he said. "What's wrong? I'll walk with you."

"No," she said. "I have to go, Saf." She turned and ran.

NEVER AGAIN. I must never even visit them again, no matter how much I want to.

Am I mad? Am I positively mad? Look at the kind of queen I am. Look what I would do to one of my own people.

My father would be pleased with my perfect lie.

SHE WAS BEYOND any care as she ran with her hood low, beyond taking notice of anything around her. And so she was woefully unprepared when a person reared out of a dark doorway just outside the castle and clamped a hand to her mouth.

19

Training kicked in. Bitterblue did what Katsa had taught her and dropped like a stone, surprising her assailant with her sudden weight, then connecting her elbow to some soft part of a torso. The person lost his balance and she fell with him, scrabbling for her knives, cursing, shouting, gasping. And then a small cart parked across the street transformed into something with shrouded arms and legs that burst toward them, flapping, swinging, knife flashing, chasing her assailant away.

Bitterblue lay in the gutter where she'd been flung, stunned, slowly realizing that she was alone. *What in the skies just happened?*

Shoving herself to her feet, she assessed the damage. Aching head and shoulder and ankle. But nothing broken or unworking. When she touched her stinging forehead, blood came away on her fingers.

Paying much greater attention now, she ran the rest of the way to the castle and, once inside, set out to find Po.

He was not in his rooms.

Katsa's rooms seemed particularly far away in the dead of night. By the time Bitterblue got there, her head was splitting with pain and consumed with a specific question: Had the person who attacked her known whom he was attacking, or had it been a random attack on a stranger? And if he had known, *what* had he known? Had he thought himself to be attacking the queen, or merely the queen's spy? Or perhaps a miscellaneous friend of Saf and Teddy's? Had their struggle on the ground elucidated her identity to him? She had not recognized him. Nor had she heard him speak, so she couldn't say if he was Monsean. She knew nothing at all.

Bitterblue tapped Katsa's door.

The door shot open partway and Katsa slammed herself into the crack, torso wrapped in a sheet, eyes glaring, bare shoulders blocking ingress.

"Oh, hello," she said, letting the door go. "What happened? Are you all right?"

"I need Po," Bitterblue said. "Is he awake?"

The door swung open to reveal the bed, where Po lay sleeping. "He's exhausted," said Katsa. "What happened, sweetheart?" she asked again.

"Someone attacked me outside the castle," Bitterblue said.

Katsa's eyes blazed blue and green and Po sat up in bed like a mechanical doll. "What is it?" he said blearily. "Wildcat? Is it morning?"

"It's the middle of the night and Bitterblue's been attacked," Katsa said.

"Seas," Po said, launching himself out of bed, dragging his sheet with him, knotting it around his waist and blundering back and forth like he was still half asleep. His bruised face looked thoroughly disreputable. "Who? Where? Which street? Did they speak with an accent? Are you all right? You seem all right. Which way did they go?"

"I don't even know if the attack was meant for me or for the spy I was pretending to be," Bitterblue said. "Nor do I know who it was. It was no one I recognized and he didn't speak. But I believe that the Graceling was there, Po. Holt's niece, with the Grace of disguise. I believe she may have come to my aid."

"Ah," Po said, going still all of a sudden, then placing his hands on his hips and taking on a bizarre expression. A sort of studied nonchalance.

"Holt's niece?" Katsa said, peering at Po, puzzled. "Hava? What about her? And why do you have sparkly stuff all over your face, Bitterblue?"

"Oh." Bitterblue found a chair and sat, rubbing randomly at the paint she couldn't see on her face, the entire unhappy night flowing into her at once. "Don't ask me about the paint while Po is here, Katsa, please," she said, fighting tears. "The paint is private. It has nothing to do with the attack."

Katsa seemed to understand this. Going to a side table, she poured water into a bowl. Then, kneeling, she stroked Bitterblue's face with the soft cloth and cool water, patted her stinging forehead. This gentleness was too much. Big, seeping tears began to run down Bitterblue's cheeks, which Katsa accepted in stride, patting them away.

"Po," Katsa said in a measured voice, "why are you standing there trying to look innocent? What's going on with Hava?"

"I *am* innocent," Po said indignantly. "A week or so ago I met her, is all."

"Ah," said Bitterblue, Po's perfect comprehension of the Holt-sculpture debacle last night finally making sense. "You're friends with my kidnapper. Lovely."

"She was in the castle sneaking around," Po went on, waving this away, "trying to visit Holt. I sensed her pretending to be a sculpture in one of the hallways and apprehended her. We had a little chat. I trust her. She was very out of the loop that day with Danzhol, Bitterblue. She didn't realize, until it all happened, that he'd been intending to go so far as to kidnap you. She feels awful about it. Anyway, she agreed to spend some time in the wee hours of the morning keeping an eye out for your safety. I worry that she hasn't contacted me," he added, rubbing his face with both palms, "because I asked her to get in touch if anything ever happened. How far from the castle did the attack take place, Bitterblue? I can't find her anywhere outside."

"Get in touch how?" Katsa asked, absently passing the cloth to Bitterblue.

"It was near to the east wall," Bitterblue said, "not in view of it, but one street beyond. What exactly are you doing, asking her to keep an eye out for me, Po? She's a wanted fugitive! And does this mean you've told her I go out nights?"

"How was she supposed to get in touch with you?" Katsa asked.

"I told you," Po said to Bitterblue, "I trust her."

"Then trust her with *your* secrets, not mine! Po! Tell me she doesn't know!"

"Po," Katsa said, in such a strange voice that both Po and Bitterblue stopped, turning to look at her. She had backed away nearly to the door and wrapped her bare arms around her sheet dress, as if she were cold. "Po," she said again, "how was Hava to get in touch with you? Was she to come knocking on our doors?"

"What do you mean?" he asked; then swallowed; then rubbed the back of his neck, looking uncomfortable.

"How," Katsa said, "did you explain to her that you knew she was a person, not a sculpture?"

"You're jumping to conclusions," Po said.

Katsa stared at Po with an expression on her face Bitterblue didn't often see. The look of a person who's been punched in the gut. "Po," Katsa whispered. "She's a total stranger. We don't know the first thing about her."

Hands on hips, head hanging, Po blew a breath of air at the floor. "I don't need your permission," he said, rather helplessly.

"But you're being reckless, Po. And devious! You made a promise that you would tell me whenever you decided to tell someone new. Don't you remember?"

"Telling you would have meant fighting a war with you about it, Katsa. I should be able to decide about my own secrets without having to go into battle with you every single time!"

"But if you've changed your mind about a promise," Katsa said desperately, "you must tell me. Otherwise, you're breaking the promise, and I'm left feeling that you've lied. How is it that I should need to explain this to you? This is the sort of thing you usually have to explain to me!"

"You know what?" said Po suddenly, forcefully. "I can't do this with you around. I can't work through this thing when I know every moment how much it frightens you!"

"If you imagine that I'm going to leave you while you're in this mind-set—"

"You have to leave. It's been agreed. You go north to look for the tunnel to Estill."

"I won't go. None of us will! If you're determined to ruin your own life, at least your friends will be here for you when it happens!"

Katsa was yelling now; they were both yelling, and Bitterblue had made herself small in her chair, flinching at the terrible noise, clutching the damp cloth to her chest with both hands. "Ruin my life?" Po cried. "Perhaps I'm trying to save my life!"

"Save your life? You—"

"Remember the deal, Katsa. If you won't leave, then I will, and you'll let me go!"

Katsa was holding the door handle, her fingers so tight that Bitterblue half expected the handle to snap off. Katsa stared at Po for a long time, saying nothing.

"You were leaving anyway," Po said quietly, taking a step toward her, reaching out a hand. "Love. You were leaving, and then you were going to come back. That's all I need right now. I need time."

"Don't come any closer," Katsa said. "No. Don't say any more," as he opened his mouth again to speak. A tear slid down Katsa's face. "I understand you," she said, "completely." And she pulled on the door, slipped through the crack, and was gone.

"Where is she going?" Bitterblue asked, startled. "She's not dressed."

Po sank onto the bed. Dropping his head into his hands, he said, "She's going north to search for the tunnel to Estill."

"Now? But she has no supplies! She's wearing a sheet!"

"I've located Hava," he said roughly. "She's hiding in the art gallery. She has blood on her hands and she's telling me that your attacker is dead. I'll get dressed and go up to her to see what she knows."

"Po! Will you let Katsa go like this?"

He made no response. She understood, from the tears he was trying to hide from her, that he had no wish to discuss it.

Bitterblue watched him for a moment. Then, going to him, she touched his hair. "I love you, Po," she said. "Whatever you do."

Then she left.

A LAMP WAS lit in her sitting room. The blue of the room was swallowed in darkness and a silver sword lay gleaming on the table, seeming to hold all the light.

Beside it was a note.

Lady Queen,

It's been decided I must leave for Estill in the morning, but I wanted to deliver this from Ornik first. I hope you're as pleased with it as I am and will have no cause to use it while I'm gone. I'm sorry I won't be around to help you with your various puzzles.

Yours, Giddon

Bitterblue lifted the sword. It was a solid shaft, weighty and well-balanced, well-fitted to her hand, her arm. Simple in design, dazzling in the darkness. *Ornik did well,* she thought, holding it aloft. *I could have used it tonight.*

In her bedroom, Bitterblue made a place for the sword and belt on her bedside table. The mirror showed her a girl with a scrape on her forehead, raw and ugly; a girl who was tear-stained, paint-smudged, chap-lipped, messy-haired. All that she'd done tonight was visible on her face. She almost couldn't believe that the morning had started with her dream, her visit to Madlen. That only last night, she'd run with Saf across the city roofs and learned about the truth killers. Now Katsa was gone, on her way to some tunnel. Giddon was soon to leave too, and Raffin and Bann. How did so much happen in so little time?

Saf.

Her mother's embroidery, happy fish and snowflakes and castles in their rows, boats and anchors, the sun and stars, filled Bitterblue with loneliness. Before she even laid herself down properly, she was asleep.

IN THE MORNING, both Thiel and Runnemood were quite taken aback by the scrape on her forehead. Thiel, in particular, acted as if her head were hanging on by a mere thread, until she snapped at him to take hold of himself. Runnemood, seated in the window as usual, pushed his hand through his hair, jeweled rings glinting, eyes glinting. He would not stop staring at her. Bitterblue got the feeling that when she told him the scrape was from practice with Katsa, he didn't believe her.

When Darby came bounding in, sober, bright-eyed, and alarmed that the queen should exhibit something as dreadful as a scratch, Bitterblue decided it was high time to take a break from her tower. "Library," she said in response to Runnemood's inquiring eyebrow. "Don't get your pants in a knot. I won't stay long."

Making her way down the spiral steps, leaning on the wall to steady herself, Bitterblue changed her mind. She wasn't spending much time in her High Court these days. There never seemed to be anything interesting going on. But today, she'd like to sit with her judges for just a short while, even if it meant gritting her teeth through a tedious boundary dispute or some such. She'd like to look into their faces and measure their manners, get a feel for whether any of those eight powerful men might be the type to silence the city's truthseekers.

The city's truthseekers. Whenever she touched them with her thoughts today, her heart was a bright burst of sadness and shame.

When she walked into the High Court, a trial had already begun. At the sight of her, the entire court stood. "Catch me up," she said to the clerk as she crossed the dais to her chair.

"Accused of murder in the first degree, Lady Queen," said the clerk briskly. "Monsean name, Birch; Lienid name, Sapphire. Sapphire Birch."

Her mouth had dropped open and her eyes had whipped to the accused before her brain had even processed what it was hearing. Frozen, Bitterblue stared into the bruised, bloody, and utterly dumbfounded face of Sapphire.

BITTERBLUE COULD NOT breathe and, for a moment, she saw stars.

Turning her back to the judges, the floor, the gallery, she stumbled in confusion to the table behind the dais where supplies were kept and where the clerks stood, so that as few people as possible would see her confusion. Clinging to the table so that she wouldn't fall, she reached for a pen, touched it to ink, blotted. She pretended to be jotting something down, something of dire importance that she'd just remembered. She had never held a pen so hard.

When her lungs seemed to be accepting air again, she said, almost whispering, "Who hurt him?"

"If you'll sit, Lady Queen," said the voice of Lord Piper, "we'll put the question to the accused."

Carefully, Bitterblue turned to face the standing court. "Tell me," she said, "this instant, who hurt him."

"Hmm," Piper said, scrutinizing her in puzzlement. "The accused will answer the queen's inquiry."

A moment of silence. She didn't want to look at Saf again but it was impossible not to. His mouth was a bloody gash and one eye was swollen almost shut. His coat, so familiar to her, was rent at one of the shoulder seams and spattered with dried blood. "The Monsean Guard hurt me," he said, then stopped, then added, "Lady Queen." Then, "Lady Queen," he repeated in bafflement. "Lady Queen."

"That will do," Piper said sternly.

"Lady Queen," Saf said again, suddenly falling into his chair, giggling hysterically, and adding, "How could you?"

"The queen is not the one who hit you," Piper snapped, "and if she had, it would not be yours to question. Stand up, man. Show respect!"

"No," Bitterblue said. "Every single person here, sit."

A suspended moment of silence followed. Then, hastily, hundreds of people sat. She spotted Bren in the audience, golden-haired, tight-faced, sitting four or five rows behind her brother. She caught Bren's eye. Bren stared back at her with a look like she wanted to spit in Bitterblue's face. And now Bitterblue was thinking of Teddy, at home in his cot. Teddy would be so disappointed in her when he heard this truth.

Holding tight to her own fingers, Bitterblue moved to her seat and also sat; then jumped up, startled; then sat again, this time not on her own sword. *Po. Can you hear me? Will you come? Oh, come quickly!*

Keeping a channel open to Po but directing her attention to the large guard presence in the prisoner's hold with Saf, she said, "Which of you soldiers would care to explain the Monsean Guard's abuse of this man?"

One of the soldiers stood, squinting at her through two impressively bruised eye sockets. "Lady Queen," he said, "I am the captain of this unit. The prisoner resisted arrest, to the extent that one of our men is in the infirmary with a broken arm. We wouldn't have touched him otherwise."

"You little bitch," Saf said wonderingly.

"Don't!" Bitterblue yelled, rising, extending a finger at the guard, who'd drawn a fist back to strike Saf again. "I don't care what he calls you," she said to the guard, knowing perfectly well whom Saf had meant. "There will be no striking of prisoners, except in self-defense." *Oh, Po, he's not making this easy. If he starts telling the truth, I don't know what I'll do. Pretend he's insane? Insanity won't help to free him.* And everyone was half standing again, which made her want to scream. Dropping into her seat once more, she said, "What evidence have I missed? Who's he supposed to have murdered?"

"An engineer in the east city named Ivan, Lady Queen," Piper said.

"Ivan! The one who built the bridges and stole the watermelons? He's dead?"

"Yes, Lady Queen. That Ivan."

"When did it happen?"

"Two nights ago, Lady Queen," said Piper.

"Two nights ago," Bitterblue repeated, then understood what that meant. Her eyes bored into Piper's. "The night before last night? At what time?"

"Just before midnight, Lady Queen, under the clock tower on Monster Bridge. There is a witness who saw everything. The hour struck moments later."

Her heart sinking into her boots, into the floor, into the earth beneath her castle, Bitterblue forced herself to look at Saf. And yes, of course he stared back at her with crossed arms and a nasty, twisted smirk to his broken mouth, for Saf knew perfectly well that just before midnight the night before last, he'd been holding her hands on the roof of the shop, answering her third question, and keeping her from feeling that she would fall off the face of the earth. He'd tossed her his watch to comfort her height sickness. They'd heard the clock chime together. *Oh, Po, I don't understand what's happening here. Someone is lying. What am I to do? If I tell the truth, my advisers will know I've been sneaking out, and I can't bear them knowing, I just can't, they'll never trust me again, they'll fight me on everything, they'll try to control me. And the whole kingdom will speculate about whether I'm having a secret affair with a Lienid sailor who's a thief. I'll lose my credibility with everyone. I'll shame myself and everyone who supports me. What do I do? What's the way out of this?*

Where are you?

You don't hear me, do you. You're not coming.

"The accused has offered an alibi, Lady Queen," Piper continued. "He claims to have been stargazing with a friend on his roof. He further claims that his friend lives in the castle but that he doesn't know the friend's true identity. Perversely, he then refuses to describe the friend for us so that we might produce him. Which is all in the way of saying that he has no alibi at all."

Which is all in the way of saying that even when faced with the charge of murder, Saf protects the secrets of the people he considers to be friends. Even when he doesn't have the privilege of knowing those secrets himself.

Saf's expression hadn't changed, except to grow harder, tighter, more bitterly amused. She saw no softness for herself there. The softness had been for Sparks, and Sparks was gone now.

Po. I have no choice.

Bitterblue rose and said, "Everyone remain seated." She couldn't control her trembling. To stop herself from hugging her own arms, she took hold of her sword hilt. Then she looked into Saf's face and said, "I know his companion's true name."

The doors at the back of the courtroom crashed open and Po exploded through so forcefully that the audience spun around on their benches, craning to see what the ruckus was. Standing in the center aisle, himself bruised and gasping, Po called up to Bitterblue,

"Cousin! Sticky door you've got there!" Then he pretended to pass his eyes over the people in the room. What followed was the most masterly impression of shocked recognition that Bitterblue had ever seen. Po's body went still and his face registered perfect amazement. "Saf," he said. "Great seas, is that you? You're not accused of something, are you?"

Bitterblue's relief was premature, she knew that. Still, it was the only emotion she could feel as she fell into her chair. She wasn't going to say a thing until she understood exactly what Po was up to, other than, perhaps, the single word *Piper*, so that Piper would know to run through the charges against Saf once more and Po could go through the dramatics of pretending to be astonished and appalled.

"But, this is extraordinary," Po said, walking up the aisle, coming alongside the prisoner's hold, where Saf sat gaping at Po as if Po were a dancing bear that had just jumped out of a cake. In one easy motion, Po swung himself over the gate, pushed through Saf's startled, rising guards, and took Saf's shoulder. "Why are you protecting me, man? Don't you know what happens to murderers in Monsea? Lady Queen, he didn't murder that man. He *was* on the roof that night, just as he says, and I was with him."

THANK YOU, PO. Thank you. Thank you.

She was like the paper glider she'd watched Po fling into the wall. She thought she might slide right off the edge of her chair and crumple onto the floor.

A furious argument had begun between Po and her judges.

"My business is none of your business," Po said flatly when Lord Quall asked, with a smarmy smile, why he'd been stargazing on a roof with a sailor in the east city at midnight. "Nor does it have anything to do with whether Saf is innocent or guilty." And later, "What do you mean, how long have I been friends with him? Haven't you asked him?" *I don't know if they've asked him,* Bitterblue thought to him; but apparently Po had already determined that they hadn't—which was lucky—for he continued without missing a beat. "We met for the first time that night. Can you wonder that I fell in talking with him? Look at him! I don't ignore my own people!"

Don't draw any more attention to him than you need to, Po. He's not coping well. For if Po's apparent surprise at finding his new best friend on trial for murder was well acted, it paled in comparison to Saf's confoundedness at finding the Graceling prince of Lienid at his side, knowing who he was, claiming to be his friend, knowing obscure details about his whereabouts two nights ago, and lying to the High Court on his behalf.

Quall asked Po if he could furnish any other witnesses.

Po took a step to the front of the hold. "Am I on trial here? Perhaps you think the two of us killed the man together."

"Naturally not, Lord Prince," said Quall. "But you'll understand our hesitation in trusting a Lienid Graceling who claims to have no Grace."

"When have I ever claimed to have no Grace?"

"Not you, of course, Lord Prince. The accused."

Po spun back to Saf. "Saf? Did you tell these judges that you have no Grace?"

Saf swallowed. "No, Lord Prince," he whispered. "I only claimed not to know my Grace, Lord Prince."

"You do perceive the difference?" Po asked, rather sarcastically, turning back to Quall.

"And still, it's certain that the accused lied, Lord Prince, for he also claimed not to know your true identity."

"It's obvious he lied to protect me and my business," Po said impatiently. "He is loyal to a fault."

"My Prince," Saf piped up miserably, "I would rather be convicted of a crime I didn't commit than put you in jeopardy."

Oh, finish this, Po, please, thought Bitterblue. *I cannot bear how pathetic he is.*

And then Po shot Bitterblue the briefest of sardonic expressions. Bitterblue, hardly able to believe it, studied Saf more closely. Surely his humility wasn't an act? *Could* Saf act in a moment like this?

"He is proud of lying!" Quall said triumphantly.

Bitterblue had given up on identifying the authenticity of anyone's emotions. She only knew that Po seemed genuinely fed up with Quall. Swinging himself over the gate of the hold—not quite as smoothly as he had before—he came to stand before the dais. "What is your problem?" he asked Quall. "Do you doubt the truth of my testimony?"

Quall worked his mouth. "Not at all, Lord Prince."

"Then you acknowledge that he must be innocent; but still, you can't let it go. Why don't you like him? Is it because he's Graced? Or might it be because he's Lienid?"

"He's a funny sort of Lienid," said Quall, with a touch of contempt that suggested some personal disregard.

"To your eyes, perhaps," Po said coolly, "but he would not be wearing those rings or that gold in his ears if the Lienid didn't consider him to be Lienid. Many Lienid look just like him. While your Monsean king was murdering people indiscriminately, our Lienid king was opening his arms to Gracelings seeking freedom. A Lienid is the reason your queen is alive today. Her Lienid mother had a mind stronger than any of the rest of you. Your Monsean king killed my father's Lienid sister. Your own queen is half Lienid!"

Po, Bitterblue thought, beginning to be thoroughly confused. *We're getting off course here, don't you think?*

"Your Monsean witness is the one who's a criminal liar," Po said, extending his hand toward a broad, handsome man in the first row of the audience.

Po! No one's told you which one is the witness! Bitterblue jumped to her feet so that everyone would have to focus on figuring out whether to rise or remain seated, rather than on Po's strange perceptiveness. *Pull yourself together,* she snapped at him. "Arrest the witness," she snapped at the guards around Sapphire, "and release the accused from the hold. He's free to go."

"He did break the arm of a member of the Monsean Guard, Lady Queen," Piper reminded her.

"Who was arresting him for a murder he didn't commit!"

"Nonetheless, Lady Queen, I don't believe we can tolerate behavior like that. He also lied to the court."

"I sentence him to the black eye and bloody mouth he already has," Bitterblue said, gazing at Piper squarely. "Unless every one of you objects to that, he's free to go."

Piper cleared his throat. "That's acceptable to me, Lady Queen."

"Very well," Bitterblue said. She turned and, without another glance at Saf or Po or any of the gaping audience, marched to the exit at the back of the dais.

Po, don't let him get away. Bring him somewhere where I can talk to him privately. Bring him to my rooms.

WHEN BITTERBLUE BURST into her sitting room, Fox was
polishing the royal crown.

"Shall I come back later, Lady Queen?" she asked, with one
glance at the queen.

"No. Yes. No," said Bitterblue, a bit wildly. "Where is Helda?"

"Lady Queen?" Helda's voice came from the doorway behind
her. "What on earth is the matter?"

"Helda," said Bitterblue, "I did something terrible. Don't let
anyone in but Po and whoever he brings, all right? I can't talk to
anyone else."

"Of course, Lady Queen," said Helda. "What happened?"

Bitterblue began to pace. She couldn't begin to explain. To get
away from the need to do so, she waved her hands hopelessly, then
pushed past Helda to the foyer and her bedroom and shut the door.
Inside, she commenced pacing again, her sword slamming against
her leg every time she turned.

Where is Po? Why must they take so long?

Not certain when or how she'd crossed the room, she found herself bent over her mother's chest, clinging to its edges. The figures
carved into its lid blurred with her tears.

Then the door opened and Bitterblue scrambled to her feet,
turned, tripped, sat down hard on the trunk. Po came in and shut
the door behind him.

"Where is he?" Bitterblue asked.

"In your sitting room," Po said. "I've asked Helda and that girl to step out. Is there any way I can convince you not to do this now? He's had an awful lot thrown at him and no time to absorb it."

"I need to explain."

"I really think that if you gave him some time—"

"I promise I'll give him cartloads of time, after I explain."

"Bitterblue—"

Bitterblue stood, swept toward Po, and stopped before him, chin raised, staring at him.

"Yes, all right," Po said, rubbing his face with both ring-covered hands, defeated. "I'm not leaving," he added flatly.

"Po—"

"Be as queeny as you like, Bitterblue. He's angry, he's hurt; he's clever and slippery; this morning he broke someone's arm. I will not leave you alone in these rooms with him."

"Can't you just extract some sort of Lienid oath of honor from him or something?" she shot at him sarcastically.

"I already have," Po said. "I'm still not leaving." Marching to the bed, he sat, crossing legs and arms.

Bitterblue watched him for a moment, knowing that she was releasing feelings of one kind or another to him, not knowing herself exactly what they were. Managing, through some heroic effort of will, to contain how much she wished he would get past this addleheaded crisis about his Grace. Po said, "That ass Quall on your High Court hates the Lienid. He tells himself he thinks that we're inbred, over-muscled simpletons, but really what bothers him is that, in his opinion, we're better looking than he is. There's no logic to it, either, for he's lumped Saf into it, even though, as he himself pointed out, Saf doesn't look Lienid. He's jealous of how well Saf

and I look in our gold. Can you believe that? If he could've convicted us both of murder and taken our freedom away by virtue of
that alone, he would have. He kept trying to imagine us without it."

"Without . . . your freedom?"

"Without our gold," Po said. "I'll stay in here while you talk to
Sapphire. If he touches you, I'll come in and choke him to death."

SAF'S GOLD WAS the first thing she saw when she entered the sitting
room, sunlit in his ears and on his fingers. She understood all at
once that she wouldn't like to see him without it. It would be like
seeing him with eyes that weren't his, or hearing him speak in a
different voice.

The gash in his coat broke her heart. She wanted to touch him.

Then he turned to her and she saw the disgust carried in every
feature of his battered face and in every line of his body.

He dropped to his knees, eyes raised, staring straight into hers—
the perfect mockery of subservience, for no man on his knees ever
raised his eyes to a sovereign's face. It defeated the purpose of lowering oneself.

"Stop that!" she said. "Get up."

"Whatever you wish, Lady Queen," he said sarcastically, leaping
to his feet.

She was beginning to understand the game. "Please don't do this,
Saf," she pleaded. "You know it's just me."

Saf snorted.

"What? What is it?"

"Nothing at all," he said, "Lady Queen."

"Oh, just tell me, Saf."

"I wouldn't dream of contradicting the queen, Lady Queen."

In another place, in another conversation between them, she might have slapped his smug face. Perhaps Sparks would have slapped him right now. But Bitterblue couldn't, for Bitterblue, slapping Saf, would only be playing into his game: The mighty queen slaps the lowly subject. And the more like a subject she treated him, the more control he had over the situation. Which confused her, because it made no sense that a queen should transfer power to her subject by mistreating him.

She just wanted to be able to talk to him. "Saf," she said. "Until now, we've been friends and equals."

He shot her a look of pure derision.

"What?" she begged. "Tell me. Please talk to me."

Saf took a few steps toward the crown on its stand and put his hand full on it, stroking the soft gold of its face, measuring the gems between his fingers. She kept her mouth shut, even though it felt like a bodily assault. But when he went so far as to lift it, placing it on his own head, turning to stare at her balefully, a ruin-eyed, bloody-mouthed, tattered-coat king, she couldn't stop herself. "Put that down," she hissed.

"Hm?" he murmured as he removed the crown, setting it back on its velvet cushion. "We're not equals after all, then, are we?"

"I don't care about the stupid crown," she said, flustered. "I only care that my father was the last man I ever saw wear it, and when you put it on, I remember him."

"Ironic," he said, "for I've been thinking of how much you make me think of him."

It didn't matter that she'd had the same thoughts herself. It hurt far more coming from Saf. "You have lied just as much as I," she whispered.

"I have never once lied," he snarled in an ugly voice, taking a step toward her, so that she had to step back, startled. "I've kept things from you when I needed to. But I've never lied!"

"You knew I wasn't who I said. That was no secret!"

"You're the queen!" Saf yelled, taking another step forward. "The rutting queen! You manipulated me! And not just for information!"

Po appeared in the doorway. He took hold of the door frame above his head, casually, with one hand. Raising his eyebrows, he leaned and waited.

"Forgive me, Lord Prince," Saf said miserably, confusing Bitterblue by lowering his eyes before Po, hanging his head, stepping back from her with no equivocation.

"The queen is my cousin," said Po calmly.

"I understand, Lord Prince," Saf said meekly.

I, on the other hand, do not understand, Bitterblue thought to Po, *and I could kick you. I want him angry. When he's angry, we get to the truth.*

Po assumed a bland expression, turned on his heel, and left the room.

"He has no idea," Saf said, "does he. He has no idea what a snake you are."

Taking a breath, Bitterblue said quietly, "I didn't manipulate you."

"Horseshit," Saf said. "You told Prince Po every last detail about me, every minute of everything we've ever done, yet I'm to believe you never told your little people? You think I'm so naïve that I haven't figured out how I got pulled in for a murder I didn't commit, or who's paying that witness to lie? Or who's responsible for the attacks on Teddy and me?"

"What?" she cried. "Saf! No! How can you think I'm behind all those things when Po and I just saved you? You're not thinking!"

"And that last little bit of fun—did you enjoy that? Do you get a kick out of debasing yourself with commoners and then telling others? I cannot believe how much feeling I wasted in worry," he said, voice going low, stepping toward her again. "Fearing I would injure you somehow. Thinking you were innocent!"

Knowing it was a wild and unwise thing to do, she took hold of his arm. "Saf, I swear to you, I'm not your villain. I'm as baffled about that as you are. I'm on your side! I'm trying to find the truth! And I've never told anyone your every last detail—anyone but Po," she amended desperately, "and even he doesn't know the private things. Hardly anyone else even knows I go out at night!"

"You're lying again," he said, trying to push her off. "Let go."

She clung to him. "No. Please."

"Let go," he said between his teeth, "or I'll punch you in the face and shame myself before my prince."

"I want you to punch me in the face," she said, which wasn't true, but at least it would be fair. Her guards had punched him in the face.

"Of course," he said, "because then I'll land right back in prison." He twisted his arm away and she gave up, turned her back to him, wrapping arms around herself, hugging herself desolately.

Finally, she said in a small, clear voice, "I have lied, Saf, but never with the intention of hurting you or your friends, or any truthseekers, or *anyone*, I swear it. I only ever went out to see what my city was like at night, because my advisers keep me blind in a tower and I wanted to know. I never meant to meet you. I never meant to like you and I never meant to become your friend. Once I did, how was I to tell you the truth?"

She couldn't see him, but he seemed to be laughing. "You're unbelievable."

"Why? What is it? Explain what you mean!"

"You seem to have this daydream," Saf said, "that when we were spending time together and I didn't know you were the queen, we were friends. Equals. But knowledge is power. You knew you were the queen and I didn't. We have never once been equal, and as far as friendship goes," he said—then stopped. "Your mother is dead," he said in a different kind of voice, bitter, and final. "You've lied to me about everything."

"I told you things that were more precious to me than the truth," she whispered.

A silence stretched between them, empty. A distance. It lasted a long, long time.

"Let's suppose for a minute that you're telling the truth," he finally said, "about not being the person behind the attacks."

"I am telling the truth," she whispered. "Saf, I swear it. The only thing I lied about is who I am."

Another short silence. When he spoke again, it was with a sadness and a quietness that she did not know how to associate with the Saf she knew. "But I don't think you understand who you are," he said. "I don't think you realize how big it is, or how it maroons me. You're so high in the world that you can't see down as far as me. You don't see what you've done." And Saf moved around her, vanishing into the foyer without leave, shouldering through the outside doors, so abruptly that, finding herself alone, she made a small noise of surprise.

Slowly, Bitterblue unfolded herself, turning to take in the room, the midday light. She searched for the clock on the mantel, to see how many hours of this day were left to live through before she could hide in the covers of her bed.

Her eyes didn't make it as far as the clock, for the crown was missing from its velvet cushion.

Bitterblue spun frantically, her body refusing her mind's immediate comprehension, but of course, the crown was nowhere else in the room either. Hissing Saf's name, she ran after him, burst through her outside doors, and found herself staring into the faces of two very startled Lienid guards.

"Is anything wrong, Lady Queen?" the guard to the left inquired.

And what was she going to do, anyway? Race through the castle, higgledy-piggledy, having no idea of his route, in the hopes that she'd cross his path in a courtyard somewhere? And then what? Ask him, before an audience of passersby, to please give back the crown he was hiding in his coat? Then, when he refused, grapple with him for it? He'd be arrested all over again, and this time for a crime he *had* committed.

"Everything is marvelous," Bitterblue said. "This is the best day of my life. Thank you for asking."

Then she went to kick in her bedroom door and demand of Po why he'd let this happen.

The answer was straightforward enough. Po was asleep.

22

W<small>HEN</small> P<small>O</small> <small>BURST</small> back into her rooms an hour later, he was not carrying the crown.

"Where is it?" Bitterblue hissed from her place on the sofa, where she'd spent the hour pushing away the food Helda pressed on her, fending off visits from her puzzled advisers, and pulling at her cuticles.

Po collapsed beside her, rumpled and soaking wet. "I lost him."

"You lost him! How?"

"He had a head start, Bitterblue, and his sister met him just outside, and they ran together, splitting up sometimes. And it's raining, which makes things harder for me. And I cannot keep all your streets in my mind, and all the houses, and all the moving people, while also focusing on someone who grows farther and farther away; I got lost, I had to backtrack. And all the hundreds of folk who saw me were having dramatic reactions at me, wanting to know why I was running around like a lunatic, and I cannot even begin to describe how distracting that is. The power of the rumor mill, if you could feel it as I do, would boggle your mind. Too many people out there know, somehow, that Katsa left abruptly in the middle of the night, sobbing her eyes out, wearing Raffin's clothing, and taking a horse over Winged Bridge. Every one of them who looked at me wanted to know what horrible thing I'd done to her."

"In addition to that," a dignified voice said from the doorway, "look at what a sight he is, Lady Queen. I've never tried running after young men through the city streets myself, but I expect it's difficult with heavy legs and tired eyes. He looks as if he hasn't slept in days, and who can blame him, with his lady up and leaving him?" Coming into the room, Helda went to a side table, poured a cup of cider, and brought it to Po.

"She left because I asked her to, Helda," he said quietly, accepting the cup.

Sitting down across from them, sniffing, Helda said, "Who's going to tell me what's going on?"

Bitterblue was lost. Had Po told Helda his truth, then? Or was he revealing it to her this very moment? Had he even meant to, or had she snuck up on him somehow? If one of the Lienid guards stepped in, or one of the spies, would Po reveal it to them too? *Why not hang a banner from the windows?*

She tore a hangnail too close to the root and sucked her breath in through her teeth. "Well," she said to Helda, watching the bead of blood grow. "Today, a city person I know was arrested for a murder he didn't commit. He was acquitted. Then Po brought him here so that I could talk to him."

"I saw him when he came in, Lady Queen," Helda said severely, "before Prince Po shooed me back to my rooms and told me to stay there. He looked like an incurable ruffian. And when he began yelling at you, and I came out to knock some sense into him, Prince Po shooed me away again."

"His name is Sapphire," Bitterblue said, swallowing, "and he didn't know until he saw me in the High Court today that I was the queen. I'd told him that I worked in the kitchens."

Helda narrowed her eyes. "I see."

"He's a friend, Helda," Bitterblue said hopelessly. "Except that on the way out, he stole the crown."

Settling herself more firmly into her chair, Helda said again, dryly, "I see."

"I can't see with my eyes," Po said to Helda, perhaps a bit out of the blue, thrusting a hand through his soggy hair. "I believe you've gathered the rest, but if you're to know the whole truth, I should tell you I lost my eyesight eight years ago."

Helda opened her mouth; closed it.

"I sense things," Po went on. "Not just thoughts, but objects, bodies, force, momentum, the world around me, and so my blindness, much of the time, is not the hindrance it would otherwise be. But it's the reason I can't read. I can't see color; the world is gray shapes. The sun and moon are too far away for me to sense and I can't see light."

Still working her mouth, Helda reached into her pocket for a handkerchief, which she handed to Bitterblue. After a moment, she extracted another handkerchief, then set to folding it precisely, as if matching corner to corner were the day's most critical task. When she pressed it to her lips, then dabbed her eyes, Po's head dropped. "Regarding the crown," he said, clearing his throat. "They seemed to be heading east, perhaps toward the silver docks, before I lost them."

"Did you go to the shop?"

"I don't know the location of the shop, Bitterblue. No one's thought the map straight at me. Do it yourself and I'll go there now."

"No," she said, "I'll go."

"I don't advise that."

"I must."

"Bitterblue," Po said, beginning to lose his patience, "I advised you against meeting him the first time and he stole your crown. What do you think he'll do the second time?"

"But if I keep trying—"

"While I stand outside ready to come bursting in to cover for you when he, oh, I don't know, gets it into his head to drag you into the street and start screaming that the boy in the hood is really the queen of the kingdom? I don't have time for this, Bitterblue, and I don't have the energy to keep straightening your tangles!"

White-lipped, Bitterblue rose to her feet. "Shall I stop straightening your tangles, then, too, Po? How often do I lie for your sake? How often did you lie *to* me in the first years of our acquaintance? You, who are immune to being lied to yourself. How inconvenient it must be when you have to complicate your peace by lying for the sake of others."

"Sometimes," Po said with bitterness, "you are utterly without pity."

"I'd say you've enough pity for yourself," said Bitterblue. "You, of all people, should understand my need for Saf's forgiveness. What I've done to him, you do to everyone all the time. Help me or don't help me; fine. But don't talk to me as if I'm a child who trips around carelessly making messes. There are situations in my city and my kingdom that you know nothing about." Then she sat down again, suddenly, dismal and deflated. "Oh, Po," she said, dropping her face into her hands. "I'm sorry. Please, give me your advice. What should I say to him? What do *you* say when you've hurt someone with a lie?"

Po was quiet for a moment. Then he almost seemed to be laughing, mournfully, under his breath. "I apologize."

"Yes, I've done that," Bitterblue said, her mind running through the horrible conversation she'd had with Saf. Then running through it again. "Oh." She stared at Po in dismay. "I never once said I was sorry."

"You must," Po said, gently now. "Beyond that, you must tell him as much of the truth as you possibly can. You must ensure, by whatever means necessary, that he doesn't use it to ruin you. And then you must let him be as angry as he'll be. That's what I do."

And so I must throw myself into my own guilt, and into the hatred of a person I've grown fond of.

Bitterblue contemplated her ruined cuticles. She was beginning to better understand, starkly, Po's crisis. Leaning into him, she touched her head to his shoulder. He put a wet arm around her and held on.

"Helda," Bitterblue said, "how long do you think we can keep everyone from noticing that the crown is missing?"

Helda pursed her lips. "A good long time," she decided with a staunch nod. "I don't anticipate anyone caring about the crown until your uncle's visit, do you, Lady Queen? It's only your spies, your servants, your Council friends, and I in these rooms, and of those, it's only one or two of the servants I'd rather not trust. I'll construct something and throw a cloth over the cushion so it looks like nothing's amiss."

"Don't forget that it depends on Saf as well," Po said. "He's perfectly capable of making it known citywide in any number of ways that your crown is not where it should be, Bitterblue, and plenty of people saw him and me walking to your rooms together after the trial."

Bitterblue sighed. She supposed it was the sort of thing he would do, if he were angry enough. "We've got to find out who framed him for the murder," she said.

"Yes," Po said. "That's an important question. Let me go confront him about the crown, won't you? Please? I'll see if I can learn anything about the framing as well. I also think I should talk to that false witness, don't you agree?"

"Yes. All right." Bitterblue let go of him, sighing. "I'll stay here. I've some things I need to think through. Helda, will you continue to chase my advisers away?"

IN HER BEDROOM, she paced.

Could Saf really, truly, honestly think I'm behind the silencing of the truthseekers? Behind all of it? When I ran with him over the roofs? When I brought Madlen to them! Could he honestly—

Numbly, she sat on the chest, pulling hairpins out. *Could he honestly think I would want misfortune to befall him?*

Massaging her scalp, working her newly freed hair into a rat's nest, she found herself at a panicky dead end with that question. She had no control over what Saf thought.

He said that I don't see what I've done or how high I am in the world. That I marooned him. He said we've never been friends, never been equals.

Crossing to the vanity where she sat when Helda did her hair, Bitterblue threw her hairpins into a silver bowl and glared into the mirror. Sunken circles stood like bruises under her eyes, and her forehead, still raw from the attack last night, was purple and grisly. Behind her was reflected the enormity of the room, the bed high and big enough to be a dining table for all her friends, the silver, gold, scarlet walls. The dark ceiling dotted with stars. *Fox, or someone, must clean away my cobwebs,* she thought. *Someone must care for this beautiful rug.*

Bitterblue thought of the printing shop, messy and bright. She thought of the apartments behind, small enough to fit into this room, tidy, walls and floors made of rough-hewn wood. She looked in the mirror at her own gown of pale gray silk, perfectly fitted, beautifully tailored, and thought of Saf's rougher clothing, the places where his sleeve-ends frayed. She remembered how fond he was of Leck's gold pocket watch. She remembered the choker she had pawned without a second thought, barely caring how much money it made her.

She did not think that they were poor. They had work, they had food, they threw sparkling parties. But she supposed that she didn't really know what poor would look like, if she saw it. Would she recognize it? And if they weren't poor, what were they? How did it work, to live in the city? Did they pay someone rent? Who decided how much things cost? Did they pay taxes to the crown that were a strain on them?

Somewhat uncomfortable now, Bitterblue returned to her mother's chest, sat down, and forced herself to touch the edges of the question of just how, exactly, she had marooned Saf. What if the situation were reversed? What if she were the commoner and it had turned out that Saf was the king? Would she have been left marooned?

It was nearly impossible for her to conceive of such a situation. In fact, it was flatly absurd. But then she began to wonder if her inability even to imagine it had to do with her being too high to see that low, as Saf had said.

For some reason, her mind kept returning to the night Saf and she had taken a route along the silver docks. They'd talked of pirates and treasure hunting, and they'd run past the looming ships of the queen. The ships had been lined with the queen's fine soldiers who guarded the silver destined for her treasury, her very own fortress of gold.

* * * * *

WHEN PO ENTERED the bedroom sometime later, even wetter than before and with mud-streaked clothing, he found Bitterblue sitting on the floor, head in hands.

"Po," she whispered, looking up at him. "I'm very wealthy, aren't I?"

Po came and crouched before her, dripping. "Giddon is wealthy," he said. "I'm exceedingly wealthy, and Raffin is more. There's no word for what you are, Bitterblue. And the money at your disposal is only a fraction of your power."

Swallowing, she said, "I don't believe I quite appreciated it before."

"Yes," Po said. "Well. Money does that. It's one of the privileges of wealth never to have to think about it, and one of the dangers too." He shifted, sat. "What's wrong?"

"I'm not sure," Bitterblue whispered.

He sat quietly, accepting that.

"You don't seem to have the crown with you," she added.

"The crown is not in the shop," he said. "Saf has passed it on to the subordinates of a black market underlord who calls himself Spook and is said to live hidden away in a cave, if I was reading him right."

"My crown is already on the black market?" cried Bitterblue. "But how will we ever exonerate him?"

"I get the impression that Spook is only involved for safekeeping, Beetle. We may still be able to get it back. Don't despair yet. I'll work on Saf, I'll flatter him with an invitation to a Council meeting or something. When I left, you know, he knelt, kissed my hand, and wished me good dreams. This, after I'd accused him of royal theft."

"How gratifying for you that it's only the Monsean nobility he hates," she said bitterly.

"He would hate me well enough if I broke his heart," said Po quietly.

Bitterblue raised her face to him. "Have I broken his heart, then, Po? Is that what I'm to believe?"

"That's a question for you to ask him, sweetheart."

She noticed, then, that Po was shivering. More than that: She saw, as she studied him more closely, something wild and pained flashing in his eyes. Reaching out, she touched his face. "Po!" she said. "You're burning! Do you feel all right?"

"I feel like my insides are made of lead, actually," he said. "Do you think I have a fever? That would explain why I fell."

"You fell?"

"My Grace sort of starts warping things when I have a fever, you know? Without eyesight, it's disorienting." He grabbed his head vaguely. "I think I fell more than once."

"You're ill," she said, upset, standing up, "and I've sent you twice into the rain, and made you fall. Come, I'm taking you to your rooms."

"Helda is trying to find some way whereby the fact of my being blind explains what she believes to be the perversity of Katsa and me not having children," he said at random.

"What? What are you talking about? That makes no sense whatsoever. Get up."

"I really can't stand it sometimes," he said a bit erratically, still sitting on the floor, "hearing other people's thoughts. People are ridiculous. By the way, Saf is not lying about his Grace; he doesn't know what it is."

He told me so many times that he never lies to me. I suppose I didn't want to believe it. "Po." Taking Po's hands and pulling, leaning back, yanking, Bitterblue persuaded him to stand. "I'm going to walk you to your rooms and bring you a healer. You need to sleep."

"Did you know that Tilda and Bren live as a couple and they want Teddy to give them a baby?" he asked, swaying, wincing at the room as if he couldn't remember how he got there.

This was too astonishing for words. "I'm bringing you to Madlen," Bitterblue said sternly. "Now, come along."

BY THE TIME Bitterblue returned to her rooms, the light was fading. The sky was purple like Saf's eyes, and her sitting room glimmered with lamps Helda had taken care to light. In her bedroom, she lit candles for herself, sat on the floor by her mother's chest, and ran her fingers over the carvings on its top.

How lonely she felt, trying to understand all that had happened today on her own. *Mama? Would you be ashamed of me?*

Wiping a tear that had fallen onto the lid of the chest, she found herself peering more closely at the carved designs. She'd noticed before that Ashen had used some of the carvings as models for her embroidery, of course, but she'd never made a study of it. They were arranged in neat rows atop the lid—none repeated—star, moon, candle, sun, for example. Boat, shell, castle, tree, flower, prince, princess, baby, and so on. She knew, from years of staring at the edges of her own sheets, exactly which ones Ashen had borrowed.

The realization crept into her and all through her. Even before she'd bothered to count, she knew. She counted anyway, just to make sure.

The carvings on the chest numbered a hundred. The carvings her mother had borrowed for her embroidery numbered twenty-six.

Bitterblue was looking at a cipher alphabet.

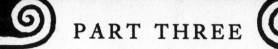

PART THREE

Ciphers and Keys

(Late September and October)

23

It was not a straightforward cipher alphabet. When Bitterblue isolated Ashen's twenty-six embroidery designs on the chest and applied the top left-most design, a star, to the letter *A*, the next in the row, a waning moon, to the letter *B*, and so on, then tested the resulting symbol alphabet against her mother's sheets, she got nothing but gibberish.

She tried applying the bottom right-most symbol to the letter *A* and working her way up the chest backward. She tried running up and down the chest in columns.

None of it worked.

Very well, then; perhaps there was a key. What key would Ashen have used?

Taking a steadying breath, Bitterblue removed the repeating letters from her own name and armed herself with the resulting alphabet.

B I T E R L U V W X Y Z A

C D F G H J K M N O P Q S

Then she applied it to the symbols on the chest, starting again at the upper left:

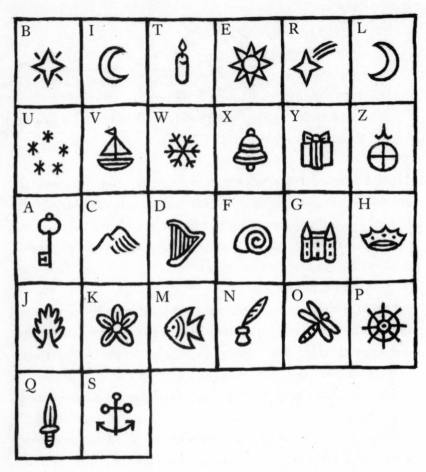

Holding tight to the sheet in her lap, she tried it against Ashen's embroidery.

When it yielded results, she separated those results into words and sentences, and added punctuation. Where Ashen had skipped letters, presumably for the sake of speed, she added them too.

Ara comes back limping.

She can't remember until I show it to her. When she sees then it hurts and she screams.

Will I stop telling Ara then? Is it better she not know?

Should I kill them when I know he's marked them for death? Would that be merciful or mad?

HELDA FOUND BITTERBLUE, that first day, in a mountain of sheets on the floor, arms wrapped around herself, shivering. "Lady Queen!" Helda exclaimed, kneeling beside her. "Are you ill?"

"My mother had a servant named Ara who disappeared," whispered Bitterblue. "I remember."

"Lady Queen?"

"She embroidered in cipher, Helda! Mama did. She must have been trying to create a record she could read to remember what was real. It must have taken her hours to write a single small passage! Here, help me. My name is the keyword. A star is a *B*. A waning moon is an *I,* a candle a *T,* the sun an *E,* a falling star an *R,* a waxing moon an *L,* the ring constellation a *U*. My name is made of light," she cried out. "My mother chose symbols of light for the letters of my name. Is Po—" Po was ill. "Is Giddon truly gone?"

"He is, Lady Queen. What in the world are you going on about?"

"Tell no one else," Bitterblue said. "Helda. Until we know what it means, tell no one, and help me arrange them."

They pulled the sheets out of her closets and off her bed and took an inventory: 228 sheets with embroidery lining the edges; 89 pillowcasings. Ashen seemed not to have dated anything; there was no way to determine the order to place them in, so Bitterblue and Helda arranged them in neat, arithmetically divided piles on her bedroom floor. And Bitterblue read and read and read.

Certain words and phrases recurred often, sometimes filling up an entire sheet. He lies. He lies. Blood. I can't remember. I must remember. I must kill him. I must get Bitterblue away.

Tell me something helpful, Mama. Tell me what happened, tell me what you saw.

IN HER OFFICES, Bitterblue's advisers, as requested, had begun to educate her about the lords and ladies of her kingdom. They began with those who lived the farthest away: their names, their property, families, tax paid, their particular personalities and skills. None of them were introduced to her as "the lord with a predilection for murdering truthseekers"—none, in fact, were remarkable at all— and Bitterblue knew she would get nowhere this way. She wondered if she could ever ask Teddy and Saf for a list of the lords and ladies who'd stolen most grievously from their people. Could she ever ask Teddy and Saf for anything again?

Then, as the days led to October, there was an explosion of urgent paperwork in the offices. "What on earth is going on?" she asked Thiel as she signed work orders blearily, pushed charters about, and fought with piles of paper that grew faster than she could keep up with them.

"It's always like this in October, Lady Queen," Thiel reminded her sympathetically, "as everyone across the kingdom tries to wrap up their business and prepare for the freeze of winter."

"Is it?" Bitterblue couldn't remember an October like this one. Then again, particular months were so hard to isolate in her memory; every month was the same. Or, every month had been, until the night she'd stepped into the city and changed a hundred facets of her life.

She tried again one day to broach the topic of truthseekers being killed. "That trial I went to," she said, "with the Lienid-Monsean who turned out to have been framed—the one who was friends with Prince Po—"

"The trial you went to without informing us, Lady Queen, then invited the accused to your rooms afterwards," Runnemood said in an oily voice.

"I invited him because my court had wronged him and he was a friend of my cousin's," Bitterblue said calmly. "And I went because it's my right to go wherever I like. His trial has gotten me thinking. In my High Court, I want witnesses to the witnesses from now on. In my prisons, I want everyone retried. Everyone, you understand? If this Lienid-Monsean was nearly convicted of a murder he didn't commit, so could everyone else in my prisons have been. Couldn't they?"

"Oh, of course not, Lady Queen," said Runnemood with a weariness and an exasperation that Bitterblue had no sympathy for. She was also weary and exasperated, her mind returning too often to bright little pictures on sheets that revealed too little that was helpful, and too much pain.

I wish I'd given my child a kind father. I wish I'd been unfaithful then. Such choices don't occur to a girl of eighteen when Leck has chosen her. Choice vanishes in his fog. How can I protect her in this fog?

One day at her desk, Bitterblue lost her breath. The room was tilting, she was falling; she could not get the air she needed into her throat and lungs. Then Thiel was kneeling beside her, holding tight to her hands, instructing her to take one slow breath after another.

"Lorassim tea," he said firmly to Darby, who'd just climbed the stairs with a stack of correspondence, his footsteps pounding like the hammer blows that would bring her tower down.

"Lady Queen," Thiel said after Darby had gone. His distress was clear in his voice. "Something is wrong in recent days; I can tell that you're suffering. Has someone hurt you? Are you injured, or ill? I beg you to tell me what I can do to help you. Give me a task, Lady Queen, or tell me what to say."

"Did you ever give comfort to my mother?" she whispered. "I remember you were there sometimes, Thiel, but I can't remember much beyond that."

A moment passed. "When I was lucid," he said, his voice a deep well of sadness, "I tried to give comfort to your mother."

"Are you going to disappear from your eyes now?" she asked accusingly, glaring into those eyes.

"Lady Queen," he said, "it's no use if we both disappear. I'm still here with you. Please tell me what's going on, Lady Queen. Is it to do with that fellow who was wrongly tried? Have you become friends with him?"

Rood came into the office then, carrying a cup of tea, which he brought to her, kneeling as well. "Tell us what we can do, Lady Queen," he said to her, wrapping her hands around the cup with his own.

You can tell me what you saw, she responded mutely to the kindness in his eyes. *No more lying. Just tell me!*

Runnemood came in next. "What's all this?" he demanded at the sight of Thiel and Rood on their knees beside Bitterblue's chair.

"Just tell me," Bitterblue whispered.

"Tell you what?" snapped Runnemood.

"What you saw," said Bitterblue. "Stop torturing me and just tell me. I know you were healers. What did he do? Just tell me!"

Rood backed away from her and found a chair.

"Lady Queen," said Runnemood grimly, squaring his feet. "Do

not ask us to call those things to mind. It was years ago and we have made our peace."

"Peace!" Bitterblue cried. "You have not made your peace!"

"He cut them," Runnemood said through gritted teeth, "often until they were dying. Then he brought them to us to mend. He thought himself a medical genius. He thought he was turning Monsea into a land of medical marvels, but all he was doing was hurting people until they died. He was a madman. Are you happy? Is this information worth forcing us to remember? Worth risking our sanity and even our lives?"

Runnemood went to his brother, who was shaking and crying now. Runnemood helped Rood up, then practically carried him out the door. And then she was alone with Thiel, who had turned into a shell after all, still kneeling beside her, cold, stiff, and empty. It was her fault. They'd been talking of something real and she'd ruined it with questions she'd never meant to ask. "I'm sorry," she whispered to him. "Thiel. I'm sorry."

"Lady Queen," he said after a moment. "These are dangerous topics to speak aloud. I beg you to be more careful in what you say."

Two weeks passed and she did not go to see Saf. There was too much, with the embroidery, with her mountains of work, with Po ill. Also, she was ashamed.

"I've been having the most wonderful dreams," Po told her when she visited him in the infirmary. "But not the kind that are depressing to wake from when you realize they're not true. You know what I mean?"

He lay on sheets soaked with sweat, the covers thrown back, fanning himself with his own open shirt. As Madlen had instructed her to do, Bitterblue dipped a cloth in cold water, wiped his sticky face, and tried not to shiver, for the fire was kept low in this room. "Yes," she said, lying, because she didn't want to burden her sick cousin with the terrible dreams she'd been having, dreams of Ashen being shot in the back by Leck's arrow. "Tell me your dreams."

"I'm myself," Po said, "and I'm as myself, with all the same powers and limitations and secrets. But there's no guilt about my lies, no doubt, because I've made a choice, and it's the best choice available to me. When I wake, everything feels a bit lighter, you know?"

His fever lingered; seemed to improve; then flared up again worse than it had been before. Sometimes when she checked in on him, he shivered and thrashed and said the strangest things, things that made no sense whatsoever. "He's hallucinating," Madlen told her once when Po had grabbed Bitterblue's arm and cried out that the bridges were growing and the river was swimming with the dead.

"I wish his hallucinations could be as pleasant as his dreams," she whispered, touching Po's forehead, stroking his sweaty hair, trying to shush him. And she wished for Raffin and Bann, who were better at sickbeds than she. She wished for Katsa, who would surely lose her anger if she saw Po like this. But Katsa was in a tunnel somewhere, and Raffin and Bann were en route to Sunder.

"It was Randa's order," Po cried, bundled under blankets this time, violently shivering. "Randa sent Raffin to Sunder to marry Murgon's daughter. He will come back with a wife and babies and grandbabies."

"Raffin marry the Sunderan king's daughter?" Bitterblue exclaimed. "Not in a million years."

A *tsk* came from the table where Madlen was mixing one of the vile concoctions she liked to make Po gag down. "Let's ask him about it again when he's not raving, Lady Queen."

"When will that be, Madlen?"

Madlen added a sour-smelling paste to the bowl, mashed it in with the rest, and didn't answer.

HELDA, IN THE meantime, had employed Ornik the smith to make a replica crown. He did this so effectively that Bitterblue's heart surged with relief the first moment she saw it, thinking that the real crown had returned—until she realized that it lacked the solidness and the luster of the true crown, and that the jewels were painted glass.

"Oh," Bitterblue said. "Goodness, Ornik is good at his job. He must have seen the crown before."

"He hadn't, Lady Queen, but Fox has, of course, and Fox described it to him."

"And so we've pulled Fox into this fiasco?"

"She saw Saf, of course, Lady Queen, on the day of the theft, and went to finish polishing the crown again the day after. Remember? There was no way not to involve her. And she's useful as a spy. I'm using her to locate this Spook character who supposedly has the crown."

"And what have we learned?"

"Spook specializes in royal contraband, Lady Queen, all kinds of noble treasure. It's been his family's business for generations. Right now, he's keeping silent on the matter of the crown. It's said that no one but his subordinates know the location of this cave he lives in. Good for our own need for silence; bad for our need to locate him and figure out what the hills is going on."

"Saf will know what's going on," said Bitterblue grudgingly, watching as Helda covered the fake crown with a cloth. "What's the punishment for royal theft, Helda?"

Sighing shortly, Helda said, "Lady Queen, perhaps it has not occurred to you that stealing a monarch's crown is more than royal theft. The crown isn't just an ornament; it's the physical manifestation of your power. Stealing it is treason."

Treason?

Death was the punishment for treason. "That's ridiculous," Bitterblue hissed. "I would never let the High Court condemn Saf to death for stealing a crown."

"For treason, you mean, Lady Queen," said Helda. "And you know as well as I do that even your own rulings may be overturned by a unanimous vote from your judges."

Yes. It was another of Ror's funny provisions, this one to put a check on the monarch's absolute power. "I'll replace my judges," she said. "I'll make you a judge."

"A person Middluns-born cannot be a judge on the Monsean High Court, Lady Queen. I don't need to tell you that the requirements for such an appointment are particular and extreme."

"Find Spook," Bitterblue said. "Find him, Helda."

"We are doing the best we can, Lady Queen."

"Do more," she said. "And I'll go to Saf, soon, and—I don't know—beg. Perhaps he'll give it back when he understands the implications."

"Do you really think he hasn't worked it out, Lady Queen?" asked Helda soberly. "He's a professional thief. He's reckless, but he's not actually stupid. He may even be enjoying this bind he's put you in."

HE ENJOYS PUTTING me in a bind.

Why am I so afraid of going to see him?

In bed that same night, Bitterblue reached for paper and pen and began a letter to Giddon. It was a letter she had no intention of ever actually showing Giddon. It was only to straighten her thoughts, and it was only addressed to him because he was the person she told the truth to, and because whenever she imagined him listening and asking questions, his questions were less worried, less fraught than anyone else's.

Is it because you're in love with him? Giddon asked.

Oh, balls. How can I even begin to think about that, she wrote, *with all that's on my mind?*

It is a rather simple question, actually, he said crisply.

Well, I don't know, she wrote impatiently. *Does that mean I'm not? I liked kissing him an awful lot. I liked going out into the city with him and the way we trusted each other without trusting each other at all. I would like to be his friend again. I would like him to remember that we got along, and to realize that he knows my truths now.*

Giddon said, *You told me once that you sat on a roof with him, hiding from killers. And now you've told me about the kissing. Can't you imagine how much trouble a townsman could get into if he were caught involving the queen in such things?*

No trouble, if I forbade it, she wrote. *I would never allow him to be blamed for a thing he did in innocence, not knowing who I was. Frankly, I don't intend him to be blamed for stealing the crown either, and he is not innocent of that crime.*

Then, Giddon said, *isn't it possible that a person who thought you a commoner might feel betrayed to learn that you have so much power over his fate?*

Bitterblue didn't write anything for a while. Finally, the pen held tight and the letters small, as if she were whispering, she wrote: *I have been thinking about power a great deal lately. Po says that one of the privileges of wealth is that you don't need to think about it. I think it's the same with power. I feel powerless more often than I feel powerful. But I am powerful, aren't I? I have the power to hurt my advisers with words and my friends with lies.*

Those are your examples? said Giddon, with a small touch of amusement.

Why? she wrote. *What's wrong with those examples?*

Well, he said, *you risked the well-being of every citizen in your kingdom when you invited the Council to use your city as a base for the overthrow of the Estillan king. Then you sent King Ror a letter asking him for the support of the Lienid Navy in the case of war. You do recognize these things for what they are, don't you? They are power in the extreme!*

Do you mean you think I shouldn't have done it?

Well, perhaps you shouldn't have done it so lightly.

I did not do it lightly!

You did it so your friends would stay near! Giddon said. *And you have not seen war, Lady Queen. Could you have understood the decision you made? Did you truly comprehend its implications?*

Why are you telling me this now? You were at that meeting, she wrote. *You were practically in charge of that meeting! You could have objected!*

But this is a conversation you're having with yourself, Lady Queen, Giddon said. *I'm not actually here, am I? I'm not the one objecting.*

And Giddon faded away. Bitterblue was left with herself again, holding her strange letter to the fire, wound up in too many different kinds of confusion. Knowing that in the end, she needed Saf's help finding out who was targeting truthseekers, whether or not he could ever forgive her abuses of power.

Ashen had made bad choices because of Leck's fog. Bitterblue didn't have that excuse; her bad choices were all her own doing.

With that depressing thought in mind, Bitterblue went to the dressing room and pulled out her hood and trousers.

T ILDA ANSWERED HER knock. Seeing the queen on her doorstep, Tilda stood there surprised, but gentle-eyed. "Come in, Lady Queen," she said.

It was a reception Bitterblue hadn't been expecting, and one that stabbed her with shame. "I'm sorry, Tilda," she whispered.

"I accept your apology, Lady Queen," said Tilda simply. "We're heartened to realize that all this time, the queen has been on our side."

"You do realize that?" said Bitterblue.

Stepping inside, she found herself exposed in a pool of light. Bren was at the press, looking back at her levelly. Saf was perched on a table behind Bren, glaring, and Teddy stood in the doorway to the back room. "Oh, Teddy," she said, too pleased to check herself. "I'm so happy to see you standing on your own."

"Thank you, Lady Queen," he said with a small smile that made her know she was forgiven.

Tears choked her eyes. "You're too kind to me."

"I always trusted you, Lady Queen," said Teddy, "even before I knew who you were. You're a person of generosity and feeling. It warms my heart to know that such a person is our queen."

Sapphire snorted dramatically. Bitterblue forced herself to look at him. "I'm sorry," she said. "I imposed myself on your lives here and I lied. I'm sorry for tricking all of you."

"That's not much of an apology," said Saf, sliding down from his table, crossing his arms.

Antagonism was helpful. It gave her guilt something solid and sharp to throw itself against. Bitterblue set her chin and said to Saf, "I apologize for the things I did wrong, but I won't apologize for my apology. I'd like to talk with you alone."

"That's not going to happen."

Bitterblue shrugged. "Then I suppose everyone will get to hear my side of things. Where should we start? With your upcoming trial for treason, where I'll be called to testify that I saw you steal the crown?"

Sapphire walked right up to her. "I look forward to explaining why I was in your rooms in the first place," he said calmly. "It'll be fun to ruin your reputation. This is a boring conversation. Are we done?"

Bitterblue slapped him, as hard as she could. When he grabbed her wrists, she kicked him in the shin, then kicked him again, until finally, swearing, he let her go. "You're a bully," he spat out.

"You're a brat," she said, shoving at him, tears spilling onto her cheeks. "What good is it for both of us to be ruined? What utter, useless good? Treason, Saf? Why did you have to do something so blazingly *stupid*?"

"You played with me!" he said. "You humiliated me and you insulted my prince by compelling him to lie for me!"

"And so you committed a hanging crime?"

"I only took the rutting thing to spite you," he said. "That there are consequences that make you unhappy is just a bonus! I'm glad it's a hanging crime!"

The room had emptied around them; they were alone. Too close to his hard-breathing body, she pushed past him toward the press and clung to it, trying to think. There was something underneath the words he'd said that she needed to get straight.

"You understand that I'm unhappy," she said, "because you know that I'm frantic for your safety."

"Mmph," he said, close behind her. "Who cares?"

"You know that the nearer you get to danger, the more unhappy I'll be and the harder I'll work to protect you. Which is apparently a thing you find amusing," she added bitterly. "But your joy over this delightful situation presupposes how much I care about you."

"So?"

"So," she said, "that means that you know perfectly well that I care about you. You know it so well that you're getting pleasure out of hurting me with it. And since you already know it, there's nothing I need to convince you of and nothing I need to prove." Turning to face him, she said, "I'm sorry I lied. I'm sorry I humiliated you and I'm sorry I compelled your prince to lie for you. I did wrong and I won't make excuses. You can decide whether to forgive me or not. You can also decide whether to reverse this stupid thing you've done."

"It's too late to reverse it," Saf said. "Other people know."

"Get the crown back from this Spook person and give it to me. If I can show that I have it, no one's going to look me in the face and accuse me of lying when I go on to say I've always had it."

"I don't think I could get it back," Saf said after a moment's pause. "I'm told that Spook has sold it to her grandson. My agreement was with Spook as a caretaker, to hide it for me, but Spook broke that agreement when she sold it. I have no agreement with the grandson."

"It doesn't sound as if you had much of an agreement with Spook either," said Bitterblue, trying to navigate through all the surprising things he'd just said. Spook was a woman? "What are you talking about, she sold the crown to her grandson? What does that mean?"

"Spook has a grandkid, apparently, that she's bringing up in the business."

"The business of black-market thievery?" said Bitterblue scornfully.

"Spook is more of a manager and dealer than a thief. Other people do her thieving for her. So, she's sold the crown to the grandkid, probably for almost nothing, and now the kid gets to decide what to do. It's like a test, see. It'll make him a name."

"If he publicizes his possession of it, it'll also get him arrested and hanged."

"Oh, you won't find him. *I* don't even know who he is and I'm much closer to their world than you could ever be. He's called Gray, apparently."

"What will he do with it?"

"Whatever he likes," Saf said carelessly. "Maybe put it up for public auction? Hold it for ransom? Spook's family has a lot of expertise at exploiting the nobility, at no harm to themselves. If your detectives poke so hard that they manage to find Gray and put him on trial, a dozen of his grandmother's women and men will vouch for him."

"How, exactly? Maybe by incriminating someone else instead? *You,* for example?"

"I suppose so, now that you mention it."

Bitterblue took a deep, angry breath. At this moment, she hated his smirking face; she hated him for the enjoyment he was getting out of this. "Find out how much Gray wants for it."

"You would buy back your own crown?"

"Rather than see you hanged?" Bitterblue said. "This surprises you?"

"More like, disappoints me," he said. "It's not very interesting, is it? Throw money at the problem? Anyway, if it came to that, I wouldn't hang. I'd run. It's time I left anyway."

"Oh, fabulous," Bitterblue sputtered. "You'll leave. What a stupendous solution to a blazingly stupid problem you created for both of us. You're sick, you know that?" she said, turning away from him again. "And you're wasting my time with this. Time is the thing I have least of."

"How onerous for you to be so important," Sapphire said caustically. "Go home to your gold rooms and sit on a silk cushion while servants bring you every pleasure and Graced guards keep you safe."

"Right," Bitterblue said, touching the place on her forehead where the scrape from the attack outside the castle had only just healed. "Safe."

The door opened suddenly. Teddy stuck his head in. "Forgive me," he said sheepishly. "I felt the need to check that everything was all right."

"You don't trust me," said Saf to him, disgusted.

"Should I, when you're like this?" Teddy came a bit farther into the room and rested his eyes on Bitterblue. "I'll leave if I'm in the way," he said.

"We're not getting anywhere," Bitterblue responded wearily. "You're not in the way, and Teddy, you remind me that I'd like your help."

"What can I do for you, Lady Queen?"

"Could you tell me which lords and ladies in my kingdom stole the most for Leck's sake? Do you have that kind of information? It would give me a place to start as I try to find out who's behind the killing and framing of truthseekers."

"Ah," said Teddy, sounding pleased. "I could come up with a

few people who have reason to be ashamed of themselves. But it wouldn't be a complete list, Lady Queen. There are plenty of towns we haven't heard from. Would you like the list nonetheless?"

"Yes, please," said Bitterblue. *If I could leave with a list, then maybe this visit could be more than a heartbreaking waste of time.*

And so Teddy went to a desk to cobble together a list. Bitterblue stared at the table beside the press, not really seeing it, trying not to look at Saf. He stood too near her, glaring at the floor with his arms crossed, sullen and silent.

Then, gradually, the stacks of paper before her came into focus. It was printed material, but not Death's *Kissing Traditions* or Teddy's dictionary. As she began to understand what she was looking at, she said out loud, "This cannot possibly be what you've been hiding from me all this time. Teddy? Can it?" Taking one of the top sheets in her hand, she noted that the page beneath was identical.

"Hello," Saf said, reaching out, pushing against her, trying to take the paper from her.

"Oh, let her have it, Saf," Teddy said tiredly. "What does it matter now? We know she's not going to try to hurt us for printing it."

"Find out how much Gray wants for the crown, Saf. And get off me," Bitterblue said, giving him such a ferocious look that he actually stopped trying to grab at the paper and backed away, momentarily confused.

Bitterblue took a sample from each of the piles on the table. Rolling them up in one hand, she went to Teddy and accepted the short list of names he proffered. Then she left the shop.

OUTSIDE, SHE STOPPED under a light. Unrolling the papers, she leafed through them, studying each carefully. They all had the same title, "Reading and Writing Lesson," and each lesson was numbered. The Number Ones contained, in large type, the letters of the alphabet and the numerals zero through ten. The Number Twos contained a scattering of simple words, such as *cat, pan, cart, rat*. The words increased in complexity, and more numerals were introduced, as the lesson numbers rose. At the bottom corner of each page was printed a tiny geographic identifier: Flower District, East City. Monster Bridge, East City. Winter Park, Fish Dockyards. Castle's Shadow, West City.

Reading lessons? *So much secrecy over reading lesson—*

Something whacked Bitterblue so hard in the back of her shoulder that it spun her around. Someone tackled her and papers went flying. Falling, crashing awkwardly against the rise of the gutter, her arm broke beneath her and she screamed in pain.

25

THE THOUGHTS CAME clearly and with an astonishing calm. Bitterblue was being choked by a woman with iron strength who sat on her and pinned her to the ground. There were others too, other small battles exploding around them, cries and grunts, flashes of steel. *I do not consent to die,* thought Bitterblue, desperate for air, but she couldn't reach the woman's eyes or throat and she couldn't reach the knives in her boots, and she tried to find the one in the sleeve of her broken arm but the pain undid her. Suddenly she understood what that burning pressure was in the back of her shoulder: a knife. If only she could reach it with her good hand—she tried, scrabbled, found the hilt and pulled. The knife came away with a blast of pain that was almost unendurable but she slashed wherever she could at her attacker. Her head was going to burst, but she kept slashing. Her vision went black. She lost consciousness.

SHE WOKE TO pain. When she tried to cry out, there was more pain, for her throat was ragged.

"Yes, that woke her," a deep male voice said. "I'm sorry for it, but it has to be done with broken bones. It will make for less pain later."

"What'll we do with all these bodies?" someone else whispered, a female voice.

"Help me get them inside and my friends and I will deal with them," said a third voice that made Bitterblue want to cry out again, for it was Saf.

"Some of the Lienid Guard will stay and help you," said the original male voice firmly. "I'm taking the queen home."

"Do you know who they are?" asked Saf. "Should the bodies go with you in case castle people can identify them?"

"Those aren't my instructions," said the male voice.

Recognizing that voice now, Bitterblue croaked out a name. "Holt."

"Yes, Lady Queen," said her Graceling guard, leaning over her, coming into view. "How are you, Lady Queen?"

"I don't consent to die," she whispered.

"You're far from dead, Lady Queen," Holt said. "Can you manage some water?"

Holt passed a flask to someone above Bitterblue. Only then did Bitterblue realize that her head was cradled in a person's lap. Moving her eyes up to look into the face of that person, for an instant, she saw a girl. Then the girl transformed into a marble statue of a girl, and Bitterblue was rocked with dizziness.

"Hava," said Holt sharply. "Stop that. You'll give the queen a headache."

"I think someone else should take over," said the statue hastily. Then she was a girl again and extricating herself from Bitterblue, thunking the queen's head on the ground. As Bitterblue gasped at this new pain, there was the sound of feet scurrying away.

Holt came quickly to Bitterblue's aid, supporting her head and bringing the flask to her lips. "I apologize for the behavior of my niece, Lady Queen," he said. "She assisted you quite bravely until you noticed her."

Swallowing water was like swallowing fire. "Holt," whispered Bitterblue. "What happened?"

"A team of thugs was waiting outside the shop to kill you, Lady Queen," said Holt. "Hava and I were here at Prince Po's request. We did what we could. That friend of yours heard the noise and came out to help. But we were strapped, Lady Queen, if I may say so, until half a dozen of your Lienid Door Guard came running onto the scene."

"My Lienid Door Guard?" said Bitterblue in bewilderment, registering now the sound of boots on pavement, grunts as men lifted bodies. "How did they know to be here?"

Holt put the flask away somewhere. Then, carefully, he lifted her in both arms. Being carried by him was like gliding. The parts that hurt did so floatingly, without a single jolt. "As I understand it, Lady Queen," he said, "Thiel came running to your rooms tonight to check on you. When he found you gone, he exhorted Helda to send a contingent of your Lienid Door Guard after you."

"Thiel?" said Bitterblue. "Thiel knew I was in danger?"

"Hey," said Saf's voice, suddenly near. "I think that's her own blood—your sleeve is turning black with it, man." A hand explored her back, her shoulder, and Bitterblue cried out. "She's been stabbed," said Saf as the world went dark.

SHE WOKE AGAIN to the murmuring voices of Helda and Madlen. All of her parts felt stuffed with wool, especially her head. A cast of some kind immobilized her left wrist and forearm, and the back of her left shoulder was on fire. Blinking her eyes, she saw the red and gold stars of her own bedroom ceiling. Through the window, light was just beginning to build. It was a new day.

It seemed safe now, with Madlen and Helda near, to believe that she really wasn't going to die. The moment it seemed safe, it also seemed impossible that she should have survived. A tear made a single track into her hair, and then that was that, for crying meant gasping and deep breaths, and it only took one deep breath to remember how much breathing hurt.

She whispered, "How did Thiel know?"

The murmuring voices stopped. Both Helda and Madlen came and leaned over her, Helda's face tight with tension and relief, her hand reaching down to stroke the hair at Bitterblue's temples. "It's been quite a night, both in and out of the castle, Lady Queen," she said quietly. "What a fright Madlen had when Holt came running into the infirmary with you, and I didn't fare much better when Madlen brought you to me."

"But how did Thiel know?" she whispered.

"He didn't say, Lady Queen," said Helda. "He came here frantic, looking like he'd been fighting with a bear, and told me that if I knew where you were and what was good for me, I'd send your Lienid Guard to you."

"Where is he now?" Bitterblue whispered.

"I've no idea, Lady Queen."

"Send someone to bring him to me," said Bitterblue. "Is everyone else all right?"

"Prince Po had a terrible night, Lady Queen," said Madlen. "Agitated and inconsolable. I had to drug him when Holt came in with you, for he was wild. He put up a fight; Holt had to hold him down for me."

"Oh, poor Po," said Bitterblue. "Is he going to be all right, Madlen?"

"He's in the same shape you're in, Lady Queen, which is to say that I firmly believe he'd be on the mend if he would only consent to rest. Here, Lady Queen," she said, pressing a folded note into

Bitterblue's good hand. "Once we'd gotten the medicine into him and he knew he was a lost cause, he went to great effort to dictate this to me. He made me promise to give it to you."

Bitterblue opened the note one-handed, trying to remember the key she was using with Po these days. Poppyseed cake? Yes. With that key, Po's ciphered message in Madlen's loopy hand showed itself to say, more or less: *Runnemood went to prisons eleven o'clock stabbed nine sleeping prisoners in one room then set room on fire. In and out through secret passage. I wasn't hallucinating. One was Saf's lying witness. One was that mad murderer you asked Madlen to examine. Later, Runnemood and Thiel entered another passage that led down and under east wall. I lost them.*

WHEN HER LIENID Guard could not find Runnemood, Bitterblue called in the Monsean Guard. They couldn't find him either. He was nowhere to be found in the castle, nor were they having any luck in the city.

"He's run for it," said Bitterblue in frustration. "Where is his family? Have you talked to Rood? Runnemood's supposed to have a thousand friends in the city. Find out who they are, Captain, and find him!"

"Yes, Lady Queen," said Captain Smit, standing before her desk, looking appropriately stern but also befuddled. "And you have definite reason to believe that Runnemood was behind the attack on your person, Lady Queen?"

"He is certainly behind something," said Bitterblue. "Where's Thiel? Where is everybody? Send someone up, will you?"

The person the captain sent up was, in fact, Thiel. His hair was worried into a vertical arrangement and his color was gray. When he saw her arm and the purple marks on her throat, he began to blink with bright, wet eyes. "You should be in bed, Lady Queen," he said hoarsely.

"I had to get out of it," said Bitterblue flatly, "to deal with the question of why Runnemood murdered nine of my prisoners, then snuck into a passage under the east wall with you."

Thiel collapsed, shaking, into a chair. "Runnemood murdered nine prisoners?" he said. "Lady Queen, how do you know all this?"

"We're not discussing what I know, Thiel. We're discussing what I don't. Why did you go into a secret passage with Runnemood last night, how did you know to send my Lienid Guard to my rescue, and what does one have to do with the other?"

"It's because he told me, Lady Queen," said Thiel, sitting hopeless and confused in his chair. "I came upon him very late. He didn't seem himself, Lady Queen. He was wild-eyed, smiling too much, making me nervous. I followed him into that passage, hoping that if I stayed with him, I could learn what was wrong. When I pressed him, he told me he'd done something brilliant, but of course I didn't know about the prisoners. Then he told me you'd gone out into the city and he'd sent a team to kill you."

"I see," said Bitterblue. "Just like that, he told you?"

"He was nothing like himself, Lady Queen," Thiel said again, grasping his hair. "He seemed to have some crazy idea that I'd be pleased to hear what he was saying. Truly, I believe he'd gone mad."

"And were you surprised?"

"Well, of course, Lady Queen. I was flabbergasted! I left him and ran back, straight to your rooms, hoping he'd lied and I'd find you safely there!"

"Where is Runnemood, Thiel?" said Bitterblue. "What's going on?"

"I don't know where he is, Lady Queen," said Thiel in amazement.

"I don't even know where that passage leads. Why do I feel you don't believe me?"

Bitterblue shot up from her seat, unable to contain her heartache. "Because Runnemood did not suddenly go mad," she said, "and you know it. He's the most sane of you all. And you've been telling me not to speak out loud about Leck's time, you've been telling me to bring my worries about the past to you before anyone else. You've been at odds with him, and giving me subtle warnings. Haven't you? What's your reason for those things if you didn't know he had a vendetta against truthseekers?"

Thiel was beginning to recede from her. She recognized the signs. He was pulling into himself, drawing his arms close, and he hadn't risen when she'd done so. "Now I don't know what you're talking about, Lady Queen," he whispered. "You're confusing me."

There was a knock at that moment. Fox poked her red head into the room. "Lady Queen," she said, "forgive me."

"What is it?" Bitterblue cried in vexation.

"The scarf Helda promised, Lady Queen, to hide your bruises," said Fox.

Bitterblue waved her inside impatiently, then gestured her away. And then she stared in wonderment at the scarf Fox had left on her desk. Memories flashed through her, for this scarf had belonged to Ashen. It was soft gray with flecks of silver and she hadn't thought of it once, not once in eight years; but now she remembered Ashen counting Bitterblue's fingers and kissing them. She remembered Ashen laughing—laughing! Bitterblue had said something funny and made Ashen laugh.

Lifting the scarf with utter gentleness, as if a breath could blow it apart, Bitterblue wrapped it twice around her neck, then sat down. Patted it, smoothed it.

She looked up at Thiel and found him gawking at her with stricken eyes.

"That was your mother's scarf, Lady Queen," he said. Then tears began to run down his face. Something within his eyes seemed to collapse, but it was a living thing in there—not emptiness, but life struggling with pain. "Forgive me, Lady Queen," he said, crying harder now. "I have known since that trial two weeks ago that Runnemood was involved in something terrible. He'd framed that young Lienid-Monsean, you see. I walked in on his anger after it failed, and forced the truth from him. I've been trying to deal with it myself. He was my friend for fifty years. I thought that if I could try to understand why he would do such a thing, then I could bring him to his senses."

"But, you hid it from me?" cried Bitterblue. "You knew what he'd done, and you hid it?"

"I have always wanted your path to be easy, Lady Queen," he said hopelessly, dashing his tears away. "I've wanted to shield you from any more pain."

THERE WASN'T A great deal more that Thiel could tell her.

"But why did he do it, Thiel? What was he trying to achieve? Was he working for someone? Was he, perhaps, working with Danzhol?"

"I don't know, Lady Queen. I couldn't get him to tell me any of that. I could make nothing logical of it at all."

"I can see some logic," she said grimly. "He had a logical understanding of the need to go into the prisons and stab the innocent, and all those he'd paid to lie or kill. Especially after I'd ordered that everyone be retried. Then he set the place on fire to hide what he'd done. He was cleaning up after himself, wasn't he? I wonder, was he responsible for the attack on me that left that scrape on my head? And did he know who I was?"

"Lady Queen," said Thiel, alarmed. "You're speaking of a great many things I know nothing about and am distressed to hear of. You never told us you were attacked before this. And Runnemood never spoke of paying people to kill other people."

"Until tonight," Bitterblue said, "when he told you he'd hired people to kill me."

"Until tonight," Thiel whispered. "He told me that you'd made friends with the wrong sorts of people, Lady Queen. Do not ask me to explain it beyond that, because all I can think is that he was mad."

"Madness is such a convenient explanation," Bitterblue said sarcastically, rising to her feet again. "Where is he, Thiel?"

"Truly, I don't know, Lady Queen," Thiel said, beginning to rise. "I didn't see him again after I left him in the passage."

"Sit down," Bitterblue snapped, wanting to be taller than him, wanting to be able to look down on him. He sat abruptly. "Why did you send no one after him? You let him go!"

"I was thinking of you, Lady Queen," he cried. "Not him!"

"You let him go!" she said again in frustration.

"I'll find out where he is, Lady Queen. I'll find out about all these things you've said, all these crimes you think he's been committing."

"No," she said. "Someone else will find out for me. You're no longer in my employ, Thiel."

"What?" he exclaimed. "Lady Queen, please. You can't!"

"Can't I? Can't I really? Do you understand what you've done? How can I trust you if you shield me from the atrocities of my own advisers? I'm trying to be a queen here, Thiel. A queen, not a child to be protected from the truth!" Her voice, rough and broken, forced its way out of her injured throat. He'd hurt her with this thing, more than she'd thought it possible for a stiff, emotionless old man to do. "You lied to me," she said. "You led me to believe that I could count on you to help me be a righteous queen."

"You are a righteous queen, Lady Queen," he said. "Your mother would be—"

"Don't you dare," she hissed, talking over him. "Don't you dare use the memory of my mother to call on my mercy."

There was a moment of silence. He hung his head, seeming to understand. "You must consider, Lady Queen," he whispered, "that we were students together. He was my friend long before Leck. We suffered a great deal together. You must also consider that you were ten years old. Then before I knew it you were a woman of eighteen, going around on your own, discovering perilous truths, and, apparently, running through the streets at night. You must allow me time to adjust."

"I'm going to allow you plenty of time," she said. "Stay away until you've decided to make a habit of the truth."

"I decide it now, Lady Queen," he said, blinking back his shocked tears. "I will not lie to you again. I swear it."

"I'm afraid I don't believe you."

"Lady Queen," he said, "I beg you. Now that you're injured, you'll have even greater need of help."

"Then I shall only wish to be surrounded by those who are helpful," she said to the man who kept everything running. "Get out," she said. "Go to your rooms and think things through. When you suddenly remember where Runnemood went, send us a note."

He pushed himself to his feet, not looking at her. Quietly, he left the room.

"While I have this horrible cast on my arm," she said that night to Helda, "I need to be able to dress and undress without this rigmarole."

"Yes," Helda said, breaking the seam of Bitterblue's sleeve and easing the garment over the cast. She'd had to sew Bitterblue into her dress that morning. "I've a few ideas, Lady Queen, to do with open sleeves and buttons. Sit down, my dear. Don't even move; I'll untie this scarf and deal with all these underthings. I'll put you into your shift."

"No," Bitterblue said. "No shift."

"Far be it from me, Lady Queen, to stop you if you wish to sleep with nothing on, but you have a small fever. I do believe you'll be more comfortable with an extra layer of warmth."

She wasn't going to fight with Helda about the shift, because she didn't want Helda to suspect her reason for not wanting it. But, oh, how much she ached, and how wearying to add removing the rutting shift to the list of impossible tasks she was going to have to complete in order to sneak out tonight. When Helda began to pull her hairpins out and unravel her hair, Bitterblue stopped herself again from arguing, and said, "Would you braid it in one long braid for me, please, Helda?"

Finally, Helda was gone, the lamps were extinguished, and Bitterblue lay on her right side in bed, throbbing so mightily that she wondered if it was possible for one small queen in one big bed to start an earthquake.

Well. No point in delaying.

Sometime later, with gasping breath and a pounding head, Bitterblue left her rooms and began the long trek through corridors and down stairways. She wouldn't think about her one-armedness, or the lack of knives in her sleeves. There were a great many things she wouldn't think about tonight; she would trust to luck and hope she encountered no one.

Then, in the great courtyard, a person stepped out of the shadows and stood in her path. He let off gleams of light, softly visible in the torches, as he always did.

"Please don't make me stop you," Po said. It wasn't a joke or a warning. It was a true plea. "I will if I have to, but it'll only make both of us more sick."

"Oh, Po," she said, then went to him and hugged him with her one good arm.

He put his arm around her uninjured side, held her tight, and sighed, slowly, into her hair, balancing himself against her. When she rested her ear against his chest, she could hear his flying heartbeat. Slowly, it calmed. He said, "Are you determined to go out?"

"I want to tell Saf and Teddy about Runnemood," she said. "I want to ask if anything's changed with the crown, and I need to tell Saf again that I'm sorry."

"Will you wait until tomorrow, and let me send someone to bring them to you?"

It was bliss, the very idea of being allowed to turn around and go back to her bed. "Will you do it early?"

"Yes. Will you sleep, so that when they come, it won't exhaust you to talk to them?"

"Yes," she said. "All right."

"All right," he said, sighing again above her. "When Madlen stepped out for a moment today, Beetle, I followed the tunnel under the east wall."

"What? Po, you'll never get healthy!"

Po snorted. "Yes, we should all take your advice on such matters. It starts at a door behind a hanging, in an east corridor on the ground floor. It lets out into a teeny, dark alleyway in the east city, near the base of Winged Bridge."

"Do you think he escaped into the east city, then?"

"I suppose so," Po said. "I'm sorry my range doesn't extend that far. And I'm sorry I never took time to talk to him and pick up that something was wrong. I haven't been much use to you since I got here."

"Po. You've been ill, and before that, you were busy. We'll find him, and then you can talk to him."

He didn't respond, just rested his head on her hair.

She asked, once, whispering, "Have you heard anything from Katsa?"

He shook his head no.

"Are you ready for her to come back?"

"I'm not ready for anything," he said. "But that doesn't mean I don't want things to happen."

"What's that supposed to mean?"

"I want her to come back. Is that a good enough answer?"

Yes.

"To bed?" he said.

Yes, all right.

BEFORE FALLING ASLEEP, she read a fragment of embroidery.

Thiel reaches his limit every day yet goes on. Perhaps only because I beg him. Most would rather forget and obey unthinking than face truth of mad world Leck tries to create.

Tries and, I think, sometimes fails. He destroyed sculptures in his rooms today. Why? Also took his favorite sculptor Bellamew away. We'll never see her again. Success at destruction. But failure at something, for he cannot be satisfied. Fits of temper.

He's too interested in Bitterblue. I must get her away. That's why I beg Thiel to hold on.

26

"I'M SURPRISED TO see you," Bitterblue said the next morning to Rood as she entered her tower office. He was quiet and grim in the absence of his brother, but not meek, not shaking. Clearly not in the throes of a nervous episode.

"I've had a bad twenty-four hours, Lady Queen," he said quietly. "I won't pretend otherwise. But Thiel came to me last night and impressed upon me how much I'm needed right now."

When Rood suffered, his suffering was present and material; he didn't hide behind emptiness. It was a frankness that made Bitterblue want to trust him. "How much of this did you know?" she ventured.

"I haven't been my brother's confidant for some years, Lady Queen," he said. "Frankly, it's best that it was Thiel he encountered in the halls that night. He might have walked right past me and never said a word, and it was his speaking that saved your life."

"Has the Monsean Guard questioned you about where he might have gone, Rood?"

"Indeed, Lady Queen," he said. "I fear I was useless to them. I, my wife, my sons, and my grandchildren are his only living family, Lady Queen, and the castle is the only home we've ever known. He and I grew up here, you know, Lady Queen. Our parents were royal healers."

"I see." This man who tiptoed around cringing at everything had a wife, sons, and grandchildren? Were they joys for him? Did he eat with them every night and wake up with them in the morning, and did they comfort him when he was ill? Runnemood seemed so cold and aloof in contrast. Bitterblue couldn't imagine having a sibling and walking past that person blindly in the halls.

"Do you have family, Darby?" she asked her yellow-green-eyed adviser the next time he came rattling up the stairs.

"I had family once," he responded, wrinkling his nose in distaste.

"You . . ." Bitterblue hesitated. "You weren't fond of them, Darby?"

"It's more that I haven't thought of them in some time, Lady Queen."

She was tempted to ask Darby what he did think of, ever, while he was running around like a manic apparatus designed for dispensing paperwork. "I confess I'm surprised to see you in the offices today too, Darby."

Darby looked into her eyes and held them, which startled her, because she couldn't remember him ever having done that before. She saw then how dreadful he looked, his eyes bloodshot and too wide, as if he were forcing them open. A tremor in the muscles of his face that she hadn't noticed before. "Thiel threatened me, Lady Queen," he said. Then he handed her one paper and one folded note, swept up her outgoing pile, and flipped through it with an expression as if he'd like to punish any piece of paper in the stack that was not in perfect order. Bitterblue imagined him poking holes in the papers with a letter opener, then holding them too close to the fire while they screamed.

"You are an odd bird, Darby," she said aloud.

"Hmph," Darby said, then left her alone. Being in her tower office without Thiel gave her a strange sense of suspension, as if she were waiting for the workday to begin. For Thiel to walk back in from whatever errand he was on and keep her company. How furious she was with him for doing something that had forced her to send him away.

The piece of paper Darby had brought listed the results of Runnemood's latest literacy survey. In both castle and city, the statistics hovered around eighty percent. Of course, there was no earthly reason to believe that they were accurate.

The note, written in graphite, was in Po's large, careful hand. Briefly, it told her that Teddy and Saf had been summoned and would meet her in her library alcove at noon.

She went to an east-facing window, worried, suddenly, about how Teddy was going to manage the trip. Leaning her forehead against the glass, she breathed through pain and dizziness. The sky was the color of steel, a late-autumn sky, though it was only October. The bridges stood like mirages, gorgeously grand as they reached across the river. Squinting, she understood what was happening with the air that seemed to change color and move. Snowflakes. Not a storm, just a spitting, the first of the season.

Later, when she left for the library, she stopped in the lower offices to look out over all the clerks who worked here every day. She supposed they numbered thirty-five or forty at any time, depending on . . . well, she didn't really know what it depended on. Where did her clerks go when they weren't here? Did they march around the castle checking on . . . things? A castle was chock-full of *things* to check on, wasn't it?

Bitterblue made a mental note to ask Madlen whether the medications she was taking for pain were dulling her intellect or whether she actually was stupid. A youngish clerk named Froggatt, perhaps thirty years old with bouncy dark hair, stood bent over a table nearby. He straightened himself and asked her if she needed anything.

"No, thank you, Froggatt," she said.

"We're all extremely relieved that you survived the attack, Lady Queen," said Froggatt.

Surprised, she looked into his face, then studied the other faces in the room. They'd all stood, of course, when she'd walked in, and now stared back at her, waiting for her to go, so that they could get back to work. Were they relieved? Really? She knew their names, but nothing about their lives, their personalities, or their histories, other than that they had all worked in her father's administration, for varying lengths of time, depending on their ages. If one of them disappeared and no one told her, she might never notice. If told, how much would she feel?

And it wasn't relief she saw in their faces. It was a blankness, as if they didn't see her, as if their lives existed only inside the paperwork each of them was waiting to return to.

No one was in her library alcove except for the woman in the hanging and the young, castle-turning version of herself.

It seemed ironic, somehow, to stand before the sculpture in the state Bitterblue was in now. The sculpture girl's arm was turning into a rock tower with soldiers, strengthening itself, becoming its own protection. Bitterblue's real-life arm was affixed to her side with a sling. *Like a reflection in a depressing, distorted mirror,* she thought.

She heard steps. Then Holt appeared through the bookshelves, one hand clamped on Teddy's arm and the other on Saf's. Teddy kept turning in circles and, whenever he reached the end of his tether, spinning back again, eyes big as saucers. "*The Linguistic Geography of Estill, East and Far East!*" he exclaimed, reaching to the shelves for that title, then grunting as Holt tugged him on.

"Easy with the manhandling, Holt," Bitterblue said, a little alarmed. "Teddy doesn't deserve it. And I expect Saf gets too much pleasure out of it," she added, taking in Saf's righteous indignation as he tried to shake Holt off. Saf had fresh bruises. They gave him the look of a hooligan.

"I'll be within calling distance, Lady Queen, should you need me," Holt said. With one last, silver-gray glare at Saf, he stalked away.

"Did you get here all right, Teddy?" she asked. "You didn't walk?"

"No, Lady Queen," Teddy said. "We were picked up in a lovely carriage. And you, Lady Queen? You're all right?"

"Yes, of course," Bitterblue said, moving to the table, pulling out a chair for him one-handed. "Sit down."

Teddy sat carefully, then touched the leather of the manuscript on the table before him. His eyes widened as he read the label. Then filled with wonder as he began to read more labels.

"You may take as many of them as you like, Teddy," Bitterblue said. "I hoped to hire you to print them. If you have friends with presses, I'd like to hire them too."

"Thank you, Lady Queen," Teddy whispered. "I accept gladly."

Bitterblue dared a glance at Saf, who stood with his hands in his pockets, carefully looking bored. "I understand that I owe you my gratitude," she said to him.

"I like a fight," he said shortly. "Are we here for a reason?"

"I have news to tell you about my adviser Runnemood."

"We know it," said Saf.

"How?"

"When the Monsean Guard, the Queen's Guard, *and* the Lienid Door Guard are scouring the city for a queen's man who tried to have her killed, people tend to hear about it," said Saf coldly.

"You always know more than I expect."

"Don't condescend," Saf snapped.

"I would very much like if we could talk," she said tightly, "rather than fight. Because you tend to know so much, I wonder what else you might be able to tell me about Runnemood. Namely, how much crime he's responsible for, why on earth he's doing it, and where he's gone. I've learned that he's the one who arranged to have you framed, Saf. What else can you tell me? Was he behind your stabbing, Teddy?"

"I've no idea, Lady Queen," said Teddy. "About that or about all the rest of the killing. It is a bit difficult to believe that one man could be behind it all, isn't it? We're talking about dozens of deaths in the last few years, and when I say that, I mean all kinds of victims. Not just thieves or other criminals like us; people whose greatest crime is teaching others to read."

"Teaching others to read," said Bitterblue desolately. "Truly? Then you *were* hiding those reading lessons from me. It's dangerous for you to print them, I suppose? But I don't understand. Aren't people taught to read in the schools?"

"Oh, Lady Queen," said Teddy, "the city schools, with few exceptions, are in a shambles. The court-appointed teachers aren't qualified to teach. The children who can read are taught at home, or by people like me, or Bren or Tilda. History is also neglected—no one is taught Monsea's recent history."

Bitterblue fought down a rising fury. "As usual, I had no idea," she said. "And schooling in the city does fall under Runnemood's jurisdiction. But what can it mean? It almost seems like Runnemood took the policy of forward-thinkingness and ran completely amok with it. Why? What do we know of him? Who could have influenced him?"

Teddy reached into a pocket. "That reminds me, Lady Queen. I made you a list again, in case you lost yours when you were attacked."

"A list?"

"Of lords and ladies who stole most grievously for Leck's sake, Lady Queen. Remember?"

"Oh, yes," said Bitterblue. "Of course. Thank you. And Teddy, anything you can tell me to keep me appraised of the situation in the city will help me, do you understand? I can't see it from my tower," she said. "The truth of the lives of my people is never in any of the papers that cross my desk. Will you help me?"

"Of course, Lady Queen."

"And the crown?" she asked, resting her eyes again on Saf's hard face.

He shrugged. "I can't find Gray."

"Are you looking?"

"Yes, I'm looking," he said peevishly. "It's not my biggest worry at the moment."

"What worry could be greater?" she snapped at him.

"Oh, I don't know," he said, "perhaps your insane adviser who tried to kill me once and is now loose in the east city somewhere?"

"Find Gray," Bitterblue ordered.

"Of course, Your Royal Majestic Highness."

"Saf," said Teddy quietly. "Think about whether you're being fair when you continue to punish our Sparks."

Saf turned and marched to the hanging, where he glared at the strange-haired lady with his arms crossed. And it took Bitterblue a moment to catch her breath, for she hadn't dreamed she'd ever be allowed to hear that name again.

After a moment, she said, "Will you take a few of the books, then, Teddy?"

"We'll take them all," Teddy said, "every one, Lady Queen. But perhaps only two or three at a time, for Saf is right. I don't want to attract the wrong kinds of attention. I've had enough of fire."

After they'd gone, Bitterblue sat for a few moments with Death's rewritten manuscripts, trying to decide which one to start next. When Death stumped along and waved a reread at her, she said, "What is it about?"

"The artistic process, Lady Queen," he said.

"Why did my father want me to read about the artistic process?"

"How should I know, Lady Queen? He was obsessed with art and his artists. Perhaps he wanted you to be too."

"Obsessed?" she said. "Really?"

"Lady Queen," said Death, "do you walk around the castle with your eyes closed?"

Bitterblue grasped her temples and counted to ten. "Death," she said, "what would you say to my giving a few of these rewrites to a friend who has a printing press?"

Death blinked. "Lady Queen," he said, "these manuscripts, like everything else in this library, are yours with which to do whatever you like." He was silent for a moment. "I can only hope that you'll find yourself wishing to give *all* of them to this friend."

Bitterblue peered at him. "I would like to keep the transfer secret," she said, "for my friend's sake, at least until Runnemood is found and all this mystery is cleared up. You'll keep the secret, won't you, Death?"

"Of course I will, Lady Queen," said Death, clearly insulted by the question. He dumped the book about the artistic process onto the table and retreated in a huff.

* * * * *

"I'm worried about Teddy and Saf," Bitterblue said to Helda later. "Would it be unreasonable to ask my Lienid Door Guard to spare a few men to keep an eye out for them?"

"Of course not, Lady Queen," said Helda. "They'd do anything you ask."

"I know they'll do what I order. That doesn't make my order reasonable."

"I meant they'll do it out of loyalty, of course, Lady Queen," Helda chided her, "not obligation. They worry about you and your worries. You realize that they're the reason I've always known about your sneaking out, don't you? They're the ones who always told me."

Bitterblue absorbed this with some embarrassment. "They weren't supposed to have recognized me."

"They've been guarding you for eight years, Lady Queen," said Helda. "Do you really think they haven't learned your stance, your walk, your voice?"

I've walked past them countless times, Bitterblue thought, *thinking of them as nothing more than bodies standing beside a door. Liking their presence because they look and sound like my mother.* "When will I truly wake up?"

"Lady Queen?"

"How much more is there that I'm not seeing, Helda?"

Bitterblue was in Helda's rooms because she wanted to take a look at all of the scarves Helda kept producing from the back of her wardrobe to hide Bitterblue's bruises. "I don't understand," Bitterblue went on as Helda pushed the doors open further, revealing shelves full of fabrics that slung little arrows of memory into Bitterblue's heart. "I didn't know you had them. Why do you have them?"

"When I came to serve you, Lady Queen," said Helda, pulling

scarves out and handing them to Bitterblue to touch, to wonder at, "I found that the servants assigned to the task had done rather an over-zealous cleaning of your mother's cabinets. King Ror had saved a few things he'd recognized as Lienid, like the scarves, and anything very valuable, Lady Queen. But the rest, her gowns, her coats, her shoes, were all gone. I took what was left. I put the jewelry in your chest, as you know, and decided to keep the scarves for you until you were older. I'm sorry it was the need to hide the marks of an attack that brought them to mind again, Lady Queen," she added.

"But that's how memory works," Bitterblue said quietly. "Things disappear without your permission, then come back again without your permission." And sometimes they came back incomplete and warped.

There was an aspect of memory that Bitterblue had been trying to come to terms with lately, one so hurtful that she had not managed yet to face it full on. Her memories of Ashen were a series of snippets. Many of them were moments that had transpired in Leck's presence, which meant that Bitterblue had not even been in her right mind. When they'd been without Leck, they'd spent much of that time fighting Leck's brain fog away. Leck hadn't just stolen Ashen from Bitterblue by killing her. He'd stolen her before that, as well. Bitterblue could not imagine the person Ashen would be today, were she alive. It was not fair that she should find herself doubting, at times, how well she'd ever known her mother.

Even Helda's rooms, the simple, small bedroom in green and the bathing room in turquoise, disconcerted Bitterblue, for they had been her own bedroom and bathing room while Ashen was alive. Bitterblue's current bedroom had been Ashen's. Ashen had bathed her in what was now Helda's turquoise tub, locking the door against Leck, talking with her about all kinds of things. Ror City, where she'd lived in the king's castle, the most massive building in the world, its domes and turrets high in the sky above the Lienid Sea. Ashen's father, her brothers and sisters, nieces and nephews. Her oldest brother, Ror, the king. The people she missed who'd never met Bitterblue but would someday. Her rings, flashing in the water.

All of that was real, thought Bitterblue stubbornly.

She remembered a rough spot on one of the tiles of the tub that had scraped her arm from time to time. She remembered pointing it out to Ashen. Marching now to the tub, she was able to find the sharp little spot immediately. "There," she said, fingering it with a furious sort of triumph.

It was the minutes spent in Helda's room, remembering the feeling of a different time, that caused Bitterblue to become curious about another missing piece, and wonder if it might answer any of her questions. She wanted, finally, to see the rooms that had been Leck's.

THE HORSE IN the sitting room hanging that covered Leck's door had sad green eyes that stared into Bitterblue's. Its forelock hung into those eyes, a more violet blue than the dark, deep blue of its fur, making her think of Saf. Helda helped her push the hanging aside.

The investigation of the door behind did not take long. It was solid, immovable wood, tight in its frame, and it seemed to be locked. There was a keyhole, and Bitterblue remembered Leck using a key. "Who do we know who can pick locks?" she asked. "I've never seen Saf do it, but I wouldn't put it past him. Or, I wonder if Po could find us the key?"

"Lady Queen," said a voice behind them, making Bitterblue jump. She turned to find Fox in the doorway.

"I didn't hear the doors open," said Bitterblue.

"Forgive me, Lady Queen," said Fox, stepping into the room. "I didn't mean to take you by surprise. If it's any use to you, Lady Queen, I have lock picks that I've been learning how to use. I thought it might be a practical skill for a spy," she said, a bit defensively, when Helda gazed at her with eyebrows raised. "It was Ornik's idea."

"You seem to be developing a friendship with the handsome young smith," said Helda evenly. "Just remember that while he is a Council ally, Fox, and though he helped us with the matter of the crown, he is not a spy. He has no right to your information."

"Of course not, Helda," said Fox, sounding mildly offended.

"Well," Bitterblue said. "Do you have the lock picks with you?"

Fox produced from her pocket a cord on which hung an assortment of files, picks, and hooks, tied together so they wouldn't jingle. When she pulled away the tie, Bitterblue saw that the metal was scratched and rough in places, rust smoothed away.

It took Fox several minutes of fiddling, which she performed carefully, on her knees, her ear to the door. Finally, a heavy click sounded. "That's it," she said, standing, grasping a handle, then pushing. The door didn't move. She tried pulling.

"I remember that it opened in," said Bitterblue. "And I never saw him struggling with it."

"Well then, something is blocking it, Lady Queen," said Fox, pushing harder on the wood with her shoulder. "I'm quite sure I've unlocked it."

"Ah," said Helda. "Look." She pointed to a place in the middle of the door where the sharp tip of a nail peeked through the surface of the wood. "Perhaps it's boarded up from the inside, Lady Queen."

"Boarded and locked," said Bitterblue, sighing. "Is either of you any good at mazes?"

*　*　*　*　*

As Fox and Bitterblue descended the stairway that had dropped Bitterblue into Leck's maze once before, Fox explained her theory about mazes: once inside, one should choose one hand, the left or the right, put it to the wall, then follow the maze all the way through, keeping that same hand to the wall. Eventually, one would reach the heart of the maze.

"A guard did something like that with me last time," said Bitterblue. "But it won't work if we happen to start against a wall that's an island, detached from the rest of the maze," she added, thinking it through. "We'll put our hands on the right-hand wall. If we end up where we started, then we'll know it's an island. We'll take the next possible left turn, then return to putting our hands on the right-hand wall. That'll work. Oh," she said in dismay. "Unless we come up against another island. Then we'll have to do it all over again, plus, keep remembering what we've already done. Balls. We should've brought markers to put down in the passageway."

"Why don't we just try it, Lady Queen," Fox said, "and see how it goes?"

It was quite disorienting. Mazes were made for Katsa, with her unreal sense of direction, or Po, who could see through walls. Luckily, Fox had had the foresight to bring a lamp. After exactly forty-three turns with their hands on the right wall, they came upon a door in the middle of a corridor.

The door, of course, was locked.

"Well," said Bitterblue as Fox knelt again and began her patient poking, "at least we know this one can't be boarded up from the inside. Unless the person boarded up both doors, then stayed inside to die, and we're about to find his rotted corpse," she said, chuckling at her own morbid joke. "Or unless, of course," she added, groaning, "there's a third way to exit Leck's rooms. A secret passage we don't know about yet."

"Secret passage, Lady Queen?" said Fox absently, her ear to the door.

"The castle seems to be full of them, Fox," said Bitterblue.

"I had no idea, Lady Queen," said Fox. A quiet click sounded. When Fox grasped the door handle and pushed, the door swung open.

Holding her breath, not certain what to steel herself against, but steeling herself nonetheless, Bitterblue stepped into a dark room full of tall shadows. The shadows were so human in form that she let out a gasp.

"Sculptures, Lady Queen," said Fox calmly, behind her. "I believe they're sculptures."

The room smelled of dust and had no windows. It was cavernous and square with no furniture, except for a single, massive, empty bed frame in the center of the room. The sculptures, on pedestals, filled the rest of the space; there must have been forty of them. Walking among them with Fox and the lantern was a bit like walking among the shrubberies of the great courtyard at night, for they loomed in just the same way, all seeming as if they were about to come alive and start striding around.

She could see that they were the work of Bellamew. Animals turning into each other, people turning into animals, people turning into mountains or trees, all with a vitality, a sense of movement and feeling. Then the lamp caught a strange blotch of color and Bitterblue realized something was peculiar about these sculptures. Not just peculiar, but wrong: They were slapped over with gaudy, bright paint of every color, paint that made spatters all across the rug.

She had expected weapons of torture in this room, perhaps. A collection of knives, stains of blood. But not ruined art arranged on a ruined rug, surrounding the skeleton of a bed.

He destroyed the sculptures in his rooms. Why?

The walls all around were covered with continuous hangings. A field of grass, turning to wildflowers, then into a thick forest of trees that gave way to wildflowers again, then to the field of grass it had started with. Bitterblue touched the forest on the wall, just to assure herself that it wasn't real, only a hanging. Dust rose; she sneezed. She saw a tiny owl, turquoise and silver, sleeping in the limbs of one of the trees.

Built into the back wall of the room was a door. It led to nothing more than a bathing room, functional, cold, ordinary. Another door opened to a closet space, empty and choked with dust. She could not stop sneezing.

A third doorway in the back wall, this one a simple opening with no door, led to a spiral staircase climbing up. At the top of the stairs was a door so thoroughly nailed over with boards that it was difficult to catch a glimpse of the door itself. Bitterblue pounded and called Helda's name. When Helda responded, her question was answered: This was the staircase that led up to Bitterblue's sitting room and the blue horse hanging.

Down the steps again, Bitterblue said to Fox, "It's creepy, isn't it?"

"It's fascinating, Lady Queen," said Fox, stopping before the room's tiniest sculpture, staring at it, mesmerized. It was a human child, perhaps two years old, kneeling with arms outstretched. A girl with something knowing in her eyes. Her arms and hands were turning to wings. Her wispy hair was sprouting feathers, her toes turning into talons. Leck had slapped a streak of red paint across her face, but it didn't manage to deaden the expression in her eyes.

Why would he try to ruin something so beautiful? What is the world he was trying, and failing, to create?

What is the world Runnemood is trying to create? And why must they both create their worlds by destroying?

In the morning, Madlen arrived, rebandaged Bitterblue's shoulder wound, gave her medicines, and commanded her, with clear and specific instructions, to take them, even the bitter ones that were nauseating to swallow. "They will help your bones knit together, Lady Queen," she said, "faster than they could on their own. Are you doing the exercises I prescribed?"

The sun rose while Bitterblue grumbled over breakfast, but dimly. When she dragged herself to the windows in search of light, she discovered a world of fog. Fighting to make out the back garden through the whiteness, she thought she saw a person standing on the garden wall. The person threw something into the garden, a small, slender, gliding thing, bright white and slashing a streak through the thick air.

It was Po with his stupid paper glider. As she recognized him, he raised an arm in greeting to her, then lost his balance, spun both arms like a windmill, and promptly fell off the wall. Somehow he managed to propel himself into the garden rather than into the river. Most certainly Po, and most certainly not well enough to be doing gymnastics in the back garden.

Bitterblue glanced at Madlen and Helda, who sat at the sitting room table murmuring over their morning cups. If Po had escaped from the infirmary again, she didn't want to give him away. "I feel like a bit of air before I go to my office," she said. "If Rood or Darby come for me, tell them to stuff themselves."

A grand production followed this announcement. The choosing and placement of a scarf, the positioning of her sword, the draping of a cloak over her bound arm. Finally, feeling like a moving coatrack, Bitterblue left them. Helda had altered her skirts so that they made wide, flowing trouser legs like Fox's, and found time yesterday, somehow, to fit the left sleeve of this particular gown with buttons. It seemed that Bitterblue had only to mention a species of attire she liked, and Helda would hand it to her a few days later.

Except, of course, the crown.

IN THE GARDEN, the sculpture of the woman turning into a mountain lion stood stark, screaming. Patches of fog hugged her and drifted away. *How did Bellamew make her eyes so alive?* Then recognition settled into Bitterblue. She registered the shape of the face, the eyes full of determination and pain. This figure was her mother.

For some reason, the fact of it didn't surprise her. Neither did the sadness of it. It seemed right to her; the sculpture didn't just look, but felt, like Ashen. She was grateful to it for grounding her in the certainty that she had indeed, at least some of the time, known her mother.

"What are you holding there?" Po called to her, for Bitterblue had brought Teddy's list of guilty lords and ladies.

"What are *you* holding?" she asked him as she approached him, meaning the paper glider. "Why are you throwing that thing around my garden?"

He shrugged. "I wondered how it would do in cold, wet air."

"Cold, wet air."

"Yes."

"How it would do what, exactly?"

"Fly, of course; it's all about the principles of flight. I study birds, especially when they're gliding, and this paper thing is my attempt to study it further. But my progress is slow. My Grace isn't so finely tuned that I can grasp all the details of what happens in the few seconds before it crashes."

"I see," Bitterblue said. "And you're doing this why?"

He propped his elbows on the wall. "Katsa has wondered if a person could ever build wings to fly with."

"What do you mean, to fly with?" said Bitterblue, suddenly irate.

"You know what I mean."

"You'll only encourage her to believe it can be done."

"I have no doubt it can be done."

"To what purpose?" snapped Bitterblue.

Po's eyebrows rose. "Flying would be its own purpose, Cousin. Don't worry, no one would ever expect the queen to do it."

No, I'll be left with the honor of planning the funerals.

The smallest grin lighting his face, Po said, "Your turn. What did you bring me?"

"I wanted to read the names on this list to you," she said, shaking the paper open one-handed, "so that if you ever hear anything about any of them, you can tell me."

"I'm listening," he said.

"A Lord Stanpost who lives two days' ride south from the city collected more girls from his town for Leck than any other person," said Bitterblue. "A Lady Hood came in a close second, but she is dead now. In central Monsea, townspeople starved to death in a town governed by a lord named Markam who taxed them cruelly. There are a few more lords' names here"—Bitterblue listed them—

"but half of them are dead, Po, and none of them are names I know, beyond useless statistics given me by my advisers."

"None of the names are familiar to me either," said Po, "but I'll make a few inquiries, when I can. Who've you shared the list with?"

"Captain Smit of the Monsean Guard. I've told him to look for connections between Runnemood and these names, and also try to find if Runnemood arranged Ivan's murder, or just Saf's framing."

"Ivan?"

"The engineer Runnemood framed Saf for killing. I shared it with my spies too, just to see if they came back with information that matches Smit's."

"Don't you trust Smit?"

"I'm not sure I trust anyone, Po," said Bitterblue, sighing. "Though it is a relief to be talking with the Monsean Guard about the truthseeker killings, and finally have their help."

"Give the list to Giddon too, when he gets back from Estill. He's been gone nearly three weeks; he should return soon."

"Yes," said Bitterblue. "I do trust Giddon."

Po paused. "Yes," he said, a bit gloomily.

"What is it, Po?" Bitterblue asked softly. "You know he'll forgive you in time."

Po snorted. "Oh, Beetle," he said. "I'm scared to death to tell my father and brothers about it. They'll be even more angry than Giddon."

"Hm," said Bitterblue. "Have you decided for certain to do so?"

"No," he said. "I want to talk it over with Katsa first."

Bitterblue took a moment to take better hold of all the opinions and anxieties she knew she was flinging at him, including her worries over how a talk like that would go, and why Katsa wasn't back yet if all she was doing was exploring a tunnel somewhere. "Well, Ror knows about you and the Council," she said, "doesn't he?"

"Yes."

"And he's learned about Skye's preference for men. Hasn't he made his peace with those surprises?"

"It wasn't a small matter in either case," Po said. "There was a great deal of yelling."

"You seem like a person who can handle a bit of yelling," she said lightly.

His smile was both hopeless and teary. "Ror and me yelling and Katsa and me yelling are two different creatures entirely," he said. "He's my father, and a king. And I've been lying to him for my entire life. He's so proud of me, Bitterblue. His disappointment is going to be crushing, and I'll feel it in his every breath."

"Po?"

"Yes?"

"When my mother was eighteen and Leck chose her, who gave permission for the match?"

Po considered. "My father was king. It would have been him, at Ashen's request."

"I think Ror must know how it feels to have betrayed someone he loves, Po."

"But of course, it wasn't his fault. Leck came to his court and manipulated everyone there."

"How much comfort do you suppose Ror gets from that?" she asked quietly. "He was her king and her older brother. He sent her away to be tortured."

"I expect you're trying to comfort me," Po said with slumped shoulders. "But all I can think is that if Ror had known I was a mind reader at the time, he could have introduced me to Leck during that visit, for the purpose of investigating his sister's potential husband. And maybe I could have prevented the entire thing."

"How old were you?"

Po took a moment to calculate. "Four," he said, seeming surprised by the answer.

"Po," she said. "What do you think Leck would have done to a four-year-old who knew his secret and was trying to get others to see it too?"

Po didn't answer.

"It was your mother who compelled you to lie about your Grace, wasn't it?"

"And my grandfather," Po said. "For my own safety. They feared my father would use me."

"They did right," Bitterblue said. "If they hadn't, you'd be dead. When Ror thinks all this through, he will see that everyone has done the best they could think to do at every moment. He'll forgive you."

IN HER OFFICE, there were certain things Bitterblue no longer felt the need to pretend she didn't know. Rood and Darby might not know the origins of her friendship with Teddy and Saf, but the fact that she might be privy to the things they knew was no longer a secret.

"I understand that Runnemood has made a shambles of the city schools," she said to Rood and Darby both. "I understand that hardly anyone is taught history or how to read, which is an utter disgrace, and a problem we're going to address immediately. What do the two of you suggest?"

"Forgive me, Lady Queen," said Darby, who was sweating, his face clammy and wet. As he spoke, he began to tremble. "I feel terribly ill." He turned and ran out the door.

"What is wrong with him?" asked Bitterblue pointedly, knowing the answer.

"He's trying not to drink, Lady Queen, now that Thiel's absence makes a necessity of our presence," said Rood in a calm voice. "The sickness will pass once he succeeds."

Bitterblue studied Rood. His sleeve-ends were stained with ink, and his white hair, combed carefully across the bald part of his head, was slipping out of place. His eyes were quiet and sad. "I wonder why I haven't worked more closely with you, Rood," she said. "I think you pretend less than the others."

"Then perhaps, Lady Queen," said Rood, with a small hesitation that she took for modest embarrassment, "we can work closely on this matter of the schools. What if we were to create a new ministry, dedicated to education? I could present you with suitable candidates to fill the role of minister."

"Well," said Bitterblue, "I can see that it would make sense to assemble a dedicated team, though perhaps we're already getting ahead of ourselves." She glanced at the tall clock against the wall. "Where's Captain Smit?" she added, for Smit had promised a report to her on the Runnemood search in person every morning. The morning was nearly past.

"Shall I seek him out, Lady Queen?"

"No. Let's discuss this more. Will you start by explaining to me the way the schools are run now?"

It was a bit odd to spend such focused time with a person who was liable, at unexpected moments, to bring Runnemood sharply to her mind. Rood's unassuming personality could not have been more different, but the timbre of his voice was similar, especially when he began to feel confident about a thing. So was his face, from certain angles. She glanced at her empty windows now and then, trying to absorb how a man who'd sat in those windows so many times could have been capable of stabbing people to death in their sleep and trying to kill her.

WHEN NOON CAME and Smit had not yet arrived, Bitterblue decided to go looking for him herself.

The barracks of the Monsean Guard were just west of the great courtyard, on the castle's first level. Bitterblue swept in.

"Where is Captain Smit?" she demanded of a tense young man who sat at a desk inside the door. He gawked at her, leapt up, then shuffled her through another door into an office. Bitterblue found herself staring at Captain Smit, who was leaning across an extraordinarily tidy desk and talking to Thiel.

Both men rose hastily. "Forgive me, Lady Queen," said Thiel in embarrassment. "I was just leaving." And Thiel faded from the room before she was even able to gather how she felt about finding him there.

"I hope he's not interfering," said Bitterblue to Smit. "He's no longer my adviser. As such, he has no power to compel you to do anything, Captain Smit."

"On the contrary, Lady Queen," said Captain Smit, bowing neatly. "He was not interfering or commanding, merely answering some questions I had about how Runnemood spent his time. Or rather, trying to answer, Lady Queen. One problem I'm coming up against is that Runnemood was highly secretive and told conflicting stories about where he was going at any given time."

"I see," said Bitterblue. "And your reason for not reporting to me this morning?"

"What?" said Captain Smit, glancing at the clock on his desk;

then startling her by pounding on the top of it with his fist. "I'm dreadfully sorry, Lady Queen," he said in vexation. "My clock keeps stopping. As it happens, I've little to report, but that's no excuse, of course. We've made no progress in the search for Runnemood, nor have I managed to learn anything about any connections he may have had with the individuals on your list. But we've only just begun, Lady Queen. Please don't lose hope; perhaps I'll have something to report to you tomorrow."

IN THE GREAT courtyard, Bitterblue paused to glare at a shrubbery of a bird, bright with autumn leaves. She was clenching her one good fist, hard.

Going to the fountain, she sat on the cold edge, trying to work out what she was so frustrated about.

I suppose this is part of being a queen, she thought. *And part of being injured, and part of Saf not wanting me around, and part of everyone knowing where, and who, I am all the time: I must sit and wait while other people run around investigating things, then come back and give me reports. I'm stuck here, waiting, while everyone else has adventures.*

I don't like it.

"Lady Queen?"

She looked up to find Giddon standing over her, snowflakes melting in his hair and on his coat. "Giddon! Po was just saying this morning that you should be back soon. I'm so pleased to see you."

"Lady Queen," he said gravely, running a hand through wet hair. "What happened to your arm?"

"Oh, that. Runnemood tried to kill me," she said.

He stared at her in amazement. "Runnemood, your own adviser?"

"There's a lot going on, Giddon," she said, smiling. "My city

332 — KRISTIN CASHORE

friend stole my crown. Po's inventing a flying machine. I've dismissed Thiel and discovered that my mother's embroidery is all ciphered messages."

"I wasn't even gone three weeks!"

"Po's been sick, you know."

"I'm sorry to hear that," he said, with no expression.

"Don't be an ass. He's actually been quite unwell."

"Oh?" Now Giddon was looking uncomfortable. "What do you mean, Lady Queen?"

"What do you mean, what do I mean?"

"I mean, is he all right?"

"He's a bit better now."

"Is he—he's not in danger, Lady Queen?"

"He'll be fine, Giddon," she said, relieved to hear the touch of anxiety in his voice. "I've a list of names to give you. Where are you going first? I'll walk with you."

GIDDON WAS HUNGRY. Bitterblue was racked with shivers from the cold air and moisture of the fountain, and wanted to hear about Piper's tunnel and Estill. And so he invited her to join him for a meal. When she accepted, he led her through the east vestibule and into a crowded corridor.

"Where are we going?" she asked.

"I thought we'd go to the kitchens," Giddon said. "Do you know your kitchens, Lady Queen? They abut the southeast gardens."

"Once again," said Bitterblue dryly, "you're giving me a tour of my own castle."

"The Council has contacts there, Lady Queen. I'm hoping Po will join us too. Are you as cold as you look?" he asked.

She saw what he saw, an approaching man who balanced a colorful tower of blankets in his arms. "Ah, yes," she said. "Let's corral him, Giddon."

Moments later, Giddon helped her drape a mossy green-gold blanket over her injured arm and her sword. "Very nice," he said. "This color reminds me of my home."

"Lady Queen," said a woman Bitterblue had never seen before, bustling between her and Giddon. She was tiny, old, wrinkled—shorter even than Bitterblue. "Allow me, Lady Queen," said the woman, grabbing the front of Bitterblue's blanket, which Bitterblue was holding closed with her tired right hand. The woman produced a plain, tin brooch, gathered both sides of the blanket together, and pinned them tight.

"Thank you," Bitterblue said, astonished. "You must tell me your name so that I can return your brooch to you."

"My name is Devra, Lady Queen, and I work with the cobbler."

"The cobbler!" Bitterblue patted the brooch as the traffic in the corridor swept her and Giddon on their way. "I didn't know there was a cobbler," she said aloud to herself, then glanced sidelong at Giddon, sighing. Her blanket trailed behind her like the train of a grand and expensive cape, making her feel, oddly, like a queen.

BITTERBLUE HAD NEVER heard so much roaring noise or seen so many people working at such a frantic pace as in the kitchens. She was amazed to discover that there was a rather wild-eyed Graceling who could tell from the look and, especially, the smell of a person what would, at that moment, be most satisfying for her or him to eat. "Sometimes it's nice to be told what you want," she said to Giddon, inhaling the steam that rose from her cup of melted chocolate.

When Po arrived, coming to stand warily before Giddon, mouth tight and arms crossed, Bitterblue saw him as Giddon would and realized that Po had lost weight. After a moment of mutual assessment, Giddon said to him, "You need food. Sit down and let Jass sniff you."

"He makes me nervous," said Po, obediently sitting down. "I worry about how much he senses."

"The ironies abound," said Giddon dryly around a spoonful of ham and bean soup. "You look terrible. Have you got your appetite back?"

"I'm ravenous."

"Are you cold?"

"Why, so you can lend me your soggy coat?" asked Po with a sniff at the offending article. "Stop flitting around me like it's my last day. I'm fine. Why is Bitterblue wearing a blanket cape? What did you do to her?"

"I've always liked you better when Katsa's around," Giddon said. "She's so rotten to me that you seem positively pleasant in contrast."

Po's mouth twitched. "You provoke her on purpose."

"She is so easy to provoke," said Giddon, shoving a board of bread and cheese to where Po could reach it. "Sometimes I can do it just with the way I breathe. So," he said brusquely. "We have a few problems and I'll state them plainly. The people of Estill are determined. But it's just as Katsa said: They have no plan beyond deposing Thigpen. And Thigpen has a small orbit of favorite lords and ladies, avaricious types, loyal to their king, but even more loyal to themselves. They'll need to be neutralized, every one of them, or else one of them is likely to rise to power in Thigpen's place and be no sort of improvement whatsoever. The people I talked to don't want to have anything to do with the Estillan nobility. They're deeply mistrusting of anyone in Estill who hasn't been suffering as they have."

"And yet, they trust us?"

"Yes," Giddon said. "The Council is out of favor with all the worst kings, and the Council helped depose Drowden, so they trust us. I believe that if Raffin went to them next, as the next King of the Middluns and as Randa's disgraced son, he might get through to them, for he's so unpushy. And you need to go too, of course, and do"—Giddon gestured aimlessly with his spoon—"whatever it is you do. I suppose it's best that you didn't join me this time if you were about to fall sick as a dog. But I could've used your company in that tunnel, and I needed you in Estill. I'm sorry, Po."

Surprise sprang onto Po's face. It was not a thing that Bitterblue got to see there very often. Po cleared his throat, blinking. "I'm sorry too, Giddon," he said, and that was that. Bitterblue was stung with the wish that Saf would forgive her so gracefully.

Jass came, sniffed Po, resniffed Giddon, and apparently decided that the two of them would find it satisfying to eat half the kitchen. Bitterblue sat, listening to them plot and plan, sipping her chocolate, trying to find a position that hurt less than the others, pulling apart every word of their conversation, and occasionally offering an argument, especially whenever Po veered to the topic of Bitterblue's safety. All the time, she was also absorbing the wonder that was the castle kitchens. The table at which they sat was in a corner near the bakery. From that corner, the walls seemed to spread endlessly in both directions. To one side were the ovens and fireplaces, which were built into the castle's outer walls. The high kitchen windows had no glass, and snowflakes gusted through them now, plopping wetly on stoves and people.

A mountain of potato peels sat on the floor under a table nearby.

Anna, the head baker, went to a row of enormous bowls that were covered with cloths, lifted the cloths, and, one after the other, punched down the dough in the bowls. A sharp yell brought a cavalcade of helpers with sleeves rolled, who lined themselves up at the table, took the great gobs of dough from the bowls, and kneaded them, throwing backs and shoulders into the work. Anna also stood in the line, kneading, with one arm. She held her other arm close to her body. There was something in the stiff way it hung that made Bitterblue suspect an injury of some kind. Her working arm muscles bulged as she kneaded, her neck and shoulders bulging too. The strength of her mesmerized Bitterblue, not because she was kneading one-handed but simply because she was kneading, it was work that was both rough and smooth, and Bitterblue wished she could know what that silky dough felt like. She understood that sometime soon—if not tonight, then perhaps tomorrow—if not this batch of dough, then the next one—she would be eating potato bread with her meal.

It gratified her, in a way that almost hurt, to sit beside the bakery. The warm, yeasty air was so familiar. She breathed it deeply, waking her lungs with it, feeling that she'd been taking shallow breaths for years. The smell of baking bread was so comforting; and the memory of a story she had told to herself, a story she had told Saf, about her work and about her living mother, was so real, so tangible as she sat in this place, and so sad.

WHEN CAPTAIN SMIT reported the next morning—and the morning after, and the morning after that—that there was nothing to report, Bitterblue began to be amazed by the depths to which her own frustration could plumb. Runnemood had now been missing for six days and no progress whatsoever had been made.

On the seventh day, when Captain Smit's report was the same, Bitterblue shot up from her desk and began a systematic exploration. If she could pound her feet down every hallway of the castle and clap her hand to every wall, if she could see into every workshop and learn what vista to expect around every corner, then maybe she could calm her restlessness—and her anxieties about Saf as well. For that was part of what was making these empty days so hard to bear: There was no news of Spook or the crown either, and no communication from Teddy or Saf.

She stomped down the stairs of her tower, greeted the clerks who stared back at her blankly, then went off to look for the cobbler's shop, so that she might return Devra's brooch.

She found it in the artisan courtyard, which rang with the raps and dings of coopers, carpenters, tinkers. It smelled too of the leather-worker's bitter oils and the chandler's beeswax, and in one shop, a wizened old woman made harps and other musical instruments.

Why did she never hear music in her castle? For that matter, why did she never encounter a single soul, other than Death, in the library? Surely *some* people could read. And why, when she walked through the halls, did she get a sense sometimes, looking into people's faces, of a strange thing she couldn't shake—a hard-driven sort of emptiness? They bowed to her, but she wasn't certain that they truly saw her.

On an upper level in the west castle, she found a barber shop, and beside it, a tiny shop for wig-making. Unaccountably, this delighted her. The next day, she found the children's nursery. The children did not have empty eyes.

On the day after that—nine days, and no news—she returned to the bakery, sat in the corner for a few minutes, and watched the bakers at work.

Anna offered an unsolicited explanation for something Bitterblue had, indeed, been wondering. "I was born with an un-working arm, Lady Queen," she said. "You needn't worry that your father was responsible."

Bitterblue couldn't hide her surprise at being spoken to so candidly. "It's none of my business, but I do thank you for telling me."

"You seem to like the bakery, Lady Queen," said Anna, kneading a mountain of dough as they conversed.

"I hesitate to intrude, Anna," said Bitterblue, "but I should like to try kneading the bread one day."

"Kneading might be just the exercise you need to return your arm to strength once you're out of that cast, Lady Queen. Ask your healer her advice. You're small," she added with a decisive nod. "You may come anytime, work in a corner, and not fear that you'll be in our way."

Bitterblue reached out. When Anna stilled the dough, Bitterblue laid her palm upon it. It was soft, warm, and dry, and her hand came away with a dusting of flour. For the rest of the day, when she brought her fingers to her nose, she could almost smell it.

It helped to touch things and know that they were real. Discovering this made her miss Saf with an ache she carried down every hallway, for once upon a time she had been allowed to touch him too.

ON THE FOURTEENTH day after Runnemood's disappearance, Death came to Bitterblue in her alcove in the library, where she still spent whatever time she could spare on the rewrites and rereads. He dropped a newly rewritten manuscript onto the table from a great height, turned on his heel, and marched away.

Lovejoy, curled up at Bitterblue's elbow, sprang into the air, yowling. Landing, he began immediately to groom himself with enthusiasm, as if some instinct told him to look purposeful and hide the fact that he had no idea what was going on.

"I agree that becoming conscious should not be so traumatic," Bitterblue said to him, attempting to be civil. Lovejoy had recently begun alternating between two personalities, one that hissed at her with a seething hatred whenever he saw her, the other that followed her around morosely and sometimes fell asleep pressed against her. He would not shoo when she told him to, so she'd given up on trying to influence him.

The new manuscript was called *Monarchy Is Tyranny*.

Bitterblue burst out laughing, which caused Lovejoy to pause in his grooming, peering at her suspiciously, one foot stuck in the air like a roast chicken. "Oh, dear," Bitterblue said. "No wonder Death threw it at me. I'm sure he found it quite satisfying." And then it stopped being funny. Turning in her chair, she looked at the sculpture girl, at her stubborn, defiant face. She thought that perhaps the girl had an understanding of tyranny; that she was changing into rock to protect herself from it. Then Bitterblue looked past her to the woman in the hanging, whose eyes looked back at her, deep and placid, seeming to have an understanding of everything in the world.

I would like to have her as my mother, Bitterblue thought; then almost cried out, stung by her own disloyalty. *Mama? Of course I didn't mean it. It's just—she's stuck in a moment of time when everything is simple and clear. Our simple, clear moments were never allowed to last. And how I would like some clarity, some simplicity.*

She tried to return her attention to the book she'd been rereading when Death had arrived, the book about the artistic process. She hated this book. It went on for pages and pages to say a thing it could've said in two sentences: The artist is an empty vessel with a spout. Inspiration pours in and art pours out. Bitterblue knew nothing about the process of art; she wasn't an artist, nor were her friends. Still, this book didn't feel right. Leck had liked people to be empty so that he could pour himself in and the reaction he wished for would pour out. Most likely, Leck had wanted to control his artists; control them, then kill them. Of course Leck had liked a book that characterized inspiration as a kind of . . . tyranny.

ON DAY FIFTEEN since Runnemood's disappearance, Bitterblue stumbled upon something interesting in the embroidery.

His hospital is at bottom of river. River is his graveyard of bones. I followed him and saw the monster he is. I must get Bitterblue away soon.

That was all it said. Sitting on her crimson rug with the sheet in her lap and her shoulder aching, Bitterblue remembered something

Po had said while hallucinating: "The river is swimming with the dead."

Po, she thought to him, wherever he might be. *If I drained my river, would I find bones?*

NO BONES, CAME Po's ciphered answer, but written in ink rather than Po's graphite, and in Giddon's neat hand. It was a long note, so she was glad Giddon was doing Po the favor of writing for him. *No hospital. I don't know where hallucinations came from. The words I said don't match what I saw. What I saw was Thiel crossing Winged Bridge, though my range doesn't even reach Winged Bridge. Also saw my brothers staging hand fights on ceiling, so consider that before asking me to pay closer attention to Thiel in future. My mind can't be everywhere, you know. Though, as it happens, I have sensed him, twice in recent nights, entering that tunnel that goes under wall to east city.*

I've also sensed you wandering around like a lost sheep. Why not wander to art gallery? Hava spends most nights there. Meet her. She's useful and you should know her. Be aware she has history of compulsive lying. Developed habit quite young out of necessity. Grew up in castle with mother and uncle too close to king, disguising herself to escape notice. Consequently has no friends and ended up wandering Monsea, eventually in company of likes of Danzhol. She tries to tell truth now. I really, really wish you would meet her.

Fine, Bitterblue thought back to Po grumpily. *I'll go meet your friend the compulsive liar. I'm sure we'll get along smashingly.*

THAT NIGHT, BITTERBLUE set out for her art gallery with a lamp in hand. Not knowing the best route, but knowing it was on the top level several floors above the library, she walked south through glass-ceilinged corridors. Tiny pieces of ice bounced on the glass above.

Then Bitterblue stopped in her tracks, astonished, for through the glass above her, a person was perched on hands and knees, polishing the glass with a rag. On the roof in the cold, at midnight, working in the frozen rain. It was Fox, of course. Seeing the queen below, she raised her hand.

Her Grace is madness, Bitterblue thought as she continued on. *Pure madness.*

The art gallery, when she found it, was not unlike the library. Rooms led from one to the other with unexpected nooks and circling turns that confused Bitterblue's sense of direction. In the light of her single lamp, the empty expanses and the flashes of color on the walls were eerie, unsettling. The floor was marble, but her feet barely made a sound against it. From her own sneezing, she wondered if this might be because she was stepping on a carpet of dust.

Bitterblue stopped before an enormous hanging that was the cousin, clearly, of all the others she'd seen. This one depicted a number of bright, colorful creatures attacking a man, on a cliff overhanging the sea. Every animal in the scene was a color it should not be, and Bitterblue thought that the man, screaming in agony, might be Leck. He wore no eye patch and his features weren't clear, but still, for some reason, it was the impression the hanging gave her.

Bitterblue was beginning to be tired of being gutted by her castle's art.

Leaving the hanging, she crossed the room, climbed a step, and found herself in a sculpture gallery. Remembering why she'd come here, she studied each sculpture carefully, but couldn't find what she was looking for. "Hava," she said quietly. "I know you're here."

Nothing happened for a moment. Then there was a rustling noise, and a statue near the back transformed into a girl with a hanging head. Bitterblue fought off a rising nausea. The girl was weeping, wiping at her face with a tattered sleeve. She took a step toward Bitterblue, turned into a sculpture again, then wavered back into a girl.

"Hava," Bitterblue said desperately, trying not to retch. "Please. Stop it."

Hava came to Bitterblue and fell to her knees. "Forgive me, Lady Queen," she said, choking on her tears. "When he explained it to me, it made sense, you see? He didn't use the word *kidnap*. But still, I knew it was wrong, Lady Queen," she cried. "I was excited to disguise the boat, for it's more of a challenge than disguising myself. It does not involve my Grace. It requires artistry!"

"Hava," said Bitterblue, bending down to her, at a loss for what to say to a compulsive liar who seemed to be in genuine pain. "Hava!" she cried as the girl grabbed her hand and sobbed over it. "I forgive you," she said, not feeling it in her heart, but sensing that forgiveness was necessary to calm Hava's wildness. "I forgive you," she said. "You've saved my life twice since, remember? Take a breath, Hava. Calm down and explain to me how your Grace works. Do you actually change something in yourself, or is it my perception of things that you change?"

When Hava raised her face to Bitterblue, Bitterblue saw that it was quite a pretty face. Open, like Holt's, forlorn and frightened, but with a sweetness it was a shame she felt the need to hide. Her eyes were flatly beautiful—or, at least, the one that caught the light of the lamp was beautiful, glowing copper, as brightly as Po's eyes glowed gold and silver. Bitterblue couldn't tell the color of the other eye in the darkness.

"It's your perception, Lady Queen," said Hava. "Your perception of what you're seeing."

It was what Bitterblue had assumed. The other way made no

sense; it was too improbable, even for a Grace. And here, she knew, was one of the many reasons she kept resisting Po's exhortations to trust Hava. Trusting someone who was able to change the way her mind perceived things did not come comfortably to Bitterblue.

"Hava," she said, "you're out in the city often, hiding. You're in a position to see things, and you knew Lord Danzhol. I'm trying to find a way to connect the things Runnemood does with the things people like Danzhol once did; I'm trying to sort out who Runnemood might be working with, and what truth he's trying to hide when he kills truthseekers. Do you know anything about it?"

"Lord Danzhol communicated with a lot of people, Lady Queen," said Hava. "He seemed to have friends in every kingdom, and a thousand secret letters, and visitors to his estate who would come in a back door at night and never be seen by the rest of us. But he didn't talk to me about it. And I haven't seen anything in the city that would explain anything either. If you ever wanted me to follow anyone, Lady Queen, I would do it in a heartbeat."

"I'll remember that, Hava," said Bitterblue doubtfully, not knowing what to believe. "I'll mention it to Helda."

"I have heard a strange rumor about your crown, Lady Queen," said Hava, after a pause.

"The crown!" said Bitterblue. "How do you know about the crown?"

"From the rumor, Lady Queen," said Hava, startled. "Some whispers in a story room. I was hoping they weren't true; they're ridiculous enough to be lies."

"Perhaps they are lies. What did you hear?"

"I heard of someone called Gray, Lady Queen, who's the grandchild of a famous thief who steals the treasures of Monsean nobility. The family has done so for generations, Lady Queen—it's their mark in trade. They live in a cave somewhere, and Gray is claiming to be in a position to sell your crown. It's priced at a figure so high, only a king could afford it."

Bitterblue clutched her temples. "That will not make it easy if I end up having to buy it, and I should probably do it soon, before the word spreads further."

"Oh," Hava said, distressed. "Unfortunately, the other thing I heard is that Gray won't sell to you, Lady Queen."

"What? Then who does he think will buy it? None of the other kings would part with a fortune just for the sake of what would be a senseless prank. And I won't allow my uncle to buy it back for me!"

"I'm afraid I can't explain it, Lady Queen," said Hava. "It's what I heard whispered. But rumors are often untrue, Lady Queen. Perhaps this one is. I hope it is!"

"Tell no one, Hava," said Bitterblue. "If you doubt the importance of your silence, ask Prince Po."

"If you say it's important, Lady Queen," said Hava, "then I have no need to ask Prince Po."

Bitterblue studied this Graceling liar, this odd young woman who seemed to go wherever she wanted and do whatever took her fancy, but did so in fear, and in the most utter solitude. Hava was still kneeling. "Stand please, Hava," said Bitterblue.

She was tall. As she stood, her face caught the light, and Bitterblue saw that her other eye was a deep and strange red. "Why do you hide in my art gallery, Hava?"

"Because there's no one else here, Lady Queen," said Hava softly. "And I can be near my uncle, who needs me. And I can be with my mother's work."

"Do you remember your mother?"

Hava nodded. "I was eight when she died, Lady Queen. She taught me to hide from King Leck, always."

346 — Kristin Cashore

"How old are you now?"

"Sixteen, Lady Queen."

"And—are you not lonely, Hava, hiding all the time?"

Something in Hava's pretty face wavered.

"Hava?" said Bitterblue, struck with a sudden doubt. "Is this what you really look like?"

The girl hung her head. When she looked up again, her eyes were still copper and red, but they sat in a face that was perhaps too plain to contain their strangeness, with a long, narrow mouth like a gash, and a snub nose.

It took Bitterblue concentrated effort to stop herself from reaching up to touch Hava's face, for she understood this. How she wanted to comfort the unhappiness that shone in those eyes and didn't need to be there. Bitterblue liked Hava's face. "I very much like how you look," Bitterblue said. "Thank you for showing me."

"I'm sorry, Lady Queen," she whispered. "It's hard not to hide. I'm so used to it."

"Perhaps it was unfair of me to ask."

"But it's a relief, Lady Queen," she whispered, "to let someone see me."

THE NEXT DAY, Captain Smit gave Bitterblue the news that Runnemood had, indeed, been responsible not just for Saf's framing but for Ivan the engineer's murder.

Finally, Bitterblue thought, *some progress. I'll ask Helda to put some pressure on my spies to confirm it.*

The day after that, Captain Smit told Bitterblue that now it was clear that Runnemood had also been responsible for the death of Lady Hood, the woman on Teddy's list who'd stolen girls for Leck.

"That was a murder?" Bitterblue said in dismay. "Runnemood is murdering other guilty parties?"

"I regret that our investigations suggest as much, Lady Queen," said Captain Smit. He had the appearance lately of a man under a great deal of strain, and Bitterblue made him drink some tea before leaving her office.

Next came the news that Runnemood had been in close correspondence with Lord Danzhol, may even have been responsible for convincing Danzhol to harm the queen. Then, the news that none of the living people on Teddy's list seemed in any way involved in killing, framing, or otherwise hurting truthseekers. The dead ones had all been killed by Runnemood.

On the next day—the nineteenth day since Runnemood's disappearance—Captain Smit marched into Bitterblue's office, set his chin, made his hands into fists, and presented her with a theory that Runnemood had been the single mastermind behind all the truthseeker killings and all related crime, possibly because the drive to be forward-thinking and leave Leck's time behind had triggered a vulnerable switch in his mind and made him insane.

Bitterblue had little to say in response to this. Her spies had not yet managed to confirm or deny any of the things Smit was telling her. But it had all begun to sound a bit ridiculous to her, and a great deal too convenient, that Runnemood and madness should be the entire explanation for something that had caused so much harm. Runnemood wasn't Leck; he wasn't even Graced. And Smit, standing before her desk, was jumping nervously at every slightest sound, though he'd never seemed the nervous type before. His eyes flashed bright with some strange agitation, and when he looked at her, he seemed to be seeing something else.

"Captain Smit," she said quietly. "Why don't you tell me what's really going on?"

"Oh, I have told you, Lady Queen," he said. "Indeed, I have. If you'll excuse me, Lady Queen, I'll go to my office and come back with the corroborating evidence."

He left, then didn't come back.

Po, she thought, pushing through papers at her desk. *I need you to talk to my Captain of the Monsean Guard urgently. He's lying to me. Something is dreadfully wrong.*

Po tried for two days, then finally sent a message to Bitterblue. *I can't find him, Cousin. He's gone.*

29

THE YOUNG MAN who sat inside the door of the Monsean Guard barracks was chewing his nails to bits when Bitterblue stepped in. At the sight of her, he dropped his hand hastily and stood, knocking over a cup.

"Where is Captain Smit?" she demanded as cider poured and dripped everywhere.

"He's gone away to investigate some criminal business at the silver refineries in the south, Lady Queen," said the soldier, eyeing the mess nervously. "Something to do with pirates."

"You're sure about that?"

"Certain, Lady Queen."

"And when will he be back?"

"It's hard to say, Lady Queen," said the soldier, straightening to look at her directly. "These matters can linger on."

He sounded a bit too hearty, as if he were rehearsing lines in a play. Bitterblue did not believe him.

But when she climbed to the lower offices and tried to convey her worry to Darby and Rood, they would not share her concern.

"Lady Queen," said Rood gently, "the captain of the entire Monsean Guard is bound to be needed in a great many places. If his duties are too heavy, or if you wish to divide his command so that he can always be present at court, we can discuss that. But I don't think there's reason to doubt his whereabouts. In the meantime, the Guard is certainly still searching for Runnemood."

Climbing to her tower, Bitterblue passed the mountains of paper on her desk, pushed herself to a southern window, and looked out across the castle roofs. So many expanses of glass, reflecting the fast-moving clouds. It unsettled her, as everything unsettled her; and the start of November was days away, yet the pace of work in these offices had not slowed. She could not keep alternating between worry, frustration, overwork, and boredom.

She'd taken to bringing her work to the lower offices sometimes, stumping down the steps with an armful of documents and sitting at a table, just so that she could be bored to death in company, rather than alone. There was never much chatting—talk in those rooms tended to restrict itself to work matters; and yet, she felt that as she sat in the presence of her clerks, they became less guarded in their stances and expressions. They softened into people who would look at her occasionally, say a word or two, and whose company was comfortable, and human. Froggatt had even smiled at her once; he was recently married, and seemed to smile more than the others.

Darby burst through the door. "Correspondence from Prince Po, Lady Queen," he said, passing her a ciphered note from Po, this time in his own hand.

Raffin and Bann back from Sunder trip. Raff and I take tunnel north into Estill day after tomorrow. Bann and Giddon stay with you. Katsa now gone five weeks, beginning to worry. If she returns while we're away will you send word through tunnel?

Did something that will annoy you. Invited Saf to Council meeting last night. On impulse hired him to recaulk castle windows in preparation for winter. Want to keep him near for many reasons. Don't be

*surprised to see him hanging from walls in great courtyard and for
mercy's sake, don't draw attention to your association.*

Bitterblue burned the note in her small fireplace. Then, aban-
doning her work plans, she began the trek down to the courtyard.

IT WAS NOT pleasant to stand among the shrubberies, crane one's
neck, and see people small as dolls dangling against the courtyard
walls. Well, all right, not dangling—the people themselves were
sitting. But the long platform on which they sat was dangling, on
ropes, and swaying an awful lot for something so far above the
ground, and joggling when Saf stood, and walked, unworriedly,
from one end to the other.

Saf's partner up there was Fox, which struck Bitterblue as advan-
tageous for two reasons. One, as a spy, Fox would report to Helda
anything interesting Saf told her. Two, if Fox observed the queen
drawing Saf aside to speak to him, Bitterblue didn't think that Fox
would gossip about it.

The windows they caulked were on the courtyard's south side.
Bitterblue crossed to the south vestibule and began to climb the
stairs.

IF SAF WAS surprised when the queen appeared on the other side of
his window, he didn't show it. What he did do was twist his mouth
just enough for her to feel the insolence through the glass, then
open the window. He looked in at her, eyebrows raised in inquiry.

She said his name, "Saf," then realized it was all she could safely
say. He waited, but she failed to find more words. When he stepped
back, she assumed he was returning to his work, but instead, he
called down the platform to Fox. "I'll be out again in a minute."

Not looking at Bitterblue, he climbed through the window. Then he unhitched a rope that was tied to a wide belt he was wearing. Throwing the rope out the window, he yanked the window shut, still not looking at her. A knit hat hid his hair and made his facial features more defined, and also adorable. Autumn hadn't faded his freckles.

"Come on," he said, walking away from the windows altogether, toward one of the ends of the empty room. Bitterblue followed. Through a window, Fox glanced at them, then returned to work.

They stood in a long, narrow room that had arrow loops overlooking the drawbridge and moat, a room meant to be filled with archers in the event of a siege. From where Saf positioned them, they could see the doorway at each end and all the trapdoors in the ceiling. She wished now that she'd taken a moment to learn more about how this space was used. What if sentries were stationed on the roof above? What if they came down through the trapdoors at the changing of the guard? It would look odd, the queen shivering in this obscure room with her window caulker.

"What do you want?" Saf asked shortly.

"My Captain of the Monsean Guard has gone missing," she managed to say, berating herself for her own stupid sadness in his presence. "After days and days of no news, he told me he believed that Runnemood was solely responsible for all the crimes against truthseekers, then disappeared. Everyone's telling me he's gone to the silver refineries on some urgent matter to do with pirates. But something doesn't feel right, Saf. Have you heard anything about it?"

"No," he said. "And if it's true, then Runnemood's alive and well in the east city, for an apartment where we store contraband was set on fire last night and a friend killed in the flames."

Po, Bitterblue thought breathlessly. *I know you're leaving soon and*

I'm sure you're buried in preparations. But before you go, do you have time for one more pass through the east city to look for Runnemood? It couldn't be more important.

"I'm sorry," she said aloud.

He flicked his hand in annoyance.

"There are rumors too," she went on, trying not to be stung by his rejection of her sympathy. "Rumors of the crown. Have you heard them? Once the Monsean Guard hears them, I won't be able to hide that I don't have it, Saf."

"Gray's only trying to make you nervous," Saf said. "So that you'll panic—as you're doing now—and do whatever he wants."

"Well, what does he want?"

"I don't know," said Saf, shrugging. "When he wants you to know it, you will."

"I'm trapped here," Bitterblue said. "Useless, powerless. I don't know how to find Runnemood or even what I'm looking for. I don't know what to do about Gray. My friends have their own priorities, and my men don't seem to understand that something is urgently wrong. I don't know what to do, Saf, and you won't help me either, because I hid my power from you once, and now it's all you can see. I think you don't realize your own power over me. I know it, from when we touched each other. I—" Her voice broke. "There is a way you and I could muddle toward a balance, if you would let me touch you."

For a moment, he didn't speak. Finally, he said with a quiet sort of bitterness, "It's not enough. It's not enough that you feel an attraction; find someone else to be attracted to."

"Saf," she cried, "that's not all I feel. Listen to the words I'm saying. We were friends."

"And so what, then?" he said roughly. "What do you imagine?

Me, stuck in this castle, your special commoner friend, bored out of my skull? Are you going to make a prince out of me? Do you think I want anything to do with any of this? What I want is what I thought I had," he said. "I want the person you weren't."

"Saf," she whispered, tears stinging behind her eyes. "I'm so sorry I lied. I wish I could tell you about so many true things. The day you stole my crown, I discovered a cipher my mother wrote and hid from my father. Reading it isn't easy. If you ever decide to forgive me and you want to hear about my real mother, I'll tell you."

He watched her for a moment, then stared at his feet, mouth tight. Then he raised his coat sleeve to his eyes and it stunned her, the notion that he might be crying; it stunned her so that she said one more thing.

"I wouldn't give it back," she said, "what we did. I'd give it back for my mother to be alive. I'd give it back to know my kingdom better and be a better queen. Maybe I'd even give it back to have caused you less pain. But you gave me a gift you don't realize you gave me. I'd never done anything like that before, Saf, not with anyone. Now I see there are things in life that are open to me that I never quite believed I could do, before I knew you. I wouldn't give that back, any more than I would give up being queen. Not even to make you stop punishing me."

He stood with his arms clasped together and his head bent. He reminded her of one of Bellamew's lonely sculptures.

"Will you say anything?" she whispered.

He made no response. Not a movement, not a sound.

Bitterblue turned and slipped down the steps.

THAT NIGHT, RAFFIN, Bann, and Po had dinner with her and Helda. She thought they were oddly subdued, for a group of reunited friends, and wondered if the worry for Katsa was becoming epidemic. If so, their worries did nothing to soothe her own worries.

"Good job not drawing attention to your association with Saf," said Po sarcastically.

"No one saw us," retorted Bitterblue, waiting patiently while Bann cut her pork chop. She worked the muscles of her injured shoulder gently, trying to work out some of the end-of-the-day soreness. "Anyway, who exactly do you think you are, giving orders around my castle?"

"Saf's a pain in the ass, Beetle," said Po. "But a useful pain in the ass. Should something happen with the crown, we're all better off if he's where we can reach him. And who knows? Maybe he'll overhear something interesting for us. I've asked Giddon to keep an eye on him after I go."

"I'll help, if he needs a few days," said Bann.

"Thank you, Bann," said Po.

Bitterblue paused, not understanding this exchange, but her mind caught on another question. "How much of my history with Saf have you explained to Giddon, Po?"

Po opened his mouth, then closed it. "I don't know all that much about your history myself, Bitterblue, and I've taken care not to ask either of you about it. Giddon," said Po, pausing to push some carrots around with his fork, "knows that if he observes Saf disrespecting you in any way, he's to put Saf through a wall."

"Saf would probably like that."

Po made an exasperated noise. "I'll go into the east city tomorrow," he said. "I wish I weren't going to Estill. I'd tear the entire city apart for Runnemood, then I'd ride down to the refineries and find your captain myself."

"Is there time for me or Giddon to go find Smit?" asked Bann.

"Good question," said Po, scowling at him. "Let's figure that out."

"And what about you two?" said Bitterblue, turning to Raffin and Bann. "Did you accomplish your Council business in Sunder?"

"It was not actually a Council trip, Lady Queen," said Raffin, looking abashed.

"No? What were you doing?"

"It was a royal mission. My father insisted I talked to Murgon about marrying his daughter."

Bitterblue's mouth dropped open. "You can't marry his daughter!"

"And so I told him, Lady Queen," Raffin said, and that was all he said. His lack of elaboration pleased her. It was none of her business.

Of course, it was impossible, in this company, not to think about balances of power. Raffin and Bann glanced at each other now and then, sharing silent agreement, teasing each other, or just resting their eyes on each other, as if each man was a comfortable resting place for the other. Prince Raffin, heir to the Middluns throne; Bann, who had no title, no fortune. How she longed to ask them questions that were too nosy for asking, even by her standards. How did they balance money matters? How did they make decisions? How did Bann cope with the expectation that Raffin marry and produce heirs? If Randa knew the truth about his son, would Bann be in danger? Did Bann ever resent Raffin's wealth and importance? What was the balance of power in their bed?

"Where is Giddon, anyway?" she asked, missing him. "Why isn't he here?"

The reaction was immediate: The table went quiet and her friends considered each other with troubled expressions. Bitterblue's stomach dropped. "What is it? Is something wrong?"

"He's not injured, Lady Queen," said Raffin in a voice that didn't convince her. "Not in body, anyway. He wished to be alone."

Now Bitterblue shot to her feet. "What happened?"

Taking a breath, letting it out slowly, Raffin answered in the same bleak voice. "My father has convicted him of treason, Lady Queen, on the basis of both his participation in the overthrow of the King of Nander and his continued monetary contributions to the Council. He's been stripped of his title, land, and fortune, and if he returns to the Middluns, he'll be executed. Just to be thorough, Randa has burned his estate and leveled it to the ground."

BITTERBLUE COULD NOT get to Giddon's rooms fast enough.

He was in a chair in the far corner, his arms flung and his legs spread and his face frozen with shock.

Going to him, Bitterblue dropped to her knees before him, took his hand, and wished that she had more than one hand to give.

"You should not kneel before me," he whispered.

"Shut up," she said, bringing his hand to her face and cradling it, hugging it, kissing it. Tears slid down her cheeks.

"Lady Queen," he said, leaning toward her, cupping her face gently, tenderly, as if this were the most natural thing in the world for him to do. "You're crying."

"I'm sorry. I can't help it."

"It's comforting to me," he said, wiping her tears away with his fingers. "I can't feel anything."

Bitterblue knew that species of numbness. She also knew what followed, once it passed. She wondered if Giddon realized what was coming, if he had ever known that kind of catastrophic grief.

IT SEEMED TO help Giddon to ask him questions, as if by answering, he was filling in the blank spaces and remembering who he was. And so she asked him things, letting each answer supply her next question.

This was how Bitterblue learned that Giddon had had a brother who'd died in a fall from a horse at the age of fifteen—Giddon's horse, which had not liked to be ridden by others and which Giddon had goaded him to ride, never anticipating the consequences. Giddon and Arlend had fought incessantly, not just over horses; they would probably have fought over their father's estate had Arlend lived. Giddon now wished Arlend had lived and won. Arlend might not have been a fair landlord, but nor would he have provoked the king. "He was my twin, Lady Queen. After he died, every time my mother looked at me, I believe she saw a ghost. She swore not, and she never blamed me for it openly. But I could see it in her face. She didn't live long after that."

This was also how she learned that Giddon didn't know yet if everyone had gotten out.

"Out?" she said, then understood. *Oh. Oh no.* "Surely murder was not Randa's intention. Surely the people were warned to leave the house. He's not Thigpen or Drowden."

"I worry that they'll have tried—foolishly—to save some of the family keepsakes. My housekeeper will have tried to save the dogs, and my stable master, the horses. I—" Giddon shook his head in confusion. "If anyone has died, Lady Queen—"

"I'll send someone to find out," she said.

"Thank you, Lady Queen, but I'm sure word is already on its way."

"I—" It was intolerable, being unable to make anything better. She stopped herself before she could say something rash, like an offer of a Monsean lordship, which struck her, when she took a moment to examine the notion, as no comfort whatsoever and probably insulting. If she was deposed and her castle leveled, how would it feel to be offered as a gift the queenship of some other people she knew nothing of, in some other place that was not Monsea? It was unthinkable.

"How many people were under your care, Giddon?"

"Ninety-nine in the house and on the immediate grounds, who now have no home or occupation. Five hundred eighty-three in the town and on the farms, who will not find Randa a careful landlord." He dropped his head to his hands. "And yet, I don't know what I would have done differently, Lady Queen, even knowing the consequences. I could never have continued to be Randa's man. I've made such a mess of things. Arlend should have lived."

"Giddon. This was Randa's doing, not yours."

Lifting his face from his hands, Giddon directed an expression at her that was baleful, ironic, and certain.

"All right," she said, then paused, thinking through what she wanted to express. "It is your doing, in part. Your defiance of Randa made those for whom you were responsible vulnerable. But I don't think it follows that you could have prevented it, or should have anticipated it. Randa shocked everyone with this. His empty gestures have never been so extreme before, and no one could have foreseen that the entirety of the consequences would fall on you." For this was another thing Giddon had told her: Oll, still in Nander, had been stripped of his captaincy, but Oll had lost Randa's confidence years ago, so it hardly mattered. Katsa was re-banished and re-declared fortuneless, but Katsa had been banished and fortuneless for ages. It had never stopped her from entering the Middluns when she wanted to, or stopped Raffin from advancing her money when she needed it. Randa railed at Raffin, threatened him, threatened to disown him, threatened to unname him, but never did. Raffin seemed to be Randa's sticking point; Randa was unable to do a serious injury to his own son. And Bann? Randa had an extraordinary capacity for pretending that Bann didn't exist.

Giddon, on the other hand, was a coward king's perfect target: a noble man of considerable noble wealth who didn't terrify Randa and whom it would be fun to ruin.

"Perhaps we could have anticipated it, had we not had a thousand other things to consider," Bitterblue admitted. "But I still doubt that you could have prevented it. Not without becoming a lesser man."

"You've promised never to lie to me, Lady Queen," said Giddon.

Giddon's eyes were damp and too bright. Exhaustion had begun to pull at his features, as if everything, his hands, his arms, his skin, were too heavy for him to support. Bitterblue wondered if the numbness was passing. "I'm not lying, Giddon," she said. "I believe that when you gave your heart to the Council, you chose the right path."

IN THE MORNING, Bann and Raffin came to breakfast. She watched them as they ate, subdued, half asleep. Bann's hair was wet and curling at the ends, and he seemed to be thinking hard about something. Raffin kept sighing. He was leaving for Estill tomorrow with Po.

After a while, she said, "Is there nothing the Council can do about Giddon? Has Randa's behavior not sunk him to the level of the worst kings?"

"It's complicated, Lady Queen," said Bann after a moment, clearing his throat. "Giddon *was* actually funding the Council with the wealth of his noble estate, as both Po and Raffin do, and as such, he was committing a crime that could be construed as treason. A king is justified in seizing the possessions of a treasonous lord. Randa's behavior was extreme, but he did everything by the book." Bann touched his eyes on Raffin, who sat like a man made of wood. "Perhaps more relevantly, Lady Queen," Bann continued quietly, "Randa is Raffin's father. Even Giddon opposes any action on our part that would set Raffin in direct opposition to his father. Giddon has lost all that mattered to him. Nothing we did could change that."

They ate again in silence for a while. Then Raffin said, as if deciding something, "I've also lost something that mattered. I still cannot believe he did it. He's made himself my enemy."

"He's always been our enemy, Raffin," said Bann gently.

"This is different," Raffin said. "I've never wanted to reject him as my father before. I've never wanted to be king, just so that he isn't."

"You've never wanted to be king at all."

"I still don't," said Raffin with sudden bitterness. "But he shouldn't be. I'll be lost as a king, but at least," he said, enunciating each word, "I won't be a damn cruel man."

"Raffin," said Bitterblue, her heart swelling with how much she understood this. "I promise you," she said, "when that day comes, you won't be alone. I'll be with you, and all the people who help me will too. My uncle will go to you if you want him. Both of you will learn how to be king," she said, meaning Bann, of course, and more grateful than she'd ever been before for Bann's groundedness, to balance out Raffin's abstraction. Perhaps they could make a king together.

Helda walked into the room and opened her mouth to speak; then paused as the outer doors were heard to creak open. Moments later, Giddon surprised them all by yanking Saf into the room by one arm. Giddon looked bleary-eyed and rumpled.

"What did he do now?" Bitterblue asked sharply.

"I found him in your father's maze, Lady Queen," said Giddon.

"Saf," said Bitterblue, "what were you doing in the maze?"

"It's not against the law to walk through the castle," Saf said, "and anyway, what's *his* excuse for being in the maze?"

Giddon backhanded Saf across the mouth, grabbed him by the collar, looked straight into his astonished eyes, and said, "Speak to the queen with respect or you'll never work with the Council in any capacity."

Saf's lip was bleeding. He touched it with his tongue, then grinned at Giddon, who released him roughly. Saf turned back to Bitterblue. "Nice friends you've got," he said.

Bitterblue knew that Giddon had almost certainly been in the maze because Po had sent him in there, to find out what Saf was up to. "Enough," she said, angry with both of them. "Giddon, no more hitting. Saf, tell me why you were in the maze."

Reaching into his pocket, Saf pulled out a ring with three keys on it, followed by a set of lock picks Bitterblue recognized. Without ceremony, he deposited both into Bitterblue's hand.

"Where did you get these?" Bitterblue asked in confusion.

"They look like Fox's lock picks, Lady Queen," said Helda.

"They are," said Bitterblue. "Did she give them to you, Saf, or did you steal them?"

"Why would she give me her lock picks?" asked Saf blandly. "She knows exactly who I am."

"And the keys?" asked Bitterblue evenly.

"The keys came out of her pocket when I nicked the lock picks."

"What are they the keys to?" Bitterblue asked Helda.

"I couldn't say, Lady Queen," said Helda. "I wasn't aware of Fox having any keys."

Bitterblue studied the keys in her hand. All three were large and ornate. "They're familiar," she said vaguely. "Helda, these keys are familiar. Come, help me," she said, going to the blue horse hanging. As Helda took the hanging in both arms, Bitterblue began to try each key in the lock. The second one successfully unlocked the door.

Bitterblue looked into Helda's eyes, sharing with Helda the question of why Fox would have had Leck's keys in her pocket. And why, having them, she would have made a show of using the lock picks. "I'm certain there's a satisfactory explanation, Lady Queen," said Helda.

"So am I," said Bitterblue. "Let's wait to see if she volunteers it to me when she discovers Saf took them."

"I trust her, Lady Queen."

"I don't," said Saf from the other side of the room. "She has holes in her earlobes."

"Well," Helda said, "that's because she spent her childhood in Lienid, just like you did, young man. Where do you suppose she got a name to match her hair?"

"Then why doesn't she talk to me about Lienid?" Saf said. "If her family was alert enough to send her away, why doesn't she talk to me about the resistance? Why tell me nothing of her family, her home? And where is her Lienid accent? She's trying to make herself into nothing, and I don't trust it. Her conversation is too selective. She told me the location of Leck's rooms but didn't say a word about there being a maze. Was she hoping I would get caught?"

"Did she instruct you to go snooping?" retorted Bitterblue. "You're complaining about the mistrustful behavior of someone you stole from, Saf. Maybe she doesn't talk to you because she doesn't like you. Maybe she didn't like Lienid. Anyway, the list of people you trust is shorter than the number of keys on this ring. What do we have to do to make you stop behaving like a child? We won't always go into contortions to protect you, you know. Has Prince Po told you that the day he saved your life in my courtroom and you rewarded him by stealing my crown, he spent hours running through the rain in pursuit of it, then fell gravely ill?"

No, Po hadn't told him. Saf's sudden, silent chagrin was evidence. "Why were you in my father's maze?" Bitterblue asked again.

"I was curious," Saf said in a defeated voice.

"About what?"

"Fox mentioned Leck's rooms," Saf said. "Then I picked her pocket and came up with the keys, and thought I could guess what they were for. I was curious to see the rooms for myself. Do you think that Teddy or Tilda or Bren would forgive me if I didn't use the opportunity of my time in the castle to uncover some truths?"

"I think that Teddy would tell you to stop wasting my time, and the Council's time too," said Bitterblue. "And I think you know I'd be happy to describe Leck's rooms to Teddy myself. Balls, Saf. If he asked, I'd take him to see them with his own eyes."

The outer doors creaked open again.

"I think we're done here," Bitterblue said, nervous now for Saf's sake, in case the person coming in was anyone other than Po or

Madlen. Or Death. Or Holt. Or Hava. *These are the people I trust,* she thought, rolling eyes at herself.

"Has Prince Po recovered?" Saf put in.

Katsa burst into the room.

"Recovered from what?" she demanded. "What happened?"

"Katsa!" said Bitterblue, limp with a sweet relief that brought tears pricking behind her eyes. "Nothing happened. He's fine."

"Has he—" Katsa registered that there was a stranger in the room. "Did he—" she began, confused.

"Calm down, Katsa," said Giddon. "Calm down," he repeated, offering his hand, which she grasped, after a moment's hesitation. "He was ill for a while, and now he's better. Everything's fine. What took you so long?"

"Wait till I tell you," Katsa said, "because you're not going to believe it." And then she went to Bitterblue and drew her into a one-sided hug.

"Who did this to you?" she demanded, running her fingers lightly along Bitterblue's bound arm. Bitterblue was so happy that she felt no pain. She buried her face in the coldness of Katsa's odd-smelling, furry jacket and didn't answer.

"It's a long story, Kat," came Raffin's voice beside them. "A lot has happened."

Katsa stood on her toes to kiss Raffin. And then she peered more closely over Bitterblue's head at Saf, narrowing her eyes on him, then on Bitterblue, then on him again. Beginning to grin while Saf stood with his mouth slightly open and the world's largest Graceling eyes. His gold flashed in his ears and on his fingers.

"Hello, sailor," Katsa said. Then to Bitterblue, "Does he remind you of anyone?"

"Yes," said Bitterblue, knowing that Katsa meant Po, but that she meant Katsa. Not caring. "Did you find the tunnel?" she asked, still burrowing against Katsa.

"Yes," said Katsa, "and followed it all the way to Estill. And I found something else too, through a crack. There were cracks everywhere, Bitterblue, and the air through them sounded funny to me somehow. It smelled different. So I moved a few rocks aside. It took me ages, and I started a small avalanche at one point, but I managed to make an opening to a whole new series of passages. Then I followed the widest one, as far as I could justify taking the time for. It killed me that I had to turn back. But there were openings aboveground now and then, and I'm telling you, Bitterblue, we've got to go back there. It was a passage east, under the mountains. Look at the rat that attacked me."

Once more, the doors opened. This time, Bitterblue knew who was coming. "Out," she said to Saf, extending her finger, because this was going to be a private and unpredictable thing, not for Saf's too-adoring eyes. "Out," she said more forcefully, motioning to Giddon to deal with it as Po appeared in the doorway, chest heaving, bracing a hand against the door frame.

"I'm sorry," Po said. "Katsa, I'm sorry."

"I am too," Katsa said, running at him. Giddon dragged Saf out. Katsa and Po held on to each other with tears running down their faces, making as big a scene as anyone could have expected, but Bitterblue had ceased to notice, her entire attention fixated on a thing Katsa had thrown onto the breakfast table as she'd run to Po. It was a small, strange something-or-other that was furry. Bitterblue reached out a hand.

Then she snatched her hand back, as if something had shocked her, or bitten.

It was a rat pelt, but there was something about it that was wrong.

It was almost a normal color, but not. Instead of gray, it was a sort of silver, with a sheen of gold at certain angles, and even beyond the oddness of the color, there was something peculiar about it that she couldn't quantify. She couldn't stop looking at it. This silverish rat pelt was the most beautiful thing Bitterblue had ever seen.

She made herself touch it. It was real, the fur of a real, once-living rat Katsa had killed.

Carefully, Bitterblue backed away from the table. Tears trickled down her face as she stood there, stuck in her own private avalanche.

31

WHAT IT SEEMED to mean was that while Leck's real world had been made up of lies, his imaginary world was true.

She sent for Thiel to join them, because she needed him, so immediately that it didn't even occur to her until later that she'd invited him straight into the room where a cloth covered a fake crown. When he appeared at her doors, surprised, but his face full of hope, Bitterblue found herself reaching for his hand. He was gaunt; he'd lost weight. But his clothing was neat, face shaved, expression attentive.

"It might upset you, Thiel," she told him. "I'm sorry, but I need you."

"I'm too happy to be needed for anything else to matter, Lady Queen," he said.

The silver pelt overwhelmed Thiel with numbness and confusion. He would have landed on the floor if Katsa and Po together hadn't managed to push a chair beneath him. "I don't understand," he said.

"You know the stories Leck told?" Bitterblue asked him.

"Yes, Lady Queen," said Thiel in bewilderment. "He was always telling stories about strangely colored creatures. And you've seen the art. The hangings," he said, flapping his hands at the blue horse across the room. "The bright flowers twined all around the sculptures. The shrubberies." Thiel shook his head back and forth as if he were ringing it like a bell. "But I don't understand. Surely it's only a pelt from a particularly unique rat. Or—could it be something Leck made, Lady Queen?"

"Lady Katsa found it in the mountains to the east, Thiel," said Bitterblue.

"To the east! Nothing lives to the east. The mountains are uninhabitable."

"Lady Katsa found a tunnel, Thiel, under the mountains. It may be that there's inhabitable land beyond. Katsa," said Bitterblue, "did it act like a regular rat?"

"No," Katsa responded firmly. "It marched right up to me. I thought, *Oh, here's a volunteer for my dinner,* but then I found myself standing there staring at it like a fool. And then it ran at me!"

"It mesmerized you," Bitterblue said grimly. "That's how Leck described them in his stories."

"It was something like that," admitted Katsa. "I had to close off my mind the way I might do around"—a quick glance at Thiel, who still shook his head back and forth ponderously—"a mind reader. Then I came to my senses. I'm dying to go back, Bitterblue. As soon as I have the time, I'll follow the tunnel all the way through."

"No," Bitterblue said. "No waiting. I need you to go now."

"Are you going to command me?" Katsa asked, laughing.

"No," Po said, tight-mouthed. "No commanding. We need to discuss this."

"I need everyone to see it," Bitterblue said, not listening. "I need everyone's opinions, everyone who knows the stories and everyone who knows anything about anything. Darby, Rood, Death—Madlen, might she have some knowledge of animal anatomy?—Saf and Teddy and all those who know the stories from the story rooms. I need everyone to see this!"

"Cousin," said Po quietly, "I advise caution. You're spinning around with a sort of a wild gleam and Thiel is sitting there like a man lost inside himself. Whatever this thing is," he said, running his fingers over the pelt with mild distaste, "and I agree that it doesn't seem normal—whatever it is, it has a powerful effect on those who knew Leck. Don't just go flinging it at people. Go slow, and keep it secret, you understand me?"

"It's where he came from," Bitterblue said. "It's got to be, Po, and that means it's where I'm from too, a place where the animals look like this and cloud your mind, the same way he did."

"It might be," Po said. He was hugging her, his shirt smelling faintly of Katsa's furry coat, which comforted her, as if she were being hugged by both of them at once. "Or it might just be a thing he knew of and made up crazy stories about. Take a breath, sweetheart. You can't figure it all out right now. We need to go a step at a time."

Po and Raffin were leaving the next day to take Giddon's tunnel into Estill and talk to the Estillan people about their plans for replacing King Thigpen. Katsa and Po spent the better part of the day snappish and irritable to everyone but each other. Bitterblue supposed it would be late before they could be alone together, and Po needed sleep if he was to spend the next day on a horse.

Then Katsa began to talk about accompanying the princes to Estill. Hearing this, Bitterblue called Katsa to her tower.

"Katsa," Bitterblue said, "why would you go with them? Do they need you, or is it a wish for more time with Po?"

"It's a wish for more time with Po," Katsa said frankly. "Why?"

"If you're considering going, then you mustn't be needed here. Right?"

"There's a lot I can do here with Bann, Helda, and Giddon. There's a lot I can do in Estill with Po and Raff. My presence isn't crucial right now in either place. I think I know where you're going with this, Bitterblue, and I'm afraid it's bad timing."

"Katsa," Bitterblue said. "It matters so desperately to me where you were and what you saw, but even forgetting my personal reasons, even forgetting the rat, it matters that a passage has opened and we don't know where it leads. If there's a part of the world that we don't know about, nothing is more important than finding out about it. Not even the Estillan revolution is more important. Katsa—Leck told stories about a whole other kingdom. What if there are people over there, on the other side of the mountains?"

"If I go," Katsa said, "I could be gone a long time. Just because the Council doesn't need me now doesn't mean they won't need me in two weeks."

"*I* need you."

"You're a queen, Bitterblue. Send the Monsean Guard."

"I could do that, even not trusting the Monsean Guard at the moment, but a company of soldiers doesn't move as fast as you, or as discreetly. And what'll happen when my soldiers get there? They won't have your mental strength or your Grace when they're beset by a pack of colorful wolves or some such. Nor will they be able to move without being seen, as you can, and I need someone to spy on what's over there, Katsa. You were made for this. It would be so neat and easy!"

"It would not be easy," said Katsa, snorting.

"Oh, how hard do you think it would be?"

"Not hard to follow the tunnel, face wolves, poke around, and come back," said Katsa, her voice growing sharp. "Hard to leave Po just now."

Bitterblue took a breath. She focused for a moment, centering herself around her stubbornness. "Katsa," she said, "I don't like to be cruel. And I know I can't make you do anything you don't want to do. But—please—add it to the possibilities you're considering. Think about what it would mean if another kingdom exists on the other side of the mountains. If we're capable of discovering them, then they're capable of discovering us. Which would you rather happened first? Couldn't Po and Raffin delay their trip just a little bit longer?" she suggested. "What's one more day? I'm sorry, Katsa," she said, alarmed now, for big, round tears had begun to slide down Katsa's face. "I'm sorry to ask for this."

"You have to," Katsa said, smearing the tears away, wiping her nose on her sleeve. "I understand. I'll think about it. May I stay with you for a few minutes until I've got hold of myself?"

"You don't ever have to ask," said Bitterblue, astonished. "You may always stay as long as you like."

And so Katsa sat in a chair, shoulders straight, breath even, scowling into the middle distance, while Bitterblue sat across from her, glancing at her worriedly now and then. Otherwise pushing her eyes across finance reports, letters, charters, and more charters.

After a short while, the door opened and Po slipped in. Katsa began to cry again, silently. Bitterblue decided to take her charters downstairs to work on them in the lower offices.

As she left the room, Po went to Katsa, pulled her up, sat himself in her chair, and drew her into his lap. Shushing her, he rocked her, the two of them holding on to each other as if it were the only thing keeping the world from bursting apart.

*   *   *   *   *

THEY SENT HER a note later in the day. Ciphered in Katsa's hand, it read: *Po and Raffin delay one day. When they go, I'll return to the mystery tunnel and follow it east.*

We're sorry for kicking you out of your office.

I'll come for your lesson in the morning. I'll teach you how to fight with one arm bound.

"Is it always like that?" asked Bitterblue at dinner.

Giddon and Bann, her two dinner companions, turned to blink at her, puzzled. The others had dined with them too, but then they'd all run back to their plans and preparations, which was as Bitterblue liked it. Giddon and Bann were the people she most wanted to ask about this, though Raffin would also have been welcome.

"Is what always like what, Lady Queen?" asked Giddon.

"I mean," said Bitterblue, "is it possible to have a—" She wasn't sure what to call it. "Is it possible to share someone's bed without tears, battles, and constant crises?"

"Yes," said Bann.

"Not if you're Katsa and Po," said Giddon at the same time.

"Oh, stop it," Bann protested. "They go long stretches of time without tears, battles, or crises."

"But you know they both love a good blowup," said Giddon.

"You make it sound as if they do it on purpose. They always have good reason. Their lives are not simple and they spend too much time apart."

"Because they choose to," Giddon said, rising from the table, going to bank up the dying fire. "They don't need to spend so much time apart. They do it because it suits them."

"They do it because the Council requires it," Bann said to Giddon's back.

"But they decide what the Council requires, don't they? As much as we do?"

"They put the Council ahead of themselves," Bann said firmly.

"They also like to make scenes," Giddon muttered with his head in the fireplace.

"Be fair, Giddon. They're just not good at containing themselves in front of their own friends."

"That's the definition of a scene," said Giddon dryly, coming to sit down again.

"It's just—" Bitterblue began, then stopped. She wasn't sure what it just was. Her own experience was miniscule, but it was all she had, so she couldn't help referring to it. She had liked sparring with Saf. She had liked playing trust games. But she didn't like fighting with him, not at all. She didn't like being the object of his fury. And if the crown situation counted as a crisis, well, then she didn't like crises either.

On the other hand, she saw clearly enough that Katsa and Po had something sustaining, deep, and fierce. It was a thing that she envied sometimes.

Bitterblue stabbed a mystery pie across the table with her fork and was delighted when it turned out to be made of winter squash. She pushed her plate closer and shoveled herself a generous portion. "It's just that while I'm sure I would like the making up, I don't think I have the heart for constant fighting," she said. "I think I might prefer something—more peaceful in execution."

Giddon cracked a grin. "They do give the impression that no one else has nearly as much fun making up."

"But people do, you know," said Bann, perhaps a bit slyly. "I wouldn't worry about them, Lady Queen, and I wouldn't worry about what it means. Every configuration of people is an entirely new universe unto itself."

IN THE MORNING, Giddon left to meet a Council ally from Estill who was visiting a town called Silverhart, half a day's ride east along the river. Then he surprised them all by not coming back by nightfall.

"I hope he gets in before morning," Po said over dinner. "I didn't want to leave until he was back."

"So he can protect me?" said Bitterblue. "You think I'm not safe with both you and Katsa away, don't you? Don't forget, I have my Queen's Guard and my Lienid Guard, and it's not like I ever leave the castle anymore."

"I finally got into the east city today, Beetle," said Po. "I walked practically every street, and spent some time in the south city too. I could not find Runnemood. And Bann and I tried to work it out, but we can't get around that it'd be a great strain right now for him or Giddon to take off in search of your captain."

"Someone set a fire three nights ago and killed another of Saf and Teddy's friends," said Bitterblue.

"Oh," said Po, dropping his silverware. "I wish this Estill thing weren't happening now. Too much is going on and nothing is right."

With the rat pelt tucked in her pocket, Bitterblue couldn't really argue. Early in the day, she'd gone to the library and shown it to Death. At the sight of it, he'd turned eight shades of gray.

"Merciful skies above," he'd said hoarsely.

"What do you think?" asked Bitterblue.

"I think," said Death, then paused, truly seeming to be think-ing. "I think I need to rethink the current shelving of King Leck's stories, Lady Queen, for they're in a section reserved for fantastical literature."

"That's what you're worried about?" demanded Bitterblue. "The shelving of your books? Send someone for Madlen, will you? I'm going to my table, where I intend to read about how monarchy is tyranny," she said, then stormed away in annoyance, realizing that it hadn't been a particularly incisive retort.

Madlen produced a much more satisfactory reaction. Narrowing her eyes on the pelt, she announced "Hm-hm!" then proceeded to ask a thousand questions. Who'd found it, and where? How had the creature behaved? How had Lady Katsa defended herself? Had Lady Katsa encountered any people? How far had Lady Katsa followed the tunnel? Where, precisely, did this tunnel start? What was going to be done about it, when, and by whom?

"I hoped you might have some medical insight," Bitterblue managed to interject.

"It's rutting peculiar, Lady Queen," said Madlen, then glanced at the hanging of the wild-haired woman, spun on her heel, and marched off.

Sighing, Bitterblue turned to Lovejoy, who was sprawled on the table, peering at her with his chin resting on one paw. "It's a good thing I employ all these experts," she said. Then she held the tip of the pelt out to him, poking his nose with it. "What do you think of it?"

Lovejoy made a point of having no opinion whatsoever.

I WON'T LET him into our rooms. Perversely, he honors my barricades, while setting up his own guards outside our door. When he goes away to his graveyard I explore his rooms. I'm looking for passage out, but find nothing.

If I knew his secrets and plans, could I stop him? But I can neither read them nor find them. The sculptures watched me look. They told me the castle has secrets and he'd kill me if he found me snooping. It was a warning, not a threat. They like me, not him.

Bitterblue sat that night with legs crossed on her bedroom floor, wondering if it was worthwhile to try to find any sense in the passage when half of it seemed raving mad.

"Lady Queen?" said a voice from the doorway.

Bitterblue turned, startled. It was Fox.

"Forgive me for the intrusion, Lady Queen," said Fox.

"What time is it?" asked Bitterblue.

"One o'clock, Lady Queen."

"Perhaps a bit late for intrusions."

"I'm sorry, Lady Queen," said Fox. "It's just that there's something I've got to tell you, Lady Queen."

Bitterblue extricated herself from the sheets and went to stand by her dressing table, wanting to be away from her mother's secrets, her father's secrets, while Fox was in the room. "Go on," she prompted, guessing what this was about.

"I found a set of keys, Lady Queen," Fox said, "in a corner, in a deserted back room of the smithy. I'm not certain what they were the keys to. I—could have asked Ornik his opinion," she said, hesitating, "but I was snooping when I found them, Lady Queen, and didn't want him to know. He came in and thought I was waiting for him, Lady Queen, and I thought it might be best to let him go on thinking that."

"I see," said Bitterblue dryly. "Mightn't they simply have been keys to the smithy?"

"I tried that, Lady Queen," said Fox, "and they weren't. They were big, grand, important-looking keys, not like any I've ever seen. But before I could bring them to you, Lady Queen, they disappeared from my pocket."

"Oh?" said Bitterblue. "Do you mean that someone stole them?"

"I couldn't say, Lady Queen," said Fox, looking down at her own folded hands.

Fox knew perfectly well that Bitterblue knew perfectly well that Fox was spending her daylight hours on a platform with a thief who had every appearance, on the basis of recent events, of being involved with the queen somehow. Bitterblue couldn't blame Fox for deciding not to accuse Saf outright of theft. For all Fox knew, it risked angering the queen.

At the same time, if it weren't for Saf, would Bitterblue be hearing about the keys at all? Once Saf had stolen them, Fox *had* to tell Bitterblue about them, in case Saf did. Regardless of her original intentions, and regardless of where she'd actually gotten them.

"Have you learned anything new about the crown, Fox?" she asked as a sort of test, to see if everyone's stories matched up.

"The Gray fellow refuses to sell to you, Lady Queen," said Fox. "And he's spreading rumors. But it's only to make you nervous, Lady Queen, and tighten the net around you. He'll keep it from the people you most need not to know of it, then blackmail you for whatever he wants by threatening to tell them."

Unhelpfully, the stories matched. "Very clever," said Bitterblue. "Thank you for telling me about the keys, Fox. Helda and I will keep our eyes out for them."

And then, after Fox had gone, she opened her mother's chest, reached under the rat pelt, and fished the keys out.

She'd practically forgotten them, what with the arrival of the pelt and the plans of all her friends. Now she left her rooms with a lamp in her good hand. Dropping down the staircase into the maze, she put her right shoulder to the wall and took the necessary turns.

The very first key she tried opened her father's door with a great click.

Inside, Bitterblue stood under the watchful eyes of the paint-splattered sculptures. "Well?" she said to them. "My mother asked you where the castle keeps its secrets, but you wouldn't tell her. Will you tell me?"

Looking from one sculpture to another, she couldn't help feeling that Ashen had written nothing mad. It took effort not to think of them as living creatures with opinions. The silver and turquoise owl in the hanging peered at her with round eyes.

"What is the third key for?" she asked them all. Then she went into the bathing room, climbed into the tub, and pressed on every tile in the wall behind it. She pressed on every other tile she could reach too, just to be thorough. Going to the closet space, she ran her good hand along the shelves and other surfaces, sneezing, but persistently pushing. Back inside the room, she pushed and patted the hangings.

Nothing. No hidden compartments full of Leck's musty, secret thoughts.

Forty-three turns with her shoulder hugging the left wall brought her back to her staircase. As she climbed the steps, the sound of some lonely musical instrument rose to her ears. Melancholy strings being touched by someone's hand. *Someone in my castle does play music.*

In her bedroom, Bitterblue returned to her place on the rug and began with a new sheet.

Thiel says he'll get me knife if he can. Won't be easy, Leck keeps track of all knives. He'll have to steal one. Must tie sheets together and go out window. Thiel says it's too dangerous. But there's only one guard in garden, too many guards by any other route. He says when it's time he'll keep Leck away.

T HE NEXT DAY, Po and Raffin left before dawn, taking their horses into the east city and quietly across Winged Bridge. Katsa followed soon after, leaving Bann, Helda, and Bitterblue to stare at one another gloomily over breakfast. Giddon still hadn't returned from Silverhart.

Then, in late morning, Darby ran up her tower stairs and dropped a folded note onto her desk. He sniffed. "This seems urgent, Lady Queen."

The note was written in Giddon's hand, unciphered. *Lady Queen,* it said, *please come to your stables as soon as possible and bring Rood. Be discreet.*

She couldn't think why Giddon would ask for such a thing, and doubted it could be for any cheerful reason. Well, at least he was safely back.

Rood followed her to the stables like a timid dog, folded in on himself, as if trying to make himself disappear. "Do you know what this is about?" she asked him.

"No, Lady Queen," he whispered.

Stepping into the stables, she couldn't spot Giddon anywhere, so she chose the closest row of stalls and began to walk down them past horses that stomped and snorted. Around the first corner, she saw Giddon in the door of a faraway stall, bending over something on the ground. Another man was with him—Ornik, the young smith.

Rood let out a sob beside her.

Giddon heard, turned, and came to them quickly, blocking their advance. With one arm outstretched to stop Bitterblue and his other arm practically holding Rood upright, he said, "It's dreadful, I'm afraid. It's a corpse that's been in the river for some time. I—" He hesitated. "Rood, I'm sorry, but we think it's your brother. Would you know his rings?"

Rood collapsed to his knees.

"It's all right," Bitterblue said to Giddon as he looked at her helplessly. She put her hand on his arm. "You deal with Rood. I know his rings."

"I'd rather you didn't have to see it, Lady Queen."

"It will hurt me less than it hurts Rood."

Giddon spoke over his shoulder to Ornik. "Stay with the queen," he said, unnecessarily, for Ornik had already come forward, smelling of vomit.

"That bad, Ornik?" said Bitterblue.

"It's very bad, Lady Queen," Ornik said grimly. "I'll show you his hands only."

"I would like to see his face, Ornik," she said, not knowing how to explain that she needed to see all there was to see. Just so that she would know, and possibly understand.

And yes, she recognized the rings constricting the skin of the horrible balloon hand, though the rest of him was unrecognizable. Barely human; fetid; the sight of him barely sufferable. "Those are Runnemood's rings," she told Ornik. *And this answers the question of whether Runnemood is the only person targeting truthseekers. This body wasn't setting any fires in the city*—she counted days in her head—*four nights ago.*

He would have died anyway, if he'd been convicted of his crimes. So why is seeing him dead so horrible?

Ornik covered the body with a blanket. When Giddon came to stand beside them, Bitterblue looked back and saw that Darby had come and was kneeling with an arm around Rood. And beyond them, Thiel, hovering, with empty eyes, like a ghost.

"Is there any way of knowing what happened?" Bitterblue asked.

"I don't think so, Lady Queen," said Giddon. "Not with a body that's been in the river as long as this one seems to have been. As long as three and a half weeks, I suppose, if he died the night he disappeared, right? Rood and Darby are both speculating that it was suicide."

"Suicide," she repeated. "Would Runnemood have committed suicide?"

"Unfortunately, Lady Queen," said Giddon, "there's more I need to tell you."

"All right," Bitterblue said, noticing that behind Giddon, Thiel had turned and was gliding away. "Just give me a minute, Giddon."

She ran to catch up with Thiel, calling his name.

He turned to her woodenly.

"Do you also think it was suicide, Thiel? Don't you think he must have had enemies?"

"I can't think, Lady Queen," said Thiel in a voice that cracked and strained. "Would he have done such a thing? Had he gone so mad? Perhaps it is my doing," he said, "for letting him run off that night, alone. Forgive me, Lady Queen," he said, backing away in confusion. "Forgive me, for this is my doing."

"Thiel!" she said, but he pushed himself away.

Turning back, Bitterblue saw Giddon down another row of stalls, hugging a man she'd never seen before, hugging him like a long-lost cousin. And now Giddon was hugging the horse that had apparently just come in with the man. Giddon had tears running down his face.

What on earth was going on? Was everyone mad? She focused on the tableau of Darby and Rood on their knees. Runnemood's wrapped corpse lay on the floor beyond them, and Rood was weeping inconsolably. Bitterblue supposed one might over a brother, no matter who the brother had grown up to be.

She went to him to tell him she was sorry.

THE MAN GIDDON had been hugging was the son of Giddon's housekeeper. The horse Giddon had been hugging was one of Giddon's own horses, a mare who'd been on an errand in town when Randa's raid had begun. No one had felt the need to tell Randa's men that their inventory of Giddon's stables that day was off by one horse.

All the people had gotten out of the buildings. All the horses had survived, as had all the dogs, down to the smallest runt puppy. As for Giddon's things, little was left. Randa's men had gone through the place beforehand, collecting items of value, then carefully set the sort of fire that would produce the maximum destruction.

Bitterblue walked with Giddon back into the castle. "I'm so sorry about all of it, Giddon," she said quietly.

"It's a comfort to talk to you about it, Lady Queen," he said. "But do you remember that there was more I needed to tell you?"

"Is it about your estate?"

It was not about Giddon's estate. It was about the river, and Bitterblue's eyes widened as she listened.

The river at Silverhart was full of bones. The bones had been discovered at the same time as Runnemood's body, for, as it happened, the corpse had gotten hung up on what turned out, upon investigation, to be a reef of bones. Ice had then formed around the body and frozen solid, anchoring it into place. All of this had occurred at a bend in the river where water pooled, slowing nearly to a stop. It was a deep spot the townspeople tended to avoid, for the very reason that dead things accumulated there, fish and plants washing up to the banks, lingering until they rotted away. It was a putrid place.

The bones were human.

"But how old are they?" Bitterblue asked, not understanding. "Are they the bodies Leck burned on Monster Bridge?"

"The healer didn't think so, Lady Queen, for he could find no signs of burning, but he admitted to having little experience with reading bones. He wasn't comfortable speculating about their age. But it's possible they've been collecting there for some time. If people hadn't had to row in among them to free Runnemood's corpse, they wouldn't have been discovered. No one makes a point of going to this stretch of river, Lady Queen, and no one steps into the pool, for the footing there is dangerous."

And now Bitterblue was thinking about something else entirely: Po and his hallucinations. *The river is swimming with the dead.* Ashen and her embroidery. *The river is his graveyard of bones.* "We need to bring the bones out," she said.

"I understand that there are underwater caverns in this place, Lady Queen, with quite deep water. It may be difficult."

A memory opened to Bitterblue like a crack of light. "Diving for treasure," she muttered.

"Lady Queen?"

"According to something Saf said to me once, he knows a bit about recovering things from the ocean floor. I expect he could extrapolate to a river floor. Can one do such a thing in cold weather? He is discreet," she added grudgingly, "with information, anyway. Not so much with his behavior."

"At any rate, I'm not sure discretion is an issue here, Lady Queen," said Giddon. "The whole town knows about the bones. They were discovered just before I arrived, and I'd heard them talked about several times before I even reached my contact. If we have a bone-retrieval operation going on in the river half a day's ride from the city, I don't see it staying quiet."

"Especially if we decide to search other parts of the river as well," Bitterblue said.

"Should we be doing that?"

"I think they're the bones of Leck's victims, Giddon," she said. "And I think there must be some in the river here, near the castle. Po couldn't sense them when he looked for them specifically, but when he was sick and hallucinating, his Grace swelling and distorting, some part of him knew. He told me the river was swimming with the dead."

"I see. If Leck dumped bones into the river, I suppose we could find them practically to the harbor. How well do bones float?"

"I have no idea," Bitterblue said. "Perhaps Madlen knows. Perhaps I should make a team of Madlen and Sapphire and send them out to Silverhart. Oh, my shoulder aches and my head is splitting," she said, stopping in the great courtyard, rubbing at her scalp under its too-tight braids. "Giddon, how I wish a few days would go by without any upsetting news."

"You've too much to worry about, Lady Queen," Giddon said quietly.

"Giddon," she said, caught by his tone, and ashamed of herself for complaining. Looking into his face and seeing a kind of desolation in his eyes that he was managing to keep out of his voice. "Perhaps this is a useless, unhelpful thing to say," she said. "I hope it will not be insulting. But I want you to know that you're always welcome in Monsea and you're always welcome at my court. And if any of your people have no employment, or wish, for whatever reason, to be elsewhere, they're all welcome here. Monsea is not a perfect place," she said, taking a breath, clenching her fist to ward off all the feelings that rose with that statement. "But there are good people here, and I wanted you to know."

Giddon took her small, clenched fist in his hand, raised it to his mouth, and kissed it. And Bitterblue was lit up inside, just a little bit, with the magic of knowing she'd done a small thing right. Oh, to feel that way more often.

BACK IN HER office, Darby told her that Rood was in bed, being looked after by his wife and, supposedly, bounced on by grandchildren, though Bitterblue couldn't imagine Rood being bounced on by anything without breaking. Darby did not react well to the news of the bones. He blundered away and, as the hours went on, became a bit erratic in his gait and his speech. She wondered if he was drinking at his desk.

It had never occurred to Bitterblue to inquire before this exactly where Thiel kept his rooms. She only knew they were on the fourth level, northish, though obviously not within Leck's maze. That evening, she asked Darby for more specific directions.

In the correct hallway, she consulted a footman, who stared at her with fish eyes and pointed wordlessly at a door.

Somewhat unsettled, Bitterblue knocked. There was a pause.

Then the door swung inward and Thiel stood before her, staring down at her. His shirt was open at the throat and untucked. "Lady Queen," he said, startled.

"Thiel. Did I bring you out of bed?"

"No, Lady Queen."

"Thiel!" she said, noticing a small patch of red above one of his cuffs. "You're bleeding! Are you all right? What happened?"

"Oh," he said, looking down, searching his chest and arms for the offending spot, covering it with his hand. "It's nothing, Lady Queen, nothing except my own clumsiness. I'll see to it immediately. Would you—would you care to come in?"

He pulled the door fully open and stood aside awkwardly while she passed through. It was a single room, small, with a bed, a washstand, two wooden chairs, no fireplace, and a desk that seemed far too small for such a large man, as if he must knock his knees against the wall when he used it. The air was too cold and the light too dim. There were no windows.

When he offered her the better of the straight-backed chairs, Bitterblue sat, uncomfortable, embarrassed, and unaccountably confused. Thiel went to the washstand, turned his injured side away from her, rolled up his sleeve, and did something or other with pats of water and bandages. A stringed instrument stood in an open case against the wall. A harp. Bitterblue wondered if, when Thiel played it, its sound reached all the way to Leck's maze.

She also saw a bit of broken mirror on the washstand.

"Has this always been your room, Thiel?" she asked.

"Yes, Lady Queen," he said. "I'm sorry it's not more welcoming."

"Was it—assigned to you," Bitterblue asked carefully, "or did you choose it?"

"I chose it, Lady Queen."

"Do you never wish for a larger space?" she asked. "Something more like mine?"

"No, Lady Queen," he said, coming to sit across from her. "This suits me."

It did not suit him. This bare, comfortless square of a room, the gray blanket on the bed, the dreary-looking furniture did not in any way match his dignity, his intelligence, or his importance to her or to the kingdom.

"Have you been making Darby and Rood go to work every day?" she asked him. "I've never known either of them to go so long without a breakdown."

He studied his own hands, then cleared his throat delicately. "I have, Lady Queen. Though of course I could not insist it of Rood today. I confess that whenever they've asked for my guidance, I have given it. I hope you don't feel that I've been imposing myself."

"Have you been very bored?" she asked him.

"Oh, Lady Queen," he said fervently, as if the question itself were relief from boredom. "I've been sitting in this room with nothing to do but think. It is paralyzing, Lady Queen, to have nothing to do but think."

"And what have you been thinking, Thiel?"

"That if you would let me come back to your tower, Lady Queen, I would endeavor to serve you better."

"Thiel," she said quietly, "you helped us escape, didn't you? You gave my mother a knife. We wouldn't have gotten away if you hadn't; she needed that knife. And you distracted Leck while we ran."

Thiel sat huddled within himself, not speaking. "Yes," he finally whispered.

"It breaks my heart sometimes," Bitterblue said, "the things I can't remember. I don't remember that the two of you were such friends.

I don't remember how important you were to us. I only remember flashes of moments when he took you both downstairs to punish you together. It's not fair, that I don't remember your kindness."

Thiel let out a long breath. "Lady Queen," he said, "one of Leck's cruelest legacies is that he left us unable to remember some things and unable to forget others. We are not masters of our minds."

After a moment, she said, "I would like you to come back tomorrow."

He looked at her with hope growing in his face.

"Runnemood's dead," she said. "That chapter is over, but the mystery is not solved, for my truthseeking friends in the city are still being targeted. I don't know how it'll be between us, Thiel. I don't know how we'll learn to trust each other again, and I know you're not well enough to help me with every matter I face. But I miss you, and I'd like to try again."

A thin line of blood was seeping through another part of Thiel's shirt, high on his sleeve. As Bitterblue stood up to go, her eyes touched on all the parts of the room once more. She couldn't shake the feeling that it was like a prison cell.

BITTERBLUE WENT NEXT to the infirmary. She found Madlen's room warm from the heat of braziers, well lit against the autumn early darkness, and, as always, full of books and paper. A haven.

Madlen was packing.

"The bones?" asked Bitterblue.

"Yes, Lady Queen," said Madlen. "The mysterious bones. Sapphire has gone home and is also readying himself."

"I'm going to send a couple soldiers from my Lienid Guard with you, Madlen, because I'm concerned about Saf—but will you keep a close watch on him too, in your capacity as healer? I don't know how much he actually knows about recovering things from water, especially in the cold, and he thinks he's invincible."

"I will, of course, Lady Queen. And perhaps when I come back, we can take a look under that cast. I'm eager to test your strength and see how my medicines have worked."

"May I knead bread once the cast is off?"

"If I'm satisfied with your progress, then yes, you may knead bread. Is this why you came here, Lady Queen? For permission to knead bread?"

Bitterblue sat on the end of Madlen's bed, beside a mountain of blankets, papers, and clothing. "No," she said.

"I thought not."

She practiced the words in her mind before speaking them aloud, worried that they might prove she was mad. "Madlen. Would a person ever cut himself," she said, "on purpose?"

Madlen stilled her rummaging hands and peered at Bitterblue. Then she shoved the mountain of things on the bed aside with one powerful arm and sat beside her. "Are you asking for yourself, Lady Queen, or someone else?"

"You know I wouldn't do such a thing to myself."

"I would certainly like to think that I know it, Lady Queen," Madlen said. Then she paused, looking quite grim. "There are no limits to the ways people you think you know can astonish you. I can't explain the practice to you, Lady Queen. I wonder if it's meant to be punishment for something one can't forgive oneself for. Or an external expression, Lady Queen, of an internal pain? Or perhaps it's a way to realize that you actually do want to stay alive."

"Don't talk about it as if it's a life-affirming thing," Bitterblue whispered, furious.

Madlen studied her own hands, which were large, strong, and,

Bitterblue knew, infinitely gentle. "It's a relief to me, Lady Queen, that in your own pain, you take no interest in hurting yourself."

"Why would I?" Bitterblue flared. "Why should I? It's foolish. I would like to kick the people who do it."

"That would, perhaps, be redundant, Lady Queen."

IN HER ROOMS, Bitterblue stormed to her bedroom, slamming, even locking the door, then yanking at her braids, yanking at her sling and her gown, tears making silent tracks down her face. Someone knocked at the door. "Go away," she yelled, stomping back and forth. *How am I to help him? If I confront him, he'll deny it, then go empty, and fall apart.*

"Lady Queen," Helda's voice said on the other side of the door. "Tell me you're all right in there or I'll have Bann knock the door in."

Half crying, half laughing, Bitterblue found a robe. Then she went to the door and pulled it open.

"Helda," she said to the woman who stood there imperiously, holding a key in her hands that rendered her threat a bit overdramatic. "I'm sorry for my rudeness. I was—upset."

"Mmph. Well, there's more than enough to be upset about, Lady Queen. Pull yourself together and come into the sitting room, if you would. Bann has come up with a place for us to hide your Sapphire, should things reach a crisis point with the crown."

"IT WAS KATSA'S suggestion, Lady Queen," said Bann. "Do you think he'd go willingly to a hiding place of ours?"

"Possibly," Bitterblue said. "I could try to talk to him. Where is it?"

"On Winged Bridge."

"Winged Bridge? Isn't that part of the city rather populated?"

"He's to go up *onto* the bridge, Lady Queen. Hardly anyone goes onto it. And it happens to be a drawbridge, did you know? On its near side it has a sort of a room—a tower—for the drawbridge operator. Katsa discovered it the first time she left for her tunnel, for her route took her across the bridge, and she had no supplies that night, remember?"

"Isn't Winged Bridge high enough that practically three full-rigged ships stacked on top of each other could pass under it with room to spare?"

"In a manner of speaking, yes," said Bann mildly. "I don't expect there's ever been a need to raise the drawbridge. Which means it's a drawbridge tower no one looks at twice. It's furnished and functional, supplied with pots and pans and a stove and so on. It would be just like Leck to station a man there with no work to do, wouldn't it? His kind of illogic? But it's empty now. According to Katsa, everything is under years of dust. Katsa broke in and took a knife and a few other things, but left the rest."

"I'm beginning to warm to this idea," Bitterblue said. "It'd do Saf some good to sit in a cold room, sneezing and thinking about his mistakes."

"It's better than trying to hide him in one of our wardrobes, at any rate, Lady Queen. And it would be the first step in moving him to Estill."

Bitterblue raised her eyebrows. "You seem to have plans for him."

Bann shrugged. "Of course, we would try to help him regardless, Lady Queen, because he's your friend. But he's also a person we could use."

"I believe his own preference, if he decided to run, would be Lienid."

"We're not going to force him to go anywhere, Lady Queen," Bann said. "A person who doesn't want to work with us is no use to us. He follows his gut. It's one of the reasons he appeals to us, but we know it means he'll do whatever he likes. Tell him about the bridge, won't you? I'll go there myself one of these nights to make sure it suits our purposes. Sometimes, the best hiding places are in plain sight."

THAT NIGHT, INSTEAD of pushing herself through more embroidery, Bitterblue found herself padding to the art gallery. She wasn't sure why she did, and in her robe and slippers, no less. Helda and Bann had gone to sleep, and Giddon had his own problems. She had a vague sense of wanting company.

But Hava was nowhere to be found. "Hava?" she called once or twice, in case the girl was hiding. No response.

She ended up standing before the hanging of the man being attacked by the colorful beasts. Wondering, for the first time, if she might be looking at a true story.

A click sounded and the hanging she was staring at moved, billowed. There was a person behind it. "Hava?" she said.

It was Fox who emerged, blinking at Bitterblue's lantern. "Lady Queen!"

"Fox," Bitterblue responded. "Where on earth did you come from?"

"There's a spiral staircase that leads all the way up from the library, Lady Queen," said Fox. "I was just trying it for the first time. Ornik told me about it, Lady Queen. Apparently it runs past Lady Katsa's rooms as well, and the Council uses it sometimes for meetings. Do you think I'll ever be allowed to attend Council meetings, Lady Queen?"

"That will be for Prince Po to decide," said Bitterblue evenly, "and the others. Have you met any of them, Fox?"

"Not Prince Po," said Fox, then went on to talk about the others. Bitterblue only half attended, because Po was the one who mattered. She wished she'd had Po chat with Fox before he'd gone. And she was also distracted because something else entirely had captured her thoughts: She was seeing, in her mind, a succession of hidden entrances behind wild, strangely colored creatures. The door to Leck's stairway, hidden behind the blue horse in her sitting room. The secret entrance to the library, hidden behind the wild-haired woman in the hanging. The strange, colorful insects on the tiles of Katsa's bath; and now, a door in the wall behind this horrible scene.

"Forgive me, Fox," Bitterblue said, "but I'm exhausted. It's time I went to bed."

Then she walked back to her rooms and collected the keys. Going out again past her guards, dropping down the appropriate stairs, winding through the maze, she tried not to rush, because it was silly, only a hunch, and it was foolish to hope too hard.

Inside the room, she went to the tiny owl in the tapestry, lifted the bottom of the great, heavy, woven cloth, and crawled beneath it.

She couldn't see a thing and spent the first minute coughing at the dust. Eyes watering, nose itching like crazy, pressed up against the wall and half suffocated by art, she asked herself what in the blazes she expected to happen now: a door that swung open? A tunnel of light? *Feel around,* she thought. *Po opened the door behind Katsa's tub by pressing on a tile. Feel the wall. Reach high! Leck was taller than you.*

Feeling the wall, finding nothing but smooth wood, she grew disheartened, and also slightly embarrassed. What if someone intelligent whose opinion mattered came into the room, saw the bulge in the hanging, and lifted it to find the queen in her robe groping idly at the wood of the wall? Or, worse, what if they assumed she was an intruder and began whacking at her through the hanging? What if—

Her finger hooked into a knot in the wood, very high, so high that she was on tiptoe when she found it. Stretching herself as tall as she could, Bitterblue pushed her finger farther into the hole. A click sounded, followed by a rolling noise. A space opened before her.

She had to crawl back into the room for her lantern. Once under the hanging again, she lifted her light. It illuminated a stone spiral staircase leading down.

Bitterblue gritted her teeth and began the descent, wishing she had a free hand to steady against the wall. The staircase straightened eventually to a long, stone, descending passage. Continuing on, she found that it curved in places and contained occasional steps leading down. It was difficult to keep track of where she was in relation to Leck's room.

When her lamp found a glowing design on the wall, she stopped to examine it. A painting, painted directly onto the stone. A pack of wolves, silver, gold, and palest pink, howling at a silver moon.

She knew better than to pass on by without trying. Setting her lantern on the floor, she ran her hand over the stone, searching for something, anything that might be anomalous. Her finger caught in a hole on one side of the painting. The shape of the hole was strange. Familiar. Bitterblue touched its edges and realized it was a keyhole.

Breathing shakily, she pulled the keys from the pocket of her robe. Separating the third key from the others, she slipped it into the lock and carefully turned it. A click sounded. The stone wall before her pushed forward.

Taking the lamp again, Bitterblue squeezed into a shallow, low-ceilinged sort of closet, with shelves lining the back wall. On the shelves were books bound in leather. She set the lamp on the floor. Pulling a book down at random, her whole body shaking now, Bitterblue knelt. The leather was a sort of folder enclosing loose papers. Opening the folder awkwardly with one hand, holding a sheet of paper to the lamp, she saw squiggles, strange dips, curves, and slashes.

Now she remembered it: her father's peculiar, squiggly writing. She'd thrown some of it into the fire once. She hadn't been able to read the letters then. Now she understood why.

More secrets in cipher, Bitterblue thought, breathing through the fact. *My father wrote his secrets in cipher.*

If no one Leck hurt is left to tell me what he did, if no one will tell me the secrets everyone's trying to hide, the secrets that trap everyone inside pain, perhaps it doesn't matter. For Leck can tell me himself. His secrets will tell me what he did to leave my kingdom so broken. And finally, I'll understand.

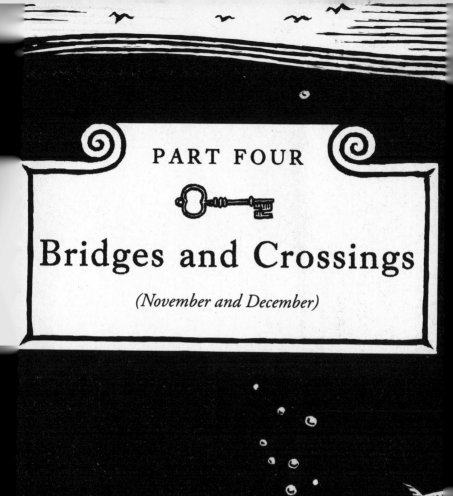

PART FOUR

Bridges and Crossings

(November and December)

33

THE BOOKS NUMBERED thirty-five. Bitterblue needed help, fast; she needed Helda, Bann, and Giddon. And so, locking all doors behind her, she went to wake each of them up.

At her persistent knocking, three bleary people came to three doors, listened to her frantic explanation, then went to get dressed. "Will you find my guard Holt?" she asked Bann, who leaned against his own door frame with no shirt on, looking like he would collapse unconscious on the floor if only she'd let him. "We need him to pull down the wooden boards blocking my sitting room door and he has to do it quietly, because we've got to get the journals up into my rooms without anyone knowing, and for rot's sake, hurry up!"

When Holt arrived, Hava was with him, for Holt had been visiting his niece in the art gallery when Bann had found him. Bitterblue, Hava, Holt, Giddon, and Bann snuck down the stairs and into the maze with a scattering of lamps, a strange, silent, late-night search party. They glided around corners to Leck's door.

Bitterblue forgot to warn them; unlocking the door and pushing everyone in, she forgot to warn Holt and Hava that the room was full of Bellamew's sculptures. Hava, shocked at the sight of them, flickered in confusion, turning into a sculpture, then back to a girl.

"He destroyed them," she said in a low, furious voice, holding her lantern close to one. "He covered them with paint."

"They're still beautiful," Bitterblue said quietly. "He tried to destroy

402 — Kristin Cashore

them, but I think he failed, Hava. Look at them. I don't need your help with the books—stay here and spend time with them."

Holt stood before the sculpture of the child growing wings and feathers. "This is you, Hava," he said. "I remember."

"I need your help, Holt," said Bitterblue. "Come with me."

Holt took one long look around the room. His gaze lingered on the empty bed frame. The eyes he finally turned to Bitterblue made her a bit nervous, for there was something unsteady there that she would rather not see in the eyes of a man Graced with strength and known for unpredictable behavior. "Holt?" she said, holding out her hand. "Will you come with me?"

Holt took her hand. She led him, like a child, to the back of the room and up the steps, and showed him the boards nailed to her sitting room door. "Can you pull them away, quietly, so that if any members of the Monsean Guard should be patrolling the maze, they won't overhear?"

"Yes, Lady Queen," he said, grasping a board with both hands, then tugging on it gently, so that it came out of the wall with nothing more than a small scraping sound.

Satisfied, Bitterblue left Holt to his work and scuttled down the steps to Giddon and Bann, who were waiting to be led under the hanging and through the tunnel to Leck's books.

WHEN THEY REACHED the closet with the books, she sent Giddon on down to follow the passage to its end and discover where it led. Someone had to, and she couldn't bear to leave the books herself. Then she and Bann began to pull the volumes down from the shelves and carry them back up to Leck's room, where they piled them on the rug. Muted sounds indicated that Holt was still pulling boards away from the door. Hava wandered from sculpture to sculpture, touching them, wiping dust away, not saying a word.

Bitterblue was in the closet reaching for the last few books when Giddon returned. "It goes on for some time, Lady Queen," he said, "and ends at a door. It took me forever to find the lever to open the door. It opens into the same corridor in the east castle where the tunnel to the east city starts, and it's hidden behind a hanging, just as all these doors seem to be. I only saw the hanging from the back, but it looked like a big, green wildcat tearing out the throat of a man. I peeked out into the corridor. I don't think anyone saw me."

"I hope no one else has made the colorful-animal-hidden-tunnel connection," breathed Bitterblue. "I'm furious with Po for not realizing."

"Not fair, Lady Queen," said Giddon. "Po can't see colors, and anyway, he hasn't had time to be mapping your castle."

Now she was angry with herself. "I'd forgotten about the colors. I'm an ass."

Before Giddon could respond, an enormous, distant crash interrupted them. They stared at each other in alarm. "Here, take these," Bitterblue said, shoving most of the remaining books at him, cradling the rest in her arm. The noises continued; they came from above, from the direction of Leck's room. Giddon and Bitterblue ran up the slope.

In the bedroom, Holt was lifting the bed frame into the air and crashing it down again onto the rug, breaking it into pieces. "Uncle," Hava cried, trying to grab his arm. "Stop it. Stop it!" Bann was struggling with Hava, trying to pull her away, but letting go every time she flickered into something else. Grabbing on to his own head, moaning.

"He ruined her," Holt said over and over, deliriously, lifting a piece of the bed frame and smashing it into the floor. "He ruined her. I let him ruin my sister." The bed frame he shattered so easily was a solid, huge thing. Splintered pieces of wood flew around the room, knocking against sculptures, raising explosions of dust. Hava fell down and he didn't even glance at her. Bann dragged Hava out of Holt's range and she huddled on the floor, weeping.

"Did he take all the boards down from the door?" Bitterblue asked Bann, shouting over the noise. Bann nodded, breathless. "Then get the books up the stairs to my rooms," she ordered both Bann and Giddon, "before the entire Monsean Guard breaks through the door to see what the noise is about." Then she went to Hava and held on to the girl as best she could, closing her eyes, because Hava kept changing shape and it was sickening.

"There's nothing we can do," Bitterblue told her. "Hava, we must just let him be until he's done."

"He'll hate himself when it's over," said Hava, gasping with tears. "That's the worst thing about it. When he comes back to his senses and realizes he went berserk, he'll hate himself for it."

"Then we must stay out of the way, where he can't hurt us," Bitterblue said, "so that we're able to reassure him that the only thing he injured was a bed frame."

No guards came. When the bed frame was well and truly smashed, Holt sat among the pieces on the floor, crying. Hava and Bitterblue went to him; they sat with him while he began his apologies and his expressions of shame. They tried to take that burden away from him, with gentle words of their own.

THE NEXT MORNING, Bitterblue walked into the library with a journal under her arm and stopped before Death's desk.

"Your Grace of reading and remembering," she said to Death. "Does it work with symbols you don't understand, or only with letters you do?"

Death wrinkled his nose in a way that made it seem as if he were wrinkling his entire face. "I have no earthly idea what you're talking about, Lady Queen."

"A cipher," Bitterblue said. "You've rewritten entire pages in cipher, from the book about ciphers that Leck destroyed. Were you able to do that because you understood the ciphers? Or can you remember a string of letters even if they mean nothing to you?"

"It's a complicated question," said Death. "If I can make them mean something—even if it's something silly that they don't actually mean—then yes, to some extent—if the passage isn't too long. But in the case of the ciphers in the cipher book, Lady Queen, I rewrote them successfully because I understood them and had their translations memorized. Passages of that length, had they been random strings of letters or numbers with no meaning, would have been much more difficult. Luckily, I do have a mind for ciphers."

"You have a mind for ciphers," Bitterblue repeated vaguely, talking more to herself than to him. "You have a gift for looking at letters and words and seeing patterns and meaning. That is how your Grace works."

"Well," Death said, "more or less, Lady Queen. Much of the time."

"And if it's a cipher in symbols, rather than letters?"

"Letters are symbols, Lady Queen," Death said with a sniff. "One can always learn more of them."

Bitterblue handed him the book she was carrying and waited while he opened it. At the first page, his eyebrows furrowed in puzzlement. At the second page, his mouth began to hang open. He sat back, dumbfounded, lifting his eyes to her face. Blinking too fast. "Where did you find it?" he asked in a hoarse, throaty voice.

"Do you know what it is?"

"It's his hand," Death whispered.

"His hand! How can you tell that, when none of the letters are the same?"

"His handwriting is odd, Lady Queen. You'll remember. He consistently wrote some letters strangely. The way he wrote them is similar, and in some cases, identical, to the symbols in this book. Do you see?"

Death pointed one thin finger to a symbol that looked like a U with a tail.

𝒰

Leck had, indeed, always written the letter *U* with that strange little tail at its top right. Bitterblue recognized it, and realized suddenly that she'd intuited the similarity the very first time she'd opened the first book. "Of course," she said. "Do you think this symbol corresponds to our *U*?"

"It wouldn't make for much of a cipher if it did."

"This cipher is your new job," Bitterblue said. "When I came to you, it was only to ask you to read it, in the hopes that you could memorize it, or even copy it, so that if we lost them, they wouldn't truly be lost. But now I see you're the man to break the cipher. It's not a simple substitution cipher, for there are thirty-two symbols. I counted. And there are thirty-five books."

"Thirty-five!"

"Yes."

Death's strange eyes were damp. He pulled the book toward him and held it to his chest.

"Break the cipher," Bitterblue said, "I beg you, Death. It may be the only way I ever understand anything. I'll work on it as well, and so will a couple of my spies who have a talent for ciphers. You may keep as many of the books as you want here, but no one else must ever, ever see them. Understand?"

Not speaking, Death nodded. Then Lovejoy sat up in Death's lap, his head poking above the desktop, his fur sticking out in oddball directions, as it always did, as if his hide fit him poorly. Bitterblue hadn't even known he was there. Death pulled Lovejoy against his chest and held him tight, gripping both cat and book as if he expected someone to try to take them from him.

"Why did Leck let you live?" Bitterblue asked Death quietly.

"Because he needed me," said Death. "He couldn't control knowledge unless he knew what the knowledge was and where to find it. I lied to him, when I could. I pretended his Grace worked on me even more than it did; I preserved what I could; I rewrote what I could and hid it. It was never enough," he said, his voice breaking. "He raped this library and all other libraries, and I couldn't stop him. When he suspected me of lying, he cut me, and whenever he caught me in a lie, he tortured my cats."

A tear ran down Death's face. Lovejoy began to struggle from being held so hard. And Bitterblue understood that a cat's fur might lie strangely on its body if its skin has been cut by knives. A man's spirit might shiver unpleasantly around his body if he has been alone with horror and suffering for too long.

There was nothing she could do to mend that kind of suffering. Nor did she want to frighten Death with demonstrative behavior. But leaving without an acknowledgment of all he'd said was not an option. Was there a right thing to do? Or only a thousand wrong things?

Bitterblue walked around the desk to him and placed her hand gently on his shoulder. When he breathed in and out once, raggedly, she obeyed an astonishing instinct, bent, and kissed his dry forehead. He took another great breath. Then he said, "I will break this cipher for you, Lady Queen."

* * * * *

IN HER OFFICE with Thiel at the helm, paper passed more smoothly across Bitterblue's desk than it had in weeks.

"Now that it's November," she said to him, "we can hope for a response soon from my uncle with advice on how I'm to provide remuneration to the people Leck stole from. I wrote to him at the start of September, remember? It'll be a relief to get to work on that. I'll feel like I'm actually doing something."

"I theorize that those bones in the river are from bodies dumped by King Leck, Lady Queen," responded Thiel.

"What?" Bitterblue said, startled. "Does that have something to do with remuneration?"

"No, Lady Queen," said Thiel. "But people are asking questions about the bones, and I wonder if we shouldn't release a statement explaining that King Leck dumped them. It will put an end to the speculation, Lady Queen, and allow us to focus on matters like remuneration."

"I see," said Bitterblue. "I'd prefer to wait until Madlen has concluded her investigation, Thiel. We don't actually know yet how the bones got there."

"Of course, Lady Queen," said Thiel, with utter correctness. "In the meantime, I'll draft the statement, so that it's ready for release at the slightest moment."

"Thiel," she said, putting her pen down and giving him a look. "I'd much rather you spent your time on the question of who's burning buildings and killing people in the east city than on drafting a statement that might never be released! Now that Captain Smit is *away*," she said, trying not to imbue the word with too much sarcasm, "find out for me who's in charge of the investigation. I want daily reports, just like before, and you may as well know that I've rather lost my faith in the Monsean Guard. If they want to impress me, they should find some answers that match the answers my own spies are finding, and fast."

Of course, her own spies weren't finding any answers. No one in the city had anything helpful to offer; the spies sent to investigate the names on Teddy's list uncovered nothing. But the Monsean Guard didn't need to know that, and neither did Thiel.

Then, a week after Madlen and Saf had gone to Silverhart, Bitterblue received a letter that elucidated—possibly—*why* her spies still weren't finding any answers.

The first part of the letter was written in Madlen's strange, childish handwriting.

We're recovering hundreds of bones. Thousands, Lady Queen. Your Sapphire and his team are bringing them up faster than I can keep count. I am afraid that I can tell little about them beyond the basics. Most of them are the smaller bones. I have found pieces from at least forty-seven different skulls and am attempting to articulate the skeletons. We have set up an impromptu laboratory in the guest rooms of the inn. We are lucky that the innkeeper has an interest in science and history. I doubt all innkeepers would wish their guest rooms full of bones.

Sapphire wishes to write you a line. He says that you will know the key.

What followed was a paragraph in some of the most indecipherable handwriting Bitterblue had ever seen, so tangled that it took her a moment to confirm that it was, indeed, ciphered. Two possible keys sprang to mind. To spare her own heart, she tried the hurtful one first. *Liar.* It didn't work. But the second one produced this message: *you were right to send your lienid guard and i must thank you for it. they stopped man with knife who came at me in camp when i was wet freezing in no state to fight. wild man, raving, could give no reason, no names for who hired him. pockets full of money. this is how they do it. they choose lost souls to do their work, desperate people with no reason who couldn't identify them even if wanted to, so looks like random senseless crime. be careful, watch your back. are guards watching shop?*

Guards are watching the shop, Bitterblue wrote back, using his key. She hesitated, then added, *You be careful too, in that cold water, Saf.*

The key was *Sparks.* Bitterblue couldn't help the tiny hope that rose in her heart that she was forgiven.

IN THE MEANTIME, Ashen's embroidery lay, neglected, in piles on her bedroom floor, with three of Leck's books hidden beneath it. She spent as much time as she could spare with her nose in one of those books, scribbling at scrap after scrap of paper, pushing her mind through every kind of decipherment she'd ever read about—or, trying to, anyway. She'd never had to do this before. She'd ciphered messages using the most complicated ciphers she could imagine, and enjoyed the neatness of it, the rapid calculations of her own mind. But deciphering was an entire other beast. She understood the basic principles of decipherment, but when she tried to transfer that understanding to Leck's symbols, everything kept falling apart. She could find patterns, in places. She could find strings of four or five or even seven symbols that reappeared here and there in the exact same sequence, which should have been a good thing. Repetitions of a particular sequence of symbols within any ciphered text suggested a repeated word. But the repetitions were exceedingly rare, which suggested a revolving series of more than one cipher alphabet, and it did not help a bit that the total number of different symbols in use was thirty-two. Thirty-two symbols to represent twenty-six letters? Were the extra symbols blanks? Were they used as alternates for the most common letters, like *E* and *T,* to make it difficult for a cipher-breaker to break the cipher by means of examining letter frequency? Did they represent consonant blends like *TH* and *ST*? It gave Bitterblue a headache.

Death hadn't made much progress on the cipher either, and was more harried and snappish than usual. "I may have determined that there are six different revolving alphabets," Bitterblue said to him one evening. "Which suggests that the key is six letters long."

"I determined that days ago!" he practically shouted. "Don't distract me!"

Watching Thiel as he tottered around her tower sometimes, Bitterblue wondered what her greater reason was for hiding the existence of the journals from him. Was she more afraid of his interference? Or of the damage it would do to his fragile soul to know that secret writing of Leck's had been found? She'd been furious with him for shielding her from the truth, and now found herself with the same instinct.

Rood was back, shuffling around slowly, taking small breaths. Darby, on the other hand, flung himself around the offices and up and down the stairs, flung papers and words about, stank like old wine, and finally, one day, collapsed on the floor in front of Bitterblue's desk.

He muttered incomprehensible gibberish while healers attended to him. As they carried him out of the room, Thiel stood frozen, staring out the windows. His eyes seemed fixed on something that wasn't there.

"Thiel," said Bitterblue, not knowing what to say. "Thiel, can I do anything for you?"

It seemed, at first, as if he hadn't heard. Then he turned away from the window. "Darby's Grace prevents him from sleeping the way we do, Lady Queen," he said quietly. "Sometimes, the only way for him to switch his mind off is to make himself blind drunk."

"There must be something I can do to help him," Bitterblue said. "Perhaps he should have less stressful work to do, or even retire."

"Work comforts him, Lady Queen," said Thiel. "Work comforts all of us. The kindest thing you can do is allow us to continue working."

"Yes," she said. "All right," for work kept her own thoughts from spinning out of control too. She understood him.

She sat on her bedroom floor that night with two of her spies who were cipher breakers. The books lay open before them as they hypothesized, argued, passed weariness and frustration back and forth to each other. Bitterblue was too exhausted to realize how exhausted she was, and how unequal to the task.

At the edge of her vision, a largeness filled the doorway. Turning, trying not to lose her thought, she saw Giddon leaning against the door frame. Behind him, Bann rested his chin on Giddon's shoulder.

"Can we convince you to join us, Lady Queen?" asked Giddon.

"What are you doing?"

"Sitting," Giddon said, "in your sitting room. Talking about Estill. Complaining about Katsa and Po."

"And Raffin," Bann said. "There's a sour cream cake."

The cake was motivation, of course, but mostly, Bitterblue wanted to know what sorts of things Bann said when he was complaining about Raffin. "I'm not getting anywhere with this," she admitted blearily.

"Well, and we need you," Giddon said.

Half stumbling in her slippers, Bitterblue joined them. Together, they walked down the corridor.

"Specifically, we need you to lie supine on the sofa," Bann said as they entered the sitting room.

This struck Bitterblue as suspicious, but she complied, and was deeply gratified when Helda loomed out of nowhere and slapped a plate of cake on her stomach.

"We're having some luck with military defectors in south Estill," began Giddon.

"This raspberry filling is amazing," said Bitterblue fervently, then fell asleep, with cake in her mouth and her fork in her hand.

MADLEN AND SAF were away for nearly two weeks. When they returned, they made a path through November snow with upward of five thousand bones, and few answers.

"I have managed to reassemble three or four nearly complete skeletons, Lady Queen," said Madlen. "But mostly I've got fragments, and not enough time or space to work out which goes with which. I've found no evidence of burning, but some of sawing. I believe we're looking at hundreds of people, but I can't be any more specific. What would you say to having that cast off tomorrow?"

"I would say it's the first good news I've had in—" Bitterblue tried to calculate back, then eventually gave up. "Forever," she said grumpily.

Leaving the infirmary, stepping into the great courtyard, she came face-to-face with Saf. "Oh!" she said. "Hello."

"Hello," he said, also taken by surprise.

He was, apparently, about to climb onto the window-caulking platform and haul it, with Fox, to whatever obscene height today's work called for. He looked well—the water didn't seem to have hurt him—and there was something quiet in the way he stood there before her, looking at her. Less antagonism?

"I've something to show you, and a request," Bitterblue said. "Will you come to the library sometime in the next hour?"

Saf gave a small nod. Behind him, Fox tied a rope to her belt, not seeming to notice them.

DEATH STORED ALL the journals Bitterblue wasn't working on in a low cabinet in his desk. When Bitterblue asked to borrow one, he unlocked the cabinet and handed it to her impatiently.

When, shortly thereafter, Saf walked into her library nook with high eyebrows, she passed it to him. Flipping pages, he said, "What is this?"

"A cipher we can't break," she said, "written in Leck's hand. We've found thirty-five volumes."

"One for each year of his reign," Saf said.

"Yes," Bitterblue said, trying to look as if she'd already noticed that. As if, in fact, he hadn't just given her a tool to take back to the deciphering team. If each book represented a year, could they isolate similarities between corresponding parts of different journals? Would each book's opening language, for example, relate to winter?

"I want you to take it," Bitterblue said, "but you must keep it close, Saf. Show no one outside Teddy, Tilda, and Bren, *tell* no one, and if no one has any useful thoughts, return it directly. Don't get caught with it."

"No," Saf said, shaking his head, holding it out to give back to her. "I'm not taking it, not with the way things have been. Someone'll find out. I'll be attacked, they'll get it from me, and your secret will be ruined."

Bitterblue sighed shortly. "I suppose I can't argue. Well then, will you look through it now and tell the others about it, and let me know what they say?"

"Yes, all right," he said, "if you think it'll help."

He'd gotten his hair cut. It was darker now, and bits of it stuck up endearingly, in new directions. Confused by his willingness to be helpful and conscious that she was staring, she walked to the hanging while he flipped through the book again. The sad, green eyes of the woman in white calmed her.

"What's the request?" he said.

"What?" she said, spinning around.

"You said you had something to show me," Saf said, gesturing with the book, "and a request. I'll do it, whatever it is."

"You—you will?" she said. "You're not going to fight me?"

He rested his eyes on her face with a frankness she hadn't seen there since the night he'd kissed her, then found her crying in the graveyard and blamed himself for it. He looked a bit embarrassed. "Maybe the cold water unblocked my head," he said. "What's the request?"

She swallowed. "My friends have found you a hiding place. If a crisis arises with the crown and you need to hide, will you go to the drawbridge tower on Winged Bridge?"

"Yes."

"That was it," she said.

"I'll go back to my work, then?"

"Saf," she said, "I don't understand. What does this mean? Are we friends?"

The question seemed to confuse him. He placed the journal back on the table carefully. "Maybe we're something else," he said, "that hasn't figured itself out yet."

"I don't understand what that means."

"I think that's the point," he said, pushing his hand through his hair a bit hopelessly. "I see I acted like a child. And I see you clearly again. But it's not like anything can ever be how it was. I'll go now, Lady Queen," he said, "if that's all right."

When she didn't respond, he turned and left her. After a while, she went to her table and tried to push herself through a bit more of the book about monarchy and tyranny. She read something about oligarchies and something about diarchies, but none of it sank in.

She wasn't sure that she had any idea who Saf was now, and his use of her title had devastated her.

THE NEXT MORNING, Bitterblue opened her bedroom door to the prospect of Madlen brandishing a saw.

"This is not a reassuring sight, Madlen," said Bitterblue.

"All we need is a flat surface, Lady Queen," said Madlen, "and everything will go swimmingly."

"Madlen?"

"Yes?"

"What happened to Saf in Silverhart?"

"What do you mean, what happened?"

"Yesterday, when he talked to me, he seemed changed."

"Ah," said Madlen thoughtfully. "I couldn't say, Lady Queen. He was quiet, and I did think that the bones sobered him. Perhaps they encouraged him to consider who you are, Lady Queen, and what you're dealing with."

"Yes, perhaps," said Bitterblue, sighing. "Shall we go into the bathing room?"

One of Leck's journals lay open at the foot of the bed, where Bitterblue had been puzzling it over. Walking past the pages, Madlen paused, struck by it.

"Are you any good at ciphers, Madlen?" Bitterblue asked.

"Ciphers?" Madlen said in apparent bewilderment.

"You mustn't tell a soul about it—not a soul, do you understand? It's a cipher written by Leck, and we're having a terrible time cracking it."

"Indeed," Madlen said. "It's a cipher."

"Yes," said Bitterblue patiently. "So far, we haven't managed to identify the meaning of even a single symbol."

"Ah," Madlen said, peering at the page more closely. "I see what you mean. It's a cipher, and you believe each symbol represents a letter."

Bitterblue came to the conclusion that Madlen wasn't much good at ciphers. "Shall we get this over with?" she said.

"How many symbols are in use, Lady Queen?" asked Madlen.

"Thirty-two," said Bitterblue. "Come this way."

BEING WITHOUT THE cast was marvelous. Bitterblue could touch her arm again. She could scratch the skin, she could rub it; she could wash it clean. "I will never break a bone again," she announced as Madlen introduced her to a new series of exercises. "I love my arm."

"Someday you'll be attacked again, Lady Queen," said Madlen sternly. "Pay attention to the exercises so that you'll be strong on that day."

Then, when Bitterblue and Madlen stepped out of the bathing room together, they found Fox standing at the end of the bed, staring at Leck's ciphered book and holding one of Ashen's sheets in her hands.

Bitterblue made an instant decision.

"Fox," she said pleasantly. "I'm sure you know better than to trifle with my things when I'm out. Put that down and come away."

"I'm so sorry, Lady Queen," Fox said, dropping the sheet as if it were on fire. "I'm thoroughly ashamed of myself. I couldn't find Helda, you see."

"Come along," said Bitterblue.

"Your bedroom door was open, Lady Queen," Fox continued eagerly as they walked. "I heard your voice beyond, so I poked

418 — Kristin Cashore

my head in. The sheets were piled on the floor and the top one was so beautiful with embroidery that I went to it to see it closer. I couldn't resist, Lady Queen. I apologize. I had a report for you, you see."

Bitterblue saw Madlen out, then brought Fox into the sitting room. "Well then," she said calmly. "What is this report? Have you found Gray?"

"No, Lady Queen. But I've been hearing more rumors in the story rooms about Gray having the crown, and about Sapphire being known to be the thief."

"Mm," Bitterblue said, not finding it difficult to playact concern, for her worry was genuine, even while her mind spun with a hundred other things. Fox, who was always around when delicate things were happening. Fox, who knew an awful lot of Bitterblue's secrets, but about whom Bitterblue knew practically nothing. Where did Fox live when she was outside the castle? What kind of city people encouraged their daughter to work such odd hours, run around with lock picks in her pocket, snoop and ingratiate herself?

"How did you become a castle servant, Fox, not living in the castle?" asked Bitterblue.

"My family has been the servants of nobility for generations, Lady Queen," Fox said. "We've always tended to live outside the homes of our patrons; it's just been our way."

When Fox had gone, Bitterblue went looking for Helda. She found her in Helda's own bedroom, knitting in a green armchair. "Helda," she said. "What would you say to us having Fox followed?"

"Goodness, Lady Queen," said Helda, needles calmly clicking. "Has it come to that?"

"I just . . . I don't trust her, Helda."

"What's caused this?"

Bitterblue paused. "The hair that stands up on the back of my neck."

BITTERBLUE WAS IN the royal bakery a day later, thudding her tired arm determinedly against a ball of dough, when she looked up to find Death bouncing before her.

"Death," she said in astonishment. "What in the blue sky—"

His eyes were wild. A pen behind his ear dripped onto his shirt, and there were cobwebs in his hair. "I've found a book," he whispered.

Wiping her hands, moving him away from Anna and the bakers, who were trying not to look too curious, Bitterblue said quietly, "You found another ciphered book?"

"No," said Death. "I found a whole new book. A book that will crack the cipher."

"Is it a book about ciphers?"

"It's the world's most wonderful book!" he exclaimed. "I don't know where it came from! It's a magical book!"

"All right, all right," said Bitterblue, pulling him away into the clatter of the rest of the kitchen, toward the doors. Trying to soothe him and shush him and keep him from bursting into song or dance. She wasn't worried about his sanity, at least no more than she worried about anyone's sanity in this castle. She understood that books could be magical. "Show me this book."

THE BOOK WAS big and fat and red, and it was spectacular. "I understand," said Bitterblue, flipping through it, sharing his excitement.

"No, you don't," said Death. "It's not what you think."

What she thought was that this book was a sort of enormous, extended key that showed what each of Leck's symbol words really meant. The reason she thought this was that the first half of the book contained page after page of words Bitterblue knew, and each word was followed by a symbol word.

care . . . . ᛒᛁᚻᛏᛃ

careful . . ᛒᛁᚻᛏᛃᚩᛒᚹᛈ

carry . . . . ᚻᚠᛃᚳ

case . . . . ᛒᛁᚻᛏᚦ

cat . . . . . ᚻᚠᛞ

catch . . . ᚻᚠᛞᚠᚣ

cause . . . ᚻᚴᛈ

cell . . . . . . ᚦᛣᛈ

The back half of the book seemed to be the same information reversed: symbol words, followed by the real words they represented. And it was interesting that the symbol spellings seemed utterly random. A four-letter word, like *care*, might have a three-symbol spelling, and another word also made of *c*'s, *a*'s, and *r*'s, like *carry*, might, in its symbol spelling, share only one of the symbols used to spell *care*.

Also interesting that anyone would take such a risk with a cipher, allowing a book like this to exist. Leck's cipher was, indeed, uncrackable, only as long as this book was where it couldn't be found. "Where did you get this?" she asked, frightened, suddenly, of it disintegrating—of fires. Of thieves. "Are there more copies?"

"It's not the key to his cipher, Lady Queen," said Death. "I know you think that, and you're wrong. I tried it. It doesn't work."

"It's got to be," Bitterblue said. "What else would it be?"

"It's a dictionary for translating our language into an entire other language, and vice versa, Lady Queen."

"What do you mean?" Bitterblue plopped the book onto the desk beside Lovejoy. It was huge and her arms were tired, and she was beginning to be annoyed.

"I mean what I said, Lady Queen. Leck's symbols are the letters of a whole other language. This is the lexicon of our shared languages: all the words of our language translated into their language, and all the words of theirs translated into ours. Look, here," he said, flipping to a page at the book's very beginning, where all thirty-two symbols were listed in columns, each with a letter, or a combination of letters, beside it.

Symbol		Symbol		Symbol		Symbol	
𝑓	ah	𝛬	h	⊳	n	𝑑	s
𝑅	b	₵	ee	ⱻ	ng	𝑦	sh
ᴒ	v	𝑏	oe	ⱺ	oh	𝑓	t
𝑦	g	𝛿	y	ᴓ	yoh	𝑈	oo
𝑒	gh	𝑋	k	𝑊	w	𝑢	ue
𝑃	d	𝑁	kh	𝐻	p	𝑉	z
𝐾	ay	𝑄	l	𝑒	f	𝐴	zh
𝐻	way	𝑔	m	𝑧	r	𝐸	'

422 — KRISTIN CASHORE

"I theorize that this page is a pronunciation guide for speakers of our language," said Death. "It shows us how to pronounce the letters of the new language. You see?"

A whole other language. It was an alien concept to Bitterblue, so alien that she wanted to believe it was Leck's own personal language, one he'd made up for cipherment purposes. Except that the last time she'd assumed Leck had made something up, Katsa had come marching into her rooms with a rat pelt the color of Po's eyes.

"If there is another land to our east," Bitterblue whispered, "I suppose they would be likely to have a language and a lettering that differed from ours."

"Yes," Death said, hopping with excitement.

"Wait," she said, realizing something more. "This book isn't handwritten. It's printed."

"Yes!" cried Death.

"But—where is there a press with letter molds of these symbols?"

"I don't know!" cried Death. "Isn't it marvelous? I broke into the castle's defunct printing shop, Lady Queen, and fairly ransacked the place, but found nothing!"

Bitterblue hadn't even known there was a defunct printing shop. "That accounts for the cobwebs, then?"

"I can tell you this language's word for *cobwebs*, Lady Queen!" cried Death, then said something that sounded like it should be the word for a delightful new kind of cake: *hopkwepayn.*

"What?" Bitterblue said. "Have you learned it already? Dear skies! You've read the book and learned an entire language." Needing to sit down, she rounded the desk and collapsed into Death's own chair. "Where did you find this book?"

"It was on that shelf," Death said, pointing to the bookshelf directly across from his desk, perhaps five paces away.

"Isn't that the mathematics section?"

"It is exactly that, Lady Queen," said Death, "full of dark, slender volumes, which is why this enormous red thing caught my eye."

"But—when—"

"It appeared in the night, Lady Queen!"

"That's extraordinary," Bitterblue said. "We need to find out who put it there. I'll ask Helda. But are you telling me that this book doesn't make Leck's books coherent?"

"Using it as a key, Lady Queen, Leck's books contain gibberish."

"Have you tried using the pronunciation key? Perhaps if you pronounce the symbols, they sound like our words."

"Yes, I tried that, Lady Queen," said Death, joining her behind the desk, kneeling, unlocking the low cabinet with the key he kept on a string around his neck. Bringing out one of Leck's journals at random, he opened to the middle and began to read aloud. "*Wayng eezh wghee zhdzlby mzhsr ayf ypayzhgghnkeeoh*-DASH-*khf*—"

"Yes," Bitterblue said. "You've made your point, Death. What if you transcribed that horrible sound into our lettering? Does that become a cipher we could crack?"

"I think it's much less complicated than that, Lady Queen," said Death. "I believe King Leck wrote in cipher in this other language."

Bitterblue blinked. "The way we do in our language, but in his."

"Exactly, Lady Queen. I believe that all our work identifying the use of a six-letter key was not in vain."

"And—" Bitterblue was now resting her face flat on the desk. She moaned. "That strikes you as less complicated? To break this cipher, not only will we need to learn the other language, but we'll need to learn *about* the other language. What letters are used most often, and in what ratio to the others. What words tend to be used together. And what if it's *not* a cipher with revolving alphabets and a six-letter key? Or what if there's more than one six-letter key? How can we ever guess a key in another language? And if we do ever manage to decipher anything, the deciphered text will still be in the other language!"

"Lady Queen," said Death solemnly, still kneeling at her side, "it will be the most difficult mental challenge I have ever faced, and the most important."

Bitterblue raised her eyes to his. His entire being was glowing, and she understood him suddenly; she understood his devotion to difficult but important work. She said, "Have you really learned the other language already?"

"No," he said. "I've barely begun. It's going to be a slow and difficult process."

"It's too much for me, Death. I might learn some words, but I don't think my mind is going to be able to follow yours into the decipherment. I won't be able to help. And, oh, it terrifies me that you carry so much responsibility, all alone. Something this big shouldn't depend so entirely on a single person. No one must learn what you're doing, or you won't be safe. Is there anything you want or need that I could give you to make things easier?"

"Lady Queen," he said, "you've given me all I want. You're the queen a librarian dreams of."

Now, IF ONLY she could learn to be the queen those with more practical considerations dreamed of.

She finally received a ciphered letter from her uncle Ror, who agreed, with some cantankerousness, to travel to Monsea with a generous contingent of the Lienid Navy. *I'm not happy about it, Bitterblue,* he wrote. *You know I avoid involving myself in the matters of the five inner kingdoms. I cannot recommend strongly enough that you do the same, and I don't appreciate that you've left me with little choice but to offer my navy as your protection from their whims. We will have a serious talk about this when I arrive.*

Her cousin Skye enclosed a ciphered letter as well, as he always did, for the eighteenth letter in every sentence of Skye's deciphered text always combined to make the key for the next of Ror's letters. *Father would do almost anything for you, Cousin, but this one definitely ruffled his feathers. I took an extended vacation to the north just to get away from the yelling. I'm quite impressed with you. Keep it up. We wouldn't want him to get complacent in his old age. How is my little brother?*

It couldn't be too terribly bad if Skye was joking about it. And it was a great relief to Bitterblue both that she was in a position to influence Ror and that Ror was strong-minded enough to protest. It suggested the potential, someday, for an even balance of power between them—if she could ever convince him that she was grown up now, and that sometimes, she was right.

She did think he was wrong about some things. Lienid's seclusion from the five inner kingdoms was the luxury of an island kingdom, but she thought perhaps it was a trifle disingenuous on Ror's part. Ror's niece was the Monsean queen and his son a Council leader, Ror's kingdom was the seven kingdoms' wealthiest and most just, and at a time when kings were being deposed and kingdoms being born again on shaky legs, Ror had the potential to be a powerful example for the rest of the world.

Bitterblue wanted to be a powerful example with him. She wanted to find the way to build a nation that other nations would like to imitate.

How strange that Ror had mentioned nothing about the remuneration issue in his letter, for Bitterblue had sent her letter asking for remuneration advice before she'd sent the letter asking Ror to bring his navy. Perhaps the navy letter had upset him so much that he'd forgotten the other issue? Perhaps—perhaps Bitterblue could begin without his advice. Perhaps it was a thing she could plan herself, with the help of the few people she trusted. What if she had advisers, clerks, ministers who would listen to her? What if she had advisers who were unafraid of their own pain, unafraid of the kingdom's unhealed parts? What if she weren't always fighting against those who should be helping her?

What a strange thing a queen was. She found herself thinking sometimes, especially during the few minutes a day Madlen allowed her to knead bread dough: *If Leck came from some land to the east and my mother came from Lienid, how am I the supreme ruler of Monsea? How can I be, without a drop of Monsean blood in my veins?* And yet, she couldn't imagine being anyone else; her queenness was something she couldn't separate from herself. It had happened so fast, in the throwing of a dagger. Bitterblue had looked across a room at her dead father's body and known, to her very core, what she'd just become. She'd said it aloud. "I'm the Queen of Monsea."

If she could find the right people, the people she could trust who would help her, would she begin to assume the true purpose of a queen?

And what then? Monarchy was tyranny. Leck had proven that. If she found the right people to help her, were there ways she could change that too? Could a queen with a queen's power arrange her administration such that her citizens had power too, to communicate their needs?

There was something about the kneading of bread that connected Bitterblue's feet to the earth. Her wanderings did it too, her continued castle explorations. Needing candles for her bedside table one day, she went to get them herself at the chandler. Noticing her fast-growing wardrobe of trouser-skirt gowns, and the sleeves that were converted now back to buttonlessness, she asked Helda to introduce her to her dressmakers. Curious, she burst in on the boy who came every night to clear her dinner dishes away—then wished she'd planned that one more wisely, for he wasn't a boy. He was a young man with startling, dark good looks and fine shoulders and a beautiful way with his hands, and she was wearing a bright red robe with too-big pink slippers, her hair a mess and a smear of ink on her nose.

It was deeply satisfying, the workings of the castle around her. When she crossed the great courtyard in cold that sliced through her, she saw Saf on his platform, and workers clearing the ice from the drains. She saw snow falling onto the glass and meltwater pouring into the fountain. In the middle of the night in the corridors, men and women shined the floors on their knees with soft cloths while snow piled on the ceilings above them. She began to recognize the people she passed. No progress was made in the search for a witness to the red dictionary delivery, but when Bitterblue visited Death in the library, she learned the new alphabet, watched him draw alphabet grids and letter frequency diagrams, and helped him keep track of the numbers. "They call their language by a name we might pronounce as 'Dellian,' Lady Queen. And they—or, at any rate, Leck—calls ours, more or less, 'Gracelingian.'"

"Dellian, like the false name of the river? Like the River Dell?"

"Yes, Lady Queen."

"And Gracelingian? The name of our language is 'Gracelingian'?!"

"Yes."

Even Madlen's work of articulating skeletons, which had taken over the infirmary laboratories and one of the patient wards, comforted Bitterblue. These bones were the truth of something Leck had done, and Madlen was trying to return them to themselves. It felt, to Bitterblue, like a way of showing respect.

"How is your arm, Lady Queen?" Madlen asked her, holding what looked like a handful of ribs, staring at them as if they might speak to her.

"Better," Bitterblue said. "And kneading the bread grounds me."

"There's power in touching things, Lady Queen," said Madlen, echoing something Bitterblue herself had once thought. Madlen held the ribs out for Bitterblue to take. Bitterblue took them, feeling their peculiar smoothness. Tracing a raised line on one.

"That rib broke once, and rehealed, Lady Queen," said Madlen. "Your own arm, where the bone broke, is probably a bit like that."

Bitterblue knew Madlen was right: There was power in touching things. Holding this once-broken bone, she felt the pain its person had felt when it broke. She felt the sadness of a life that had ended too soon, and of a body that had been dumped as if it meant nothing; she felt her own death, which would happen someday. There was a sharp sadness in that too. Bitterblue had no peace with the notion of dying.

In the bakery, leaning over the bread dough, pushing and shaping it into an elastic thing, she began to find clarity on one point: Like Death, Bitterblue also had a taste for difficult—impossible—slow—messy work. She would figure out how to be queen, slowly, messily. She could reshape what it meant to be queen, and reshaping what it meant to be queen would reshape the kingdom.

And then, one day at the very start of December, as she pushed her tired arms to their daily limit, she looked up from the baker's table. Death stood before her. She didn't need to ask. From the luminous look on his face, she knew.

I~N THE LIBRARY~, Death handed her a piece of paper.

KEY: ⅀𝒜𝔉𝒴Ȼ𝒪, pronounced, roughly, *Ozhaleegh*

	𝔉	𝒮	𝛺	⅄	𝒪	𝖯	Ⴆ	Ħ	⋏	Ȼ	ᕋ	ꙟ	𝕏	Ħ	𝖄	Ջ	⊦	⅀	Ⴀ	𝔶	Ꝺ	Ə	3	ʤ	𝒴	𝒻
1.	⅀	Ⴀ	𝔶	Ꝺ	Ə	3	ʤ	𝒴	𝒻	𝒰	𝕎	𝒱	◿Ħ	𝔉	𝒮	𝛺	⅄	𝒪	𝖯	Ⴆ	Ħ	⋏	Ȼ	ᕋ	𝕏	𝖄	Ջ	⊦	⅀
2.	◿Ħ	𝔉	𝒮	𝛺	⅄	𝒪	𝖯	Ⴆ	Ħ	⋏	Ȼ	ᕋ	𝕏	ꙟ	𝖄	Ջ	⊦	⅀	Ⴀ	𝔶	Ꝺ	Ə	3	ʤ	𝒴	𝒻	𝒰	𝕎	𝒱
3.	𝔉	𝒮	𝛺	⅄	𝒪	𝖯	Ⴆ	Ħ	⋏	Ȼ	ᕋ	𝕏	ꙟ	𝖄	Ջ	⊦	⅀	Ⴀ	𝔶	Ꝺ	Ə	3	ʤ	𝒴	𝒻	𝒰	𝕎	𝒱	◿Ħ
4.	𝖄	Ջ	⊦	𝒻	⅀	ᕋ	𝛺	ꙟ	𝕏	Ə	3	ʤ	𝒴	𝒻	𝒰	𝕎	𝒱	◿Ħ	𝔉	𝒮	𝛺	⅄	𝒪	𝖯	Ⴆ	Ħ	⋏	Ȼ	𝕏
5.	Ȼ	ᕋ	𝕏	ꙟ	𝖄	Ջ	⊦	𝒻	⅀	ᕋ	ꙟ	Ə	3	ʤ	𝒴	𝒻	𝒰	𝕎	𝒱	◿Ħ	𝔉	𝒮	𝛺	⅄	𝒪	𝖯	Ⴆ	Ħ	⋏
6.	𝒪	𝖯	Ⴆ	Ħ	⋏	Ȼ	ᕋ	𝕏	ꙟ	𝖄	Ջ	⊦	𝒻	⅀	ᕋ	ꙟ	Ə	3	ʤ	𝒴	𝒻	𝒰	𝕎	𝒱	◿Ħ	𝔉	𝒮	𝛺	⅄

"The key is *ozhaleegh*," said Bitterblue, the pronunciation awkward in her mouth.

"Yes, Lady Queen."

"What does that word mean?"

"It means monster, Lady Queen, or beast. Aberration, mutant."

"Like him," Bitterblue whispered.

"Yes, Lady Queen. Like him."

"The top line is the regular alphabet," said Bitterblue. "The six subsequent alphabets began with the six letters that spell the word *ozhaleegh*."

"Yes."

"To decipher the first letter of the first word in a passage, we use alphabet number one. For the second letter, alphabet number two, and so on. For the seventh letter, we go back to alphabet number one."

"Yes, Lady Queen. You understand it perfectly."

"Isn't it rather complicated for a journal, Death? I use a similar ciphering technique in my letters to King Ror, but my letters are brief, and perhaps I write one or two a month."

"It wouldn't have been terribly difficult to write, Lady Queen, but it would have been a tangle to try to reread. It does seem a bit extreme, especially since presumably no one else spoke the Dellian language."

"He overdid everything," said Bitterblue.

"Here, let's take the first sentence of this book," said Death, pulling the closest book forward and copying down the first line:

ᐁᐃ ᒪᘇᕊᓇᘿ ᕊᔎᕟᙏ ᕲᐃᔿᔼᕳᙆᐁᘘᕟ ᔾᕼᗉ ᘇᘇ ᑌᕲᕊ
ᕟᙏ ᙭ᔼᕟᕟᒡᘿᕍᕼ ᑲᔎᕳ ᘇᘇ ᑌᕥᕟᒡᐃ ᙭ᕲᕊᕍ

"Deciphered, it reads—"

Both Death and Bitterblue scribbled on Death's blotter. Then they compared their results:

ᕟᔎ ᒪᙏᕟᐃᕍᔎ ᙭ᔎᕟᕟᔎ ᔾᕟᒪᕟᕍᕍᔎᙏᙏᑊ ᔾᕟ ᑲᕟᕥ ᕟᕳᕍᕊ
ᕟᔎ ᕍᔎᕟᕟᑲᙏᕟᑊᕟ ᕲᔎᕍ ᑲᕟᕥ ᕟᙏᕟᕳᕍᕟ ᕍᔾᕟ

"Are those real words?" asked Bitterblue.

"*Yah weensah kahlah ahfrohsahsheen ohng khoh nayzh yah hahntaylayn dahs khoh neetayt hoht,*" Death said aloud. "Yes, Lady Queen. "It means . . ." He screwed his lips tight, thinking. "'The winter gala approaches and we haven't the candles we need.' I've had to make some guesses about verb endings, Lady Queen, and their sentence structure differs from ours, but I believe that's accurate."

Touching her deciphered scribbles, Bitterblue whispered the strange Dellian words. In places, they sounded like her own language, but not quite: *yah weensah kahlah,* the winter gala. They felt like bubbles in her mouth: beautiful, breathy bubbles. "Now that you've cracked the cipher," she said, "should you try to memorize all thirty-five volumes before you start translating?"

"In order to memorize so much, Lady Queen, I'd need to decipher as I read. As long as I'm doing that, I may as well complete the translation as well, so that you have something to look at."

"I hope it isn't thirty-five books about party supplies," she said.

"I'll spend the afternoon translating, Lady Queen," he said, "and bring you the results."

HE ENTERED HER sitting room that night, while she was eating a late dinner with Helda, Giddon, and Bann. "Are you all right, Death?" Bitterblue asked him, for he looked—well, he looked old and miserable again, without the glow of triumph he'd had earlier in the day.

He handed her a small sheaf of paper wrapped in leather. "I leave it to you, Lady Queen," he said grimly.

"Oh," Bitterblue said, understanding. "Not party supplies, then?"

"No, Lady Queen."

"Death, I'm sorry. You know you don't have to do this."

"I do, Lady Queen," he said, turning to leave. "You do too."

A moment later, the outer doors closed behind him. Looking at the leather in her hands, she wished that he hadn't gone so soon.

Well, none of it would ever end if she was too afraid for it to begin. She pulled at the tie, pushed the cover aside, and read the opening line.

Little girls are even more perfect when they bleed.

Bitterblue slapped the cover over the page again. For a moment, she sat there. Then, raising her eyes to each of her friends in turn, she said, "Will you stay with me while I read this?"

"Yes, of course," was the response.

She carried the pages to the sofa, sat herself down, and read.

Little girls are even more perfect when they bleed. They are such a comfort to me when my other experiments go wrong.

I am trying to determine if Graces reside in the eyes. I have fighters and mind readers, and it is a simple matter of switching their eyes, then seeing whether their Graces have changed. But they keep dying. And the mind readers are so troublesome, too often understanding what is happening, so that I must gag them and restrain them before they spread their understanding to the others. Female fighter Gracelings are not limitless, and it infuriates me that I must waste them this way. My healers say it is blood loss. They say not to conduct so many experiments simultaneously on one person. But tell me, when a woman is lying on a table in her perfection, how am I not to experiment?

Sometimes I feel that I am doing all of it wrong. I have not made this kingdom into what I know it can be.

If I could be allowed my art, then I would not have these head-aches that feel as if my head is splitting open. All I want is to surround myself with the beautiful things that I have lost, but my artists won't be controlled like the others. I tell them what they want to do and half of them lose their talent completely, hand me work that is garbage, and stand there proud and empty, certain they've produced a masterpiece. The other half cannot work at all and go mad, becoming useless to me. And then there are those very few, those one, those two who do the literal of what I instruct, but imbue it with some genius, some terrible truth, so that it is more beautiful than what I asked for or imagined, and undermines me. Gadd created a hanging of monsters killing a man and I swear that the man in the hanging is me. Gadd says not, but I know what I feel when I look at it. How did he do it? Bellamew is a world of problems unto herself; she will not take instruction at all. I told her to make a sculpture of my fire-haired beauty and it began as such, then turned into a sculpture of Ashen in which Ashen has too much strength and feeling. She made a sculpture of my child and when it looks at me, I am convinced that it pities me. She will not leave off sculpting these infuriating transformations. Their work mocks my smallness. But I cannot turn away because it is so beautiful.

It is a new year. I will think about killing Gadd this year. A new year is a time for reflection, and really, what I ask for is so simple. But I cannot kill Bellamew yet. There is something in her mind that I want, and my experiments show that minds cannot live without bodies. She is lying to me about something. I know it. Somehow, she has found the strength to lie to me; and until I know the nature of this lie, I cannot be done with her.

My artists cause me more grief than they are worth.

It has been a hard lesson to learn, that greatness requires suffering.

Men are hanging lamps from the frames of the courtyard ceilings in preparation for the winter gala. They can be so stupid with me in their heads that it's insufferable. Three fell because they'd barely secured the ends of their rope ladder. Two died. One is in the hospital and will live for some time, I think. Perhaps, if he is mobile, I can involve him in the experiments with the others.

This was the sum of what Death had given her. He'd done a neat job of it, copying a Dellian line and then working out the translation just beneath it, so that she could see both, and perhaps begin to learn some of the Dellian vocabulary.

At the table, Bann and Helda conversed quietly about the problem of factions in Estill, noble versus citizen—with interjections from Giddon, who was dripping single drops of water into an extremely full glass, waiting to see which drop would cause the water to spill over the edge. From across the table, Bann tossed a bean. It plopped itself neatly into Giddon's glass and caused a deluge.

"I can't believe you just did that!" said Giddon. "You brute."

"You're two of the largest children I've ever known," scolded Helda.

"I was doing science," Giddon said. "He threw a bean."

"I was testing the impact of a bean upon water," Bann said.

"That's not even a thing."

"Perhaps I'll test the impact of a bean upon your beautiful white shirtfront," said Bann, with a threatening wave of a bean. Then both of them noticed that Bitterblue was watching. They turned their grins upon her, which was like a bath of silliness for her, a bath to clean away the dirty, crawling, panicky feeling she'd gotten from Leck's words.

"How bad was it?" asked Giddon.

"I don't want to ruin your good moods," said Bitterblue.

This earned her a look of mild reproach from Giddon. And so she did what she most wanted to do: Held it out for him to take. Coming to sit beside her on the sofa, he read it through. Bann and Helda, coming to sit in armchairs, read it next. No one seemed inclined to speak.

Finally, Bitterblue said, "Well, at any rate, it doesn't tell me why people in my city are killing truthseekers."

"No," said Helda grimly.

"This book begins at the new year," Bitterblue said, "which supports Saf's theory that each book chronicles a year of his reign."

"Is Death deciphering them out of order, Lady Queen?" asked Bann. "If Bellamew is making sculptures of you and Queen Ashen, then Leck's married, you've been born, and this is a book from late in his reign."

"I don't know that they're labeled in any way that would make it easy to put them in order," Bitterblue said.

"Maybe it'll be less upsetting to read them without having to mark the particular progression of his abuses," Giddon said quietly. "What was Bellamew's secret, do you suppose?"

"I don't know," Bitterblue said. "The location of Hava? It seems like he had a particular interest in Gracelings, and girls."

"I fear this will be just as horrible for you as the embroidery, Lady Queen," said Helda.

Bitterblue had no response to that either. Beside her, Giddon sat with his head thrown back, eyes closed. "When's the last time you left the castle grounds, Lady Queen?" he asked without moving.

Bitterblue sent her mind back. "The night that wretched woman broke my arm."

"That's almost two months ago, isn't it?"

Yes, it was. Two months, and Bitterblue was a bit depressed thinking about it.

"There's sledding on the hill that leads up to the ramparts of the castle's western wall," Giddon said. "Did you know that?"

"Sledding? What are you talking about?"

"The snow is dry and fine, Lady Queen," said Giddon, sitting up, "and people have been sledding. No one'll be there now. I expect it's well-enough lit. Does your fear of heights extend to sledding?"

"How should I know? I've never been sledding!"

"Get up, Bann," said Giddon, whacking Bann's arm.

"I'm not going sledding at eleven o'clock at night," said Bann with finality.

"Oh, yes you are," said Helda significantly.

"Helda," said Giddon, "it's not that I don't want Bann's involuntary company, but if, as you seem to be implying, it's not decent for the queen to go sledding with one unmarried man in the middle of the night, then how is it decent for her to go sledding with two?"

"It will be decent because I'm going," Helda said. "And if I must subject myself to late-night larks in freezing climes all for the sake of decency, then Bann will suffer beside me."

This was how Bitterblue came to discover that sledding, in a nighttime snowfall, with bewildered guards standing above and the earth's most complete silence, was magical, and breathless, and conducive to a great deal of laughter.

THE NEXT NIGHT, while Bitterblue was again eating with her friends, Hava came scurrying in. "Excuse me, Lady Queen," she said, trying to catch her breath. "That Fox person just came into the art gallery through the secret passage behind the hanging. I hid, Lady Queen, and followed her to the sculpture room. She tried to lift one of my mother's sculptures with her bare hands, Lady Queen. She failed, of course, and when she left the gallery, I followed her. She came nearly to your rooms, Lady Queen, then dropped down the staircase into the maze. I ran straight here."

Bitterblue jumped up from the table. "You mean that she's in the maze now?"

"Yes, Lady Queen."

Bitterblue ran for the keys. "Hava," she said, coming back and going to the hidden door, "slip down there, will you? Quickly. Hide. See if she comes in. Don't interfere—just watch her, understand? Try to figure out what she's up to. And we'll eat," Bitterblue instructed her friends, "and talk about nothing that matters. We'll discuss the weather and ask after each other's health."

"The worst of all of this is that I no longer think it's safe for the Council to trust Ornik," said Bann glumly, after Hava had gone. "Ornik associates with her."

"Maybe that's your worst," Bitterblue said. "My worst is that she knows about Saf and the crown, and has from the beginning. She may even know about my mother's cipher, and my father's too."

"We need trip wires, you know," said Bann. "Something for all our secret stairways, including the one Hava just went down, to alert us if anyone's spying. I'll see what I can come up with."

"Yes? Well, it's still snowing," said Giddon, following Bitterblue's orders to speak of the mundane. "Have you been making any progress on your nausea infusion, Bann, since Raffin left?"

"It's as pukey as ever," said Bann.

Sometime later, Hava tapped on the inside door. When Bitterblue let her in, Hava reported that Fox had, indeed, entered Leck's rooms. "She has new lock picks, Lady Queen," said Hava. "She went to the sculpture of the little child—the smallest in the room—and tried to lift it. She did just manage to budge it, though of course she couldn't lift it properly. Then she let it go again and stood staring at it for a while. She was thinking about something, Lady Queen. Then she poked around the bathing room and the closet, then ran up the steps and stood with her ear to your sitting room door. And then she came back down and left the room."

"Is she a thief," said Bitterblue, "or a spy, or both? If a spy, for whom? Helda, we are having her followed, aren't we?"

"Yes, Lady Queen. But she loses her tail every night at the merchant docks. She runs along them toward Winter Bridge, then climbs under them. Her tail can't follow her under the docks, Lady Queen, for fear of getting caught under there with her."

"I'll follow her, Lady Queen," said Hava. "Let me follow her. I can go under the docks without being seen."

"It sounds dangerous, Hava," said Bitterblue. "It's cold, it's wet under the docks. It's December!"

"But I can do it, Lady Queen," Hava said. "No one can hide as I can. Please? She put her hands all over my mother's sculptures."

"Yes," said Bitterblue, remembering those same hands on her mother's embroidery. "Yes, all right, Hava, but please be careful."

ALL I WANT is a peaceful place of art, architecture, and medicine, but the edges of my control fray. There are too many people and I am exhausted. In the city, the resistance never ends. Every time I capture a mind reader, another surfaces. There is too much to erase and too much to create. Perhaps I am pleased with the glass ceilings, but the bridges aren't big enough. I'm sure they were bigger across the Winged River in the Dells. The Winged River is more regal than my river. I hate my river for this.

I had to kill the gardener. He's always made monsters for the courtyard, he's always made them as I asked, they look and act alive, but after all, they are not alive, are they? They are not real. While I was at it, I killed Gadd too. Did I kill him too soon? His hangings are too sad and they aren't real either, they aren't even made of monster fur. I cannot get it right. I cannot get it perfect, and I hate my own attempts. I hate this cipher. It is necessary, it seems as if it should be brilliant, but it begins to give me a head-

ache. *My hospital gives me a headache. There are too many people. I tire of deciding what they should think and feel and do.*

I should have stuck with my animals in their cages. Their lack of language protects them. When I cut them, they scream, because I cannot explain to them that it doesn't hurt. They always, always know what I am doing. There is a purity in their fear, and it is such a relief to me. And it is nice to be alone with them.

There is purity in counting my knives. There is a purity sometimes in the hospital too, when I let the patients feel the pain. Some of them release such exquisite cries. It sounds almost as if the blood itself is screaming. The roundness of the ceiling and the dampness make for such acoustics. The walls shine black. But then the cries upset the others. The fog begins to lift from their minds and they begin to understand what they are hearing, and the men begin to understand what they are doing, and then I have to punish them, awe them, shame them, make them dread me and need me until they have forgotten, all of them, and that is so much more work than keeping them always blind.

There are those precious few I keep for myself and treat away from the hospital. There always have been. Bellamew is one and Ashen is another. I let no one watch, unless I am making someone watch, as punishment. It is punishment to Thiel to watch me with Ashen. I do not let him touch her and sometimes I cut him. In those moments, when it is private, in my rooms, closed away, and I hold the knives, the perfection comes back for an instant. Just for an instant, peace. My lessons with my child will be this way. It will be perfect with my child.

Is it possible that Bellamew has been lying to me for eight years?

* * * * *

Bitterblue began to give the translations to her friends to read first so that they could warn her of mentions of her mother, or herself. Every night, Death presented new pages. Some nights, Bitterblue couldn't bring herself to read them at all. On those nights, she asked Giddon to summarize, which he did, sitting beside her on the sofa, voice low. She chose Giddon for the job because Helda and Bann wouldn't promise not to edit out the worst parts, and Giddon would. He spoke so quietly, as if it would lessen the impact of the words. It didn't—not really—though if he'd spoken louder, Bitterblue agreed that that would have been worse. She sat listening, with her arms tight around herself, shivering.

She worried about Death, who saw the words first and with no buffer; who labored over them for hours every day. "Perhaps at a certain point," she said to him, not quite believing such words were coming from her own mouth, "it's enough for us to know that he was a brutal man who did mad things. Perhaps the details don't matter."

"But it's history, Lady Queen," said Death.

"But, it's not," Bitterblue said. "Not really, not yet. In a hundred years it will be history. Now it's our own story."

"Our own story is even more important for us to know than history, Lady Queen. Aren't you trying to find answers in these books to today's questions?"

"Yes," she said, sighing. "Yes. Can you really bear to read it?"

"Lady Queen," said Death, laying his pen down and looking hard into her face. "I lived outside it for thirty-five years. For thirty-five years I tried to learn what he was doing and why. For me, this fills in holes."

For Bitterblue, it was creating holes, holes in her ability to feel. Great, blank spaces where something existed that she couldn't process, because to process it would make her know too much, or make her certain she was going mad. When she stood in the lower offices now and watched the empty-eyed bustle of clerks and guards, Darby, Thiel, and Rood, she understood a thing Runnemood had said one time when she'd pushed too hard. Was the truth worth losing one's sanity?

"I don't want to do this anymore," Bitterblue said one night to Giddon, still shivering. "You have a beautiful voice, do you know that? If we continue with this, your voice'll be ruined for me. I must either read his words myself, or hear them from someone who's not my friend."

Giddon hesitated. "I do it because I'm your friend, Lady Queen."

"I know," Bitterblue said. "But I hate it, and I know you do too, and I don't like that we've developed a nightly routine of doing something hateful together."

"I won't agree to you doing it alone," Giddon said stubbornly.

"Then it's a good thing I don't need your permission."

"Take a break from it, Lady Queen," said Bann, coming to sit on her other side. "Please. Read a bigger pile once a week, instead of small, torturous bits every day. We'll continue to read it with you."

This seemed a promising idea—until the week had passed, and the day came to read seven days' worth of accumulated translation. After two pages, Bitterblue couldn't go on.

"Stop," Giddon said. "Just stop reading. It's making you sick."

"I believe he preferred female victims," Bitterblue said, "because in addition to the other mad experiments he forced them to endure, he was performing experiments that related to pregnancy and babies."

"This is not for you to read," Giddon said. "This is for some other person who wasn't one of the players in this tale to read, and then tell you the things a queen needs to know. Death can do it as he's translating."

"I believe he raped them," Bitterblue said, alone, cold, not listening, "all of them in his hospital. I believe he raped my mother."

Giddon yanked the papers from her hands and threw them across the room. Jumping at the unexpectedness of this, Bitterblue saw him clearly as she hadn't before, saw him towering over her, mouth hard, eyes flashing, and realized he was furious. Her vision came into focus and the room filled itself in around her. She heard the fire crackling, the silence of Bann and Helda, at the table, watching, tense, unhappy. The room smelled like wood fires. She pulled a blanket around herself. She was not alone.

"Call me by my name," she said quietly to Giddon.

"Bitterblue," he said just as quietly, "I beg you. Please stop reading the psychotic ramblings of your father. They are doing you harm."

She looked to the table again, where Bann and Helda watched with quiet eyes. "You're not eating enough, Lady Queen," said Helda. "You've lost your appetite, and if I may say so, Lord Giddon has too."

"What?" she cried. "Giddon, why didn't you tell me?"

"He's also been asking me for headache remedies," Bann said.

"Stop it, you two," said Giddon in annoyance. "Lady Queen, you've been walking around with this horrible, trapped look in your eyes. The smallest things make you flinch."

"I understand now," she said. "I understand all of them now. And I've been pushing them. I've been forcing them to remember."

"It's not your fault," Giddon said. "A queen needs people around her who aren't afraid of her necessary questions."

"I don't know what to do," she said, her voice cracking. "I don't know what to do."

"You need to build some criteria," said Bann, "to give to Death.

The facts you need to know now, in order to address the immediate needs of your kingdom, and only those facts."

"Will you all help me?"

"Of course we will," said Bann.

"I've already worked out what the criteria should be," said Helda with a firm nod, while Giddon collapsed onto the sofa in relief.

It was a process that involved a fair deal of argument, argument that was a comfort to Bitterblue, because it was logical, and it made the world solid around her again. Afterwards, they went to the library to look for Death. The endless, slow, silent winter snowfall continued. In the great courtyard, Bitterblue turned her face to the glass ceilings. The snow drifted down. Grief began to touch her. The edges of grief; a grief too large for her to accept all at once just now.

She would pretend she was up there in the sky, above the snow clouds, looking down on Monsea, like the moon or the stars. She would pretend she was watching the snowfall cover Monsea, like bandages from Madlen's gentle hands, so that underneath that warm, soft covering, Monsea could begin to heal.

36

THE NEXT MORNING, Thiel stood at his stand, straight and efficient, flipping through papers.

"I won't ask you any more questions about Leck's time," Bitterblue said to him.

Thiel turned, peering at her in confusion. "You—you won't, Lady Queen?"

"I'm sorry for every time I've forced you to remember a thing you wish to forget," she said. "As far as I'm able, I'll try never to do that again."

"Thank you, Lady Queen," he said, still confused. "Why? Has something happened?"

"I'll ask other people instead," she said. "I'm going to be seeking out some new people, Thiel, to help me with matters that are too painful for those of you who worked with Leck to address. And maybe some city people to inform me about city matters specifically, and help me solve some of these mysteries."

Thiel stared back at her, clutching his pen in both hands. He looked so lonely somehow, and so unhappy. "Thiel!" she hastened to add. "You'll still be my number one man, of course. But I find myself wanting a greater range of advice and ideas, you understand?"

"Of course I understand, Lady Queen."

"I'm going to meet with a few of them now," she said, rising from her chair, "in the library. I've asked them to come. Oh, please,

Thiel," she added, wanting to touch him. "Don't look like that. I can't do without you, I promise, and you're breaking my heart."

IN HER LIBRARY alcove, Tilda and Teddy stood together, brother and sister, gazing at the endless rows of books. Their faces glowed with appreciation.

"Did Bren stay at the shop?" asked Bitterblue.

"We thought it unwise to leave it unguarded, Lady Queen," said Tilda.

"And my Lienid Guard?"

"One stayed to guard Bren, Lady Queen, and the other accompanied us."

"It makes me nervous for them to split up," Bitterblue said. "I'm going to see if we can spare another man or two for you. What news can you give me?"

"Bad news, Lady Queen," said Teddy grimly. "Early this morning, a story room burned. It was empty, so no one was hurt, but no one saw how it started either."

"I suppose we're meant to think it was random," said Bitterblue in frustration. "A coincidence. And naturally, it wasn't in my morning report. And I really don't know what to do," she added, a bit hopelessly, "beyond send the Monsean Guard to patrol the streets more, except that ever since Captain Smit disappeared, I've been leery of trusting the Monsean Guard. Smit's been gone a month and a half, you know. I keep getting reports on his proceedings at the refineries that I cannot get myself to believe. Darby says they're in Smit's handwriting, but Darby hasn't been inspiring confidence of late. Oh," she said, rubbing her forehead. "Perhaps I'm just crazy."

"We could find out whether Captain Smit's truly at the refineries,

Lady Queen," said Tilda, elbowing her brother, "couldn't we, Teddy? Through our own contacts?"

Teddy's face lit up. "We could," he said. "It may take a few weeks, but we'll do it, Lady Queen."

"Thank you," Bitterblue said. "On another matter, can any of you make letter molds?"

"Bren quite enjoys it, Lady Queen," said Tilda.

Bitterblue handed Tilda a piece of paper on which she'd drawn the thirty-two letters of the Dellian alphabet. "Please ask her to make molds of these shapes," said Bitterblue. For Death's translation of the first volume was moving at a crawl and all this talk of fire was making Bitterblue distinctly anxious; what if they lost the other thirty-four volumes somehow, before Death got to them? "Leck's journals need printing," she said. "Tell no one."

THE NEXT MORNING, Bitterblue emerged from her rooms, rubbing sleep from her eyes.

In the sitting room, Helda arranged the breakfast dishes. "Hava was just here, Lady Queen," she said, banging plates around. "She's succeeded where the other tail hasn't. She's followed Fox to her nighttime lair."

"Lair." Bitterblue went to kneel before the fire, adjusting her sword, breathing in the light. It was hard to wake up when the snow never stopped and the sun never reached her windows. "That's not a friendly word. You know, Helda, I've been thinking some things through. Is Fox's lair, by any chance, a cave?"

"It is, Lady Queen," said Helda humorlessly. "Fox lives in a cave across the river."

"And Spook and Gray also live in a cave?"

"Yes. An interesting coincidence, isn't it? Fox's cave is on the other side of Winter Bridge. She gets onto the bridge, if you can believe it, by climbing up its pillars from where they start under the docks."

"Balls," said Bitterblue. "Why not just walk onto it the normal way? Why not row across the river in a boat?"

"We can only assume that she's alert to the possibility of being followed, Lady Queen. It's difficult to spot a person in dark clothing climbing the pillars of a bridge at night, even a bridge made of mirrors. Once Hava understood what Fox was doing, of course, she backtracked and ran onto the bridge in the usual way, but Fox was too fast for her, and got too far ahead. Fox crossed the bridge, shimmied down the pillars again, and, as best as Hava could tell from above, disappeared into a grove of trees."

"How does Hava know about the lair, then?"

"Because she followed the next person who came across the bridge, Lady Queen."

Something in Helda's tone gave Bitterblue a sinking feeling. "And that person was?"

"Sapphire, Lady Queen. He led Hava directly into the trees, then to an outcropping of rock that was guarded by men with swords. Hava can't be sure, of course, but she believes it's a cave and that it was Fox's destination as well."

"Tell me he didn't go in," said Bitterblue. "Tell me he hasn't been working with them all this time."

"No, Lady Queen," said Helda. "Lady Queen! Take a breath," said Helda, coming to Bitterblue, kneeling, grasping Bitterblue's hands hard. "Sapphire did not go in, nor did he make his presence known to the guards. He hid, and poked around. He seemed to be investigating the place."

For a moment, Bitterblue rested her head on Helda's shoulder, breathing through the relief. "Bring him somewhere discreet, please, Helda," she said, "so that I can talk to him."

A CIPHERED NOTE from Helda at noon told Bitterblue that Saf was waiting in her rooms.

"How is this discreet?" Bitterblue asked, blowing into the sitting room. Helda sat at the table, calmly eating her lunch. Saf stood before the sofa in coat and hat, gloves and halter belt, stamping his feet and radiating cold. "How many people saw him?"

"He came through that window, Lady Queen," said Helda. "The window faces the garden and the river, both of which are empty at the moment."

Seeing the ropes then, she went to the window in question to examine the platform. She hadn't realized how narrow the platform was. It swayed and clanked against the castle wall.

Gripping her hands into fists, she said, "Where is Fox?"

"Fox disappears for lunch, Lady Queen," said Saf.

"How do you know she doesn't disappear somewhere where she can see my windows?"

"I don't," Saf said, shrugging. "I'll factor it into whatever happens next."

"And what do you expect to happen next?"

"I was hoping you'd ask me to push her off the platform, Lady Queen," he said.

It was a relief that he was being insolent, even while using her title; it gave her a familiar patch of ground to stand on. "Fox is Gray," she said, "isn't she? My *gray-eyed* Graceling servant and spy is Spook's grand*daughter* Gray."

"It would seem so, Lady Queen," said Saf plainly. "And what your creepy girl who turns into things probably doesn't know, despite her wondrous abilities, is that last night, I found a place where, if I put my ear to the ground, I could overhear Fox and Spook talking. The crown is in that cave. I'm sure of it. Along with a lot of other royal loot, from the sound of it."

"How did you know Hava was following you?"

Saf snorted. "There was an enormous gargoyle on Winter Bridge," he said. "Winter Bridge is the mirrored bridge that disappears into the sky, and it doesn't have stone gargoyles. And I knew you'd been having Fox tailed. That's how I tailed Fox myself. By tailing your tails. Fox kept disappearing under the docks. Your spies would give up, but I was more persistent. I took a lucky guess a few nights ago and caught sight of her on the bridge."

"Have you been seen, Saf? It doesn't sound like you've been very careful."

"I don't know," he said. "It doesn't matter. She doesn't trust me and she's smart enough not to believe that I trust her. That's not how we're going to win this game."

Standing quietly, Bitterblue took Saf in, his soft, purple eyes that didn't match his blunt manner. Trying to understand him. Feeling, inconveniently, that she never did, except for when she was touching him. "Is this a game, then, Saf?" she said. "Dangling from the castle walls every day with a person who could ruin your life? Following her at night to wherever she goes? When were you going to tell me?"

"I wish you would stop being queen," he said, with a strange, sudden shyness that came out of nowhere, "and join me, when I go away. You know you have the instincts for my kind of work."

Bitterblue was utterly speechless. Helda, meanwhile, did not suffer from the same affliction. "Watch yourself," she said, taking a step toward Saf, her face like thunder. "You just watch what you say to the queen, young man, or you'll find yourself leaving by the window, and fast. You've brought her nothing but trouble so far."

"At any rate," Saf said, glancing at Helda warily, "I'm going to steal the crown tonight."

Bitterblue's breath came back in a rush. "What? How?"

"The main entrance to the cave is always guarded by three men. But I believe there's a second entrance, for there's a guard who always sits some distance from the main entrance, in a hollow where lots of rocks are piled."

"But Saf," she said, "you're basing your knowledge, and your attack plan, solely on the position of a guard? You've seen no actual entrance?"

"They're planning to blackmail you," Saf said. "They want the right to handpick a new prison master for your prisons, three new judges for your High Court, and the Monsean Guard assigned to the east city, or else they'll make it known that the queen had an affair with a common Lienid thief who stole her crown during a tryst."

Again, Bitterblue was speechless. She managed a breath. "This is my fault," she said. "I allowed her to witness so much of what was happening."

"I'm the one who allowed that, Lady Queen," said Helda quietly. "I'm the one who brought her on. I liked her Grace of being fearless without being reckless. She was so useful for the tricky tasks, like climbing up into the windows, and she had such spy potential."

"I think you're both forgetting that she's a professional," said Saf. "She positioned herself close to you a long time ago, didn't she? Her family has been stealing from this castle forever, and they positioned her near you. And I made their job easy as pie, stealing your crown, of all things, and handing it straight to them. You realize that, don't you? I handed her a bigger prize than she could've ever hoped to steal herself. I bet she knows every corner of your castle, every hidden doorway. I bet she's known how to navigate Leck's maze from the start. Those keys I nicked from her pocket were probably a family treasure—I bet her family's had them since Leck died and everyone in the castle started cleaning out his things. She's a professional, just like the rest of her family, but more insidious than they, because she's not afraid of anything. I'm not sure she has a conscience."

"That's interesting," Bitterblue said. "You think a conscience requires fear?"

"What I think is that they can't blackmail you without the crown," said Saf. "Which is why I'm going to steal it tonight."

"With the help of my Lienid Door Guard, you mean."

"No," Saf said sharply. "If you've guards to spare, send them to the shop. I can do this quietly, myself."

"How many men guard the cave, Saf?" snapped Bitterblue.

"All right, then," he said. "I'll bring Teddy, Bren, and Tilda. We know how to do this type of thing and we trust each other. Don't get in our way."

"Teddy, Bren, and Tilda," Bitterblue muttered. "All these close-knit family businesses. I'm quite jealous."

"You and your uncle rule half the world," Saf said with a snort, then dove behind an armchair as the outer doors creaked open.

"It's Giddon," Bitterblue announced as the man himself walked in.

When Saf emerged from behind his chair, Giddon made his face blank. "I'll wait till he goes, Lady Queen," Giddon said.

"Right," said Saf sarcastically. "I'll be making my dramatic exit, then. Should you give me something to steal, in case Fox sees me climbing out the window and I need an excuse?"

Helda marched to the table, grabbed a silver fork, marched back to Saf, and shoved it at his chest. "I know it's not up to your usual plunder," she said darkly.

"Right," Saf said again, accepting the fork. "Thank you, Helda, I'm sure."

"Saf," Bitterblue said. "Be careful."

"Don't worry, Lady Queen," he said, catching her eyes, holding them for a moment. "I'll bring your crown back in the morning. I promise."

His exit brought cold air rushing into the room. When he'd closed the window behind him, Bitterblue went to the fire to capture some of its heat. "How are you, Giddon?"

"Thiel was walking on Winged Bridge last night, Lady Queen," said Giddon without preamble. "It seemed a bit odd at the time, so we thought you should know."

With a small sigh, Bitterblue pinched the bridge of her nose. "Thiel on Winged Bridge. Fox, Hava, and Saf on Winter Bridge. My father would be so pleased with the popularity of his bridges. Why were *you* on Winged Bridge, Giddon?"

"Bann and I were making some improvements to Saf's hiding place, Lady Queen. Thiel walked by just as we were about to leave."

"Did he see you?"

"I don't think he saw anything," said Giddon. "He was in another world. He came from the far side of the river and he had no light, so we didn't see him at all until he walked directly past our window. Moving like a ghost—made us both jump. We followed him, Lady Queen. He took the steps down to the street and entered the east city, but I'm afraid we lost him after that."

Bitterblue rubbed her eyes, hiding her face in comforting darkness. "Do either of you know if Thiel knows about Hava's Grace for disguise?"

"I don't believe he does, Lady Queen," said Helda.

"I'm sure it's nothing," Bitterblue said. "I'm sure he's just going for melancholy walks. But perhaps we could ask her to follow him once."

"Yes, Lady Queen," said Helda. "If she's willing, it may be better to know. Runnemood is supposed to have jumped off one of the bridges, and Thiel is a bit depressed."

"Oh, Helda," said Bitterblue, sighing again. "I don't think I can bear it being anything other than melancholy walks."

THAT NIGHT, EXHAUSTION and worry pushed Bitterblue beyond sleep. She lay on her back staring at the blackness. Rubbing her arm, which still seemed marvelous to her somehow, aching with tiredness but free from that horrid cast, and, finally, dressed in her knives again.

Eventually, she lit a candle so that she could watch the gold and scarlet stars glimmer on her bedroom ceiling. It occurred to her that she was keeping a sort of vigil, for Saf. For Teddy, Tilda, and Bren, who were stealing a crown. For Thiel, who walked alone at night and shattered too easily. For those of her friends who were far away, Po, Raffin, and Katsa, perhaps shivering in tunnels.

When drowsiness began to soften the edges of her exhaustion and she knew sleep was near, Bitterblue allowed herself to linger with a thing she hadn't allowed herself in some time: the dream of herself as a baby in her mother's arms. It had been too sad to touch recently, with Leck's journals so near. But tonight she would allow it, in honor of Saf, for Saf had been the one, that night she'd slept on the hard shop floor, who'd told her to dream of something nice, like babies; Saf had pushed her nightmares away.

SHE WOKE, AND dressed, to a peculiar gray-green daylight and a shrieking wind that seemed to be racing around the castle in circles.

In the sitting room, Hava sat as close to the fire as one could without actually sitting in it. She was wrapped in blankets, drinking a steaming cup of something.

"I'm afraid Hava has a report that's going to upset you, Lady Queen," said Helda. "Perhaps you should sit down."

"Upsetting about Thiel?"

"Yes. We've heard nothing about Sapphire yet," Helda said, answering the question Bitterblue had actually been asking.

"When will—"

"Lord Giddon was out all night on other business," Helda said, "and promised not to come back without a report."

"All right," Bitterblue said, crossing the room and sitting on the hearth beside Hava, shifting to avoid her own sword. She tried to steel herself against something that she knew, somehow, would break her heart, but it was difficult. There was too much worry. "Go on, Hava."

Hava stared into her drink. "Across Winged Bridge and a short distance west, Lady Queen, there's a black cavern in the ground, tucked under the river. It smells like—something thick and cloying, Lady Queen," she said, "and in a place in the back—sort of a second room—there are piles and piles of bones."

"Bones," Bitterblue said. "More bones." *His hospital is under the river.*

"Last night, very late, Thiel left the castle through the tunnel from the eastern corridor," Hava said. "He crossed the bridge, went to the cave, and filled a box with bones. Then he carried the box back onto the bridge, stood at the center, and tipped the bones over the edge. Then he went back and did it two more times—"

"Thiel threw bones into the river," Bitterblue said numbly.

"Yes," said Hava. "And partway through, he was joined by Darby, Rood, two of your clerks, your judge Quall, and my uncle."

"Your uncle!" cried Bitterblue, staring at Hava. "Holt!"

"Yes, Lady Queen," said Hava, her strange eyes flashing with misery. "All of them filled boxes with bones and dumped them in the river."

"It's Leck's hospital," Bitterblue said. "They're trying to hide it."

"Leck's hospital?" asked Helda, appearing at Bitterblue's elbow and slipping a hot drink into her hands.

"Yes. 'The dampness and the roundness of the ceiling make for such acoustics.'"

"Ah. Yes," said Helda, then tucked her chin to her chest for a moment. "There was a bit in a recent translation about the smell in the hospital. He stacked the bodies instead of burning them, or disposing of them in any normal way. He liked the smell and the vermin. It made others ill, of course."

"Thiel was there when it was happening," Bitterblue whispered. "He saw it, and he wants the memory of it to go away. All of them do. Oh, how stupid I've been."

"There's more, Lady Queen," said Hava. "I followed Thiel, Darby, and Rood back into the east city. They met some men in a broken-down house, Lady Queen, and they all passed each other things.

Your advisers gave the men money, and the men gave your advisers papers, and a little sack. They hardly said a word, Lady Queen, but something fell out of the sack. I searched for it after they'd gone."

At the sound of the outer doors opening, Bitterblue sprang to her feet, burning herself on her sploshing drink but not caring. Giddon filled the doorway. His eyes went straight to hers. "Sapphire is alive and free," he said grimly.

Bitterblue sank down onto the hearth again. "But it's not over," she said as her thoughts scrambled to interpret. "You've just given me all the good news, haven't you? He's free, but hiding. He's alive, but hurt, and he doesn't have the crown. Is he hurt, Giddon?"

"No more than Saf ever is, Lady Queen. At sunrise, I saw him step onto the merchant docks, coming from Winter Bridge, calm as calm, and begin to walk west toward the castle. He walked right past me—saw me—gave me the barest nod. I began to wrap up my own business so as to keep an eye on him. The docks were busy—work starts early on the river. He passed a small knot of men loading a brig and suddenly three of them broke off and stepped in behind him. Well, he picked up his pace, and next thing I knew, all of them were running, and so was I, and the chase was on, but I couldn't get to him before they did. There was a fight—he was getting the worst of it—and all at once he pulled the crown out of his coat and held it in his hands, clear as daylight. I'd almost reached them," Giddon said, "when he threw it."

"Threw it?" repeated Bitterblue hopefully. "To you?"

"Into the river," said Giddon, dropping himself into a chair and rubbing his face with his hands.

"Into the river!" Bitterblue could not, for the moment, comprehend this. "Why does everyone throw every troublesome thing into the river?"

"He was losing the fight," Giddon said. "He was about to lose the crown. To keep Spook and Fox from regaining their leverage over you, he threw it into the river, and then he ran."

"Incriminating himself!" cried Bitterblue. "What sort of crime is it to throw the crown into the river?"

"The bigger crime will be that he had the crown in the first place, to throw into the river," said Giddon. "A member of the Monsean Guard—not to mention too many witnesses—saw it happen. When the guard challenged Spook's three thugs, they made up a story about how they'd chased Saf, and beaten him, because he'd stolen back what he'd given them months ago."

"That isn't a made-up story," Bitterblue said miserably.

"No," admitted Giddon. "I suppose it isn't."

"But—do you mean that they admitted that they'd been in possession of the crown, and were trying to be in possession of it again?"

"Yes," said Giddon. "They themselves, for themselves. To protect Spook and Fox, you see, Lady Queen, and to keep control of what's known. Now Spook's thugs are in prison, but the Monsean Guard won't be satisfied until they've captured Saf too."

"Will Spook's thugs hang?"

"Possibly," said Giddon, "depending on what Spook can manage to do. If they do hang, Spook will see that their families become exceedingly rich and comfortable. That'll have been the deal."

"I will not let Saf hang," said Bitterblue. "I will not let Saf hang! Where did he go? Is he in the drawbridge tower?"

"I don't know," Giddon said. "I stayed behind to see what happened. We'll check once it gets dark."

"The whole day?" Bitterblue said. "We won't know until night-time?"

"I went to the shop afterwards, Lady Queen," said Giddon. "He wasn't there, of course, but everyone else was, and they had no idea he'd been planning to steal the crown."

"I'm going to kill him."

"They were dealing with their own problems," said Giddon. "There was a fire in the shop early last night, Lady Queen, before Saf left. Bren is sick from the smoke and so are two of your Lienid Door Guard, for they got trapped in there, trying to put the fire out."

"What?" cried Bitterblue. "Are they all right?"

"The consensus is that they will be, Lady Queen. Saf is the one who pulled his sister out."

"We must send Madlen. Helda, will you arrange it? And what about the shop, Giddon?"

"The shop will stand. But Tilda told me to tell you that your rewrites are mostly burned and they won't have any letter molds to show you for a while. Bren worked on some samples all day yesterday that she planned to bring you for approval, but they can't find them in the mess."

"Oh," Hava said, putting her cup down onto the hearth with a thunk. "Lady Queen," she said, reaching into a pocket and holding something out to Bitterblue. "This is what fell out of that sack."

Bitterblue took the thing from Hava and stared at it as it lay in the center of her palm. It was a tiny wooden mold of the first letter in the Dellian alphabet.

Closing her fingers around the mold, Bitterblue stood and walked numbly to the doors.

IN HER TOWER office, the sky glowed strangely through the glass ceiling. Snow blew at the windows.

As she entered, Thiel turned to greet her.

Runnemood was involved in something terrible, he'd said to her once. *I thought that if I could try to understand why he would do such a thing, then I could bring him to his senses. All I can think is that he was mad, Lady Queen.*

"Good morning, Lady Queen," said Thiel.

Bitterblue was beyond pretending, beyond feeling, her body unable to absorb what her mind couldn't help but begin to understand.

"Runnemood, Thiel?" she said quietly. "Was it only ever Runnemood?"

"What, Lady Queen?" Thiel said, freezing in place. Staring at her with those steel-gray eyes. "What are you asking me?"

How tired Bitterblue was of fighting, of people looking straight at her and lying. "The letter I wrote to my uncle Ror about beginning a policy of remuneration, Thiel," she said. "I entrusted that letter to you. Did you send it, or did you burn it?"

"Of course I sent it, Lady Queen!"

"He never received it."

"Letters are lost sometimes at sea, Lady Queen."

"Yes," said Bitterblue. "And buildings catch fire accidentally, and criminals murder each other in the streets for no reason."

A kind of desperate distress was beginning to join Thiel's confusion; she could read the beginnings of his distress, and horror too, as he continued to stare at her. "Lady Queen," he said carefully, "what has happened?"

"What did you think was going to happen, Thiel?"

At that moment, Darby pushed through the door and handed a note to Thiel. Thiel glanced at it in distraction; stopped; read it again with more care.

"Lady Queen," he said, sounding more and more confused. "This morning at daybreak, that young Graceling with the Lienid decoration—Sapphire Birch—was seen running along the merchant docks with your crown, which he then threw into the river."

"That's absurd," said Bitterblue evenly. "The crown is sitting in my rooms this very minute."

Thiel's eyebrows pinched together in doubt. "Are you certain, Lady Queen?"

"Of course I'm certain. I was just there. Have they been searching the river for it?"

"Yes, Lady Queen—"

"But they haven't found it."

"No, Lady Queen."

"Nor will they," Bitterblue said, "because it's in my sitting room. He must have thrown something else into the river. You know perfectly well that he's a friend of mine and of Prince Po's and, as such, would never throw my crown into the river."

Thiel had never been more bewildered. Beside him, Darby stood with yellow-green eyes that were narrowed and calculating. "If he did steal your crown, Lady Queen," Darby said, "it would be a hanging offense."

"Would you like that, Darby?" asked Bitterblue. "Would it solve any of your problems?"

"I beg your pardon, Lady Queen?" said Darby huffily.

"No, I'm sure the queen is right," said Thiel, blundering around for solid ground. "Her friend wouldn't do such a thing. Clearly, someone has made a mistake."

"Someone has made grievously many mistakes," Bitterblue said. "I think I'll go back to my rooms."

In the lower offices, she stopped, looking into the faces of her men. Rood. Her clerks, her guards. Holt. She thought of Teddy on the floor of an alley with a knife in his gut; Teddy, who only wanted people to know how to read. Saf running from killers, Saf framed for murder. Saf shivering and wet from diving for bones, a man coming at him with a knife. Bren fighting to save the printing shop from fire.

Her forward-thinking administration.

But, Thiel saved my life. Holt saved my life. It's not possible. I've gotten something wrong somehow. Hava is lying about what she saw.

Sitting at his desk, Rood raised his eyes to hers. Bitterblue remembered, then, the letter mold she still held tight in her fist. She took it between her thumb and forefinger and held it up for Rood to see.

Rood squinted, puzzled. Then, understanding, he slumped back in his chair. Rood began to weep.

Bitterblue turned and ran.

SHE NEEDED HELDA, she needed Giddon and Bann, but when she got to her sitting room, they weren't there. On the table sat new translations and a report, lined in Death's tidy hand. It was the last thing on earth Bitterblue wanted to see just now.

She ran into the foyer and down the hallway and burst into Helda's rooms, but Helda wasn't there either. On her way back up the hallway, she stopped for a moment, burst into her own bedroom, and ran to her mother's chest. Kneeling over it, gripping its edges, she forced her heart to hold the word that named what Thiel had done. "Betrayal."

Mama, she thought. *I don't understand. How could Thiel be such a liar, when you loved him and trusted him? When he helped us escape? When he's been so kind and gentle with me, and promised me never to lie again? I don't understand what's going on. How can this be?*

The outer doors creaked open. "Helda?" she whispered. "Helda?" she said again in a stronger voice.

There was no answer. As she rose and went to her bedroom door, a strange sound reached her, coming from the direction of the sitting room. Metal thudding on carpet. Bitterblue ran into the foyer, then stopped as Thiel came rushing out of the sitting room. He stopped too, at the sight of her. His arms were full of papers and his eyes were wild and heartsick and full of shame. He locked those eyes on her face.

Bitterblue stood in her tracks. "How long have you been lying to me?"

He spoke the words in a whisper. "As long as you have been queen."

Bitterblue cried out. "You're no better than my father!" she said. "I hate you. You've crushed my heart."

"Bitterblue," he said. "Forgive me for what I've done and for what I must do."

Then he pushed through the doors and was gone.

SHE RAN INTO the sitting room. The fake crown lay on the carpet and Death's pages were gone.

She ran back into the foyer and pushed through the outer doors. She was nearly to the end of the corridor when she turned back, ran past her own startled Lienid Guard, and pounded on Giddon's door. Pounded again and again. Giddon pulled the door open, rumpled and barefoot and clearly only half awake.

"Will you go to the library," she said, "and make sure Death is safe?"

"All right," he said, bleary and confused.

"If you see Thiel," she said, "stop him and don't let him go. He's learned about the journals and a thousand things have happened and I think he intends to do something terrible, Giddon, but I don't know what it is," and she ran.

SHE BURST INTO the lower offices. "Where is Thiel?" she cried.

Every face in the room stared back at her. Rood stood and said quietly, "We thought he was with you, Lady Queen. He told us he was going to find you and talk to you."

"He came and left," said Bitterblue. "I don't know where he went or what he intends to do. If he comes here, please don't let him go. Please?" she said, turning to Holt, who sat in a chair by the door, staring at her dazedly. Bitterblue grabbed Holt's arm. "Please," she pleaded. "Holt, don't let him go."

"I won't, Lady Queen," said Holt.

Bitterblue ran away from the offices, not reassured.

She went to Thiel's room next, but he wasn't there either.

The air in the great courtyard, when she reached it, stabbed her with its coldness. Members of the Fire Guard were running in and out of the library.

Bitterblue rushed in after them, ran through smoke, and saw Giddon on the floor leaning over Death's body. "Death," she cried, running to them, throwing herself down, her sword clunking on the floor. "Death!"

"He's alive," Giddon said.

Shaking with relief, Bitterblue hugged her insensible librarian; kissed his cheek. "Will he be all right?"

"He's been knocked on the head and his hands are scraped up, but that seems to be all. You're all right? The fire is out, but the smoke is still thick."

"Where's Thiel?"

"He was already gone when I got here, Lady Queen," said Giddon. "The desk was in flames and Death was lying on the floor behind it, so I dragged him away. Then I ran to the courtyard, screamed for the Fire Guard, and stole some poor fellow's coat to beat the fire down. Lady Queen," he said, "I'm sorry, but most of the journals were destroyed."

"It doesn't matter," Bitterblue said. "You saved Death." And then she looked straight at Giddon for the first time and cried out, for ragged gashes scored his cheekbone.

"It was only the cat, Lady Queen," he said. "I found him hiding under the burning desk, stupid creature," and Bitterblue threw her arms around Giddon.

"You saved Lovejoy."

"Yes, I suppose," said Giddon, sooty and bloody, his arms full of the tearful queen. "Everyone is safe. There, there."

"Will you stay with Death and watch over him?"

"Where are you going?"

"I've got to find Thiel."

"Lady Queen," he said, "Thiel is dangerous. Send the Monsean Guard."

"I don't trust the Monsean Guard. I don't trust anyone but us. He won't hurt me, Giddon."

"You don't know that."

"Yes, I do."

"Take your Lienid Guard," Giddon said, looking seriously into her face. "Will you promise me that you'll take your Lienid Guard?"

"No," she said. "But I'll promise you that Thiel will not hurt me." She pulled his face down and kissed him on the forehead as she had Death; then she ran.

How she knew, she couldn't say, but she did. Something in her heart, something underneath the pain of betrayal and, in fact, more fundamental, told her. Fear told her where Thiel had gone.

She did have the foresight, as she flew under the castle portcullis onto the drawbridge, to stop before one of the astonished Lienid Guard who was less loomingly tall than the others, and demand his coat.

"Lady Queen," he said as he shouldered out of it, helping her into it, "you'd best not. The snow is working itself up to a blizzard."

"Then you'd better give me your hat and gloves as well," she said, "and then go inside to warm yourself. Did Thiel come this way?"

"No, Lady Queen," the guard said.

He'd taken the tunnel, then. Pulling on the hat and gloves, Bitterblue ran east.

THE STAIRS THAT led pedestrians onto Winged Bridge were built into the side of one of the bridge's great stone foundations. Stairs with no railing, in a wind that couldn't decide on a direction, in deep shadow as the clouds packed themselves tight.

Big footprints marked the new snowfall on the steps.

Fishing under her too-big coat, she unsheathed her sword, feeling stronger with it in her hand. Then she lifted her foot and placed it into Thiel's first footprint. Then the next step, then the next.

At the top of the stairs, the surface of the bridge shone blue and white, and the wind screamed. "I'm not afraid of heights!" she screamed back at the wind. It touched some deep inner current of courage to scream that lie, so she did it again. The wind screamed to drown her out.

Through the falling snow, she could make out a person standing far ahead on the bridge. The bridge was a narrow, slippery hill of marble that she must climb in order to reach the form that was Thiel.

Thiel was at the bridge's edge. He grabbed the parapet with both hands and suddenly Bitterblue was running, sword in hand, screaming words Thiel could not hear. The surface beneath her thudding feet changed to wood, with more give, a hollow sound, snow sticking, and he hoisted his knee onto the parapet and she pushed herself, pounded, reached him, screaming, grabbed his arm and yanked him back. Crying out in amazement, losing his balance, he reeled back onto the bridge.

Pushing herself between Thiel and the parapet, Bitterblue whipped her sword point to his throat, not caring that it made no sense to threaten a person with bodily harm who was trying to kill himself. "No," she said. "Thiel, no!"

"Why are you here?" he cried, tears streaming down his face. He wore no coat and shook with the cold. The wet snow matted his hair down and made his features stand out sharply, like a living skeleton. "Why am I able to spare you none of this? You weren't meant to see this!"

"Stop it, Thiel. What are you doing? Thiel! I didn't mean what I said! I forgive you!"

He backed away, crossing the width of the bridge as she followed with her sword, until his back was to the opposite parapet. "You cannot forgive me," he said. "There is no forgiveness for what I've done. You've read his words, haven't you? You know what he made us do, don't you?"

"He made you heal them, so that he could keep hurting them," she said. "He made you watch him as he cut them and raped them. It wasn't your fault, Thiel!"

"No," he said, his eyes growing wide. "No, he's the one who watched. We're the ones who cut them and raped them. Children!" he cried. "Little girls! I see their faces!"

Bitterblue was paralyzed with dizziness. "What?" she said, understanding, all at once, the final truth. "Thiel! Leck made you do the hurting?"

"I was his favorite," Thiel said, frantic. "I was his number one. I felt the pleasure when he told me to. I feel it when I see their faces!"

"Thiel," she said, "he forced you. You were his tool!"

"I was a coward," he cried out desperately, against the wind. "A coward!"

"But it wasn't your fault! Thiel. He stole who you were!"

"I killed Runnemood—you see that, don't you? I pushed him off this bridge to stop him hurting you. I've killed so many. I've tried to make the memory end, I've needed it to go away, but all of it only gets bigger and more impossible to control. I never meant it to grow so big. I never meant to tell so many lies. It was supposed to end. It never ends!"

"Thiel," she said, "there is nothing that cannot be forgiven!"

"No," he said, shaking his head, shaking the tears from his face. "I've tried, Lady Queen. I've tried, and it won't heal."

"Thiel," she said, sobbing now. "Please. Let me help you. Please, please, come away from the edge."

"You're strong," he said. "You will make things better; you're a true queen, like your mother. I stood here while your mother burned. When he lit her body up on Monster Bridge, I stood right here and watched. I was there to honor her passing. It's right that no one will honor mine," he said, turning around toward the parapet.

"No," she said. "No, Thiel!" she cried, grabbing at him, dropping her useless sword, willing some part of her, some extension of her spirit or soul to reach out from inside her and entwine him, stop him, hold him on this bridge. Hold him here safe with her love. *Stop struggling, Thiel. Stop fighting me. No, stay here, stay here! You will not die.*

Prying her fingers away, he pushed her so hard that she fell to the ground. "Be safe, Bitterblue. Be free of this," he said to her. Then he grabbed the parapet, hoisted himself onto it, and fell over the edge.

SHE LAY FAR above rushing water.

Maybe he had pretended. Maybe he'd walked away while her eyes were closed, changed his mind, gone back home.

No. He hadn't pretended. Her eyes had never closed. She had seen.

IT WAS NECESSARY that she no longer be on this bridge. Of that, she was fairly certain. But she couldn't walk, because the bridge was too high in the air for walking on. What if she stayed here? What if she clung to a memory of a cold mountain, of Katsa's body giving her heat, of Katsa's arms holding her safe to the earth?

Crawl, she could crawl. There was no shame in crawling when one couldn't walk. Someone had said that to her once. Someone—

"Hey."

The voice from above was familiar.

"Hey, what are you doing? Are you hurt?"

The person attached to the voice was touching her with his hands, brushing off an accumulation of snow. "Hey, can you get up?"

She shook her head.

"Can you talk? Is it the heights, Sparks?"

Yes. No. She shook her head.

"You're scaring me," he said. "How long have you been out here? I'm picking you up."

"No," she managed, because being picked up was too high.

"Why don't you tell me what four hundred seventy-six times four hundred seventy-seven is, all right?"

Saf gathered her up, gathered her sword too, and carried her to the drawbridge tower while she clung to him, and tried to work that one out.

INSIDE, IT WAS warm. There were braziers. When he lowered her to a chair, she held on to one of his arms and wouldn't let him go.

"Sparks," he said, on his knees before her, taking off her gloves and hat, feeling her hands and face, "this is not cold sickness, and I get the feeling that it's more than your fear of heights. Last time you were afraid of heights, you had a tongue to curse me with."

Bitterblue was holding his arm so hard that she thought her fingers would break. And then he put his other arm around her and pulled her into a hug. She transferred all her clinging pressure to his torso, hugging him back. Shaking. "Tell me what's wrong," he said.

She tried. She really did. She couldn't.

"Whisper it in my ear," he said.

His ear was warm on her nose. The gold stud in his earlobe was hard and comforting on her lip. Three words. It would only take three words and then he would understand. "Thiel," she whispered. "Jumped off."

This was met with stillness, then an exhalation, then a tightening of his arms. Then moving, lifting, resettling, until he was in the chair, holding her in his lap, holding her tight while she shook.

SHE WOKE TO him settling her onto blankets on the floor. "Stay with me," she said. "Don't go."

He lay beside her and wrapped his arms around her. She slept.

* * * * *

SHE WOKE AGAIN to low voices. Gentle hands. People leaning over her in snow-covered coats. "She'll be all right," said Raffin.

Saf's voice said something about the snow. "Maybe you should stay here," he said.

Po's voice said something about horses, about it being too dangerous to draw attention. Po's voice! Po was holding her, kissing her face. "Keep her safe," he said. "I'll wait for her at the bottom of the bridge when the storm is over."

Then she was alone with Saf again. "Po?" she said, turning in confusion.

"He was here," Saf replied.

"Saf," she said, finding his face in the dimness. "Do you forgive me?"

"Shh," said Saf, stroking her hair, her falling-out braids. "Yes, Lady Queen. I forgave you some time ago."

"Why are you crying?"

"A lot of reasons," he said.

She wiped the tears from Saf's face. She fell asleep.

SHE WOKE FROM a nightmare of falling. Ashen, herself, bones, everyone, everything, falling. She woke crying out and thrashing and was astonished, then devastated, to find Saf there holding her, comforting her, for this time she was truly awake, and with Saf, all the other truths of the waking world rushed back. And so she clung to him to push them away, pressed herself against him. She felt the length of his body against hers; she felt his hands. She heard his whispers, let him fill her ears and her skin. She kissed him. When he responded to her kisses, she kissed him more.

"Are you certain you want this?" he whispered, when it became clear what was happening. "Are you certain that you're certain?"

"Yes," she whispered. "Are you?"

* * * * *

WHAT IT DID was return her to herself. For Saf reminded her of trust, of her capacity for comfort, her willingness to be loved. So that afterwards, when the pain came rushing back again, fresh and relentless, she had the strength to bear it, and a friend to hold her while she sobbed.

She cried for the part of her soul that had been clinging to Thiel and had fallen with him into the water, the part of herself that he'd torn away when he'd jumped. She cried for her failure to save him. Most of all, she cried for what Thiel's life had been.

"No more nightmares," Saf whispered. "Dream of something that will comfort you."

"I want to think he was happy sometimes."

"Sparks, I'm sure he was."

A picture of Thiel's room, stark and comfortless, came to her. "I never saw him happy. I know of nothing he enjoyed."

"Who did he love?"

The question sucked her breath away. "My mother," she whispered, "and me."

"Dream of that love."

She dreamed of her wedding. She couldn't see whom she was marrying, that person never entered the scene, and it didn't matter. What mattered was that there was music, played on all the castle's instruments, and the music made everyone happy, and she danced with her mother and Thiel.

IT WAS EARLY morning when her growling stomach woke her. She opened her eyes to light, and the strange comfort of the dream. Then, memory. Aches, all over, from Thiel fighting her, Thiel pushing her, from crying, loss, from Saf. The snow had stopped and the sky shone blue through three tiny round windows. Saf slept beside her.

It wasn't fair, how innocent he looked when he was sleeping. The fresh bruising around his eye and the purple that showed through the Lienid markings of his arm were also unfair. She hadn't noticed those bruises in the dimness of the day before, and he'd certainly given her no indication of them.

How loyal and gentle Saf had been with her, and without her asking it of him. As quick to love as he was to anger, as quick to warmth as to foolishness, and he had a tenderness she wouldn't have expected from him. She wondered if you could love someone you didn't understand.

His eyes flickered open, soft purples shining on her. When he saw her, he smiled.

Dream something nice, he'd said to her that night in the shop, *like babies.* And she had. *Dream of that love.*

"Saf?" she said.

"Yes?"

"I think I know what your Grace is."

IT WAS THE thing about dreams. They were so odd by nature, and they left one with such a feeling of the unreal, that how was one ever to notice when they themselves behaved strangely?

The Grace of giving dreams was a beautiful Grace for someone contrary and dear to have. She told him so as she strapped on her knives and he tried to convince her to stay a bit longer.

"We need to experiment," he said. "We need to test whether it's true. What if I can give you a dream by just wishing it and not saying a word? What if I can give you a highly detailed dream, like Teddy in pink stockings holding a duck? I have food here, you know. You must be starving. Stay and eat something."

"I'm not taking the food you need," Bitterblue said, stepping into her gown, "and people will be worried about me, Saf."

"Do you suppose I could give you bad dreams?"

"I haven't the slightest doubt. You'll stay in this room, won't you, now that it's daylight?"

"My sister is sick."

"I know," she said. "I'm told she'll be all right. I've sent her Madlen. I'll send someone to you with news as soon as we have it, I promise. You understand you've got to stay here, don't you? You won't risk being seen?"

"I'm going to go out of my skull with boredom in this room, aren't I," said Saf, sighing, then pushing his blankets aside, reaching for his clothing.

"Wait," Bitterblue said.

"What?" he said, glaring at her. "What—"

Bitterblue had never seen a man naked, and she was curious. She decided the universe owed her a few minutes, just a few, to satisfy her curiosity. So she went to him and knelt, which shut him up.

"I'll give you a dream," he whispered to her. "A wonderful dream. I won't tell you."

"An experiment?" said Bitterblue with the tiniest smile.

"An experiment, Sparks."

SHE KNEW THAT the bridge would be more or less horrible. She pushed herself quickly to the middle, as far from the edge as possible. The wind had died down at some point in the night and snow had accumulated, which was welcome. Pushing through it distracted her from focusing on where she was.

It also helped to know that Saf was watching from the draw-bridge tower and would come out into broad daylight to help her if she stopped, or visibly panicked, or fell. She would hide her panic from him and push on; yes, as long as she was panicking, she may as well push on.

A lifetime later, she was even with the staircase, and here, she ceased to care what Saf saw. On her hands and knees, she approached the steps, then appraised them. The snow had drifted across them unevenly. A person stood at the bottom, his face and hair hidden behind a hood. He pushed the hood back. Po.

Bitterblue sat down on the highest step and began to cry.

He climbed up to her, sat on the outer edge beside her, and put his arm around her. Such a relief not to have to talk or explain. Such a relief for her to remember, and him to know.

"It's not your fault, sweetheart."

Don't, Po. Just—don't.

"All right," he said. "I'm sorry."

What he did do was pull off her hat, wind up her loose hair, and stick the hat back on so that her hair wasn't visible. Then pulled her collar up and tugged the hat even lower. And then he stood at the outer edge as they climbed down, keeping his arm around her, and led her through empty alleys to a narrow door in a wall.

Through the door was a very long, very dark and dank tunnel.

When they finally reached the tunnel's end and light seeped through the crack at the bottom of another door, he said, "Hang on a minute. There are too many people just now."

"Are we about to step into the east corridor?" Bitterblue asked.

"Yes, and cross over to the secret passage that leads up to your father's rooms."

"Why are we sneaking?"

"So that everyone believes that you came back to the castle yesterday, told us about Thiel, and have been in your rooms ever since," said Po.

"So that no one will remember the existence of the drawbridge tower," she said.

"Yes."

"Or wonder how you all knew about Thiel."

"Yes."

"You've already told everyone?"

"Yes."

Oh, thank you. Thank you for taking that job from me.

"All right," said Po. "Let's move quickly."

Brilliant light as they stepped into the corridor. They crossed to a hanging of a green wildcat, behind which they passed through another door and into more darkness. They had no lamp as they climbed the winding passage, so Po warned her of steps in the path.

Finally, they clambered out from behind another heavy hanging, into Leck's rooms. Bitterblue stumbled up the stairs. At the top, Po knocked. A key was heard to turn in the lock. When the door opened, Bitterblue fell into Helda's waiting arms.

THE PACKETS OF seabane were in a cabinet in her bathing room. She hadn't imagined that she would feel so—lost—the first time she swallowed those herbs down.

Back in the corridor, she pushed toward the doors.

"A bath and breakfast would do you good, Lady Queen, before you face your staff," said Helda gently. "Clean clothing. A fresh start."

"There's no such thing as a fresh start," said Bitterblue numbly.

"Do you need to see Madlen for anything, Lady Queen?"

Bitterblue wanted to see Madlen, but she didn't need to see Madlen. "I suppose not."

"Why don't I ask her here, just in case, Lady Queen?"

And so Helda and Madlen helped her soak away sweat and dirt in the bath, helped her wash her hair, took her soiled clothing and brought her fresh, clean things to wear. Madlen chatted quietly, her familiar, strange accent grounding Bitterblue. She wondered if there were signs on her body of her night with Saf, if Helda and Madlen could tell. Signs of her struggle with Thiel. She didn't mind, as long as no one asked questions. She had a vague feeling that questions would shatter her shell. "Are Bren and my guards all right?" she asked.

"They're extremely uncomfortable," said Madlen, "but they'll be fine. I'll go back to Bren later today."

"I promised Saf updates," said Bitterblue.

"Lord Giddon will check in on Sapphire after dark, Lady Queen," said Helda. "He'll convey all the news we have."

"And is Death all right?"

"Death is deeply depressed," said Madlen. "But otherwise recovering."

She didn't expect breakfast to do her any good. When it did, it was her first experience of a new kind of guilt. It shouldn't be so easy to nurture herself, her stomach should not be so comforted by food that was filling. She shouldn't want to live when Thiel had wanted to die.

IN THE INFIRMARY, her two Lienid guards seemed grateful for her visit and her thanks.

Death sat propped up in bed with a lopsided bandage around his head.

"All those books," he moaned. "Lost. Irreplaceable. Lady Queen, Madlen says I'm not to work until my head stops aching, but I believe it's aching from lack of work."

"That sounds a bit unlikely, Death," said Bitterblue gently, "seeing as you were bashed over the head. But I do understand what you mean. What work would you like?"

"The remaining journals, Lady Queen," he said fervently. "The one I was working on survived the fire, and Lord Giddon tells me that a very few others did as well. He has them. I'm dying to see them, Lady Queen. I was so close to understanding things. I believe that some of his odder and more particular renovations to the castle and city were an attempt to bring another world to life here, Lady Queen. Presumably the world he came from, with the colorful rat. I believe he was trying to turn this world into that one. And I believe that it may be a land of considerable medical advancement, which is why he was obsessed with his mad hospital."

"Death," she said quietly. "Have you ever gotten the impression, from reading about his hospital, that it was not him, but his staff, that did the hurtful things to the victims? That he often stood back and watched?"

Death's eyes narrowed. "It would explain some things, Lady Queen," he said, his eyes widening again. "He speaks sometimes of the few victims he 'kept for himself.' That could mean, couldn't it, that he shared the others, presumably with other abusers?"

"The abusers were also his victims."

"Yes, of course, Lady Queen. In fact, he speaks of 'moments when his men come to realize what they are doing.' It hadn't occurred to me until now, Lady Queen," he said morosely, "which men he was referring to, or precisely what they were doing."

At this reminder of her men, Bitterblue stood, grimly preparing herself. "I'd better go."

"Lady Queen," he said, "may I ask you for one more thing on your way?"

"Yes?"

"You—" He paused. "You will think it unimportant, Lady Queen, in the face of your other worries."

"Death," she said. "You're my librarian. If there's something I can do that will bring you comfort, tell me what it is."

"Well," he said. "I keep a bowl with water for Lovejoy under the desk, Lady Queen. It will certainly be empty, if it's there at all. He'll be disoriented by my absence, you see? He'll think I abandoned him. He can manage feeding himself quite well on the library mice, but he does not venture outside the library and won't know where to find water. He's very fond of water, Lady Queen."

*   *   *   *   *

Lovejoy was fond of water.

The desk was a blackened, broken-down shell, the floor under it ruined. The bowl, green as a Monsean valley, lay upside down some distance from the desk. Carrying it out of the library and into the great courtyard, shivering, Bitterblue walked to the fountain pool. The bowl, once she'd filled it, was so cold that it burned her fingers.

In the library, she considered the situation, then knelt behind the gutted desk and placed the water under its corner. It didn't seem kind to draw Lovejoy to such a smelly ruin, but if that was where he was used to finding his water, then perhaps that was where he would look for it.

She heard a growl, in a feline voice she recognized. Peeking beneath the desk, she saw a lump of darkness and the dangerous flick of a tail.

Cautiously, she slid her hand halfway under the desk toward him, so that he could decide whether to approach or ignore. He chose attack. Yowling and swift, he swiped at her, then retreated again.

Bitterblue held her bleeding hand to her chest, biting back her cries, because she didn't blame him, and she knew how he felt.

On a stairway, as she approached her offices, Po intercepted her.

"Do you need me?" he asked. "Do you want me, or anyone else, to go in there with you?"

Standing before the strange light of his eyes, Bitterblue thought about that. "I will need you," she said, "many times in the next few days. And I'll need your concentrated help at some point in the future, Po. Your help with my court and my administration and with Monsea alone, undistracted—not while you're also contributing to an Estillan revolution. Once Estill is settled, I want you back here for a short while. Will you agree?"

"Yes," he said. "I promise."

"I think I need to do this thing now alone," she said. "Though I have no idea what to say to them. I have no idea what to do."

Po tilted his head, considering her. "Both Thiel and Runnemood are dead, Cousin," he said, "and they were always in charge. Your men will be looking for a new leader."

WHEN SHE STEPPED into the lower offices, the room went still. All faces turned to her. Bitterblue tried to think of them as men who needed a new leader.

What surprised her was that it wasn't difficult. She was struck by the need transparent on their faces and in their eyes. Need for many things, for they stared at her like lost men, mute with confusion, and with shame.

"Gentlemen," she said quietly, "how many of you have been involved in the systematic suppression of truths from Leck's time? The killing of truthseekers?"

None of them answered, and many of them dropped their eyes.

"Is there anyone here who wasn't involved, in one way or another?" she said.

Again, no one answered.

"All right," she said, a bit breathlessly. "Next question. How many of you were forced by Leck to commit atrocities upon other people?"

All of them raised their eyes to her again, which stunned her. She'd been afraid that the question would cause them to break. But instead they looked into her face, with hope, almost; and looking back at them, finally she saw it, the truth hiding behind the numbness, at the back of the deadness, in all of their eyes.

"It wasn't your fault," she said. "It wasn't your fault, and now it's over. No more hurting people. Do you understand? No more hurting even one more soul."

Tears were running down Rood's face. Holt came to her, dropping to his knees. He took her hand and began to weep. "Holt," she said, bending down to him. "Holt, I forgive you."

A breath went around the room, a silence that seemed to ask if it too was worthy of forgiveness. Bitterblue felt the question from all of them, and stood there, scrambling for the answer. She couldn't sentence every guilty man here to a term in prison and leave it at that, for that would change nothing about the truer problem in their hearts. She couldn't dismiss them from their work and send them away, because left to their own devices, they would probably continue to hurt people, and some of them would hurt themselves. *No more of people hurting themselves,* she thought. *But nor can I keep them on and tell them to continue with their work—for I can't trust them.*

She had thought of the queen as a person who shaped big things, like bringing literacy back to the city and castle. Like opening her High Court to claims for remuneration from across the entire kingdom. Housing the Council while they assisted the Estillans with the overthrow of an unjust king and dealing with whatever Katsa found at the other end of that tunnel. Deciding, when Ror came with his navy, how much of a navy Monsea needed, and how much it could afford.

But it is just as important, she thought, *to thaw these men who were frozen by my father, and to stand at their sides through the pain of their healing.*

How can I ever take care of so many men?

She said, "We have a great deal of work to do, and undo. I'm going to divide you into teams and assign each team to one aspect of the task. Each team will include new people, Monseans, from outside this administration. You'll report to them, as they'll report to you, and you'll work with them closely. You understand that my reason for involving others is that I can't trust you," she said, pausing, allowing that small, necessary arrow to hit each of them. *They need me to trust them again, or they won't be able to be strong.* "But each of you has the opportunity now to regain my trust. I will not require any of you to revisit the abuses of King Leck. I'll leave that to others who weren't hurt by him so directly. I won't allow anyone to hold you responsible for, or plague you with, things you did then that you were compelled to do. I also forgive you, personally, for the crimes you've committed since," she said. "But—others may not, and those people have the same right to justice that you do. The time ahead is going to be messy and difficult," she said. "Do you understand that?"

Stricken faces looked back at her. Some of them nodded.

"I'll help each of you through it, however I can," she said. "If there are trials, I'll testify on your behalf, for I understand that few of you were at the top of this chain of command, and I understand that you were forced for years, some of you for decades, by my father, to be obedient. Perhaps some of you don't know now how to be anything but obedient. That's not your fault.

"One more thing," she said. "I've said that I won't make you revisit the time of King Leck, and I meant that. But there are people—lots of people—who see value in doing so. There are people who need to do so in order to recover. I don't begrudge you your own need to heal in your own way, but you will not interfere with other people's healing. I understand that what they do interferes with yours. I see the conundrum. But I will not tolerate any of you compounding Leck's crimes with more crimes. Anyone who continues with this suppression will lose every bit of my loyalty. Do you understand?"

Bitterblue looked into every face, waiting for an acknowledgment. How she'd worked with these men for so many years and never seen how much was in their faces was beyond her, and it shamed her; and now they were depending on her. It was in their eyes; and they didn't know that she was all talk, that the teams she talked about building had no foundation and no plan, nothing but her words. Her words were empty. She might as well have told them that they were all going to build a castle out of air.

Well. She had better start somewhere. Demonstrating trust was, perhaps, more important than actually feeling it. "Holt," she said.

"Yes, Lady Queen," he said gruffly.

"Holt, look into my face," she said. "I have a job for you and any men in the Queen's Guard that you choose."

This brought Holt's eyes to hers. "I'll do anything, Lady Queen."

Bitterblue nodded. "There is a cave on the other side of Winter Bridge," she said. "Your niece knows how to find it. It's the lair of a thief known as Spook and her granddaughter, Gray, whom you may know as my servant Fox. Late tonight, when both Spook and Fox are inside, I want you to raid the cave, arrest them and their guards, and seize any items inside. Talk to Giddon," she said, for Giddon was the man pegged to talk next to Saf. "He has access to information about the cave. He may be able to tell you how it's guarded and where the entrances are."

"Thank you, Lady Queen," said Holt, tears streaming down his face. "Thank you for trusting me with this."

Then Bitterblue looked into the faces of her two remaining

advisers, Rood and Darby, and knew that she was about to make things just a little bit worse for herself.

"Come upstairs with me," she said to the two.

"SIT DOWN," BITTERBLUE said.

Darby and Rood slumped into chairs like defeated men. Rood was still crying, Darby sweaty and shaking. They were grieving, as she was, and Bitterblue hated that she had to do this.

"I said below that I believed very few people were at the top of this chain of command," she said. "But both of you were, weren't you?"

Neither answered. Bitterblue was beginning to get a little tired of not being answered. "You set it up from the beginning, didn't you? Forward-thinkingness actually meant suppression of the past. Danzhol, before I killed him, intimated that the town charters were intended to keep me from digging into the truth of what happened in my towns, and I laughed at him, but that's exactly what they were meant to do, isn't it? Push the past under the rug and pretend it's possible to make a fresh start. The blanket pardons for all crimes committed in Leck's time too. The lack of education in the schools, because it's easier to control what's known when people can't read. And, worst of all, the specific targeting of anyone working against you. Right?" she said. "Gentlemen? Does that about cover it? Answer me," she commanded sharply.

"Yes, Lady Queen," Rood whispered. "That, and flooding you with paper so that you'd stay in your tower and be too overwhelmed to be curious."

Bitterblue stared at him in astonishment. "You will tell me how it worked," she said, "and who else was involved besides the men downstairs. And you'll tell me if anyone else was in charge."

"We were the ones in charge, Lady Queen," Rood whispered

again. "Your four advisers. We passed down the orders. But others have been deeply involved."

"Thiel and Runnemood were more culpable than we were," said Darby. "It was their idea. Lady Queen, you said you forgave us. You said you would testify on our behalves if there were trials, but now you're so angry."

"Darby!" she cried in exasperation. "Of course I'm angry! You lied to me and manipulated me! My own friends were singled out for killing! One is ill because you tried to burn her printing shop!"

"We did not want to hurt her, Lady Queen," said Rood desperately. "She was printing books and teaching people to read. She had papers and strange letter molds that frightened and confused us."

"And so you set it all on fire? Is that part of your method too? Destroy anything you don't understand?"

Neither man spoke. Neither man seemed entirely present in his chair. "Captain Smit?" she snapped. "Am I likely ever to see him again?"

"He wanted to tell you the truth, Lady Queen," Rood whispered. "It was a great strain on him to lie to your face. Thiel thought he'd made himself too much of a liability, you see?"

"How could you be so careless with people?" she said, furious.

"It is easier than you might think, Lady Queen," said Rood. "It only requires a lack of thought, an avoidance of feeling, and the realization, when one does think or feel, that being careless with people is all one is good for."

Thirty-five years. Bitterblue wasn't certain she'd ever be able to comprehend what it had been like for them. It wasn't fair that nearly a decade after his death, Leck was still killing people. Leck was still tormenting the same people he'd tormented; people were committing appalling acts in order to erase the appalling acts they'd already committed.

"Ivan?" she said. "The mad engineer? What happened to him?"

"Runnemood thought he was calling too much attention to himself and, hence, to the state of the city, Lady Queen," whispered Rood. "You yourself complained of his incompetence."

"And Danzhol?"

"Oh," Rood said, taking a breath. "We don't know what went wrong with Danzhol, Lady Queen. Leck did have a few special friends who would visit and find themselves drawn into his hospital; Danzhol was one. We knew this, of course, but we didn't know he'd gone mad and intended to kidnap you for money. Thiel was so ashamed afterwards, for Danzhol had asked him beforehand how highly your administration valued you, Lady Queen, and Thiel thought, in retrospect, that perhaps he should've guessed the purpose of the question."

"Danzhol was planning to ransom me back to you?"

"We think so, Lady Queen. No other party in the world would have paid so much for your return."

"But how can you say that," Bitterblue cried, "when you'd made a point of making me useless?"

"You would not have been useless, Lady Queen," Rood said, "once we'd eradicated all that had happened! You were our hope! Perhaps we should've kept Danzhol closer and involved him more in the suppression. We could have made him a judge or a minister. Perhaps then, he wouldn't have lost his mind."

"That doesn't seem likely," Bitterblue said in disbelief. "Nothing you say is logical. I was right when I thought Runnemood was the most sane of you all; at least he understood that your plan couldn't work while I was alive. I will testify on your behalves," she continued. "I will testify as to the injury Leck did to you, and the ways in which Thiel and Runnemood may have coerced you. I'll do whatever I can, and I'll make absolutely sure that you're treated fairly. But," she said, "you both know that in your cases, it's not a matter of 'if' there will be a trial. Both of you *must* go on trial. People have been murdered. I myself was almost choked to death."

"That was all Runnemood," Darby said, frantic. "He went too far."

"You have all gone too far," said Bitterblue. "Darby, see reason. You have all gone too far, and you know that I can't let you go free. How would that be? The queen protecting advisers who conspired to murder innocent Monseans and who used all the parts of her administration to see it done? You'll be imprisoned, both of you, as will anyone else who was deeply involved. You'll stay in prison until I've isolated people who can be trusted to investigate your crimes, and judges who can be trusted to try them justly and with an appreciation for all you've suffered. If you're found innocent and returned to me, I'll honor the court's ruling. But I will not pardon you myself."

Rood was breathing into his hands. He whispered, "I don't know how we all became trapped in this. I can't understand it. I still cannot fathom what happened."

Bitterblue felt as if her words were coming from a deep, hollow, unkind, and stupid core, but she pushed them out nonetheless. "Now," she said, "I want you both to write down for me how it worked, what was done, and who else was involved. Rood, you stay here at my desk," she said, handing him paper and pen. "Darby," she said, pointing to Thiel's stand. "You work over there. Separate reports. Take care that they match."

There was no comfort in making her distrust so obvious. There was no joy in depriving herself of two people whose minds and bodies she needed, depended on, to run these offices. And how horrible to send them to the prisons. One man who had a family and, somewhere deep inside him, a gentle soul, and another man who couldn't even call upon the escape of sleep.

When they were through, she arranged for members of the Queen's Guard to escort them to prison.

NEXT, SHE SENT for Giddon.

"Lady Queen," he said as he entered, "you don't look good. Bitterblue," he said, crossing the room in two strides, dropping down beside her, taking her arms.

"If you touch me," Bitterblue said, eyes closed, teeth clenched, "I'll lose my head, and they can't see me losing my head."

"Hold on to me," he said, "and breathe slowly. You're not losing your head, you're just under a massive amount of strain. Tell me what's going on."

"I'm facing," she said, then stopped. She wrapped her hands around his forearms and took a slow breath. "I'm facing a rather catastrophic staff shortage. I just put Darby and Rood in prison, and look at these papers."

She indicated the papers on her desk, covered with the scribbles of Darby and Rood. Four of the eight judges on her High Court had been involved in the suppression, convicting innocent people and people who needed to be silenced. So had Smit, of course, and the Master of Prisons. So had her Minister of Roads and Maps, her Minister of Taxes, various lords, and the head of the Monsean Guard in Monport. So many members of the Monsean Guard had learned to turn a blind eye that it had been impossible for Rood and Darby to list them individually. And then there were the lowest of the low, the criminals and the lost individuals in the city, who'd been paid, or compelled, to carry out the actual acts of violence.

"All right," Giddon said. "That's bad. But this kingdom is full of people, you know. Right now, you feel alone, but you're going to put together a team, a really magnificent team. Did you know that Helda has been making lists all day?"

"Giddon," she said, choking on a slightly hysterical laugh. "I feel alone because I *am* alone. People keep betraying me and people keep leaving me." And suddenly it was all right to lose control, here for two minutes of being dizzy against Giddon's shoulder, because he was safe, and he wouldn't tell anyone, and he was good at holding on to her with steady, strong arms.

When her breath had calmed, and she could wipe her eyes and nose on the handkerchief he gave her, instead of on his shirt, she thanked him.

"You're welcome," he said. "Tell me what I can do to help you."

"Do you have two hours you could give to me, Giddon? Now?"

Giddon glanced at the clock. "I have three hours, until two o'clock."

"Raffin, Bann, and Po—should I assume they're busy?"

"They are, Lady Queen, but they'll put their work aside for you."

"No, that's all right. Will you get Teddy for me, and Madlen and Hava, and bring all of them here with Helda?"

"Of course," he said.

"And ask Helda to bring her lists, and start thinking up one of your own."

"I know a lot of good Monseans who can be useful to you."

"That's why I called for you," she said. "While I've been bumbling around these last few months making messes, you've been meeting my people and learning things."

"Lady Queen," he said, "be fair to yourself. I've been creating a conspiracy, while you've been the focused target of one. It's easier to plan than to be planned against, trust me. And from now on, that's what you'll be doing."

* * * * *

HIS WORDS WERE comforting. But it was hard to believe them after he'd gone.

He came back with Teddy, Madlen, Hava, and Helda sooner than she expected. Teddy looked a bit harried, and was also rubbing his behind.

"That was fast," Bitterblue said, motioning to the chairs. "Are you all right, Teddy?"

"Lord Giddon put me on a horse, Lady Queen," said Teddy. "I haven't had much call for horses before this."

"Teddy," said Giddon, "I've told you I'm no longer a lord. Everyone seems determined to forget it."

"My bottom is seizing up," said Teddy glumly.

Bitterblue couldn't explain it, but once again, with people here, everything seemed less hopeless. Perhaps it was the reminder of a world outside this castle, where life ticked along and Teddy's bottom seized up, whether Thiel had jumped off a bridge or not.

"Lady Queen," said Helda, "at the end of this conversation, your worries will be gone."

Well, and that was ridiculous. Everything that worried her came rushing back. "There are a thousand things this conversation won't change," she said.

"What I meant, Lady Queen," said Helda more gently, "is that none of us have any doubt that you'll be able to outfit a fine administration."

"Well," said Bitterblue, trying to believe that. "I have some ideas, so we may as well start talking. Madlen and Hava," she said, "I don't expect you to have strong opinions about how my administration should be run, unless, of course, you want to. I've asked you to join us because you're two of the very few people I trust, and because you both know, or have observed, or have worked with, a lot of people. I need people," Bitterblue said. "There's nothing I need more. Any recommendations any of you have are welcome to me.

"Now," she said, trying not to show how shy she was to speak her ideas aloud. "I would like to add a few new ministries, so that we can have entire, focused teams working on matters that have been grievously neglected. I want to start over from scratch with building a Ministry of Education. And we should have a Ministry of Historical Record, but if we're to continue searching for the truth of what happened, we must be prepared to be gentle and take care with knowledge. We've got to talk more about the best way to do it, don't you think? And what would you all think of a Ministry of Mental Well-being?" she asked. "Has there ever been such a thing? What about a Ministry of Reparations?"

Her friends listened as she talked, and made suggestions, and Bitterblue began to draw charts. It was comforting to write things down; words, arrows, boxes made ideas more solid. *I used to have a small list, on a single piece of paper,* she thought, *of all the things I didn't know. It's hilarious to think it, when this entire kingdom could be an actual-sized map of the things I don't know.*

"Should we interview each person downstairs," she asked, "to see where each of their interests and expertise lie?"

"Yes, Lady Queen," said Helda. "Now?"

"Yes, why not?"

"I'm sorry, Lady Queen," said Giddon, "but I've got to go."

Bitterblue shot her eyes to the clock in amazement, unable to believe that Giddon's three hours were up. "Where are you going?"

Giddon directed a sheepish expression at Helda.

"Giddon?" said Bitterblue, now suspicious.

"It's Council business," Helda reassured Bitterblue. "He's not going to do anything to anyone Monsean, Lady Queen."

"Giddon," said Bitterblue reprovingly, "I always tell you the truth."

"I haven't lied!" he protested. "I haven't said a word." And when that didn't lessen Bitterblue's glare, "I'll tell you later. Possibly."

"This phenomenon wherein you always tell Lord Giddon the truth," said Helda to Bitterblue. "Might you consider extending that arrangement to others?"

"I'm not a lord!" said Giddon.

"Could we—" Bitterblue was losing focus. "Giddon, send one of my clerks or guards up on your way out, would you? Anyone who looks equal to an interview."

And so the interviews of her guards and clerks commenced, and Bitterblue found the ideas growing in a way that began to challenge the expediency of paper. Ideas were growing in all directions and dimensions; they were becoming a sculpture, or a castle.

And then everyone left her, to return to their own affairs; and she was alone, and empty and unbelieving again.

RAFFIN, BANN, AND Po came to dinner, late. Bitterblue sat quietly among them, letting their banter wash around her. *Helda is never happier than when she has young people to pester,* she thought. *Especially handsome young men.*

Then Giddon showed up, with a report on Saf. "He's bored to pieces and worried about his sister. But he gave me good information about Spook's cave to give to Holt, Lady Queen."

"After Spook and Fox are arrested," Bitterblue said quietly, her first contribution to the evening's conversation, "I wonder if we can let Saf out of the drawbridge tower. It may depend on how much Spook and Fox talk. I still don't feel like I've got a handle on the Monsean Guard just now." *I'd feel a lot better if I had the crown.* "How did your Council business go, Giddon?"

494 — K<small>RISTIN</small> C<small>ASHORE</small>

"I convinced a visiting spy of King Thigpen's not to return to Estill," said Giddon.

"And how did you do that?" asked Bitterblue.

"By—well—let's say, by arranging for him to have a holiday in Lienid," said Giddon.

This was met with a roar of approval. "Well done," said Bann, slapping him on the back.

"Did he *want* to go to Lienid?" asked Bitterblue, not certain why she bothered.

"Oh, everyone loves Lienid!" cried Po.

"Did you use the nausea infusion?" asked Raffin, pounding the table so hard in his excitement that the silver rattled. When Giddon nodded, the others gave him a standing ovation.

Quietly, Bitterblue took herself to the sofa. It was bedtime, but how was she to be alone in a dark room? How to face her own solitary, shaking self?

If she couldn't have anyone's arms around her as she fell asleep, then she could have the voices of these friends. She would wrap the voices around her and it would be like Saf's arms; it would be like Katsa's arms when they'd slept on the frozen mountain. Katsa. How acutely she missed Katsa. How acutely sometimes the presence or absence of people mattered. She would have fought Po tonight for Katsa's arms.

Of course, she'd forgotten that there might be a dream.

She dreamed that she was walking from rooftop to rooftop in Bitterblue City. She was walking on the castle roof. She was walking on the edges of the parapets of the glass roof of her castle tower, and she could see everything all at once, the buildings of her city, the bridges, the people trying to be strong. The sun warmed her, a breeze cooled her, and there was no pain, and she wasn't afraid to be standing at the top of the world.

I N THE MORNING, she woke to the news that Darby had hanged himself in his prison cell.

In her bedroom doorway, in her shift, Bitterblue fought against Helda, who was trying to take hold of her. She shouted, yelling abuse at Darby, yelling abuse at the Monsean Guard who'd let it happen, wild, savage in her grief in a way that seemed actually to frighten Helda, who stopped reaching for her and merely stood, quiet and tight-lipped. When Po arrived and Bitterblue transferred her yelling to him, he wrapped his arms around her even though she hit and kicked him. Caught her hard when she reached for one of her knives. Held her tighter and pulled her to the floor, wedged with her in the doorway, forcing her to be still. "I hate you," she yelled. "I hate him. I hate all of them!" she cried, and finally, her voice worn to exhaustion, gave up fighting and began to sob. "It's my fault," she sobbed in Po's arms. "It's my fault."

"No," said Po, who was also in tears. "It was his decision."

"Because I sent him to prison."

"No," Po said again. "Bitterblue, think about what you're saying. Darby did not kill himself because you sent him to prison."

"They're so fragile. I can't bear it. There's no way to stop them, if that's what they have in mind to do. There's nothing you can threaten them with. I should have been more gentle. I should have let him stay on."

"Bitterblue," said Po again. "This was not your doing."

"It was Leck's doing," said Helda, kneeling beside them. "Still Leck's doing."

"I'm sorry I screamed at you," Bitterblue whispered to her.

"It's all right, my dear," said Helda, smoothing Bitterblue's hair. And Bitterblue's heart ached for Darby, who'd been alone, without friends like these to hold him or draw strength from.

She said, "Somebody bring me Rood."

WHEN HER SLUMP-SHOULDERED former adviser was shuffled into her rooms by the Monsean Guard, Bitterblue said, "Rood. Are you thinking of killing yourself?"

"You've always been direct, Lady Queen," he said sadly. "It's one of the things I like about you. I do consider such things now and then. But the knowledge of the hurt it would do to my grandchildren has always stopped me. It would confuse them."

"I see," said Bitterblue, thinking that through. "What about house arrest?"

"Lady Queen," he said, looking into her face, then beginning to blink back tears. "Would you really allow that?"

"From now on, you're under house arrest," Bitterblue said. "Don't leave your family's quarters, Rood. If you need anything, send word, and I'll come."

THERE WAS ANOTHER person in Bitterblue's prisons this morning that she wanted to see, for Holt had done well. Not only were Fox and Spook behind bars, but a number of items had been returned to Bitterblue that she hadn't even realized were missing. Jewelry she'd kept in her mother's chest. The picture book she'd put on her sitting room shelves so long ago—Leck's *Book of True Things* with drawings of knives and sculptures and a Graceling's corpse, that made a sick sort of sense to her now. A great number of fine swords and daggers that had apparently gone missing, in recent months, from the smithy. Poor Ornik. He'd probably had his heart broken over what Fox had turned out to be.

Of course, she would not see Fox in her rooms; Fox would never again be invited to Bitterblue's rooms. Fox was brought to her office, instead, flanked by two members of the Monsean Guard.

She didn't look any the worse for wear, her hair, her face still startlingly pretty, her uneven gray eyes as striking as ever. But she snarled at Bitterblue, and said, "You can't link me or my grandmother to the crown, you know. You have no evidence of that. We won't hang."

She spoke it like a taunt, and Bitterblue watched her quietly, struck by the strangeness of seeing someone so changed. Was this, for the first time, Fox as she really was?

"Do you think I want you to hang?" she asked. "For being a common thief, and not a very impressive one? Don't forget that we handed you your prize."

"My family has been thieves longer than yours has ruled," Fox spat out. "There's nothing common about us."

"You're thinking of my father's side of the family," said Bitterblue calmly, "and forgetting my mother's. Which reminds me. Guards, see if she has a ring on her person, would you?"

Less than a minute later, after a short, ugly struggle, Fox gave up the ring she wore on a band around her wrist, under her sleeve. One of the guards, rubbing a sore shin where he'd been kicked, passed it to Bitterblue. It was the replica of the ring Ashen had worn for Bitterblue, the ring all of Bitterblue's spies carried: gold, with inset gray stones.

Holding it in her hand, closing it in her fist, Bitterblue felt that some sort of order had now been restored, for Fox had no right to wear something of Ashen's against her skin.

"You may take her away," Bitterblue said to the guards. "That's all I wanted."

CLERKS WHO'D HARDLY ever been up to her office before climbed the stairs today, to bring her reports. Whenever they left her again, she sat with her head in her hands, trying to loosen her braids. The sense of being overwhelmed slammed against her. Where was she to start? The Monsean Guard was a great worry, for it was huge and it was everywhere; it was a net that spread itself across the entire kingdom, and she depended upon it to protect her people.

"Froggatt," she said to her clerk the next time he walked through the door. "How will I teach everyone to think things through, and make their own decisions, and become real people again?"

Froggatt stared at a window, biting his lip. He was younger than most of the others and, she recalled, recently married. She remembered that she'd seen him smile once. "May I speak freely, Lady Queen?"

"Yes, always."

"For now, Lady Queen," he said, "allow us to continue to obey. But give us honorable instructions, Lady Queen," he said, turning a flushed face to hers. "Ask us to do honorable things, so that we may have the honor of obeying you."

It was as Po had said, then. They needed a new leader.

SHE WENT TO the art gallery. She was looking for Hava, though she didn't know why. There was something about Hava's fear that she wanted to be near, because she understood it, and something about being able to hide; something about turning into something one wasn't.

It was less dusty than it had been, and the fires were lit. Hava seemed to be trying to turn it into a habitable place. There was a kind of flicker in her vision that Bitterblue was becoming accustomed to, whenever Hava was hiding in plain sight, but nothing in the gallery was flickering today. Bitterblue sat on the floor to the side of the sculptures in the sculpture room, watching their transformations.

After some time, Hava found her there.

"Lady Queen," she said. "What's wrong?"

Considering the plain face of this girl, her strange, copper-red eyes, Bitterblue said, "I want to turn into something I'm not, Hava. Like you do, or like one of your mother's sculptures."

Hava walked to the windows beyond the sculptures, windows that looked out over the great courtyard. "I remain myself, Lady Queen," she said. "It's only other people who think I'm something I'm not. Which only reinforces, every time, the thing I am, which is a pretender."

"I'm a pretender too," said Bitterblue quietly. "Right now, I'm pretending to be the leader of Monsea."

"Hm," said Hava, pursing her lips and staring out the window. "My mother's sculptures aren't about people being what they're not either, Lady Queen, not really. She had a way of seeing truths about people, and showing them with her sculptures. Have you ever thought of that?"

"You mean that I really am a castle," said Bitterblue dryly, "and you're a bird?"

"I knew how to fly away," Hava said, "in a sense, anytime anyone else came near. The only person I was ever myself with was my mother. Even my uncle didn't know, until recently, that I was alive. It was our way of hiding me from Leck, Lady Queen. She pretended to him that I'd died, and then, every time he or anyone else at court came near, I used my Grace to hide. I flew away," she said simply, "and Leck never knew that my Grace was the inspiration for all her sculptures."

Bitterblue's eyes locked on Hava, suddenly wondering something. Unsettled, and trying to make a more focused study of Hava's face. "Hava," she said, "who is your father?"

Hava didn't seem to hear. "Lady Queen," she said in a peculiar voice, "who is that person in the courtyard?"

"What?"

"That person," Hava said, pointing, her nose pressed to the window, speaking in the wondering sort of voice that Teddy used when he talked about books.

Joining her carefully at the glass, Bitterblue looked down and saw a sight that was all comfort: Katsa and Po in the courtyard, kissing.

"Katsa," Bitterblue breathed happily.

"Beyond Lady Katsa," said Hava impatiently.

Beyond Katsa was a close-knit group of people that Bitterblue had definitely never seen before. At the edge of the group was a woman, an elderly woman. She leaned against a younger man who stood beside her. Her coat was pale brown fur; the hat on her head was pale brown fur. Her eyes, all at once, rose to meet Bitterblue's in the high gallery window.

Bitterblue needed to see her hair.

Like magic, the woman pulled off her hat and let her hair tumble down, scarlet and gold and pink, streaked with silver.

It was the woman from the hanging in the library, and Bitterblue didn't know why she was crying.

42

THEY WERE FROM a land east of the eastern mountains, called the Dells, and they came in peace. Except that some of them were from a land to the north of the Dells called Pikkia, a land that occasionally bickered with the Dells, but was currently at peace with them—or not? It was hard to follow, because Katsa was explaining it badly and none of them seemed to speak the Monsean language much at all. Bitterblue knew what language they must all speak, but the only words she could remember were *cobwebs* and *monster*. And she still seemed to be leaking tears.

"Death," she said. "Somebody fetch Death. Katsa, just for a minute, stop talking," she said, needing quiet, because something peculiar was happening here in the courtyard. The voices, the need to understand messy things, and all the *nattering*—all of it was keeping her from being able to focus.

Everyone stood quietly, waiting.

Bitterblue couldn't take her eyes off the woman from the hanging. And the strangeness was coming from this woman: Bitterblue realized that now; she was changing the air somehow, changing the way Bitterblue felt. She tried to breathe easily, tried not to be overwhelmed. Tried to see the woman's individual parts instead of being invaded by . . . her extraordinary whole. Her skin was brown and her eyes were green and her hair—Bitterblue understood the woman's hair, for she'd seen the rat pelt, but the pelt hadn't been a living, breathing woman, and it had not made her feel as if the top of her head were singing.

The air was soaked with the feeling of power being used.

"What are you doing to us?" Bitterblue whispered to the woman.

"She does understand you, Bitterblue," said Katsa, "though she doesn't speak our language. She can respond to you, but she'll only do so with your permission, for she does it mentally. It'll feel like she's in your head."

"Oh," Bitterblue said, stepping back. "No. Never."

"All she does is communicate, Bitterblue," said Katsa gently. "She doesn't steal your thoughts, or change them."

"But she could if she wanted to," said Bitterblue, for she'd read her father's stories about a woman who looked like this and had a venomous mind. Behind her, the courtyard had filled with servants, with clerks, guards, Giddon, Bann, Raffin, Helda, Hava—Anna the baker, Ornik the smith. Dyan, the gardener. Froggatt, Holt. And others filing in, and all of them staring in wonder at a woman who was standing there *glowing* with something.

"She doesn't want to change your thoughts, Bitterblue," said Katsa, "or anyone's here. And in your case, she tells me she couldn't, because you have a good, strong mind that is closed to her interference."

"I've had practice," Bitterblue said in a small, hard voice. "How does her power work? I want to know exactly how it works."

Po broke in. "Beetle," he said, his voice hinting that she was, perhaps, being rude, "I understand you, but perhaps you'd like to greet them and bring them in out of the cold first? They've come a long way to meet you. They'd probably like to be shown to their rooms."

Bitterblue cursed the tears that kept running down her cheeks. "Perhaps you've forgotten the events of the last few days, Po," she

said plainly. "It pains me to be rude, and I apologize for my rudeness. But, Katsa, you have brought a woman who controls minds
into a castle of people particularly vulnerable to such a thing. Look
around," she said, gesturing to the courtyard that continued to fill
with people. "Do you think this is good for them, to be standing
here, mindlessly staring? Maybe it is," she said bitterly. "If she truly
comes in peace, maybe she can be their higher power, and keep
them from committing any more suicides."

"Suicides?" said Katsa in dismay.

"I'm responsible for these people," Bitterblue said. "I'm not
going to welcome her until I understand who she is and how her
power works."

THEY WENT TO the library to talk about it: Bitterblue, her Council
friends, the Dellians and Pikkians, away from prying eyes and empty,
captive minds. Passing Death's ruin of a desk, she remembered that
Death was in the infirmary.

The strangers seemed neither surprised nor offended by
Bitterblue's lack of hospitality. But when she walked them into her
alcove, they stopped, eyes widening, and gawked at the hanging,
murmuring among themselves in words Bitterblue knew the sound
of, but couldn't understand. The woman with the power, in particular, exclaimed something to the others, then grabbed hold of one of
her companions and motioned him to say something, or do something, to Bitterblue. The man stepped forward, bowed, and spoke
in a heavy but somehow pleasant accent. "Queen Bitterblue," he
said. "Please forgive my—poor speech—but Lady Bier remembers
this—" The man gestured to the hanging. "She is moved to—" He
stopped, in frustration.

Katsa interjected quietly. "She says that Leck kidnapped her,

Bitterblue, and murdered one of her friends, a very long time ago. She believes this is a scene from the kidnapping, for that is the coat he gave her to wear, and they passed through a forest of white trees. Afterwards, she escaped, and fought him. In the fight, he fell through a crack in the ground, then presumably followed a tunnel that brought him to Monsea. She's moved to tell you how sorry she is that he found his way back here, and did harm to your kingdom. The Dells only discovered the seven kingdoms fifteen years ago, and the only tunnels they've known until now have brought them into far eastern Estill, so they were some time in discovering the problems in Monsea. She's sorry for letting Leck return and for not helping Monsea to defeat him."

It was strange to listen to Katsa interpret. It involved long, silent pauses on Katsa's part, which gave Bitterblue time to gape and wonder, and be boggled at some of the more astonishing things Katsa said. Which Katsa then followed up with even more astonishing things.

"What does she mean, *return*?" Bitterblue said.

Katsa squinted. "Lady Fire is unsure of what you're asking."

"She said that the tunnel brought him *back* here, to Monsea," Bitterblue said. "That she allowed him to *return*. Does she mean that Leck wasn't Dellian? Does she know he was Monsean?"

"Ah," said Katsa, pausing for the answer. "Leck was not Dellian. She doesn't know if he was Monsean, only that he was from the seven kingdoms. There are no Gracelings in the Dells," Katsa added, speaking for herself now. "My arrival created quite a commotion, let me tell you."

I'm from the seven kingdoms, Bitterblue thought, *completely. Dare I hope I'm Monsean? And this woman, this strange, beautiful woman. My father killed her friend.*

They discovered the seven kingdoms fifteen whole years ago? "That man called her Lady Bier," Bitterblue said. "But you called her Lady Fire, Katsa."

"*Bir* is the Dellian word for *fire*," said a worn and familiar voice behind Bitterblue. "Bee-ee-rah, or, in our letters, *B-i-r*, Lady Queen."

Spinning, Bitterblue faced her librarian, who was listing a bit to one side, like a ship taking water. He held the charred remains of the Dellian-Gracelingian dictionary in his hands. Part of its back end was gone, the pages were warped, and the red cover was now mostly black.

"Death!" she said. "I'm glad you could join us. I wonder—" She was hopelessly confused. "Perhaps we should all learn each other's names and sit down," she said, after which there were introductions all around, and hands taken, and manuscripts cleared from the table, and additional chairs found and wedged in among the others. And names almost immediately forgotten, because there was too much else going on. They were a group of nine travelers: three explorers, four guards, one healer, and the lady, who served as ambassador, and also as a silent translator, and who invited Bitterblue to call her Fire. Most of the travelers were browner-skinned than the most sun-darkened Lienid Bitterblue had ever seen, except for a couple who were paler, and one, the man who'd spoken before, who was fully as pale as Madlen. Their hair and eyes were also a range of hues—*ordinary* hues, aside from Lady Fire. And still, there was something in the way they all looked—in their jaws? In their expressions?—something they all had in common. Bitterblue wondered if they saw some sort of distinctive similarity when they looked at her and her friends too.

"I don't completely understand this," she said. "Any of it."

Lady Fire said something, which the pale man made a move to

translate, in his nice, funny accent. "The mountains have always been too high," he said. "We have had—stories, but no way across, or—" He made a motion with his hand.

"Under," said Po.

"Yes. No way under," said the man. "Fifteen years ago, a—" He paused again, baffled.

"A landslide," said Po. "Revealed a tunnel. And now the stories will no longer be mere stories."

"Po," said Bitterblue, disturbed that he was publicly displaying his own ability, even though she knew he was pretending that Lady Fire was talking to him mentally. Wasn't he? Or maybe she *was* talking to him mentally, and if so, did Lady Fire know what Po was? Wouldn't that make her a thousand times more dangerous? Or— Bitterblue grasped her forehead. Had Bitterblue, sitting here, thinking about it all, revealed Po's secret to Lady Fire?

Po's hand found its way around Katsa to Bitterblue's shoulder. "Take a breath, Cousin," he said. "This comes on the tail of too many horrible days. I believe this will seem like good news once you've had the time to absorb it."

I remember the day we all sat in a circle on this library floor, she thought to him. *The world was far smaller then, and still too big.*

Every day is so overwhelming.

The pale fellow was trying to talk again, saying something about how they were all sorry to have arrived during horrible days. Bitterblue raised her eyes and peered at him as he spoke, trying to place something.

"Whenever you talk," she said, "there's something familiar about it."

"Yes, Lady Queen," agreed Death dryly. "Perhaps that's because it's a stronger version of the accent spoken by your healer Madlen."

Madlen, thought Bitterblue, staring at the man. *Yes, how odd that*

he sounds like Madlen. And how odd that he's pale with amber eyes like
Madlen. And—

My Graceling healer, Madlen.

There are no Gracelings in the Dells.

But Madlen has only one eye.

Just like that, one of Bitterblue's anchors in this world turned, suddenly, into a perfect stranger.

"Oh," she said dumbly. "Oh dear." She thought of all the books in Madlen's room and found the answer to another question. "Death," she said. "Madlen saw Leck's journals on my bed, then that dictionary appeared on your shelf. The dictionary is Madlen's."

"Yes, Lady Queen," said Death.

"She told me she came from the far east of Estill," Bitterblue said. "Fetch her. Someone fetch her."

"Allow me, Lady Queen," Helda said, in a dark voice that made Bitterblue glad she was not Madlen at this moment.

Helda pushed herself up and swept off, and Bitterblue stared at her guests. They'd all gone over a trifle sheepish.

"Lady Fire apologizes, Bitterblue," Katsa said. "She says that it's embarrassing to be caught spying, but regrettably, *not* spying is never an option, as no doubt you understand."

"I understand that it makes for an interesting definition of the peace they claim to come in," said Bitterblue. "Did they make Madlen take out her own eye?"

"No," said Lady Fire emphatically.

"Never," added Katsa. "Madlen lost her eye as a child, doing an experiment with liquids and a powder that exploded. It made it possible for her to pretend."

"But how does she heal so well? Are all healers in the Dells truly so gifted?"

Katsa translated. "Medical knowledge is highly advanced there, Bitterblue. Medicines grow there that we don't have here, especially in the west, which is where Madlen is from, and science is paramount. Madlen has been kept supplied with the best Dellian medicines during her time here, to keep up her pretense."

Science, Bitterblue thought. *Real science. I would like that kind of progress in my kingdom, in a sane manner, without delusion.* Suddenly, she loved Po for his stupid paper glider, because it was based on reality.

Then Madlen came into the alcove. First, she went to Lady Fire and kissed the woman's hand, murmuring something in their language. Then she rounded the table to Bitterblue and fell to both knees. "Lady Queen," she said, bowing her head, speaking thickly. "I hope you'll forgive me for deceiving you. I have not liked to do so. At every moment, I've not liked it, and I hope you'll allow me to stay on as your healer."

Bitterblue understood then, something about how a person could lie and tell the truth at the same time. Madlen had made something of a fool of her. But Madlen's care of Bitterblue's body, and of her heart, had been genuine.

"Madlen," she said, "I'm relieved. I was steeling myself against the possibility of losing you."

THE TALK CONTINUED. Bitterblue's concept of the world had never been stretched like this before, and she was a bit light-headed.

The Dellians described what it had been like to discover a world to their west. The Dells knew war, and the Dellian king had no wish for it. And so, discovering a land of seven kingdoms in which too many of the kings were warmongers, the Dellians had chosen secret exploration, rather than making themselves immediately known.

They were exploring eastward as well.

"The Pikkians have a sizable navy," Katsa explained, "and the Dellians have been growing their navy slowly as well. They've been exploring their coastline and waters, Bitterblue."

They'd brought maps. A squat, tough-looking woman named Midya did her best to explain them. The maps showed wide expanses of land and water and, in the north, unnavigable ice.

"Midya is a famous naval explorer, Bitterblue," said Katsa.

"Does that make her Pikkian or Dellian?"

"Midya has a Dellian mother, and her father was Pikkian," said Katsa. "Technically, she's Dellian, because that's where she was born. I'm told there's a great deal of intermingling, especially in recent decades."

Intermingling. Bitterblue looked around the table, at these people who'd come together in her library alcove. Monseans, Middluners, Lienid, Dellians, Pikkians. Gracelings . . . and whatever Lady Fire was.

"Lady Fire is what is called a 'monster,'" said Katsa quietly.

"Monster," Bitterblue said. *"Ozhaleegh."*

Every Dellian speaker at the table looked up and stared.

"Excuse me," Bitterblue said, standing, walking away from the table. Pushing herself a good distance away. She found a dark place behind some bookshelves and sat on the rug in a corner.

She knew what would happen. Po would come to her, or send to her whoever he felt was the right person. But it wouldn't help, because no one was right. No one living, anyway. She didn't want to cry on anyone's living shoulder or be told bracing things. She wanted to be out of this world, in a meadow of wildflowers, or a forest of white trees, not knowing about the terrible things happening around her, a baker girl, with a mother who did needlework. Could she have that one back again? Could she have it for real?

The person who came was Lady Fire. Bitterblue was surprised that Po had sent her. Until, looking at the lady, she wondered if perhaps she had been calling for Lady Fire herself.

Fire knelt before Bitterblue. Bitterblue was suddenly frightened, terrified of this beautiful, old, creaky-kneed woman in brown; terrified of the impossible hair that tumbled around her shoulders; terrified of how much she wanted to look into this woman's face and see her own mother. Knowing, suddenly, that this was why Fire had mesmerized Bitterblue from that first moment: Because the love she felt when she looked into Fire's face was the love she had known once for her mother. And this wasn't right. Her mother had deserved that love and her mother had suffered and fought and died because of it. This woman had done nothing but walk into a courtyard.

"You have drugged me with false feeling for you," Bitterblue whispered. "That is your power."

A voice came to her, inside her head. It was not words, but she understood it perfectly.

Your feelings are real, it said. *But they're not for me.*

"I feel them for you!"

Look closer, Bitterblue. You love fiercely, and you carry a queen's share of sadness. When I'm near, my presence overwhelms you with all that you feel—but I'm only the music, Bitterblue, or the hanging or the sculpture. I make your feelings swell, but it's not me you feel them for.

Bitterblue began to cry again. Fire offered her own furry, brown sleeve to wipe Bitterblue's tears. Gathering the softness to her face, allowing herself to sink into it, Bitterblue was connected, for a moment, to this singular creature who had come when she'd called, and been kind when she'd made herself unpleasant. "If you wanted to," Bitterblue whispered, "you could go into my mind and see all that's in there. And steal it, and change it to whatever you like. Couldn't you?"

Yes, said Fire. *Though it would not be easy with you, for you're strong. You don't know it, but your unfriendly reception quite endeared you to us, Bitterblue. We hoped you would be strong.*

"You say you don't want to take our minds. Mine or my people's."

It's not why I'm here, said Fire.

"Would you do something for me if I asked you to?"

That depends on what it is.

"My mother said I was strong enough," Bitterblue said, beginning to shiver. "I was ten years old, and Leck was chasing us, and she knelt before me in a field of snow and gave me a knife and said that I was strong enough to survive what was coming. She said I had the heart and the mind of a queen." Bitterblue turned her face away from Fire, just for a moment, because this was hard; saying this truth aloud was hard. "I want to have the heart and mind of a queen," she whispered. "I want it more than anything. But I'm only pretending. I can't find the feeling of it inside me."

Fire considered her quietly. *You want me to look for it inside you.*

"I just want to know," Bitterblue said. "If it's there, it would be a great comfort for me to know."

Fire said, *I can tell you already that it's there.*

"Really?" Bitterblue whispered.

Queen Bitterblue, Fire said, *shall I share with you the feeling of your own strength?*

FIRE TOOK HER mind so that it was as if she were in her own bedroom, raw with crying and grief.

"This doesn't feel strong," Bitterblue said.

Wait, said Fire, still kneeling beside her in the library. *Be patient.*

She was in her bedroom, raw with crying and grief. She was frightened, and certain that she was incapable of the task ahead. She was ashamed of her mistakes. She was small, and tired of being left. Furious with the people who left, and left, and left. Heartsore on account of a man on a bridge who betrayed her and then left, and a boy on a bridge who she knew somehow would be the next one to leave her.

Then something began to change in the room. None of the feelings changed, but Bitterblue encompassed them somehow. She was larger than the feelings, she held the feelings in an embrace, and murmured kindnesses to them and comforted them. She was the room. The room was alive, the gold of the walls glowed with life, the scarlet and gold stars of the ceiling were real. She was bigger than the room; she was the corridor and the sitting room and Helda's rooms. Helda was there, tired and worried and feeling some arthritis in her knitting hands, and Bitterblue embraced her, Bitterblue comforted her too, and eased the pain in her hands. And grew. She was the outer corridors, where she embraced her Lienid Door Guard. She was the offices and the tower and she embraced all the men who were broken and frightened and alone. She was the lower levels and the smaller courtyards, the High Court, the library, where so many of her friends were now; where people gathered from an entire other land. The most amazing thing, to discover a new land! And its people were in the library now, and Bitterblue was large enough to contain such a degree of wonder. And to embrace her friends among them, feel the complications of their feelings for each other, Katsa and Po, Katsa and Giddon, Raffin and Bann, Giddon and Po. The complications of her own feelings. She was the great courtyard, where water pounded and snow fell on glass. She was the art gallery, where Hava hid and where Bellamew's work stood as evidence of something that had transcended her father's cruelty. She was the kitchen, humming along with unending efficiency, and the stables where the winter sun burnished wood and horses whickered with hair in their eyes, and the practice rooms where men sweated, and the armory, and the smithy, the artisan courtyard where people were working, and she held all those people in her arms. She was the grounds, the walls, and the bridges, where Sapphire hid, and where Thiel had broken her heart.

She saw herself, tiny, fallen, crying and broken on the bridge. She could feel every person in the castle, every person in the city. She could hold every one of them in her arms; comfort every one. She was enormous, and electric with feeling, and wise. She reached down to the tiny person on the bridge and embraced that girl's broken heart.

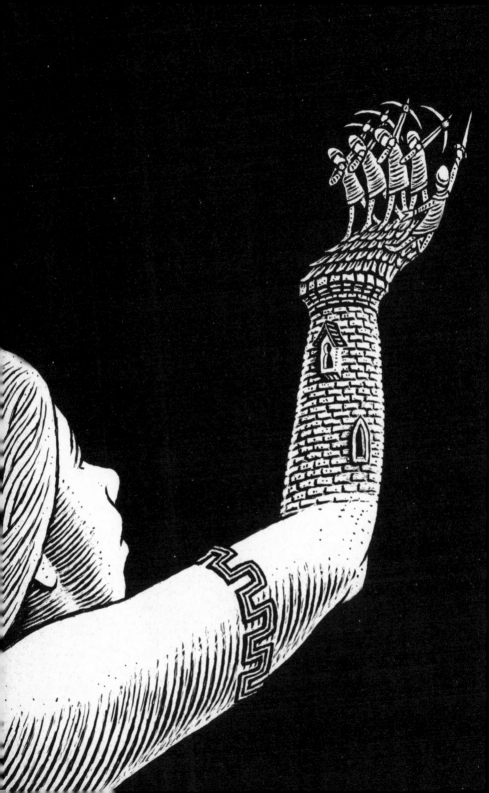

PART FIVE

The Ministry of Stories and Truth

(Late December and January)

43

IT WAS SOOTHING, when so little else in the world lent itself to clarity, to make lists of tasks that needed execution, then choose a person to entrust with each task. It was comforting to meet the person and understand, finally, why Helda or Teddy or Giddon had recommended the person. And heartening to discuss the task with that person, then leave the meeting feeling as if the execution of the task was perhaps not one of the five most hopeless undertakings on earth. She knew they couldn't all be, for there were well more than five tasks.

Hava had surprised Bitterblue with a few truly pertinent staff recommendations. The new Master of Prisons, for example, was a woman Hava had witnessed working on the silver docks, a Monsean Graceling named Goldie who'd grown up on a Lienid ship and eventually become the commander of the navy prison in Ror City. Upon returning to Monsea after Leck's death, she'd discovered that the Monsean Guard didn't employ women, at all, for anything, and certainly not to command its prisons. Goldie was Graced, of all things, with singing.

"My new prison master is a songbird," Bitterblue muttered to herself at her desk. "It's absurd." But it was no less absurd than women not being employed by the Monsean Guard. She could accept the one to change the other. And it was an exciting change.

The Dellians advised her on the matter, for they'd had women in their army for decades.

"I feel just a tad better about the Estill business now that you've made an ally in the Dellians, Bitterblue," said Po, lying on his back on Bitterblue's sofa. "At least about the danger of war. They're a serious military power. They'll back you if there's trouble."

"Does this mean you've let go of the certainty that I'm about to be attacked at every moment?"

"No," he said. "The existence of the Council endangers you."

"I'm a queen, Po," Bitterblue retorted. "I'll never be safe. Also, when it comes to war, the Dellians don't want to get involved."

"The Dellians were pretending not to exist. Now they're behaving like neighbors. And you've charmed their mind reader, which is never easily done."

"It can't be that hard, if Katsa charmed you."

"You don't find me charming?" Katsa asked her from the sitting room floor, where she sat idly with her back to the sofa. "Move over," she said to Po, shoving his legs.

"Hello," he said. "Would it kill you to ask nicely?"

"I've been asking you nicely for at least ten seconds and you've been ignoring me. Move over. I want to sit down."

Po made a show of beginning to move out of the way, then flipped himself off the sofa and flattened her. "So predictable," Bitterblue muttered as the two of them began wrestling on the rug.

"Fire is the sister-in-law of the king and the stepmother of the woman who commands the Dellian Army, Bitterblue," yelled Po, his face jammed into the carpet. "She's a valuable friend!"

"I'm right here," Bitterblue said. "You don't need to yell."

"I'm yelling because I'm in pain!" he yelled, his head under the sofa.

"I'm having a hard time with this letter," said Bitterblue vaguely. "What do you write to the elderly king of a foreign land when your kingdom is in shambles and you've only just discovered that he exists?"

"Tell him you hope to visit!" yelled Po, who seemed somehow to have gotten the upper hand. He was now straddling Katsa, trying to pin her shoulders to the ground.

Bitterblue sighed. "Perhaps I should ask him for advice. Katsa, you've met him. How did he seem?"

Katsa now sat calmly on the stomach of her vanquished foe. "He was handsome," she said.

Po moaned. "Was he beat-to-a-pulp handsome, or perhaps just push-down-a-flight-of-stairs handsome?"

"I would not push a seventy-six-year-old man down a flight of stairs," said Katsa indignantly.

"I suppose I have that to look forward to, then," Po said. "Someday."

"I've never pushed you down a flight of stairs," Katsa said, beginning to laugh.

"I'd like to see you try."

"Don't even joke. It's not funny."

"Oh, wildcat."

And now they were hugging. Bitterblue was left to roll her eyes and struggle alone with her letter to King Nash of the Dells.

"I've met a lot of kings, Bitterblue," said Katsa. "This one is a decent man, surrounded by decent people. They watched us quietly, for fifteen years, waiting to see if we could bumble ourselves into a more civilized state, rather than trying to conquer us. Po's right. You should tell him that you'd like to visit. And it would be entirely appropriate for you to ask him for advice. I have never been so happy," she added, sighing.

"Happy?"

"When I understood that the land I'd found was a land slow to war, with a king who was not an ass, and Pikkia another peaceful nation above them, I'd never been so happy. It changes the balance of the world."

ONE ADVANTAGE OF traveling by tunnel was that a tunnel made weather irrelevant. The Dellians could return in the winter, or wait until winter had passed—but, *I miss my husband,* Fire admitted to Bitterblue one day.

Bitterblue tried to imagine the kind of man who could be Fire's husband. "Is your husband like you?"

Fire smiled. *He is old like me.*

"What is his name?"

Brigan.

"And how long have you been married to him?"

Forty-eight years, said Fire.

They were tromping across the back garden, for Bitterblue had wanted to show Fire the Bellamew of her mother, fierce and strong, turning into a mountain lion. Now Bitterblue stopped, hugging herself, letting the snow soak into her boots.

What is it, my dear? asked Fire, stopping beside her.

"It's the first time I've ever heard of two people being together that long, and neither dying, and neither being awful," she said. "It makes me happy."

FIRE WAS MISSING two fingers, which had frightened Bitterblue the first time she'd noticed. *Your father did not take them,* Fire assured her; then asked her how much of a sad story she wanted to know.

This was how Bitterblue learned that forty-nine years ago, the Dells had been a kingdom with no certain shape, a kingdom recovering from a great evil. Like Monsea.

My father was a monster too, Fire told her.

"You mean, a monster like you?" asked Bitterblue.

He was a monster like me, said Fire, nodding, *in the Dellian sense. He was a beautiful man with silver hair and a powerful mind. But he was a monster the way you normally use the word here as well. He was a terror, like your father. He used his power to destroy people. He destroyed our king and ruined our kingdom. That's why I came to you, Bitterblue.*

"Because your father destroyed your kingdom?" Bitterblue said, confused.

Because when I heard about you, Fire said patiently, *my heart burst open. I felt that I knew what you'd faced and what you're facing.*

Bitterblue understood. Her voice was small. "You came just to comfort me?"

I'm not a young woman, Bitterblue, Fire said, smiling. *I did not come for the exercise. Here, I'll tell you the story.*

And Bitterblue hugged herself again, because the story of the Dells was, indeed, sad, but also because it gave her hope for what Monsea could be in forty-nine years. And what she could be too.

Fire said something else that gave Bitterblue hope. She taught Bitterblue a word: *Eemkerr.* Eemkerr had been Leck's first, true name.

Bitterblue took this information straight to the library. "Death?" she said. "Do we have birth records for the seven kingdoms for the year Leck would have been born? Will you review them for someone with a name that sounds like Eemkerr?"

"A name that sounds like Eemkerr," Death repeated, peering up at her from his new desk, which was covered with smelly, scorched papers.

"Lady Fire says that Leck told her that before his name was Leck, it was Eemkerr."

"Which is a name she remembers from almost fifty years ago," Death said sarcastically, "spoken to her, not spelled, presumably not a name from her own language, and conveyed to you *mentally* fifty years later. And I'm to recall every instance of a name of that nature in all the birth records available to me from the relevant year for all seven kingdoms, on the extremely slim chance that we have the name right and a record exists?"

"I know you're just as happy as I am," said Bitterblue.

Death's mouth twitched. Then he said, "Give me some time to remember, Lady Queen."

WHEN YOU VISIT US, Fire said, *you will see the ways Leck tried to re-create the Dells here. I hope it doesn't distress you. Our kingdom is beautiful and I would hate for it to cause you pain.*

They stood in Bitterblue's office, looking out at the bridges. "I believe," Bitterblue said, giving it careful consideration, "that if your home reminds me of mine, I will like your home. Leck was—what he was. But he did manage, somehow, to make this castle beautiful and strange, and I'd be sorry to change some things about it. He accidentally filled it with art that tells the truth," she said. "And I've even begun to appreciate the folly of these bridges. They have little reason to exist, except as a monument to the truth of all that's happened, and because they're beautiful."

Bitterblue let Winged Bridge fill her sight, floating blue and white, like a winged thing. Monster Bridge, where her mother's body had burned. Winter Bridge, glimmering with mirrors that reflected the gray of the winter sky.

She said, "I suppose those are reasons to exist."

WE WILL LEAVE before too long, said Fire. *Do I understand that you'll send a small party with us?*

"Yes," Bitterblue said. "Helda is helping me assemble it. I don't know most of them, Fire. I'm sorry not to send people I know more personally. My friends are absorbed with the Estillan situation and my own crisis here, and I fear that my clerks and guards are a bit too fragile right now for me to send with you." It was difficult to characterize the effect Fire had on Bitterblue's clerks and guards, or indeed, on any of her more empty-eyed people. She brought a deep peace to some, she made others frantic, and Bitterblue wasn't certain that one was any better than the other. Her people needed practice sitting comfortably in their own minds.

There's one who's asked to join us that I believe you know well, said Fire.

"Is there?"

A sailor. He wants to join us in our exploration of the eastern seas. I understand that he's been in some trouble with your law, Bitterblue?

Ah, said Bitterblue, taking a breath through a rush of sadness. Absorbing the inevitability of this news. *You must mean Sapphire. Yes. Sapphire stole my crown.*

Fire paused, considering Bitterblue as she stood, small and quiet, in the window. *Why did he steal your crown?*

Because, Bitterblue whispered. *He loved me and I hurt him.*

After a moment, Fire said gently, *He is welcome to join us.*

Take care of him.

We will, of course.

He can give you good dreams, Bitterblue said.

Good dreams? The sleeping kind?

Yes, the sleeping kind. It's his Grace. He can make you dream the most marvelous, comforting things.

Well, Fire said. *It's possible I've been waiting to meet your thief all my life.*

On a January morning, the day before the Dellians' departure, Bitterblue was reading Death's latest report on the journal translation. *Lady Queen,* she read, *I believe this journal I've been translating all along is from Leck's final year and is the last journal he ever wrote. In the section I just translated, he finally does kill Bellamew, as he has been threatening to do for some time.*

Froggatt ushered someone into her office and Bitterblue didn't even look up, because in her peripheral vision, the visitor looked like Po. Then he chuckled.

Her eyes shot to him. "Skye!"

"You thought I was Po," said Po's gray-eyed brother, grinning.

Bitterblue jumped up and went to him. "I'm so happy to see you! Why didn't anyone tell me you'd landed? Where's your father?"

Skye wrapped her in a hug. "I decided to be the courier myself," he said. "You look wonderful, Cousin. Father's in Monport, with half the Lienid Navy."

"Oh, right," Bitterblue said. "I forgot."

One of Skye's eyebrows jumped up and his grin widened. "You forgot that you asked my father to bring his navy?"

"No, no. There's just been—a lot going on. You've arrived in time to meet the Dellians before they go."

"The what?"

"The Dellians. They live in a kingdom to the east, under the mountains."

"Bitterblue," said Skye hesitantly, "are you in your right mind?"

Bitterblue took Skye's arm. "Let's go find Po, and I'll tell you about it."

IT WAS A pleasure to watch Po and Skye come together. Bitterblue couldn't explain why her heart swelled to see brothers kiss and hug each other, but it made her feel as if the world wasn't hopeless. The meeting took place in Katsa's rooms, where Katsa, Po, and Giddon were doing some brainstorming about Estill. After the appropriate round of greetings and explanations, Po put an arm around Skye and took him into the adjacent room. Shut the door.

Katsa watched them go. Then, crossing her arms tight, she kicked an armchair.

After a bit more kicking of furniture, walls, and floor had transpired, Giddon said to her, "Skye loves Po. This won't make him stop loving Po."

Katsa turned to Giddon with tears in her eyes. "He'll be so angry."

"He won't stay angry forever."

"Won't he?" she said. "People do sometimes."

"Do they?" he said. "Reasonable people? I hope that's not true."

Katsa gave him a funny look, but didn't answer. Resumed hugging herself and kicking things.

Bitterblue didn't want to go, but she had to; she had a meeting with Teddy in her tower. She was going to ask him if he mightn't like to work in her newly formed Ministry of Education, as an official representative adviser from the city. Part-time, of course. She wouldn't want to deprive him of the work he already loved.

* * * * *

THE MONSEAN GUARD was in too much disarray at the moment to press Bitterblue on the matter of whether her crown was missing. And so Saf had been allowed to go home, although Bitterblue was still nervous about it. The crown *was* missing, it was at the bottom of the river, and there had been witnesses. It did not seem the time in the High Court just now, while they were trying to restore a kind of honesty, for Bitterblue to lie or try to falsify evidence of a crown she could not produce.

She had not seen Saf since the night on the bridge. He was leaving with the Dellians in the morning. And so, just after sunset, Bitterblue ran through the snowy city to the shop.

Teddy answered her knock, grinned, bowed, and went away to rustle up Saf. She waited in the shop, shivering. The front wall and part of the ceiling, which had burned, were covered over with roughhewn planks that were not airtight. The room was very cold and smelled of burning; much of the furniture was gone.

Saf came in quietly, then stood there with his hands in his pockets, not saying anything. Glancing at her with a kind of shyness.

"You're leaving tomorrow," she said.

"Yes," he said.

"Saf," she said. "I have a question I need to ask you."

"Yes?"

She made herself watch his soft eyes. "If you weren't in trouble about the crown thing," she said, "would you still go away?"

The question made his eyes softer. "Yes."

She had known the answer before she'd asked. But hearing it still hurt.

"My turn," he said. "Would you stop being the queen for me?"

"Of course not."

"There, now," he said. "We've both asked each other the same question."

"We haven't."

"Have too," he said. "You asked me to stay, and I asked you to come with me."

Thinking about that, she came closer and reached for his hand. He gave it, and for a moment, she played with his rings, feeling the warmth of his skin in this cold room. Then, obeying her body, she kissed him, just to see what would happen. What happened was that he began to kiss her back. Tears slid down her face.

"It's one of the first things you told me about yourself," she whispered. "That you would go."

"I meant to do it sooner," he whispered back. "I meant to do it when things started to get tricky with the crown, to save myself. But then I couldn't. Not while we were still fighting."

"I'm glad you didn't."

"Did your dream work?"

"I walk on top of the world, and I'm not afraid," she said. "It's a beautiful dream, Saf."

"Tell me what other dream you want."

She wanted a thousand dreams. "Let me dream that we leave each other friends."

He said, "That's a true thing."

IT WAS LATE when Bitterblue returned to the castle. In her rooms, she held the fake crown in her hands, considering. Then she found Katsa and said, "Will you team up with Po on a certain matter for me? I have a special request."

Even later, Giddon came to fetch her.

"Did it work?" asked Bitterblue as they walked to Katsa's rooms together.

"It did."

"And is everyone all right?"

"Don't be alarmed when you see Po. His black eye is from Skye, not from this."

"Oh, no. Where is Skye? Should I talk to him?"

Giddon rubbed his beard. "Skye has decided to join the party going to the Dells," he said. "As Lienid's ambassador."

"What? He's leaving? He just got here!"

"I think he has a broken heart," said Giddon, "to match Po's black eye."

"I wish people would stop hitting Po," whispered Bitterblue.

"Well," Giddon said. "Yes. I'm hoping Skye is following my model. Punch Po; go on a long trip; feel better; come back and make up."

"Well," said Bitterblue, "at least we have the crown."

Inside Katsa's room, Po sat on the bed, soaked through, huddled in blankets, something like the world's most miserable clump of seaweed. Katsa stood in the middle of the room, shaking water from her hair and wringing her clothing out onto the fine rug, looking like she'd just won a swimming competition. Bann's voice came from the bathing room, where he was running a bath. Raffin sat at the dining table, trying to wipe muck off of Bitterblue's crown by applying a mysterious solution from a vial, then rubbing the crown with what looked like one of Katsa's socks.

"Where did you leave the fake crown?" asked Bitterblue.

"A good bit closer to shore," said Katsa. "We'll go make a big, noisy production of fishing it out in the morning."

And Saf could leave Monsea with his name cleared. For Bitterblue wasn't certain whether giving a fake crown to black-market lords, stealing it back, then throwing it into the river was a crime or not, but it didn't seem like much of one. And at least it wasn't treason. Saf could come back someday, and he would never hang.

THE DAY HAD started with Skye walking into her office, though it seemed ages ago. Every day was like that, so full that she stumbled into bed once it was over.

She'd been reading a report from Death when Skye had arrived. She was in her bed that night when she finally picked it up again.

He does kill Bellamew, as he has been threatening to do for some time. He kills her because he sees her, in an unguarded moment, with a child that she has claimed has been dead for years. The child disappears from the room once he has apprehended her, Lady Queen, not surprisingly, as we can only assume that the child is Hava. Bellamew refuses to produce her. Leck takes Bellamew away to his hospital, furious with her for lying about the child, has her killed with much more expediency than usual, then goes to his bedroom and tries to destroy her work with paint. Over days and weeks, he searches for the child but cannot find her, and simultaneously, his desire to be alone with you begins to grow. He begins to write of molding you into a perfect queen, and of both you and Ashen becoming increasingly unaccommodating. He writes of the anticipatory pleasure he feels in being patient.

This is the sort of intimate and painful information I would not normally burden you with, Lady Queen, except that the implications, when one considers everything together, seem significant, and I thought you would like to know them. If you will remember, Lady Queen, Bellamew and Queen Ashen were two victims Leck claimed to have "kept for himself." And his preoccupation with this child is striking, is it not?

It was striking. But it wasn't surprising. It was a thing Bitterblue had begun to wonder about on her own. It was even a thing she'd asked Hava once, but they'd gotten interrupted.

Bitterblue climbed out of bed again and found a robe.

IN THE ART gallery, she sat on the floor with Hava, trying to stop Hava from being so frightened.

"I haven't wanted you to know, Lady Queen," Hava whispered. "I've never told a soul. I intended never to."

"You mustn't call me by my title anymore," whispered Bitterblue.

"Please let me. I'm terrified of other people knowing. I'm terrified of you, or other people, or anybody, starting to think of me as your heir. I would die before I became the queen!"

"We'll make some sort of provision, Hava, I promise, so that you'll never be queen."

"I couldn't, Lady Queen," Hava said, her voice breaking in panic. "I swear to you, I couldn't!"

"Hava," Bitterblue said, taking Hava's hand and holding it tight. "I swear to you that you won't."

"I don't want to be treated like a princess, Lady Queen. I could not bear people fussing. I want to live in the art gallery, where no one sees me. I—" Tears were streaming down Hava's face. "Lady Queen, I hope you understand that I mean none of this personally. I would do just about anything for you. It's just that . . ."

"It's too big, and everything is moving too fast," said Bitterblue.

"Yes, Lady Queen," said Hava, sobbing. She flickered, once, into a sculpture. Then came back as a sobbing girl. "I would have to leave," she cried. "I would have to hide forever."

"Then we won't tell anyone," Bitterblue said. "All right? We'll swear Death to secrecy. We'll sort out what it means slowly, all right? I won't push it on you, and you'll decide what you want, and maybe we'll never tell anyone. Do you see that nothing needs to change, except what we know? Hava?" Bitterblue took a breath to prevent herself from wrapping both arms around the girl. "Hava, please," she said, "please. Don't go away."

Hava spent another moment crying against Bitterblue's hand. Then she said, "I don't actually want to leave you, Lady Queen. I'll stay."

In her bed again, Bitterblue tried to wrap sleep around herself. She had an early morning, with Dellians and Pikkians to say good-bye to. She had Skye to find and reason with, and another big day of meetings and decisions. But Bitterblue couldn't sleep. She held a word inside herself that she was too shy to say aloud.

Finally, she dared, once, to whisper it.

Sister.

"Do you suppose it tells Dellian time?" said Po two days later, lazing lengthwise across one of Bitterblue's armchairs, dangling Saf's fifteen-hour watch on his finger and occasionally trying to balance it on his nose. "I love this thing. Its inner workings calm me."

Saf had given Po the watch as a parting gift, and as thanks for saving his neck. "It'd be a funny way to keep time, wouldn't it?" said Bitterblue. "Quarter past would be twelve and a half minutes past the hour. And by the way, that's stolen property."

"But doesn't it seem that that's why Leck did everything?" said Po. "To imitate the Dells?"

"Perhaps it's another one of his botched imitations," said Giddon.

"Giddon," said Bitterblue, "what will you do after Estill?"

"Well," he said, a quiet shadow touching his face. She knew where Giddon wanted to go after Estill. She wondered if the Council would make a project of it. She also wondered if going to see something that was no longer there was a good idea—and if that mattered, when it came to a person's heart. "I suppose it depends on where I'm needed," he said.

"If there's no place you're urgently needed, or if you're unde-cided, or if, perhaps, you're thinking of visiting the Dells—would you consider coming back here for a little while first?"

"Yes," he said without hesitation. "If I'm not needed elsewhere, I'll come back here for a while."

"That is a comfort," said Bitterblue quietly. "Thank you."

Her friends were leaving, finally. In a matter of days, they were leaving for Estill, and it was the real thing this time; the revolution-aries and a few select Estillan nobles had agreed to come together, take their king by surprise, and change the lives of all Estillan people. Bitterblue was happy about her uncle's navy to the south and her strange new friends to the east. She knew she was going to have to be patient, to wait and see what would happen. And she also knew that she'd have to have faith in her friends, not dwell on thoughts of them in a war. Bann, her old sparring partner. Po, who pushed him-self too hard and was hurting now from the loss of a brother. Katsa, who would come apart if something happened to Po. Giddon. It startled her, how quickly tears came to her eyes when she thought of Giddon leaving.

Raffin was staying behind in Monsea as liaison, which was a balm to Bitterblue's heart, even though he was inclined to long silences and staring moodily into potted plants. She'd found him in the back garden that morning, on his knees in the snow, taking clippings from some dead perennials.

"Did you know," he said, peering up at her, "that in Nander, they've decided they don't want a king?"

"What?" she said. "No king at all?"

"Yes," he said. "The committee of nobles will continue to rule by vote, alongside another committee of equal power that will be comprised of representatives elected by the people."

"You mean like a sort of . . . aristocratic and democratic republic?" said Bitterblue, plucking terms from the book about monarchy and tyranny.

"Something like that, yes."

"Fascinating. Did you know that in the Dells, a man can take a husband and a woman can take a wife? Fire told me so."

"Mnph," he said, then focused his eyes on her quietly. "Is that true?"

"It is. And the king himself is married to a woman who hasn't a drop of noble blood in her veins."

Raffin was quiet for a moment, poking around in the snow with a stick. Bitterblue spent that moment in front of Bellamew's sculpture, looking into the living eyes of her mother. Touching the scarf she was wearing and gathering strength. Finally, Raffin said, "That's not the way of things in the Middluns."

"No," said Bitterblue. "But it is the way in the Middluns for the king to do as he likes."

Raffin stood, knees cracking, and came to her. "My father is a healthy man," he said.

"Oh, Raffin," she said. "May I give you a hug?"

IT WAS HARD to say good-bye.

"Do you think I could ever write you letters in embroidery that you could feel with your fingers, Po," Bitterblue asked him, "when you're away?"

He cracked a grin. "Katsa scratches me notes now and then

in wood, when she's desperate. But wouldn't you have to learn to embroider?"

"There is that," said Bitterblue, smiling with him, hugging him.

"I'll come back," Po said to her. "I promised, remember?"

"I'll come back too," said Katsa. "It's time I gave lessons here again, Bitterblue."

Katsa hugged her for a long time, and Bitterblue understood that this was always how it would be. Katsa would come and then Katsa would go. But the hug was real, and lasting, even though it would end. The coming was as real as the going, and the coming would always be a promise. It would have to be good enough.

She went to the art gallery the night they all left, because she was lonely.

And then Hava led Bitterblue downstairs, to a place in the castle Bitterblue hadn't yet been. They sat together at the top of the prison steps, listening to Goldie sing a lullaby to her prisoners.

AN UNCLE AND king was waiting for Bitterblue in Monport, with a navy on display for her pleasure. Bitterblue would go to meet him.

The day before she left, she sat in her office, reflecting. Thirty of Leck's thirty-five journals had been destroyed in the fire Thiel had lit. Terrified now of fire, Death was trying to read, decipher, and memorize the five surviving journals in one mad rush. Bitterblue understood the scope of such a catastrophic loss of information. But she couldn't make herself grieve. Her relief was too great. She thought she might like to read her father's five remaining journals, eventually, someday. Five journals did not feel undoably awful. Maybe she would be able to read them, years from now, before a fireplace, wrapped in blankets, while someone held her tight. But not now.

She'd asked Helda to take her mother's sheets away. They were also for some other day, some other time when they weren't so painful. Maybe someday, they would feel more like a memory of pain than like pain itself. And she didn't need them around to remember. She had her mother's chest and all the things in it, she had Ashen's scarves and the Bellamew sculpture, and she had her grief.

Her new sheets were smooth and even. When they touched her skin softly, without the rough bumps of embroidery at the edges, she was startled; and a kind of relief eased its way through her, as if the sores in her mind and on her heart might begin to heal.

My kingdom's challenge, she thought, *is to balance knowing with healing.*

Her clerks and guards had taken to coming to her for confessionals. Holt had started it, appearing in her office one day and saying, "Lady Queen, if you're to forgive me, I'd like you to know what you're forgiving me for."

It had not been an easy thing for Holt to do. He had killed inmates in the prisons for Thiel and Runnemood, and he couldn't even begin to force into words the things Leck had made him do. He became confused and tongue-tied, kneeling before Bitterblue with his hands clutched together and his head bowed.

"I do want to tell you, Lady Queen," he finally choked out. "But I can't."

Bitterblue didn't know what to do for her people who needed to tell things but couldn't. She thought it might be something to ask Po—who had a special insight into what would do people good— or Fire. "I'll help you with this, Holt," she said. "I promise, I won't leave you alone with this. Will you be patient with me, and I'll be patient with you?"

She had one more ministry to build. Of all of her ministries, it would be the one with which she would take the most care. She wouldn't force it on anyone, but she would make its existence widely known. It would be a ministry for all the people whose pain could be acknowledged, maybe even eased, by the telling and recording of what their own experiences had been. It would have a space of its own in the castle, a library where stories were kept, and a minister and staff that her friends would help her choose. Some of the staff would travel, to reach people who couldn't come to the city. It would be a safe place for the sharing of burdens and the capturing of memories before they disappeared. It would be called the Ministry of Stories and Truth, and it would help her kingdom heal.

"LADY QUEEN?"

The sun was setting and a light snowfall had begun. Bitterblue looked up from her desk into the familiar, sharp, and weary face of Death.

"Death," Bitterblue said. "How are you?"

"Lady Queen," said Death, "a boy named Immiker was born on a riverside estate in northern Monsea fifty-nine years ago, to a game warden named Larch and a woman named Mikra who died in childbirth."

"Fifty-nine," Bitterblue said. "That's the correct age. Is it him?"

"I don't know, Lady Queen," Death said. "Possibly. There are other records of similarly named people that I must consider."

"Could this mean I'm Monsean?"

"It matches some of the particulars, Lady Queen, and we can go on looking for clues. But I can't imagine us ever being certain that this is him. Regardless," Death said crisply, "I don't see that there's any question of whether or not you are Monsean. You are our queen, are you not?"

Death dropped a small sheaf of papers onto her desk, turned sharply on his heel, and left.

Bitterblue rubbed her neck, sighing. Then she pulled Death's papers closer.

I have completed the translation of the first journal, Lady Queen, she read. *It is, as I'd already surmised, the last journal he ever wrote. It ends with your mother's death and with your father's subsequent search of the forest for you. It also ends with the details of his punishment of Thiel, Lady Queen, for on the day you escaped with your mother, it seems that one of Leck's knives went missing. Leck decided that Thiel had stolen it and passed it to your mother. I will spare you the details.*

At her desk, Bitterblue hugged herself, feeling very high in the sky, and very alone. A memory, like a door opening onto light, unlocked itself. Thiel bursting into her mother's rooms, where Ashen had been engaged in the insane enterprise of tying sheets together and lowering them out the window. Bitterblue had been shaking with fright, for what she knew they were about to do.

Thiel's face had been running with tears and blood. "Go," he'd said, rushing to Ashen and handing her a knife that was longer than Bitterblue's forearm. "You must go now." He'd embraced Ashen, said, "Now!" in a forceful voice, then dropped on his knees before Bitterblue. He had pulled her into his arms and stopped her shaking with his tight grip. "Don't you worry," he'd said to her. "Your mother will keep you from harm, Bitterblue. Believe what she says, you understand? Believe every word she says. Go now, and be safe." Then he'd kissed her forehead and run out of the room.

Bitterblue found a fresh sheet of paper and wrote the memory down, to capture it, because it was part of her story.

Recorded by Death, the Royal Librarian of Monsea, who would merely like to note that he does not have time for this.

┌───┐
│   BEWARE: THE FOLLOWING RECORD IS AN   │
│   INCOMPLETE DRAFT.   │
│   THE ANNALIST IS OBLIGED TO FOLLOW   │
│   ORDERS AND CAN ONLY WORK WITH WHAT   │
│   HE IS GIVEN.   │
└───┘

ANNA (MONSEA): Head baker in the castle kitchens. Of questionable relevance to this record.

ASHEN (LIENID, MONSEA): First a Lienid princess, then Queen of Monsea, now deceased. Sister of King Ror of Lienid. Mother of Queen Bitterblue of Monsea. Murdered by King Leck of Monsea, her husband. This annalist remembers her as kind, highly educated, and trapped in an impossible situation. It is to be noted that she saved Queen Bitterblue's life.

BANN (MIDDLUNS): Medicine maker and reputed Council leader. Frequent traveling companion of Prince Raffin of the Middluns.

BELLAMEW (MONSEA): Sculptor, King Leck's especial favorite, murdered by him. Completed perhaps fifty or fifty-five sculptures of human transformations. Sister of Holt and mother of Hava.

BIRN (WESTER): King of Wester. Contemptible scoundrel.

BITTERBLUE (MONSEA): The Queen of Monsea and this annalist's most excellent employer. Daughter of King Leck and Queen Ashen. Niece of King Ror and Queen Zinnober of Lienid. Indubitably the finest monarch ruling in the known world today, though it is to be noted that even the finest monarchs waste their librarians' time with surprising frequency.

BREN (MONSEA): Teacher and printer in the east city; sister of Sapphire Birch. Family instrumental in the resistance. Assisting in the restoration of the castle library collection. Efficient, accurate, and highly responsible, unlike the brother she closely resembles.

DANZHOL (MONSEA): A dastardly lord from central Monsea, of questionable sanity. Grace: performing an outrage upon his own face which this annalist prefers neither to consider nor describe.

DARBY (MONSEA): Adviser to Queen Bitterblue in the years following King Leck's death. Grace: never sleeping.

DEATH (MONSEA) (PRONOUNCED TO RHYME WITH "TEETH"): This annalist, and the Royal Librarian of Monsea. Grace: speed of reading and perfect memory of all that is read.

DROWDEN (NANDER): King of Nander, now deposed. Insufferable blackguard.

DYAN (MONSEA): Head gardener to Queen Bitterblue. Of questionable relevance to this record.

EEMKERR (UNKNOWN): The childhood name of the person who would later become King Leck of Monsea. Born somewhere in the seven kingdoms. See entries for "Immiker" and "Leck."

FIRE (DELLS) (DELLIAN NAME: BIR, MORE OR LESS): A Dellian lady and what is called, in the Dells, a "monster." Most alarming woman.

FOX (MONSEA, LIENID, MONSEA): Castle servant in the years following King Leck's death. Grace: fearlessness.

FROGGATT (MONSEA): A clerk of the queen.

GADD (MONSEA): King Leck's favored creator of decorative wall-hangings. Murdered by King Leck.

GIDDON (MIDDLUNS): Once a Middluns lord, now disennobled. Reputed Council leader and frequent traveling companion of Prince Po of Lienid. It is to be noted that he saved this annalist's life.

GOLDIE (MONSEA, LIENID, MONSEA): Queen Bitterblue's new Master of Prisons. Once the master of the navy prison in Ror City, Lienid. Grace: singing.

GREENING GRANDEMALION (LIENID): Lienid prince known as Po. Reputed Council leader. Seventh son of King Ror and Queen Zinnober of Lienid and cousin of Queen Bitterblue. Famous swain of Lady Katsa of the Middluns. Grace: hand-fighting (he says). Good with cats.

GRELLA (MONSEA): A legendary Monsean mountain explorer who kept bombastic and overblown journals of his adventures and died in the pass that bears his name.

HAVA (MONSEA): Daughter of Bellamew, niece of Holt. Grace: hiding/disguise.

HELDA (MIDDLUNS, MONSEA): Queen Bitterblue's housekeeper, ladyservant, and spymaster. Formerly ladyservant to Lady Katsa of the Middluns. A person of unsurpassed dignity, though opinionated.

Holt (Monsea): A member of the Queen's Guard. Brother of Bellamew and uncle of Hava. Grace: strength.

Immiker (Monsea): A child born in Monsea in the year we believe King Leck to have been born. Possibly the Eemkerr who grew up to be King Leck, though this annalist can not confirm.

Ivan (Monsea): King Leck's favored engineer. Built the three city bridges.

Jass (Monsea): A kitchen hand of questionable relevance to this record. Grace: determining, by sight and smell, what meal would be most satisfying for a given person to eat.

Katsa (Middluns): A lady of the Middluns, banished and declared fortuneless by her uncle, King Randa of the Middluns, though this does not seem to stop her from entering the kingdom when she pleases. Reputed Council leader and that organization's founder. Cousin of Prince Raffin of the Middluns. Famous paramour of Prince Po of Lienid. Assassinated King Leck. Grace: survival, with an extreme capacity for any kind of fighting.

Larch (Monsea): Father of Immiker; therefore, possible father of King Leck.

Leck (unknown, Dells, Monsea): King of Monsea for thirty-five years; soulless psychopathic sadist. Husband of Queen Ashen and father of Queen Bitterblue. Assassinated by Lady Katsa of the Middluns. Grace: telling lies that are believed.

Lovejoy (Monsea): A cat of fine temperament.

NOTE: Lovejoy has knocked over the ink!

INSUPPORTABLE CREATURE!

MADLEN (⬛⬛⬛⬛⬛**):** A⬛⬛⬛⬛⬛⬛⬛⬛⬛⬛⬛⬛ as a Graced healer i⬛⬛⬛⬛⬛⬛⬛ Monsea.

MIDYA (DELLS): Famous Dellian naval explorer. Dellian mother, Pikkian father. Curiously, born in a Dellian prison.

MIKRA (MONSEA): Mother of Immiker; therefore, possible mother of King Leck.

MURGON (SUNDER): King of Sunder. Vile miscreant.

NASHDELL (DELLS): King of the Dells. Brother-in-law of Lady Fire. As far as this annalist knows, a good man.

OLL (MIDDLUNS): Reputed Council leader. Stripped of his captaincy by King Randa of the Middluns.

ORNIK (MONSEA): A metalsmith of the royal smithy. Of questionable relevance to this record.

PIPER (MONSEA): A Monsean lord who serves as a judge on the High Court.

PO: See entry for "Greening Grandemalion."

QUALL (MONSEA): A Monsean lord and a judge on the High Court in the years following King Leck's death.

RAFFIN (MIDDLUNS): A prince of the Middluns, King Randa's sole son and heir. Medicine maker and reputed Council leader. Cousin of Lady Katsa.

RANDA (MIDDLUNS): King of the Middluns. Not much to be said for him.

Rood (Monsea): Adviser to Queen Bitterblue in the years following King Leck's death; brother of Runnemood.

Ror (Lienid): King of Lienid. Father of Prince Po and Prince Skye, uncle of Queen Bitterblue. Presumably not the ass the other kings are.

Runnemood (Monsea): Adviser to Queen Bitterblue in the years following King Leck's death; brother of Rood.

Sapphire Birch (Monsea, Lienid, Monsea): A Monsean commoner who grew up on a Lienid ship, now identifying as Lienid; brother of Bren. Family instrumental in the resistance. A troublemaker and a squanderer of Her Majesty's energies. Of questionable relevance to this record. Grace: Her Majesty knows, but has not told this annalist.

Skye (Lienid): A Lienid prince and the sixth son of King Ror and Queen Zinnober. Brother to Prince Po and cousin to Queen Bitterblue.

Smit (Monsea): Captain of the Monsean Guard in the years following King Leck's death.

Spook (Monsea): A notorious black-market underlord.

Teddren (Monsea): Known as Teddy. Printer and teacher in the east city; brother to Tilda. Family instrumental in the resistance. An adviser to the Ministry of Education. Currently assisting in the restoration of the castle library collection. Top-rate fellow, if a bit starry-eyed.

Thiel (Monsea): Adviser to Queen Bitterblue in the years following King Leck's death.

THIGPEN (ESTILL): The King of Estill, for the moment. A vicious hoodlum.

TILDA (MONSEA): Printer and teacher in the east city; sister to Teddren. Family instrumental in the resistance. Currently assisting in the restoration of the castle library collection and the castle's defunct printing shop, with alacrity and a refreshing dedication.

Some entries are at the moment grievously incomplete, pending the final, official reports of Her Majesty. The annalist cannot be held accountable for errors or omissions caused or required by others, of which there are doubtless many.

Winged·Bridge

Monster·Bridge

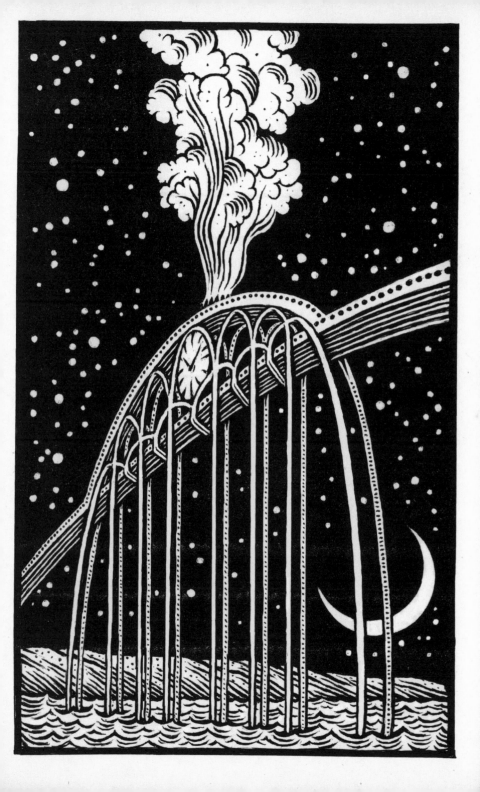

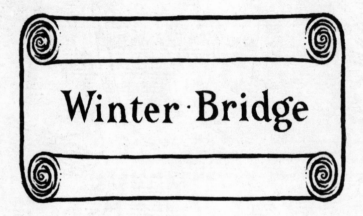

Winter·Bridge

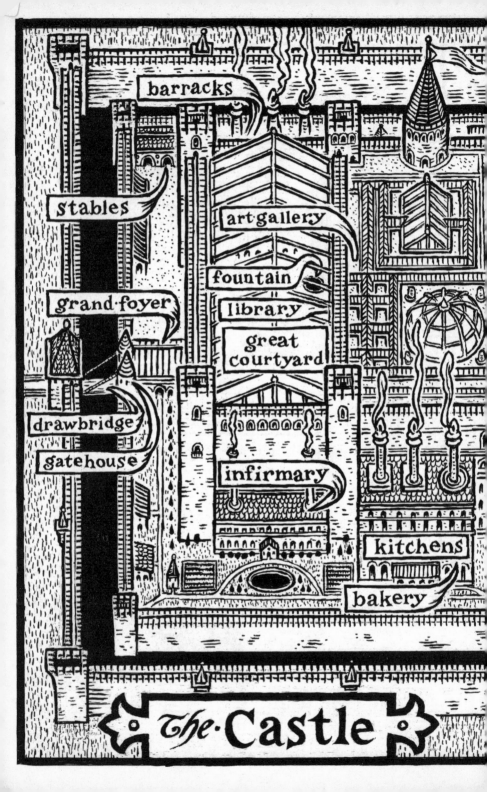

Bitterblue's·Rooms

→

→

Leck's·Room

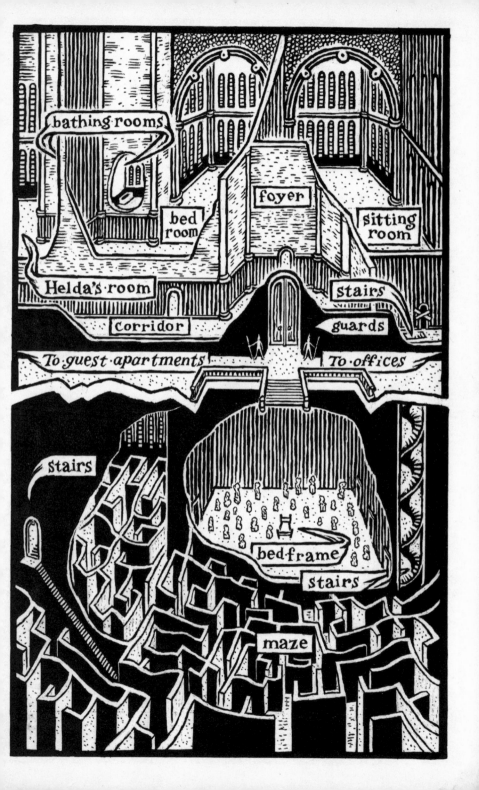

PIKKIA

THE DELLS

WINTER·SEA

ACKNOWLEDGMENTS

T HANKS TO MY editor, Kathy Dawson, for more practical help than I can quantify and especially for helping me get from the swamp of Draft One to a Draft Two I could work with. Thanks also for her love of the book, unwavering support, and hands-off *patience*. I know how lucky I am.

Thanks to Faye Bender, my agent and fierce supporter, for having my back at every moment. I would not have gotten through this book with my equanimity intact without her.

Thanks to my first round of readers, Catherine Cashore, Dorothy Cashore, and Sarah Prineas; and to my second round of readers, Deborah Kaplan, JD Paul, and Rebecca Rabinowitz. Your help has been invaluable and your generosity overwhelms me.

A note to anyone reading the acknowledgments before reading the book: The rest of the acknowledgments are full of *Bitterblue* spoilers. You've been warned!

Thanks to linguist Dr. Lance Nathan, who created both my beautiful Dellian alphabet and a Dellian language that could conceivably have developed in isolation from the same protolanguage "Gracelingian" developed from. Lance also helped by doing the initial ciphering of Leck's text for me. (Cipher enthusiasts will recognize the Vigenère ciphering method I chose for Leck's journals.) Lance *also* helped me get my head around how to navigate mazes (along with Deborah Kaplan) and how to tell time on a fifteen-hour watch, so thanks for that, as well!

Thanks to former physicist JD Paul, who answered an endless stream of questions about Po and optics so that I could determine whether Po was likely to be able to discern color or know when it's night or day. Thanks to Rebecca Rabinowitz and Deborah Kaplan, who, after reading a late draft of *Bitterblue,* counseled me on the matter of Po, disability politics, and whether there was any way to counter the consequences of my making Po's Grace grow so big that it compensated for his blindness at the end of *Graceling.* (I was not thinking about disability politics back then. It didn't occur to me, until it was too late, that I had disabled Po, then given him a magical cure for his disability—thus implying that he couldn't be a whole person and also be disabled. I now understand that the magical cure trope is all too common in F/SF writing and is disrespectful to people with disabilities. My failings here are all my own.)

Thanks to my sister Dorothy Cashore, who designed Ashen's beautiful embroidery cipher, not blinking an eye when I gave her instructions like "Make it Lienidy!" Thanks to my mother, Nedda Cashore, who served as a test subject and embroidered some of the symbols for me, even though I refused to tell her why I was asking her to do so.

Thanks to Dr. Michael Jacobson for answering questions about burns. Thanks to my uncle, Dr. Walter Willihnganz, for answering questions about knife wounds, eyeballs, and whether kneading bread is good therapy once a broken arm has healed. (The answer: Yes!)

Thanks to Kaz Stouffer at TSNY Beantown for showing me the ropes, literally, and helping me figure out how Danzhol intended to execute his dastardly plan.

Thanks to Kelly Droney and Melissa Murphy for answering strange questions about what happens to corpses in caves and bones thrown into rivers.

A number of people very kindly answered questions about specific matters from time to time, or expressed opinions when I asked for them. Some of these people, including my first- and second-round readers, have already been named here in reference to other matters; some have already been named here more than once! Chief among those not yet named are Sarah Miller (who helped me with Po in the courtroom) and Marc Moskowitz (who helped with watch parts, boat disguise, and lots of other things too). Thank you!

Any errors in the book are mine.

Thanks to Danese Joyce for her wisdom and guidance.

Thanks to Lauri Hornik and Don Weisberg for their patience and support and to Natalie Sousa for designing the beautiful Dial cover for the book. Thanks to Jenny Kelly for the beautiful interior design, and to artist Ian Schoenherr for delighting and astonishing me with his depictions of my world. A big thank you to the rest of the Penguin team who worked so hard to get Bitterblue ready and launch her into the world. Thanks also to my publishers, agents, and scouts around the world who make the business side of my work such a pleasure.

Since I seem to have made a habit of repeating myself—and because they deserve it most—thanks again to my editor and my agent.

And finally, thanks, as always, to my family.

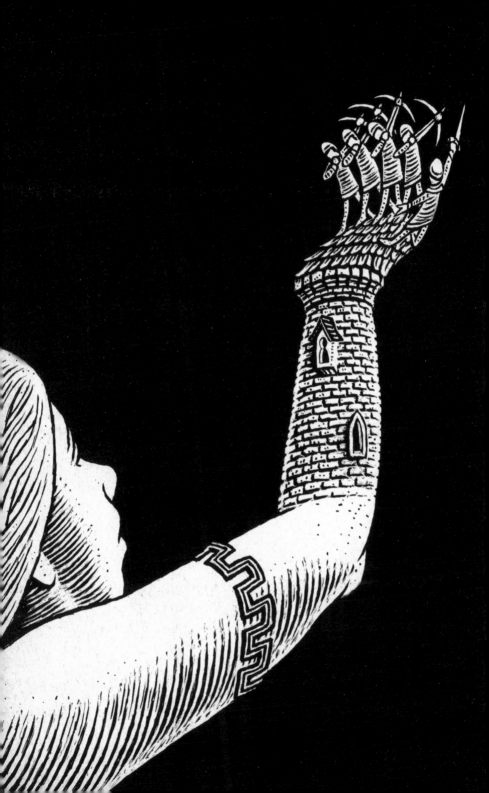

A FEW EXTRAS FOR *BITTERBLUE* FANS

FROM KRISTIN CASHORE'S BLOG,
THIS IS MY SECRET

Pictures of a Book Being Made
Sunday, December 2, 2012

To make up for my recent lack of posting—and to celebrate
Bitterblue being named a *New York Times Book Review*
Notable Children's Book of 2012—this post will be about
something :).

Disclaimer: All the photos in this post are of my own work
and are owned by me. If you use them for any purpose,
please identify them and attribute them to me. Do not
change them in any way or use them commercially.

What follows is essentially my tour presentation for
Bitterblue . . . it is the story of how the book was written.
Here goes.

As you probably know if you've spent much time on my blog, I write by hand.

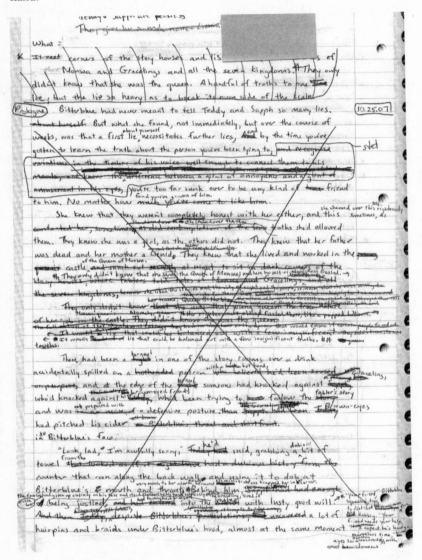

Above is the first page of the first draft of *Bitterblue*. Note that the date is October 25, 2007. Also note—if you've read *Bitterblue*—that this is not how the final book begins. And also that not a whole lot from this page made it into the final draft. What you see above is fairly typical: I write, I scratch out a word here and there, I scratch out a line, I change things; then I put it away for the day, come back the next day, realize the entire thing is crap, and cross the whole page out with a big X. Below is another fairly typical page:

Once I've written 40 or 50 pages——or, essentially, get to a point where I'm starting to worry about the house burning down (though I do keep my notebook in a fireproof, waterproof safe) —I transcribe my handwriting into my Word document using voice recognition software (because I can't type much at all without pain). The transcription, like every other moment when I'm looking at my work, is an opportunity for crossing more things out (symbolically) and changing things.

That's my essential process for every book. But, of course, there's more to it. For example, while I write, I scribble cheery, encouraging notes to myself.

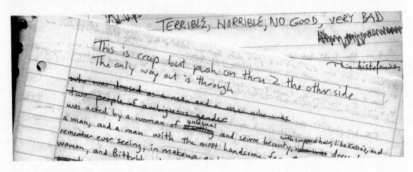

These notes are not born of modesty or low self-esteem. They are born of the simple truth that a first draft is crap; a first draft is terrible, horrible, no good, very bad; and the writer, moving forward while leaving a stream of detritus in her wake, CAN GET VERY DISCOURAGED. But she keeps moving, because, as Robert Frost said, "The best way out is always through."

Sometimes, I'm just trying to keep myself from panicking.

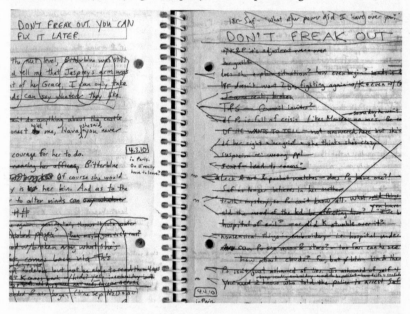

Notice the date. It's April 3, 2010. I've been writing for two and half years. I'm nowhere near the end of the first draft, which is an insufferable mess. I AM FREAKING OUT and trying very hard not to.

Bitterblue's first draft went on like that for seven notebooks.

When I finally finished the first draft, three years after I'd begun, it was 800 pages long and weighed 7000 pounds.

I sent it to my patient, PATIENT editor. She worked her way through it, poor dear, then sent me one of her typical, long, detailed editorial letters. Here's what's working, she said; here's what isn't; here's what I see you trying to do. Then she said something miraculous. I'm paraphrasing, but what she said was along the lines of: This is going to sound like a crazy idea, but now, at the beginning of the revision process, is the time to voice crazy ideas. Would you consider starting again from scratch?

!!!!!!!!

insert nervous breakdown

insert perspective

insert reconsideration

insert realization that she is 100% right

Here's the reason this ended up being the best thing my editor could have said. Within that 800-page mess, the final story was all there. If you were to read *Bitterblue*'s first draft, you would come away with essentially the same story a person reading the final book comes away with. But there was a lot of extra, unnecessary stuff in there, too; I'd spent a lot of space working things out for myself that didn't really need to be worked out for the reader. There were extra characters who could be consolidated into fewer people to simplify things. There were plot complications that didn't need to be so complicated. The themes were buried in crap; they weren't shining. There was an earthquake! (Literally. One plot point was an earthquake.) The story I was trying to tell didn't need an earthquake.

Now, normally when revising, I sit down with the printout of the draft I have and start crossing things out, working with what I've got, molding, trying to change the shape *of an existing thing* into something new. But here was my editor suggesting I start again from scratch.

I put the draft to the side, where I could reach it, but where it wasn't right in front of me. I pulled a blank sheet of paper toward me. And I played what was essentially a mental trick on myself: instead of determining to decide what to get rid of, what to change the shape of, what to mold, I said to myself, "I'm writing a book. La la la, here I am, writing a brand new book.

Hmm. What, from this pile to my side, might I *add*?"

You perceive the difference?

It was an amazing mental freedom; it allowed for a freshness in my second draft, and a freedom from the swamp of my first draft. I was able to write a second draft while NOT stuck inside that first-draft swamp. I was able to tell the same story all over again, and this time tell it *so* much better. Thank you, stellar editor Kathy Dawson. You saved my book.

Here's the first page of the second draft of *Bitterblue*.

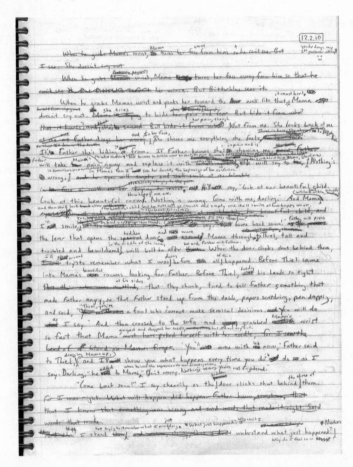

The date is December 2, 2010—more than three years since I'd started writing. Can you read what it says? It is almost word for word the way the final version of *Bitterblue* opens. I feel like this is an important point: it wasn't until I'd spent three years writing a mess of a draft that I figured out how *Bitterblue* needed to begin.

Most days during this revision, it was too depressing to acknowledge I was writing a whole new book, so I would take the printout of the old draft, cross out all the lines, and write the new book in the spaces in between. I just couldn't bear the thought of filling up seven more notebooks; writing on the old printout made me feel like I was revising rather than rewriting, which was comforting. Another mental trick (that somehow contradicted the first mental trick, I know . . . brains are complicated ^_^). In the page shown below, I've crossed out the old scene (which was related to that earthquake), written a new scene that has no connection whatsoever to the old scene, then crossed out most of the new stuff, too. Sigh.

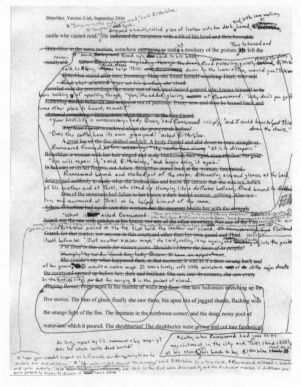

And lest you think it was worse than it actually was!, there were, in fact, pages where some of what I'd written before made it into the next draft :).

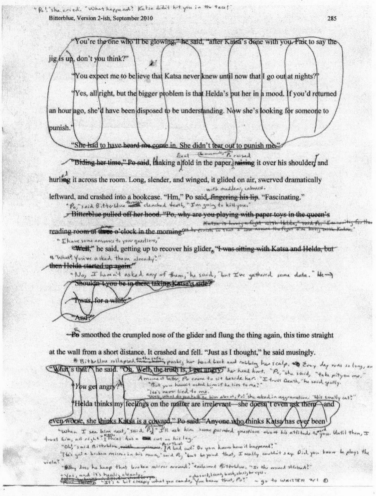

This second draft of *Bitterblue* took me about five months, if I recall correctly. Five and a half? Easily the longest revision of my life so far. And what happened after I finished Draft 2?

My editor continued to send me amazing, helpful letters; friends read and gave feedback; and I revised it several more times.

Drafts 1, 2, 3, 4, and 5, and the copyedit and the typeset manuscript.

In total, *Bitterblue* was four years of drafting and revising from start to finish.

******

There's a reason I like to tell this story. It's not because I enjoy making my audience gasp in horror (though I do). It's because I know there are always writers in the audience. I know there are people in the audience who are writing and who feel hopeless and discouraged by their own flawed work. I tell this story because I want to get this message across: THAT'S HOW IT FEELS TO BE A WRITER. It doesn't mean your book will never become what you want it to be. It doesn't mean you're not talented; it doesn't mean you're wasting your time; it doesn't mean your book isn't about anything; it doesn't mean you should give up. It only means that you're *writing*.

I think I've said this on the blog before: I imagine my self-doubt/ hopelessness/discouragement as this guy who sits next to me in my chair as I'm writing. He's always there. He is a necessary part of the process; he will never go away; so I may as well invite him to sit in a chair beside me. Sometimes I imagine myself giving him a hug, because he's so sad and pathetic; he has nothing nice to say to me, he only knows how to insult and discourage; he is, essentially, *fear*. Poor, sad little guy. I say to him, "You can sit in my company, you can say whatever it is you need to say. I know you can't help yourself. I know you're so very scared. So: you are welcome here. But," I say to him, "you're not going to stop me from writing today."

That's the story of *Bitterblue*.

Love and godspeed to all writers.

xo,
Kristin

An Incomplete List of Books I Love, by Kristin Cashore

The Handmaid's Tale, Margaret Atwood

Kushiel's Dart, Jacqueline Carey

Death Comes for the Archbishop, Willa Cather

Postcards from No Man's Land, Aidan Chambers

The House on Mango Street, Sandra Cisneros

Rebecca, Daphne du Maurier

A Candle for St. Jude, Rumer Godden

Six Feet of the Country, Nadine Gordimer

Sleeping Dogs, Sonya Hartnett

Slake's Limbo, Felice Holman

Toning the Sweep, Angela Johnson

The Principles of Uncertainty, Maira Kalman

Interpreter of Maladies, Jhumpa Lahiri

Black Juice, Margo Lanagan

Black Stars in a White Night Sky, JonArno Lawson

The Disreputable History of Frankie Landau-Banks, E. Lockhart

Jellicoe Road, Melina Marchetta

The Tricksters, Margaret Mahy

Deerskin, Robin McKinley

Anne of Green Gables, L. M. Montgomery

Care of the Soul, Thomas Moore

Shizuko's Daughter, Kyoko Mori

Beloved, Toni Morrison

Dairy Queen, Catherine Gilbert Murdock

A Step from Heaven, An Na

A Walk Out of the World, Ruth Nichols

Jacob Have I Loved, Katherine Paterson

His Dark Materials Trilogy and the
Sally Lockhart mysteries, Philip Pullman

The Satanic Verses, Salman Rushdie

Contact, Carl Sagan

The Nine Tailors, Dorothy L. Sayers

Nine Coaches Waiting, Mary Stewart

Kristin Lavransdatter, Sigrid Undset

Charlotte's Web and *Essays of E. B. White*, E. B. White

The Long Winter, Laura Ingalls Wilder

The Book Thief, Markus Zusak

A *New York Times* Bestseller
Winner of the Amelia Elizabeth Walden Award

It is not a peaceful time in the Dells. Young King Nash clings to the throne while rebel lords, in the north and south, build armies to unseat him. War is coming. The mountains and forests are filled with spies and thieves.

This is where Fire lives, a girl whose startling appearance is impossibly irresistible and who can control the minds of everyone around her.

Everyone . . . except Prince Brigan.

Chapter One

It did not surprise Fire that the man in the forest shot her. What surprised her was that he shot her by accident.

The arrow whacked her square in the arm and threw her sideways against a boulder, which knocked the air out of her. The pain was too great to ignore, but behind it she focused her mind, made it cold and sharp, like a single star in a black winter sky. If he was a cool man, certain in what he was doing, he would be guarded against her, but Fire rarely encountered this type. More often the men who tried to hurt her were angry or arrogant or frightened enough that she could find a crack in the fortress of their thoughts, and ease her way in.

She found this man's mind instantly—so open, so welcoming, even, that she wondered if he could be a simpleton hired by someone else. She fumbled for the knife in her boot. His footfalls, and then his breath, sounded through the trees. She had no time to waste, for he would shoot her again as soon as he found her. *You don't want to kill me. You've changed your mind.*

Then he rounded a tree and his blue eyes caught hold of her, and widened in astonishment and horror.

"Not a girl!" he cried out.

Fire's thoughts scrambled. Had he not meant to strike her? Did he not know who she was? Had he meant to murder Archer? She forced her voice calm. "Who was your target?"

"Not who," he said. "What. Your cloak is brown pelt. Your dress is brown. Rocks alive, girl," he said in a burst of exasperation. He marched toward her and inspected the arrow embedded in her upper arm, the blood that soaked her cloak, her sleeve, her headscarf. "A fellow would think you were hoping to be shot by a hunter."

More accurately, a poacher, since Archer forbade hunting in these woods at this time of day, just so that Fire could pass through here dressed this way. Besides, she'd never seen this shortish, tawny-haired, light-eyed man before. Well. If he was not only a poacher, but a poacher who'd accidentally shot Fire while hunting illegally, then he would not want to turn himself in to Archer's famous temper; but that was what she was going to have to make him want to do. She was losing blood, and she was beginning to feel lightheaded. She would need his assistance to get home.

"Now I'll have to kill you," he said glumly. And then, before she could begin to address that rather bizarre statement: "Wait. Who are you? Tell me you're not her."

"Not who?" she hedged, reaching again for his mind, and finding it still strangely blank, as if his intentions were floating, lost in a fog.

"Your hair is covered," he said. "Your eyes, your face—oh, save me." He backed away from her. "Your eyes are so green. I'm a dead man."

He was an odd one, with his talk of killing her, and himself dying, and his peculiar floating brain; and now he looked ready to bolt, which Fire must not allow. She grasped at his thoughts and slid them into place. *You don't find my eyes or my face to be all that remarkable.*

The man squinted at her, puzzled.

The more you look at me the more you see I'm just an ordinary girl. You've found an ordinary girl injured in the forest, and now you must rescue me. You must take me to Lord Archer.

Here Fire encountered a small resistance in the form of the man's fear. She pulled harder at his mind, and smiled at him, the most gorgeous smile she could muster while throbbing with pain and dying of blood loss. *Lord Archer will reward you and keep you safe, and you will be honored as a hero.*

There was no hesitation. He eased her quiver and her fiddle case from her back and slung them over his shoulder against his own quiver. He took up both of their bows in one hand and wrapped her right arm, her uninjured arm, around his neck. "Come along, miss," he said. He half led her, half carried her, through the trees toward Archer's holding.

He knows the way, she thought tiredly, and then she let the thought go. It didn't matter who he was or where he came from. It only mattered that she stay awake and inside his head until he'd gotten her home and Archer's people had seized him. She kept her eyes and ears and her mind alert for monsters, for neither her headscarf nor her own mental guard against them would hide her from them if they smelled her blood.

At least she could count on this poacher to be a decent shot.

ARCHER BROUGHT DOWN a raptor monster as Fire and the poacher stumbled out of the trees. A beautiful, long shot from the upper terrace that Fire was in no state to admire, but that caused the poacher to murmur something under his breath about the appropriateness of the young lord's nickname. The monster plummeted from the sky and crashed onto the pathway to the door. Its color was the rich orange-gold of a sunflower.

Archer stood tall and graceful on the stone terrace, eyes raised to the sky, longbow lightly in hand. He reached to the quiver on his back, notched another arrow, and swept the treetops. Then he saw them, the man dragging her bleeding from the forest. He turned on his heel and ran into the house, and even down here, even from this distance and stone walls between them, Fire could hear him yelling. She sent words and feeling into his mind, not mind control, only a message. *Don't worry. Seize him and disarm him, but don't hurt him. Please,* she added, for whatever it was worth with Archer. *He's a nice man and I've had to trick him.*

Archer burst through the great front door with his captain Palla, his healer, and five of his guard. He leapt over the raptor and ran to Fire. "I found her in the forest," the poacher cried. "I found her. I saved her life."

Once the guards had taken hold of the poacher, Fire

released his mind. The relief of it weakened her knees and she slumped against Archer.

"Fire," her friend was saying. "Fire. Are you all right? Where else are you hurt?"

She couldn't stand. Archer grasped her, lowered her to the ground. She shook her head numbly. "Nowhere."

"Let her sit," the healer said. "Let her lie down. I must stop the flow of blood."

Archer was wild. "Will she be all right?"

"Most certainly," the healer said curtly, "if you will get out of my way and let me stop the flow of blood. My lord."

Archer let out a ragged breath and kissed Fire's forehead. He untangled himself from her body and crouched on his heels, clenching and unclenching his fists. Then he turned to peer at the poacher held by his guards, and Fire thought warningly, *Archer*, for she knew that with his anxieties unsoothed, Archer was transitioning now to fury.

"A nice man who must nonetheless be seized," he hissed at the poacher, standing. "I can see that the arrow in her arm came from your quiver. Who are you and who sent you?"

The poacher barely noticed Archer. He stared down at Fire, boggle-eyed. "She's beautiful again," he said. "I'm a dead man."

"He won't kill you," Fire told him soothingly. "He doesn't kill poachers, and anyway, you saved me."

"If you shot her I'll kill you with pleasure," Archer said.

"It makes no difference what you do," the poacher said.

Archer glared down at the man. "And if you were so intent on rescuing her, why didn't you remove the arrow yourself and bind the wound before dragging her half across the world?"

"Archer," Fire said, and then stopped, choking back a cry as the healer ripped off her bloody sleeve. "He was under my control, and I didn't think of it. Leave him alone."

Archer swung on her. "And why didn't you think of it? Where is your common sense?"

"Lord Archer," the healer said testily. "There will be no yelling at people who are bleeding themselves to unconsciousness. Make yourself useful. Hold her down, will you, while I remove this arrow; and then you'll do best to look to the skies."

Archer knelt beside her and took hold of her shoulders. His face was wooden but his voice shook with emotion. "Forgive me, Fire." To the healer: "We're mad to be doing this outside. They smell the blood."

And then sudden pain, blinding and brilliant. Fire wrenched her head and fought against the healer, against Archer's heavy strength. Her scarf slipped off and released the shimmering prism of her hair: sunrise, poppy, copper, fuchsia, flame. Red, brighter than the blood soaking the pathway.

SHE ATE DINNER in her own stone house, which was just beyond Archer's and under the protection of his guard. He had sent the dead raptor monster to her kitchen. Archer was one of very few people who made her feel no shame for craving the taste of monster meat.

She ate in bed, and he sat with her. He cut her meat and encouraged her. Eating hurt, everything hurt.

The poacher was jailed in one of the outdoor monster cages Fire's father, Lord Cansrel, had built into the hill behind the house. "I hope there's a lightning storm," Archer said. "I hope for a flood. I would like the ground under your poacher to crack open and swallow him."

She ignored him. She knew it was only hot air.

"I passed Donal in your hall," he said, "sneaking out with a pile of blankets and pillows. You're building your assassin a bed out there, aren't you? And probably feeding him as well as you feed yourself."

"He's not an assassin, only a poacher with fuzzy eyesight."

"You believe that even less than I do."

"All right, but I do believe that when he shot me, he thought I was a deer."

Archer sat back and crossed his arms. "Perhaps. We'll talk to him again tomorrow. We'll have his story from him."

"I would rather not help."

"I would rather not ask you, darling, but I need to know who this man is and who sent him. He's the second stranger to be seen on my land these two weeks."

Fire lay back, closed her eyes, forced her jaw to chew. Everyone was a stranger. Strangers came out of the rocks, the hills, and it was impossible to know everyone's truth. She didn't want to know—nor did she want to use her powers to find out. It was one thing to take over a man's mind to prevent her own death, and another thing entirely to steal his secrets.

When she turned to Archer again, he was watching her quietly. His white-blond hair and his deep brown eyes, his proud mouth. The familiar features she'd known since she was a toddler and he was a child, always carrying a bow around as long as his own height. It was she who'd first modified his real name, Arklin, to Archer, and he had taught her to shoot. And looking into his face now, the face of a grown man responsible for a northern estate, its money, its farms, its people, she understood his anxiety. It was not a peaceful time in the Dells. In King's City, young King Nash was clinging, with some desperation, to the throne, while rebel lords like Lord Mydogg in the north and Lord Gentian in the south built armies and thought about how to unseat him.

War was coming. And the mountains and forests swarmed with spies and thieves and other lawless men. Strangers were always alarming.

Archer's voice was soft. "You won't be able to go outside alone until you can shoot again. The raptors are out of control. I'm sorry, Fire."

Fire swallowed. She'd been trying not to think about this particular bleakness. "It makes no difference. I can't play fiddle, either, or harp or flute or any of my instruments. I have no need to leave home."

"We'll send word to your students." He sighed and rubbed his neck. "And I'll see whom I can place in their houses in your stead. Until you heal, we'll be forced to trust our neighbors without the help of your insight." For trust was not assumed these days, even among long-standing neighbors, and one of Fire's jobs as she gave music lessons was to keep her eyes and ears open. Occasionally she learned something—information, conversation, the sense of something wrong—that was a help to Archer and his father, Brocker, both loyal allies of the king.

It was also a long time for Fire to live without the comfort of her own music. She closed her eyes again and breathed slowly. These were always the worst injuries, the ones that left her unable to play her fiddle.

She hummed to herself, a song they both knew about the northern Dells, a song that Archer's father always liked her to play when she sat with him.

Archer took the hand of her uninjured arm, and kissed it. He kissed her fingers, her wrist. His lips brushed her forearm.

She stopped humming. She opened her eyes to the sight of his, mischievous and brown, smiling into hers.

You can't be serious, she thought to him.

He touched her hair, which shone against the blankets. "You look unhappy."

Archer. It hurts to move.

"You don't have to move. And I can erase your pain."

She smiled, despite herself, and spoke aloud. "No doubt. But so can sleep. Go home, Archer. I'm sure you can find someone else's pain to erase."

"So callous," he said teasingly, "when you know how worried I was for you today."

She did know how worried. She merely doubted that the worry had changed his nature.

OF COURSE, AFTER he'd gone, she did not sleep. She tried, but nightmares brought her awake over and over again. Her nightmares were always worse on days when she'd spent time down among the cages, for that was where her father had died.

Cansrel, her beautiful monster father. Monsters in the Dells came from monsters. A monster could breed with a non-monster of its species—her mother had not been a monster—but the progeny was always monstrous. Cansrel had had glittery silver hair with glints of blue, and deep, dark blue eyes. His body, his face breathtaking, smooth and beautifully cut, like crystal reflecting light, glowing with that intangible something that all monsters have. He had been the most stunning man alive when he'd lived, or at least Fire had found him so. He had been better than she at controlling the minds of humans. He had had a great deal more practice.

Fire lay in her bed and fought off the dream memory. The growling leopard monster, midnight blue with gold spots, astride her father. The smell of her father's blood, his gorgeous eyes on her, disbelieving. Dying.

She wished now that she hadn't sent Archer home. Archer understood the nightmares, and Archer was alive and passionate. She wanted his company, his vitality.

In her bed she grew more and more restless, and finally she did a thing that would have turned Archer livid. She dragged herself to her closets and dressed herself, slowly, painfully, in coat and trousers, dark browns and blacks to match the night. Her attempt to wrap her hair almost sent her back to bed, since she needed both arms to do it and lifting her left arm was an agony. Somehow she managed, capitulating at one point to the use of a mirror to be sure that no hair was showing in back. Generally she avoided mirrors. It embarrassed her to lose her own breath at the sight of herself.

She stuck a knife in her belt and hefted a spear and ignored her own conscience calling, singing, screaming to her that she couldn't even protect herself from a porcupine tonight, let alone a monster raptor or monster wolf.

Next was the hardest part of all, one armed. She had to sneak out of her own house by way of the tree outside her window, for Archer's guards stood at all her doorways, and they would never allow her to wander the hills injured and alone. Unless she used her power to control them, and that she would not do. Archer's guards trusted her.

Archer had been the one to notice how closely this ancient tree hugged the house and how easily he could climb it in the dark, two years ago, when Cansrel had still been alive, and Archer had been eighteen and Fire had been fifteen and their friendship had evolved in a manner Cansrel's guards hadn't needed to know the particulars of. A manner that had been unexpected to her, and sweet, and boosted her small list of happinesses. What Archer hadn't known was that Fire had begun to use the route herself, almost immediately, first to skirt Cansrel's men and then, after Cansrel was dead, Archer's own. Not to do anything shocking or forbidden; just to walk at night by herself, without everyone knowing.

She pitched her spear out the window. What followed was an ordeal that involved much swearing and tearing of cloth and fingernails. On solid ground, sweating and shaking and appreciating fully now what a foolish idea this had been, she used her spear as a cane and limped away from the house. She didn't want to go far, just out of the trees so that she could see the stars. They always eased her lonesomeness. She thought of them as beautiful creatures, burning and cold; each solitary, and bleak, and silent like her.